DOUBLEDAY
CELEBRATES
100 YEARS OF
EXCELLENCE

gary indiana

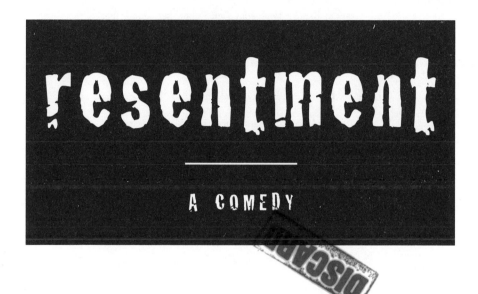

resentment

A COMEDY

doubleday

NEW YORK LONDON TORONTO SYDNEY AUCKLAND

published by doubleday

a division of Bantam Doubleday Dell Publishing Group, Inc.
1540 Broadway, New York, New York 10036

doubleday and the portrayal of an anchor with a dolphin are trademarks of Doubleday,
a division of Bantam Doubleday Dell Publishing Group, Inc.

book design by jennifer ann daddio

Library of Congress Cataloging-in-Publication Data
Indiana, Gary.
Resentment : a comedy / Gary Indiana. — 1st ed.
p.   cm.
I. Title.
PS3559.N335R47   1997
813′.54—dc21   96-46827
CIP

ISBN 0-385-48429-1

Printed in the United States of America

July 1997

First Edition

1   3   5   7   9   10   8   6   4   2

author's note

The reader will immediately glean something more than a passing resemblance between the events in *Resentment* and those epics of recent jurisprudence, *California v. Menendez, California v. Simpson* and other events of legal notoriety. I have, in fact, inserted into the action of this book many structural details, and even stray chunks of *ipsissima verba*, related to those cases, as shorthand references to generic public spectacles which millions have witnessed in one or another mediated form, and which, from the perspectives of absurdity and pathos (at least in certain piquant details), provided their own satirical embellishments. At the same time, it was and is no part of my intention to ascribe negative or fantastic characteristics to actual persons, even to comment upon any of those involved in the Menendez and other cases. Indeed, none of the characters in this novel are meant to evoke, portray, suggest or resemble specific living persons.

This is not, in other words, a "novel with a key." I had something almost opposite in mind while writing it: a kind of reverse *roman à clef* in which what has already occurred in "life" as collective spectacle functions as honorary ballast for an entirely speculative fictional narrative. Not an embroidery on actual events, but a narrative in which stray threads of reality reinforce an imaginary tapestry of the era's psychic life.

It may be useful to imagine actual trials—or other contemporary events— as they might be recounted in a hundred years, when their factual matter has become garbled, their participants confused with judges, lawyers, witnesses and defendants from unrelated legal proceedings, and time has boiled reality down to a ball of ambiguous myth. It's my guess that while there are, at any moment, myriad people who have murdered their loved ones, repeatedly, in the privacy of their imaginations, and a smaller number who have done so in fact, it should be clear that there is, currently, no superior court judge in California stalking an obsessive love object while presiding over murder trials, no eminent psychiatrist expert witness debilitated by Tourette's syndrome, no witness with a cable TV show and no prosecutor who would press the distinction between broasted and buffalo chicken wings with the zeal exhibited here. These people exist solely in the pages of this book, even if they evoke a superficial resemblance to people glimpsed on a city bus or a television screen.

for ferd eggan and larry johnson

They fuck you up, your mum and dad.
They may not mean to, but they do.

—PHILIP LARKIN, "THIS BE THE VERSE"

resentment

PART ONE

california v. martinez

In mid-August, my friend Seth arrives in Los Angeles and checks into the Chateau Marmont, full of excitement about the Martinez trial, which he's planning to write about for some magazine. He can only have the second floor suite at the Marmont for a few days, because he has a completely unrelated assignment from one of the Condé Nast publications, a profile of a famous movie star who's recently *gone out on a limb,* in the words of the movie star's publicist, by appearing as a homosexual with AIDS in a television drama about AIDS, and even though Seth is basically interested in the Martinez trial, and couldn't care less about the movie star, he needs the money from the profile to *make a dent,* as he puts it, in his spiraling debts, debts he ran up on credit cards the year before, as he frankly admits, while trying to impress Mark, a restaurant waiter he pursued for months without ever succeeding in his attempted seduction, and he also wants a few days alone at the Marmont before moving into his ex-lover Jack's ugly, inconvenient house in Mt. Washington, since the Marmont is central and private, while Jack's Mt. Washington house is remote, and everything Seth does at Jack's house is either observed by Jack or known to Jack, and even though Jack never seems to mind Seth's protracted visits, which sometimes last for months when Seth is on assignment in Los Angeles, Seth doesn't want to wear out his welcome, and avails himself whenever possible of other friends' hospitality for one or two nights here and there, though it means his papers and clothes are often scattered all over Los Angeles rather than concentrated in one place where he could easily get at them. Seth's *temporary arrangement* with Jack, as he calls it, will cover the entire duration of the Martinez trial, which could mean *six* weeks, but might easily stretch into *eight* weeks, or *ten* weeks, or even longer . . .

. . . Seth says that he's secured a courtroom pass from the State Marshal's Office giving him access to the trial on alternating days with Pacifica Radio, that he and the woman from Pacifica Radio figured out that an alternating pass shared by a Miami newspaper and a San Bernardino television station is only being used by the TV station, and only every other day by the TV station, so between the three of them it's been arranged that Seth and the woman from Pacifica Radio can attend the trial every day, rather than every other day. As for seat assignments, the so-called *network pool* has managed to secure the best seats for members of the network pool by flattering the state marshal with several pretrial profiles of the state marshal and the workings of his office, so the remaining seats are assigned on a daily basis by a kind of morning lottery drawing, which means that one day Seth might draw a good seat in the court-room, and on the following day a terrible seat, or a terrible seat followed by another terrible seat, or a good seat followed by another good seat, and so on, as luck dictates . . .

. . . the main outline of the Martinez case is undisputed by either side: one evening in August, 1989, Carlos and Felix Martinez, brothers twenty-one and eighteen years old respectively, shot and killed Fidel and Peggy Martinez, their mother and father, in the so-called rumpus room of their mansion on Woodrow Wilson Drive, blasting *two* rounds of birdshot and *three* rounds of buckshot into Fidel Martinez, *eight* rounds of buckshot and *two* rounds of birdshot into Peggy Martinez, though it is unclear how many of the shots were fired by Carlos Martinez and how many were fired by Felix Martinez, and it's also unclear if the number of shots actually correspond to the number of wounds, since far fewer birdshot and buckshot pellets were recovered than would have been consistent with *four* birdshot and *eleven* buckshot cartridges, and the exact sequence of the shotgun blasts is similarly unclear, it appears that Carlos Martinez fired first, at his father, and perhaps also fired the first shots at his mother, since Felix Martinez was initially unable or unwilling to fire his own weapon, though Felix burst through the so-called French doors of the rumpus room slightly ahead of Carlos and later fired many of the fifteen shots, though precisely how many and in what sequence Felix himself does not recall. The brothers, the papers say, *paused in the midst of the slaughter* to leave the house and reload their weapons from the trunk of Carlos's Trans Am, reportedly parked at the time in the so-called *ornamental carport,* mistaking a box of *birdshot* cartridges for a box of *buckshot* cartridges, which partially accounts for the presence of both birdshot and buckshot in the bodies of both parents, though not entirely, since only Carlos returned to the so-called rumpus room to fire the final blast of buckshot or birdshot into Peggy Martinez (a fact which may or may not weigh in Felix's favor vis-à-vis the intention to kill), suggesting that one or the other or both of the brothers initially loaded with both birdshot and buckshot. After the killings, the brothers eventually notified the police, though it is not entirely known how soon after, since imme-diately afterwards the brothers drove from the house on Woodrow Wilson Drive to Laurel Canyon to dispose of their bloodstained clothing in a dumpster be-hind the so-called Laurel Canyon Pick 'n Save, a convenience store, from Laurel Canyon to the Century City Mall, where they purchased movie tickets to establish some type of alibi, then from the Century City Mall to the Santa Monica Civic Center, where they had arranged to meet Buzz McIlheney, a former tennis coach of Carlos and Felix, at a so-called *cheese and wine tasting event,* and, not finding Buzz McIlheney at the cheese and wine tasting event, phoned Buzz McIlheney, using a Sprint telephone credit card the prosecution is making a great fuss about, from the Santa Monica Civic Center the brothers drove back to the house on Woodrow Wilson Drive, at various times the brothers estimated the hiatus between the killings and their report of the killings as *sixty minutes, sixty-seven minutes,* and *ninety minutes,* at the end of which time Carlos Martinez phoned 911 and reported the killings, in a state of apparent hysteria, somewhat ambiguously claiming to the 911 dispatcher that he and his brother had just discovered their dead parents in the so-called rumpus room, having returned home from a movie and the so-called cheese and wine tasting event, and at first, indeed not only at first but for seven months after the tragic incidents on Woodrow Wilson Drive, it was assumed that the deaths of Fidel and Peggy Martinez were *gangland killings,* or, as was sometimes reported, *gangland-style* killings, since Fidel Martinez, a video distribution company executive, was reputed to have had so-called *gangland connections* or *gangland associates,* though it was often noted that a double murder involving fifteen shotgun blasts could not be accurately described as gangland-*style* killings, even if they had in fact been *gangland* killings, since the established *style* of gangland killings is a single bullet fired from a pistol or revolver into the base of the skull, rather than five to ten rounds of birdshot and buckshot fired wildly from a shotgun. The Beverly Hills Police Department, which only handles an average of two homicides per year, in the wake of these violent deaths, surmised that the murders were indeed some type of *gang-related* or *mob-connected* killings, despite their lack of so-called gangland *style,* and pursued this avenue of thinking in its investigations . . .

. . . among the many things auguring badly for the Martinez brothers is what most newspapers characterize as the *wild spending spree* the brothers went on, together and separately, in the weeks immediately following their parents' murders. This *wild spending spree* has been variously reported as an expenditure of *seven hundred thousand dollars, eight hundred thousand dollars, eight hundred and fifty thousand dollars,* and *nine hundred thousand dollars,* and involved the purchase of three gold Rolex watches, a $60,000 Porsche convertible, a Jeep, numerous items of tennis gear and designer clothing, myriad airline tickets, the services of several bodyguards and limousine companies, as well as a condominium in Princeton, New Jersey, where Carlos had been attending college. Some of the money was spent from the *six hundred and thirty thousand dollar* life insurance payment paid out to the Martinez brothers in September, 1989, and some from the alleged *fourteen million dollar estate* left by Fidel Martinez (a figure hastily calculated after the killings and probably defective, pursuant to estate taxes, mortgages, and other outstanding debts). The Martinez money was also used by Carlos to purchase a *bistro* or *brasserie* style restaurant specializing in so-called *buffalo chicken wings,* also in Princeton, though whether this investment can really be characterized as part of a wild spending spree is a matter of considerable debate, as is the wild spending spree characterization of the condominium purchase, since it's been established that Fidel and Peggy Martinez in fact selected the condo for Carlos and had already arranged to buy the condo for Carlos, having only been prevented from doing so by their violent deaths that August.

. . . another circumstance that, in retrospect, augurs badly for the Martinez brothers is the *extravagant show of grief* they displayed right after the murders, including the eulogy given by Carlos Martinez at the funeral, and another eulogy Carlos delivered at a subsequent memorial service (held, it is sometimes noted with a certain irony, at the Screen Actors Guild), though it is also widely conceded that the brothers could not have been expected to behave otherwise, since an absence of grief would have been highly remarkable, and there is also some sentiment that the brothers may actually have been grief-stricken after committing the crime, recognizing the enormity of what they had done, regardless of the circumstances claimed by their defense attorneys, namely that Carlos and Felix Martinez had *feared for their lives,* believing that Fidel and Peggy Martinez were plotting to kill them that night in the so-called rumpus room while eating bowls of vanilla ice cream with strawberries and watching *It's a Wonderful Life* on the VCR. The newspapers, quoting various statements by the prosecutors, reflect a general reluctance to believe that someone who kills his parents can also be grief-stricken afterwards, or go on a spending spree while feeling remorse, or that human behavior, even and especially in situations where some gross transgression has been committed, can be inconsistent and contradictory . . .

. . . the involvement of the two brothers might never have come to light, Seth says, if Dr. Potter Phlegg, the so-called clinical psychologist treating both Carlos and Felix Martinez, had not had a falling out with Sabrina Wilcox, his erstwhile patient and mistress, who originally said that she overheard Felix confessing the murders to Potter Phlegg while eavesdropping at the door of Potter Phlegg's office, because Sabrina Wilcox didn't go to the police until six months later (after Potter Phlegg, or Sabrina Wilcox, depending on which you believe, ended their relationship), apparently in the erroneous belief that Potter Phlegg would then be arrested as an accessory after the fact, and charged with various crimes including rape and battery Sabrina Wilcox claims Potter Phlegg perpetrated against her (crimes, it is said, that the district attorney has so far refused to prosecute or investigate, in order to preserve Potter Phlegg as a credible witness) or else because Sabrina Wilcox was brainwashed by Potter Phlegg into thinking her own life was in danger from the Martinez brothers. Though at first Sabrina Wilcox (who says it was she and not Potter Phlegg who terminated their relationship) went to the police with the tale of having eavesdropped, now, after recovering from what Sabrina Wilcox describes as *post-traumatic stress disorder,* Sabrina Wilcox says she was brainwashed into thinking she had heard Carlos's confession, whereas she now believes she was only told about the confession by Potter Phlegg, yet because of the original claim that threats had been made against Potter Phlegg it became technically possible for Potter Phlegg, for reasons Seth has so far failed to fully grasp, to testify for the prosecution, despite the so-called doctor-patient confidentiality laws that exclude precisely such allegedly private communications between doctors and patients . . .

. . . in August, Seth tells me that as he writes up his notes at the kitchenette table in the second floor suite at the Chateau Marmont, he finds the Martinez brothers and their desperate circumstances swimming in and out of focus, like a scene revealed by a theater scrim that turns opaque with a trick of lighting. He peers out the window at the narrow drive running along the rear of the hotel, noticing a blotch of spilled yellow paint in the roadbed (a blotch that forms a kind of soft-bottomed W intersected by a jagged cross), wondering if he prefers this unaccustomed view to the easterly Sunset Boulevard view he enjoys from Room 603, his usual room at the Marmont, or whether he actually favors the westerly view from Room 511, which he habitually occupies when Room 603 is unavailable. This current view is a quieter view, he says, a desolate view, even a dead view. As he thinks about this, it strikes him that the comparatively panoramic views from Room 603 and Room 511 are also dead views, though he cannot say why, and he thinks also of the vast southerly view from the terrace of the nearby St. James Club, where he sometimes goes to stare at the wrought-iron palms along the railing, suddenly, as a dead view. The truth is, Seth says, that this is a dead city, full of dead views. Not as dead as San Francisco, which has such an odd stillness and melancholy silence about it, as if everyone who lives there died long ago, but dead all the same, because everything here is disconnected. There is no connection, Seth says, between this room and this hotel and the city around it, this room and this hotel have nothing to do with anything. Everyone in this city is in transit from one place to someplace else, crossing vast dead space to get from one dead thing to another, one moment of life to another, and in between, nothing . . .

. . . he has the same dream lately almost every night that wakes him in the dark with a sweat of relief pouring off him, that he's gone to some gathering in a confusing structure built on water, part of an abandoned airport or crumbling sanitarium at the tip of a rock jetty, at first he recognizes the other guests, or thinks he does, but the longer he stays the more they seem to be actors impersonating his friends and acquaintances, and somewhere further back, on some missing page of the narrative, he's knocked the brains out of a small boy and hidden the body in a kind of wooden shed or locker, he believes he's moved the corpse several times, concealing it in closets, under floorboards, at the back of remote rooms in this place that is sometimes a castle or luxury hotel, and now the milky white cadaver is somewhere very close, as the party becomes gayer and the guests more reckless with their dancing and drinks, the festivities spilling into all the distant corridors, servants' quarters, ballrooms full of chairs and pianos spectral under drop cloths, as things begin looking up for him, as the desperate circumstances that led to his crime reveal themselves as insignificant, he knows the discovery of the slain child will now ruin him, that he's poisoned the future with an action he no longer understands or even recalls with any clarity . . .

. . . so far Marlene Quilty, the Carlos Martinez prosecutor, who's arguing her case before the so-called *gold* jury, has described what she calls the cold-blooded lies of Carlos Martinez, beginning with the 911 phone call. When

Carlos Martinez made that call, she says, he pretended to choke back sobs while declaring that some unknown person or persons had shot his parents, and then he went on to tell police that the killings were probably some type of revenge slayings brought about by Fidel Martinez's crooked or ruthless business dealings. She says that Carlos Martinez was "cool as a cucumber" when he fired his Mossberg shotgun at his own parents. But cucumber, she says, is probably not a strong enough word, since this was no garden vegetable killing its parents, but a very cunning human being, and that two of the shots were so-called contact wounds, one to the back of Fidel's head, the other to Peggy's cheek, blowing their brains into kingdom come, and furthermore, she says, the brothers were lying in wait (one of the special circumstances that merit the death penalty) for their parents to fall asleep. Marlene Quilty says that Carlos Martinez told the police detective, Lester Zabar, that Fidel Martinez fell asleep during the first five minutes of any movie, though Carlos did not say whether movies caused Peggy Martinez to fall asleep, Marlene Quilty says she cannot prove whether both Fidel and Peggy were asleep when the brothers burst into the rumpus room, perhaps only Fidel was asleep while Peggy was fully conscious, for all we actually know, Marlene Quilty says, Fidel could have been awake and Peggy might have been asleep, but we have the defendant's own words, she says, liar though he is, that Fidel tended to fall asleep, perhaps the defendant's mother was awake when he shot her in cold blood, Marlene Quilty says, which would be bad enough, and keep in mind, she adds, that these two very real human victims were not a couple of vegetables either, but we believe she was asleep, because both Peggy and Fidel Martinez had just eaten *a rich dessert,* and you all know from your own experience, Marlene Quilty tells the so-called *gold* jury, how tired one becomes after eating a rich dessert, and the state will also show that the movie Peggy and Fidel Martinez were watching was *It's a Wonderful Life,* a movie we would guess the Martinezes had seen before, since it's so often aired on television, a movie that might easily have put them both to sleep, though tragically enough they are not here to tell us one way or another.

This brings us to the *wild spending spree,* Marlene Quilty tells the so-called gold jury, standing at a wooden podium directly behind Carlos Martinez's head (which everyone knows is partly covered by an expensive hairpiece the defense has fought bitterly to retain on Carlos's head throughout the trial, unknown to the jury, however, Carlos has to remove the glued-on hairpiece when he returns to his jail cell, and glue it back on before leaving for court each morning; some wags like Fawbus Kennedy, the famous author, claim that

Carlos worries more about his hairpiece than the outcome of the trial, at various moments in her presentation Marlene Quilty glares down into Carlos Martinez's hair as if she can barely contain an urge to rip the hairpiece off his scalp), once Carlos Martinez had *shot his parents,* she says, he wasted no time before starting to *spend their money,* and here she mentions the Rolex watches, the sticker price of the Porsche, the condominium down payment, the five hundred thousand dollars Carlos paid for the so-called buffalo chicken wing emporium in Princeton, and just in case, she says, just in case Fidel Martinez's grave and continual disappointment in his son might have swayed him into writing a new will, Carlos employed what he called *a little Jewish guy* to erase Fidel's home computer. Except for a few mistakes, declares Marlene Quilty, it was almost the perfect murder.

. . . while the so-called gold jury disperses into the basement cafeteria for the morning coffee break or out beyond the building into Little Toyko, not being sequestered and therefore free to roam the landscape at hazard from impudent reporters and the contaminating flash of newspaper headlines, Carlos's lawyer, Sarah Johnson, moves for a mistrial, in her calm methodical soft tripping voice that never rises above a kind of hospital bedside wistfulness, Sarah Johnson sounds like an intensive care nurse deftly inserting a catheter, whereas Marlene Quilty, in her flame-red suit, and her brown hair cinched back in a ponytail, has an angry impatient drilling sort of voice, a voice that tosses chunks of rubble out of sidewalks, Sarah Johnson tells the judge, Rupert Tietelbaum, that Marlene Quilty has prejudiced the jury by saying that Carlos called the computer expert *a little Jewish guy.* We know, Your Honor, Sarah Johnson says, that two members of the gold jury are Jewish, and they are going to have the statement *little Jewish guy* uppermost in their minds.

Your Honor, Marlene Quilty protests, the defendant in his own words told one of our witnesses that *a little Jewish guy* erased the hard drive on Fidel Martinez's computer. The defendant happened to characterize him that way, the same way you might say *a little Italian guy* or *a little Norwegian guy,* it isn't the state's duty to clean up the defendant's verbatim remarks anyway, but Mrs. Johnson seems to be laboring under the idea that the word *Jewish* or the word *little* or the word *guy* is some kind of racial or ethnic epithet.

In Mrs. Quilty's opening remarks, Your Honor, Sarah Johnson says, she gave a particular, scornful emphasis to the phrase little Jewish guy, as I think everyone in this courtroom clearly heard. If the Court please, I am not laboring under any idea, it is simply my impression that Mrs. Quilty gave the phrase little Jewish guy the intonation of an epithet. *Little Jewish guy,* Sarah Johnson imitates, giving the word a decided sneer.

Your Honor my intonation if it was meant to imply anything was meant to suggest the defendant's cavalier manner of describing the ease with which he had the computer erased, Marlene Quilty says, and the defendant's general attitude that all his problems could be solved by picking up a phone and hiring somebody to deal with them. Using his father's money I might add.

Oh really Your Honor that is a stretch, says Sarah Johnson in her prim fastidious way.

All right, says Judge Tietelbaum, staring into a bunch of papers on his dais, his glabrous bald scalp reflecting like a three minute egg the fluorescent light above his head, I'm going to note the defense's objection for the record, the black balloonlike sleeve of his robe passing over the scattered papers, but I'm also going to rule even though there are two Jews on the jury to deny the motion for mistrial, Tietelbaum clears his throat, makes a ruminative noise as he swallows his semidisgorged sputum, munches briefly on his copious mustache, had the prosecution quoted the defendant referring to a *kike* or a *yid,* that would be one thing, and I would suggest to you, Mrs. Quilty, that if any utterances of that nature are going to be quoted, you refrain from saying *kike* or *yid* or words of that demeanor in front of the jury, with the same precaution I have already given with regard to the term *sociopath,* but I really don't think *little Jewish guy* is strong enough language to influence the jurors one way or the other.

With all due respect, Your Honor, I think Your Honor should question the two Jews, says Sarah Johnson.

Speaking as a Jew, Mrs. Johnson, says the judge, I don't.

. . . meanwhile, in impaling files reams of dusty warrants grimly writhe into many shapes, as Seth says, as issue after issue in *The State of California v. Martinez* clogs the pipeline to appellate court, in the matter of the missing Mossberg shotguns, for example, and the audiotape of the November 9 therapy session, where Felix and Carlos explained their motives for the killings, and Dr. Potter Phlegg's audiotape of his notes from the October 30 therapy session, when Felix supposedly confessed, and the issue of the intended purpose of Sabrina Wilcox's presence outside the office of Dr. Potter Phlegg, plus the depositions given during pretrial by Dr. Potter Phlegg and Sabrina Wilcox, as well as the complaints filed by Sabrina Wilcox against Potter Phlegg alleging rape, battery, and harassment, added to the issue of Dr. Potter Phlegg's license vis-à-vis the illegal dispensing of prescription drugs, there's also the question of Daria Krapadopolos, Carlos's former fiancée, being offered money by Carlos for perjured testimony on the advice of his first attorney, who has a previous professional relationship with his present attorney, each item pressing against the other and all nuzzling forward like bald, birth-damp kittens in a greased black chute . . .

. . . after the morning break, Sarah Johnson perches at the wooden podium behind Carlos Martinez, her face like that of a large, vigilant raptor, long straight sandy hair curled inward at the ends, facing the so-called *gold* jury or Carlos jury, which sits in the raised jury box on the judge's right-hand side, while behind her are three rows of empty seats reserved for the so-called *blue* jury or Felix jury, that is, when both the *gold* jury and the *blue* jury are present, for when the *gold* jury is absent, the *blue* jury sits in the jury box, though it could as easily sit in the empty reserved seats, and in the course of the trial, when the nature of certain evidence or testimony requires that the *gold* jury be sent out while the *blue* jury remains, or the *blue* jury be sent out while the *gold* jury remains, or *both* juries be sent out and then only *one* jury be called back, and the *other jury* called back while the *first jury* is still present, it would probably be more expeditious for the *blue* jury to stay in the empty reserved seats rather than moving into the jury box, but it's also physically awkward for Felix's prosecutor and Felix's attorneys to look at the *blue* jury when the *blue* jury is seated behind them, especially since Judge Tietelbaum has issued directives restricting the attorneys' range of motion inside the space between the attorneys' table and the witness stand, and the attorneys' table and the jury box, and to address the *blue* jury when the *blue* jury is seated in the reserved seats requires the attorney to turn his or her back on the witness stand and the judge's bench, so quite often, though not always, the *blue* jury will move into the jury box in the absence of the *gold* jury, something Sarah Johnson doesn't have to think about when only speaking to the *gold* jury, since on no occasion will the *gold* jury occupy the empty reserved seats while the *blue* jury sits in the jury box, even though it would often be easier to seat them there.

In this trial, Sarah Johnson tells the gold jury, we will take you behind the luxurious facade of enormous houses and expensive cars and impressive social engagements. Things are not always how they look, says Sarah Johnson, looks can be deceiving, because on the outside, to the naked eye, anyone would have had the impression that all was hunky dory on Woodrow Wilson Drive, here you had a fabulously successful entertainment executive and his vivacious wife, and their two athletically gifted sons, the picture of Beverly Hills success. Yet everything was not hunky dory, she says, things were just the very opposite of hunky dory within, a fact known only to a few, but known to enough people whom you will hear from that you will think twice next time someone seems to have a perfect home.

Carlos and Felix Martinez killed their parents. We don't dispute how. We don't dispute where. We don't dispute when this crime occurred. We only dispute and ask the single question why. Why? Think about why. Why would two young, handsome, privileged boys who seemed to have everything find it necessary to do such an unbelievable act, and if they did do it, which we don't dispute, why such ferocity? Why so many shots? Why the incredibly messy carnage which the prosecution tells you could only be the result of hatred? Was it hatred? You will hear from many, many people who were close to this family that Carlos and Felix Martinez did not hate their parents, far from it. They lived in awe of their successful father and his accomplishments. The prosecution claims these killings were committed out of greed. Greed? These young men lived in a bubble of money. They had unlimited use of credit cards and could buy whatever they desired. The perfect crime? Far from it. In fact, it was only by chance that the Martinez brothers weren't arrested on the night of the killings, Sarah Johnson says, they certainly expected to be, they waited in the house expecting the police to arrive at any moment, you don't fire all those shots at 10 P.M. in a residential neighborhood without someone calling the police, or so they thought, she says, little did they suspect that their closest neighbors, whom you will hear from, mistook the rapid pop pop popping sound of gunshots for the rapid pop pop popping sound of Chinese firecrackers, it was only after the brothers realized that no one had called the police that they began, in their clumsy far-from-thought-out way, to consider the possibility of thinking up an alibi, collecting the shell casings, driving to the cheese and wine tasting event, and so forth. If the brothers had come anywhere near planning the perfect crime, Sarah Johnson says, we wouldn't be here having this trial, would we? I submit to you, ladies and gentlemen, that the only thing perfect about this crime was the perfect mess the Beverly Hills

Police Department made of the investigation, and we cannot blame the Martinez brothers for that.

So let's forget about hatred for a moment. Let's put aside greed. And let's not even introduce the bizarre notion that these two young men wanted to commit the perfect crime, a motive seldom if ever found outside of a detective novel. We are going to show you, instead, the life Carlos Martinez really lived. A life of dark family secrets. Secrets which could, if revealed, destroy the image of the perfect American family. This was a family in which things had been going wrong for a very long time, Sarah Johnson says. Such a very long time, stretching all the way back to Pennington, and Mugdale, and Kalamazoo, all the towns and all the houses the Martinez family lived in before arriving at Peggy's cherished zip code in Beverly Hills, back to the time when Carlos, a mere child, was sexually molested by his father. This started with inappropriate massages, usually after the harsh regimen of sports practice Fidel Martinez imposed on both his sons from an early age, and soon progressed to oral sodomy and anal penetration. Fidel Martinez used his son for his sexual gratification, and later on, his other son. They were told by their father that these sexual acts were practiced in Ancient Greece and Ancient Rome by soldiers preparing for battle, and by soldiers weary from battle. Fidel Martinez indoctrinated his sons with so-called history lessons which he said the great men of the past had learned, but had to be kept secret in the mediocre world of today. The sons, who were weary from tennis practice, believed their father was a wise man. Others would not understand these manly practices, which were nothing more or less than pedophilia, least of all Peggy Martinez, yet we have every reason to believe that Peggy Martinez did know all about the molestation and allowed it to continue for her own misguided selfish reasons.

What happened in the days leading up to the killings? A series of events, including Felix Martinez's revelation to his brother Carlos that his father had been molesting him for twelve years. Carlos Martinez confronted their father and told him this sexual activity was going to stop. He told Fidel Martinez that he was going to take his little brother out of the house. What was Fidel Martinez's reaction? He did not agree to stop. He did not agree to let Carlos take Felix away with him. He told Carlos Martinez that he, Fidel Martinez, could do what he wanted with his own son. That no one was going to threaten him. That the secret would never go outside the family, and that anyone who held the secret over him would not be allowed to live . . .

———

. . . so in Sarah Johnson's version of events, the brothers decided to arm themselves after Fidel's threat, first attempting to buy handguns at the so-called Gun-O-Rama in Venice Beach, where she says they were informed about the fifteen-day waiting period for handguns, only then, she says, in sheer desperation, they drove all the way to San Diego and purchased two Mossberg pump-action shotguns at the so-called E-Z Mart Weapons Center, she says it was Felix rather than Carlos who actually bought the guns, using a driver's license that Jocko Phelan had left, along with his wallet, when Carlos, acting on orders from Fidel, kicked Jocko Phelan out of his dormitory room at Princeton, because, Sarah Johnson says, Felix was physically similar to Jocko Phelan. Therefore the dread and panic building up to the killings resulted in quickly improvised self-defensive measures, and not some sort of master plan, and by the same token, picking up the blasted shotgun shells just seemed like the thing to do, when contrary to all expectations the police didn't zoom up to the mansion moments after the shots. Furthermore, Sarah Johnson says, you can't consider it a planned alibi to meet Buzz McIlheney at the cheese and wine event, since they never did meet Buzz McIlheney at the cheese and wine event, all these things the prosecution says reflect some type of premeditated master plan, she says, reflect the very opposite of planning, look at the so-called spending spree, if you were trying to cover up a murder would you go on a wild spending spree a few days later?

After lunch, it's Quentin Kojimoto's turn to say what the state will prove and lay out the state's theory, reminding the blue jury that Felix Martinez is a grown man, not a boy, not a child, though in fact Felix was barely eighteen at the time of the killings, Felix who drove two hundred miles to the E-Z Mart in San Diego for the sole purpose of buying shotguns, that the brothers planned the perfect murder, moreover they, the blue jurors, would hear from Dr. Potter Phlegg the spectacular confession of Felix Martinez, in which the younger brother said that Fidel Martinez had been too controlling, kept the brothers from doing what they wanted, and had disinherited them, another reason to get rid of him, furthermore, that Peggy had been killed because she would have been a witness to the killing of Fidel, that Felix had told Dr. Potter Phlegg that Peggy would have been miserable and suicidal without Fidel, and that killing her had really been a sort of mercy killing. Quentin Kojimoto has a whiffle haircut and unflatteringly chubby cheeks, his squinched features trapped in the center of a vast field of blank flesh, and something plodding and relentless and wooden about him that inspires rough comment around the courthouse that Marlene Quilty thinks he's an incompetent moron and keeps calling the district attorney trying to get him thrown off the case . . .

. . . it's true that a certain torpor descends during Kojimoto's lusterless execrations, owing possibly to the starchy ingestion of the courthouse cafeteria's plat du jour of smothered chicken à la king, a torpor communicated via courtroom camera to millions of listless Americans channel-surfing across myriad waves of cable foaming down the information superhighway, their slick residue causing mirages of toilet bowl cleansers and breath-freshening pills and tubes of hemmorhoidal cream to rise from the cerebral tarmac, viewers in Des Moines and Galveston and Chattanooga fall prey to the soporific spell of creamy rich chicken sauce prepared by an L.A. County dietician, then suddenly without preamble Lauren Nathanson tosses an electrical jolt into the neural mix, five feet two inches of galvanic response, like heat from a blast furnace, her wild mahogany hair and squarejawed fury causing everyone in court including Judge Tietelbaum to stiffen in their chairs. In the hidden heart of the Martinez case, she says, are family secrets so horrible that neither Carlos nor Felix trusted Dr. Potter Phlegg enough to tell him, especially since Potter Phlegg, prior to the killings, had reported everything Felix and Carlos told him directly back to Fidel Martinez, and the circumstances around the making of the so-called confession tape after the killings are extremely murky and open to interpretation as well.

They did not tell Potter Phlegg that Fidel Martinez molested Carlos from the age of six to the age of eight, *though he did,* and his son Felix from the age of six to the age of eighteen, *though he did,* the molestation starting in both cases with *after-sports massages* and escalating into *sodomy* and *sadistic poking* with *needles* and *tacks* and more sodomy involving *toothbrushes* and *spoons* and other household objects, which was only part of Fidel's reign of terror, aided and abetted by Peggy, who forced both boys at various times to sleep with her when Fidel was away, who regularly inspected and fondled Felix's genitals until he was fifteen, who punished both sons by making them roll around in ferret droppings left by a succession of her pet ferrets, all of them named Stinky.

They did not tell Potter Phlegg because as soon as Felix contacted Potter Phlegg in order to disburden his conscience Potter Phlegg began contriving ways to make the Martinez brothers dependent on him, began immediately to put himself forward as their advisor on investments and financial planning, and raised their suspicions that he planned to blackmail them, and so they elected to humor Potter Phlegg, to cooperate with Potter Phlegg's schemes, which included the making of the so-called confession tape, without revealing any of the true facts leading up to the homicides. For example, five days before the killings a fight broke out between Peggy and Carlos, in the course of which Peggy grabbed Carlos's hairpiece and tore it off, Felix had been unaware of Carlos's hairpiece and thought at first that his mother had ripped Carlos's hair out of his head. This shock prompted Felix to confide to Carlos, later the same night, that Fidel's sexual abuse of Felix, which Carlos believed had stopped several years earlier, had continued right up to the present day. Carlos confronted Fidel, who told him he would do as he pleased with Felix. Fidel told Carlos, "Don't throw your life away," a clear threat that Fidel would have Carlos killed if Carlos revealed as he threatened to the secret of the sexual molestation. Still later that night, Peggy told Felix that she had known all along what his father was doing to him, that she wasn't stupid, that no one had protected her—a pregnant remark we hope to explore fully in the course of this trial—and that she didn't care.

Carlos and Felix spent the remaining days in growing terror that Peggy and Fidel would have them killed. In such a family, Lauren Nathanson says, the parents seemed all-powerful, all-knowing, all-present. Felix, for example, attributed magical powers of precognition to Peggy Martinez, for she seemed to know his every movement in advance, she knew what friends he was seeing, whom he was talking to, his personal thoughts, what we now know, Lauren Nathanson says, is that Peggy Martinez bugged Felix's private phone, but the kid didn't know that. He thought his mother could get right inside his head and listen to his thoughts. And Fidel Martinez, with his loose talk about screwing his business partners and dealing with the mob, in his children's minds had the implacable reach of an octopus. In their minds there was no way they could run away and escape him. The shadowy hints of the ruthless Fidel Martinez lent chilling credence to his threats. Peggy's capricious, alcoholic self-involvement, her jealous obsessions, what seemed like her telepathic omniscience, and her resentment of the sons made her complicity all too apparent. The boys decided to arm themselves, and after a failed attempt to buy handguns at the Gun-O-Rama in Venice Beach, they drove to San Diego and bought the Mossberg shotguns from the so-called E-Z Mart. But they did so with no fixed plan in their minds, only confusion and fear.

The hiatus between Friday and Sunday of that fateful week had a dreamlike panic quality, hypervigilant yet strangely muted, a sort of underwater feeling, a silent black-and-white movie slowed down to a speed where each frame became a bleary abstract painting. Sudden noises and bursts of tense conversation eerily resonant with menace. There were 2 A.M. conferences between the brothers in Carlos's bedroom in the guesthouse, strange behavior by the parents, unexplained movements inside the mansion, speechless malevolent looks exchanged across hallways, the pool, the tennis court, the walkway between the mansion and the guesthouse, the mood weirdly deflated at odd moments by longueurs of utter normality, for as Felix himself will eventually testify, it was hard for him to believe, waking up on a clear California morning, that the whole impossible situation had carried over from the day before, that his parents were still plotting his doom, that he was still trapped in the gooey psychological web of the family. But then there was Carlos to remind him, fixed in his absolute conviction of deadly danger, and also the weird shark-fishing expedition on Saturday aboard the *Naked Movie Star,* a charter vessel in Marina Del Rey, that set off in terrible choppy waters, the boys huddled at one end of the boat with ocean spray and gelid mist soaking them from late afternoon until almost midnight, Fidel at the other end of the boat, Peggy belowdecks vomiting from seasickness but sometimes emerging to confer in whispers with Fidel, and then later, brittle silence in the house, slamming doors, the mid-August heat prickly and menacing, a still, somnolent deadness in the air, an overwhelming atmosphere of strangeness and shattered nerves, and finally, on Sunday night, Peggy's sinister ukase forbidding the boys to leave the house, Peggy joined suddenly by Fidel, the two parents boiling in unison or so it seemed with vengeful design, Fidel ordering Felix to his room, no doubt at least in Felix's mind with the purpose of having sex with Felix one final time before blowing him away, then Peggy and Fidel shutting themselves up in the rumpus room, Carlos drawn by the quarrel, finding Felix quivering at the top of the stairs, should they flee the house then and there, no, wherever they went Fidel would track them down, no relative or friend could shield them from Fidel's implacable wrath and murderous fear of exposure, it was then that Carlos told Felix, *it's now or never, let's do it,* then that Carlos went for his shotgun in the guesthouse, and Felix went for his shotgun in his bedroom, and the two of them met outside, loaded the guns from the trunk of the Trans Am, entered the hall from the side, and burst through the French windows of the rumpus room with guns drawn, firing wildly until both shotguns were spent.

In the deathly silence and gunsmoke haze they sat down and waited for the police. When nothing happened they cooked up a crude improvisation of an alibi that would have been blown full of holes by any less credulous law enforcement agency than the Beverly Hills police. Felix, Lauren Nathanson says, was ready to confess then and there, if somebody had asked the right questions. This was a kid who needed to tell. A kid the following seven months of concealment screwed up beyond belief. He had even been willing to talk to a certifiable quack like Potter Phlegg in hope of relieving the burden of guilt. But of course Potter Phlegg had betrayed him, just as Peggy had betrayed him by not protecting him from his father, just as his father had betrayed him by raping him.

So my friend Seth arrives, unpacks his jumble of wrinkled laundry at the Marmont, and steps into the Carlos and Felix story during opening arguments, his own nerves frazzled, tracking the Martinez saga with one ear tuned to a replay of the live coverage on cable TV while setting up his movie star profile, his cigarette-scarred lungs reacting badly to the orange haze of a Pacific sunset. He walks out of his room and down to the hall window to look at Sunset Boulevard. The never-ending traffic, the nimbus of promising lights along the Strip. Below, on the hotel lawn, a photographer and five assistants are arranging Drew Barrymore on a pink blanket. Across the boulevard a giant Bullwinkle the Moose catches the day's dying rays. Uneasiness sits on Seth's head like a plastic dashboard troll. The familiar trips, the familiar hotels, the familiar arrivals unsettle him more than they used to, tire him to the point of feeling old, he half expects age to strike in some terrible fashion, with a malignant lump or a coronary, for it is Seth's habit never to feel entirely at home anywhere, least of all in his own body. I'm going nowhere, he tells himself, because that is the sort of thing Seth always tells himself, with mantralike numbness, alone in a hotel.

As for Jack, who also worries about his health, frets and fusses with himself in a manner to induce paralysis of will, Jack who experiences the existential horror of being Jack with a constantly renewed sense of frustration, especially now, having gotten his death notice in the form of a blood test two years ago, he is, at the same hour, with a little help from Jose Cuervo, surveying his ken, a quarter acre of steep hillside overlooking Figueroa Street and Avenue 45, a view scumbled by overhanging tree limbs, with a vertiginous hump of residential bleakness across the way, a yawning blackness sprinkled here and there with streetlamps and dim Cornell Woolrich windows, the air fraught with the howling of dogs, a regular keening that carries on half the night and sometimes all night, for down in the Spanish slum at the base of the hill there are myriad agitated semiferal dogs chained in myriad desolate dustridden yards choked with cinder blocks piled under flapping tarpaper and slashed rubber tires and scattered auto parts and heavily tattooed slickhaired youths armed with handguns and switchblades and assault rifles, Jack's sitting in a canvas chair in his living room with most of the lights off, killing a bottle of tequila, sometimes talking to himself, experimentally, pretending to have neuropathic dementia just to see what that's like, at one moment he talks to himself but imagines he's talking to Juan, a friend slash sort of lover who's more or less left him, if people can leave you only more or less, not left him because Jack's difficult to get along with, Juan being too cool for that, but merely out of youthful fickleness, youthful in Juan's case being twenty-seven, a ripe youthfulness Jack compares in his thoughts to the oozing ripeness of a partly eaten wheel of Camembert, Jack tells this invisible cheese wheel not about his painfully intense love (because it has become more like rue or melancholy or bad digestion than what Jack would like love to be) but about his motives, explaining the tangled web of childhood disappointments and adult betrayals that make Jack all these decades later who he is, to his own sharply critical ear sounding very much like former president Richard Nixon, which leads Jack whimsically to image Nixon acting the role of a spurned homosexual.

I am not a crook, Jack tells the imaginary Juan, laughing at his own lunacy as he splashes more liquor into his glass. I've always been driven to fuck up relationships. We could get a million dollars for Hunt and his lawyer, but it would be wrong. And as for you—Jack spins in Nixonian fashion from Juan to Seth (who likewise isn't there), suddenly bilious—what gives you the right, who do you think you are . . . Jack staggers out of his seat, points his forefinger at the empty space where Seth would appear if Jack really did have dementia, holds his glass demonstratively, hears the ice cubes tinkling, the dogs baying out beyond the window screens, and smiles to himself, dropping his presidential impersonation. Dementia, he tells Seth in his own voice, as if referring to an old friend. Dementia would be just awful, but if I had it, I wouldn't know I had it, would I, so I wouldn't even know how awful it was.

———

Everyone agrees there is something monstrous and awesome about the Martinez case, but some people have different reasons for thinking this than others. Jack hasn't given it much thought at all. In Jack's mind, the Martinez case figures among a dozen current events buzzing in the zeitgeist, things you hear about without really wanting to, Jack believes that events can be tricks that keep your mind off some unchanging structural flaw in human organization, circus acts designed to numb critical scrutiny. Something hidden, a conspiracy, or some sinister condition of things. Jack's forever trying to figure such things out, attach a diagnosis, settle a meaning. Jack thinks that everything that happens hides something else. Since losing faith in dialectical materialism, Jack's inclined to analyze things in occult terms, flirting with the belief that thirteen men control the world, that planetary configurations determine random-looking events, that each person has an astral double whose actions are unseen, metaphorical, the true text of his life. In his dreams he is a butterfly that dreams about being Jack.

Seth believes the Martinez case resembles a large underwater rock, magnified by immersion, with something wriggling underneath it: blind albino fish, possibly, or eyeless eels that have grown to unbelievable length, or prehistoric flintheads encrusted in mossy crud. He thinks the Martinez drama probably illustrates something but doesn't mean anything, that you couldn't use it, for instance, to figure out the kinship system of the primitive Bororo or extract from it the chemical steps to enrich uranium. But you could turn it into a Mardi Gras float or a tableau vivant in a wax museum, serialize it into Stations of the Cross, fashion it into topiary or embroider it on exotic underpants. Seth believes it is always better for something to happen than for nothing to happen, he likes it when life speeds up and propels him through a lot of stuff he can't make heads or tails of at the time, arranging it later into complicated stories, yarns, fables, fairy tales, novellas, poems, jokes, verbal sculptures of any sort that bend in his mouth like putty.

Felix Martinez sleeps badly. He thrashes on the narrow cot in his cell and sometimes falls off. His parents visit him, tiny as mice, dragging their bleeding carcasses around the cement floor. His father never stops complaining about the bullet holes in his stomach, the blood stench he has to smell for eternity like Philoctetes with his stinking foot. And look what you've done to your mother, his father tells him, wagging an indignant furry paw at her. Half her whiskers are missing. One side of her snout looks like hamburger meat with a few pointed teeth floating inside it.

When I get through with you, his father squeaks.

You are through with me, Felix tells him with false bravado. He looks round the cell for Carlos.

Nice try, asshole, his father says. You don't get rid of us that easy.

Carlos whispers in his ear. He is somehow there but not there. Just do what he says, Carlos says. He's upset that we blew him away, you can't blame the guy.

Felix cries. He knows it disgusts his father.

Mama, he says. I'm sorry.

I forgive you, Felix. It was a stupid thing you did, but what's done is done. I never wanted to be your mother. Maybe that was it. You can't imagine what it's like, bleeding all the time. Being dead is even worse than when we lived in Kalamazoo. Nothing to do. I have to listen to your father day and night. It goes on and on just like before. He's still very angry. He was born angry and he died angry.

Damned right I'm angry. Angry is not the word. You kids had no business pulling a stunt like that. And you blew it. Don't tell me it was Carlos's idea, I'm not impressed by your excuses.

Hear that? Carlos whispers. Felix feels his brother's hot breath in his ear, his long thick body pressed against his back, his hard damp sex nestled between his buttocks. An enveloping shadow that sweats. If I go down, Carlos says, you're going with me.

The dry hot season makes everything swim before your eyes. The city a mirage of asphalt ribbons floating on a scorched white plain. One lingering image from this period is the giant crucifix on Forest Lawn, viewed from the spot where Los Feliz Boulevard dips down to the 5 Freeway. A fata morgana on the peak of a green hill. The terrible clarity of the sky the week before the fires makes faraway objects jump closer, as the winds scrape off the dreamy broth of smog.

The tense implacable progress of the trial. Immersed in its gamelike regularity, Seth finds himself living as other people do, waking at a fixed hour, projecting himself through the day as he showers and eats breakfast, drives to work. Chooses clothes that make him appear normal, inconspicuous. He stakes out a small wheeled desk in the press center two floors below the courtroom, and nobody seems to mind. It's a little bit like school. People are happy to share information, anxious to cough up, each day, a little hairball of conventional perception and whatever gossip's making the rounds. Most are working under obtuse exigencies and constraints, the house styles and potted forms of their venues.

It's fairly obvious, Seth tells me, which reporters believe in subtext, and which ones are chasing dull ironies down a dark alley to a trash dumpster. The truly awful ones, though they also have their moments of witty confusion, are the TV people, parading around in heavy makeup like manic ghouls hobbling through a cemetery, working up two minutes' worth of tripe from the labyrinth of an endless intestine, hair lacquered to their heads like Gestapo helmets. For them it's pure sensation, uncut amphetamine, they love marching out of the pressroom and onto the elevator in this tight imperial formation, and I have the impression, Seth says, that the TV reporters are actually physically larger than other people, inflated by some artificial means, a pneumatic pump for example inserted between their anal sphincters before they arrive at the courthouse, because they seem to take up a horrendous amount of space. One always has to maneuver around them in hallways and outside at the press conferences, they're just enormous, like those great floundering nudes at the beach from Picasso's surrealist period, and the really interesting thing is, they have absolutely no idea what this trial is about and they don't even care what it's about, it's just this vortex of dangerous energy they're absorbing through their pores and getting high off.

Meanwhile, all over Los Angeles, people are being murdered, some with shotguns, some with knives, some strangled in their beds, some mowed in half by automatic weapons, some hurled from moving cars, and in the vast arid bowl of the city the winds make headaches blossom, muscles twitch, furnace breezes rake along ragged nerves, while the 911 tape plays on the eighth floor of the Criminal Courts Building, a cacophony of bleeps and munching static, the dispatcher in the witness chair a slightly obese and large-breasted twenty-nine-year-old woman named Mona Swerling whose contrite sandy ponytail and thick eyeglasses and frumpy multicolored blouse convey a sadly vivacious celibacy and conventionally tiny hopes for the future, words tortured from far down in Carlos's diaphragm filling the courtroom, sobs and wails from Felix swelling in the background, a broken wall of improvised horrified noise, or else the shriek of Oedipus mixed with crisp mechanical questions the older

Martinez brother could not have anticipated. Are the people still in the house? I don't know. No. Who's been shot? My mom and dad. Are they dead? Yes. Who shot them? I don't know. Is he about to confect fleeing strangers in ski masks, a favorite sort of imaginary killer in this particular town, because some killer, sometime, the Night Stalker maybe, or the Skid Row Slasher, wore one? To Felix he yells: Get away from them! As if Felix were, who knows? Doodling in the blood with a stick, jerking off on the corpses, sucking his thumb.

Seth says that after a full day in court he drops into chaos, a sudden plenum of unstructured time. He says he cannot figure out the reverse route back to Hollywood via freeway, there are too many changes, he keeps getting lost on surface roads, winding up in Glendale or the forbidding tracts of emptiness behind Griffith Park, roads bare of traffic that look like crime scenes, derelict freight yards and cul-de-sacs, seedy nowhere villages and blank passages of useless landscape. On Friday he sticks securely to Sunset Boulevard, fighting the mild panic that a weekend with no prospects of any kind brings on. He drops into Erehwon on Beverly and buys a large economy jar of Aztec Secret, the World's Most Powerful Facial, apple cider vinegar, and a bottle of selenium tablets, which are supposed to prevent cancer. Whenever he swallows a selenium tablet, Seth visualizes powerful yellow spheres attacking some livid mass inside his liver or kidney.

Seth says that his mind is stuffed with errant nonsense, he keeps hearing words in his head ending in "ix" like "creatrix," "dominatrix," "aviatrix," while the visual part of his brain anticipates slathering the thick green goo of Aztec Secret over his face. It's this nonsense that protects him from nothingness, Seth says, because in less than a week in Los Angeles he can barely defend himself against the sameness of everything, he says that he takes a bath all day in the Martinez trial, the Martinez trial fills him up, but once the Martinez trial is over for the day, Seth says, I'm completely empty again. Opinions form in his mind, he says, like pustules, the Martinez case is like an accretion of pus in a cyst, especially the gossip that goes around the pressroom, some of it started by Fawbus Kennedy, the famous writer, who sees the Martinez case, Seth says, as his platinum meal ticket, and so far it has been, Fawbus Kennedy's always getting buttonholed by Court TV and popping up on *Larry King Live* with his theories about the Martinez case, Fawbus Kennedy's dream in life, Seth says, is to become more famous than his brother Sean, whose novels are considered more literary. And Sean Kennedy's dream in life is to become more famous than his wife Cora Winchell, whose novels are considered more highbrow than Sean Kennedy's novels. Can you imagine, Seth says, what a family dinner with the three of them must be like, Fawbus Kennedy imploding with rage that he'll never get notices as serious as Sean's notices, and Sean pretending to himself that his last book was just as good as Cora's, and Cora meanwhile thinking she's the golden canary of American letters, and of course, Seth goes on, the joke is that all three of them can't get through a paragraph without telling you which famous people they know and what tony neighborhoods they've lived in and how much money they have and how well connected they are. Fawbus is blatant and vulgar about it and Sean tries to give it a little ironic twist, whereas Cora has perfected the art of making her snobbery and name-dropping read like world-weary deprecation. Yet they are all somehow desperate to prove to people they don't even know and will never meet that they, the Kennedy and Winchell clan, belong to some exalted realm of sophistication. So these people who have so much in common, Seth says, spend all their time making each other miserable, competing for praise from other social climbers and snobs.

According to Seth, Fawbus Kennedy started the rumor that the Martinez brothers hid the Mossberg shotguns somewhere on the Martinez property in a place they selected well in advance (which of course supports Fawbus Kennedy's claim that the killings were premeditated) instead of flinging the guns off a hillside on Mulholland Drive, and then after the police finished with the crime scene retrieved the guns and disposed of them where they could never be found. Fawbus Kennedy insists that all the rumors he starts come from "sources" or "family members" or other nebulous persons, but Seth says this pretense of having secret information is only another form of competitive snobbery. Because it turns out that Sean Kennedy and Cora Winchell are friends of Lauren Nathanson, so Fawbus Kennedy has made it his business to dispute anything Lauren Nathanson claims on behalf of her client.

Seth reports this with shrill ire, feeling minimized by Fawbus Kennedy, then falls asleep and dreams that he and several friends have taken a break from some interminable legal proceeding and flown to Iceland, where it is dark all day, but the darkness in the dream is saturated by a hyperborean effusion at the horizon: refracted glacial blueness. They bathe nude in volcanic springs, steaming pools banked by mountains of slush that shed little avalanches into the water. Dream Iceland abounds with purple flowers and metallic vegetation, gingerbread Gothic cottages like ones Seth has seen in Estonia, like sets for *The Student of Prague* or *The Golem* or an early Hun folktale. In the dream, Fawbus Kennedy is married to a little Gretchen in ice-white pigtails no taller than a lawn elf, and they operate a guest house that's really an ice sculpture installed in Tavern-on-the-Green for an Oscar party. It's all loose and chaotic, mental-visual diarrhea, and in the dream, somehow, antagonisms melt in a spirit of community and reconciliation, or seem to, but Seth guesses that these friends and former enemies know that somewhere in this gelato landscape a corpse has been covered up, under the woodpile perhaps or locked in the steamer trunk that appears on the porch of Fawbus Kennedy's gingerbread chalet. The murder that happened in a different life inches its ruinous way into this one, where the same laws obtain even though Seth is not the person he was in that other life he can't remember. The phone goes off like a bomb, he crashes through webs of sleep like a bullet through glass. Morgan Talbot's voice traps him in its scissorhold before he knows he's awake, its precise tone a compound of urgent importance and liquid amiability. Some voices invite you into the uncertain flux of possibilities. Morgan's announces that life is short and time is money and the express train of Morgan Talbot is pausing at your stop just long enough for you to pitch yourself aboard. Seth has been thrown from this runaway train and cast into outer darkness so many times for so many years that he tends to think of Morgan not as the editor in chief of a magazine he occasionally writes for, but as a potentially dangerous psychopath who has to be humored by Seth's artful imitation of the person Morgan imagines him to be. Morgan's Seth is credulous, naive, sentimental about the times he and Morgan have spent together in the past, completely unresentful and even unconscious of the myriad instances when Morgan has betrayed him, and flames into instant enthusiasm for Morgan's "ideas," which he doesn't even suspect that Morgan has already tried out on four or five other writers who have turned her down. Every performance of this impersonation turns a little piece of Seth's soul into lead, and because Seth doesn't exist for Morgan except on very rare occasions when she needs something from him, Seth has been able to avoid incarnating Morgan's lousy version of himself for the better part of two years. Today his luck has run out. Even over the telephone, Morgan is turning Seth into weak-minded, sycophantic mush.

As he listens, as Morgan informs him that she's taken up residence in Bungalow 6, has blown into town for two days to supervise a photo shoot of Faye Dunaway, wants to have dinner with him, has something to talk over, Seth remembers rolling up his window in the parking lot of Ralph's the day before, there had been a man in a filthy short-sleeved shirt with one arm ending midbicep in a smooth waxy stump. He was shaking a cup with the hand of his normal arm. Long greasy hair and little piggy Charlie Manson eyes. Seth remembers thinking that some clichés really do coincide with reality, that his aversion to that dead stump and the angry bag of hopelessness it sprouted from confirmed his own survival instinct. There are people who can look at any scary specimen of humanity and think, that's me. Seth knows that he lacks this virtue. At least it doesn't live within him in any consistent way. He suspects that this lack is what connects him to Morgan, makes Morgan part of his karma. At the same time, Seth is more than dimly aware that he himself is Morgan's one-armed pariah, a stump smelling of possibly contagious failure, someone she wouldn't dream of wasting a meal on if someone more important hadn't canceled.

The transition to Morgan's bungalow is nearly unconscious: he's shaved, showered, changed his clothes in breathless irritation, smiled at Matthew Modine in the elevator, smelled the magnolias on the evening breeze and the cloying vegetation around the swimming pool, and now notes the comparative splendor of Morgan's sitting room, and the coy, goggle-eyed look she trains on him from behind her thick ugly glasses. She's been upgrading her wardrobe in a quiet way for several years, making subtle adjustments to her hair and using a bit of makeup for a change, but to Seth she will always evoke Edward G. Robinson in *Key Largo* pretending to be Edward G. Robinson in *Double Indemnity*.

I'm really glad you could do dinner on such short notice, she says, then giggles, sighs: Los Angeles, huh? with a big downtempo release of breath, as if their shared exasperation with the city were a legendary thing. Seth has always told Morgan how much he likes Los Angeles, but Morgan has never registered anything Seth's told her except the word "no," a word that invariably summons her formidable and ingenious powers of revenge. I can't tell you, Morgan tells him, what a relief it is to spend time with somebody sane out here. Seth has no idea what she means by this, what this forced complicity will lead to. And I'm really thrilled you're doing this Teddy Wade interview, Morgan adds, see if you can't get him talking about L. Ron Hubbard and stuff.

Shit, Morgan, don't tell me he's a Scientologist.

I heard something, Morgan says cryptically.

Wonderful, Seth says. He'll probably bring his own e-meter.

I can't remember if it's Scientology, Morgan says, or if he's into the Marianne Williamson, Total Love and Self-Forgiveness thing. No, wait, it's the whaddyacallit, Panchen Lama trip.

Is that like the Dalai Lama? The Panchen Lama?

I think so, says Morgan uncertainly. Aren't there two Panchen Lamas, or three, in competition? As far as which one is the incarnation of the Living Buddha?

Isn't one fucking incarnation of the Living Buddha quite enough? How can there be three of them?

Mystery of the Trinity, Morgan japes. Boo, duh, and ha.

If these people are so desperate, Seth says, why don't they just worship Santa Claus?

Oh, says Morgan, the Dalai Lama is a trip. Really amazing. Believe me.

From Morgan's tone, it's obvious she's met the Lama about a possible future cover. Seth prudently drops the subject. Morgan moves around the room, making a display of her unfamiliarity with the place, locating a couple of glasses and holding them up to the light like artifacts she's discovered on a spaceship, then moves to a sideboard and picks up a bottle of scotch with the same air of skepticism, makes a goofy inquiry with her face, pours a few drops of scotch into both glasses and laughs, same thing with the ice bucket, the ice . . . Seth's will is draining into his shoes, now he's grinning like an idiot, rattling the ice in his glass, brushing up against various pieces of furniture the way a cat in a foreign apartment does, Morgan meanwhile darts around the room for no apparent reason, picking things up, putting things down, stopping to stare at the curtains, or the telephone, or the windmill painting over the sofa, all the time Morgan darts she tosses out questions as if she were rummaging through bras and panties and skirts and blouses in a suitcase, asking his opinion on brain waves she's been having about the next issue of the magazine, articles she's lining up, concepts she's invented to pull the whole thing together in a unifying theme, and Seth, wobbling from sofa to chair arm to chair back to sideboard like a pinball flung by a flipper, weakly says Great and Too perfect and What a genius idea, his brain saying what an idiot what an idiot what an idiot, what a perfect idiot she is, what a craven idiot I am, sensing that there may be some trick questions thrown into the mix, some rotten ideas she's talking up to see if he'll agree with her because he's afraid to disagree with her, what do you think of Blank, she says, naming a current celebrity, Well, I . . . Seth makes a hesitant, hard face and watches Morgan's face go all slack and noncommittal, think he's pretty amazing, he ventures, remembering just in time that in Morgan's line of business there is nothing not to love about any celebrity getting work, and Morgan lowers her glass so her head can bob up and down emphatically. Isn't Blank amazing? she says, there are people who wouldn't agree, some people don't get how amazing Blank is, and Seth reaches down into the depths of improvisation, finding there an entire paragraph of complicated, neatly balanced praise of Blank, abundant proof that he's one of the happy many who do get it, Morgan's head bobbing and tilting and swinging back and forth in agreement. I've decided to run him on the next cover, she says, as if the next cover were the Nobel Prize, and What a terrific idea, what a great time for it, Seth assures her, shaking his head in awe at her perspicacity, assuming the mettle of an ally in Morgan's struggle against those soon-to-be former employees who don't get it, confident he can muddle through dinner without giving her an excuse to cancel his current assignment.

Seth has to admit that Morgan is no longer a shapeless ugly dyke. Success has trimmed off her baby fat and manicured her physiognomy. She now resembles the personal assistant to the sultan of Brunei, if that were a short and not unpleasantly chubby lesbian. Like many well-known and powerful homosexuals, Morgan hoarded up her homosexuality in private until the exact moment in the zeitgeist when it could be deployed as an asset, revealing it in a few unemphatic lines on the pages of a national magazine, at the tail end of what Morgan calls an essay. As they settle in a window booth in Sushi on Sunset, Seth is stricken with the insight that the very same characteristic which has typed him for all time as a *marginal eccentric* has merely added to Morgan's allure as a *media powerhouse,* that he *squandered the cash value of being a fag* by being a public fag before it could do his career any good, Seth considers that his timing is off as far as being a fag is concerned, whereas Morgan announced her lesbianism at just the right moment, draping herself in the AIDS epidemic a few months before AIDS compassion swept through the media world as a mark of deep humanity and social conscience, whereas Seth was a fag when being a fag was considered disreputable and menacing. Seth orders a cold saki in a box, Morgan a hot saki in a tumbler. Seth looks out the window at the foyer of the Bel Age Hotel, evening is settling in a dark orange strip behind the airport, Seth remembers that Morgan can tuck away any number of drinks without becoming the least bit loose or indiscreet, Morgan is no doubt counting on him to get plastered and spill any secrets he knows, Seth doesn't think he knows any secrets but he does have information, thoughts, ideas, plans, notions, enthusiasms, dreads, things in his brain which Morgan, a born brain rapist, can easily burglarize and turn to her own advantage. The pity of it is, Seth thinks, she has no ideas and a million ways to exploit ideas, whereas I have a million ideas and no way to exploit them, Morgan can take half an idea and worry it into an endless dull-minded magazine article, whereas I have to reduce the number of ideas to keep my articles from turning into philosophical treatises, Morgan can sell one-fifth of an idea buried in a mound of bullshit to the *New Yorker,* whereas I am considered difficult to work with at the *New Yorker* and any number of other places, mainly because Morgan, behind my back, tells every editor she comes in contact with that I have a drug problem, or a drinking problem, or that I'm psychotic, she's been doing it for years, for years editors and subeditors at magazines have been telling me that Morgan tells everyone I have *substance abuse problems,* and now here I am ordering little pieces of raw fish with Morgan, pretending to be Morgan's good friend, laughing at Morgan's jokes, Morgan has wrecked my career and yet there's something about Morgan that's sort of touching, she's so awkward, and she has to work so hard just to be mediocre, ideas come easily to me but Morgan has to butt her brain against a wall and burglarize every head she comes in contact with just to get the beginning of an idea. You have to admire people like Morgan in the end because they want what they want so desperately, Morgan wants to be seen as a person who thinks about things even though she doesn't know how to think, thinking doesn't cost me anything but wishing she could think costs Morgan everything, even if she destroys my career I will still know how to think, Morgan will never know how to think no matter how many people she destroys, Morgan hates me and hates people like me because we have something she can't have, Seth thinks, flushing with sodden optimism as he drains his third box of saki, she can't buy herself a brain with all that money, can she.

Jack drives a Celebrity Cab four nights out of seven, a refurbished midnight-blue Subaru with a huge crumpled gash in the driver door, ferrying drunks and license-suspended lounge lizards through darkling mists and palm-laced barrens of the county. When he closes his eyes in his living room freeway signs flash overhead under bruise-bordered evening clouds, the city's architectures scroll along his peripheral vision like military gravestones yellowing in the desert sun. Jack tells friends who really expected more from him by this late date that he's collecting material for a screenplay. Most of Jack's friends are, like him, lapsed anarcho-Leninists, residual members of Action Group 4, a collective that started in the sixties as Action Group 1, and now meets once a month, with less and less conviction and certainly no action aside from the rolling of joints and the snapping of cerveza poptops, its members uncomfortably privy to the locations and new identities of various members of Action Groups 1 through 3 who, somewhere in the middle past, took the concept of smashing the state a shade too literally and ended up with their pictures hanging in post offices. What's left of AG4, aboveground, are middle-aged intellectuals trying to cobble lives together from vestigial career instincts after decades of menial public service jobs and other forms of voluntary poverty. Jack, who used to fancy himself the Kropotkin or Lenin of the group, feels he could, at the very least, scribble down two hours' worth of darkness and pay off the house before he croaks. It's true that movies flicker in his mind while he's driving: scenes that bleed at both ends, garbled dialogue, stories that open with a taxi passenger paying the fare and walking up a gated flagstone path to a dark bungalow. Jack thinks the name of his movie is probably *Dark Bungalow*, though he also likes the title *Snatch*, if it turns out to be a kidnapping thriller, and he's also partial to the title of a book he came across in a secondhand store in Glendale, *Every Man a Murderer.*

When Jack switches on his brand-new computer and logs his ideas, the delicate narratives he's spun like glass threads in his mind melt like passages in a dream. He forgets what's behind the door of the eucalyptus-shaded bungalow, his passenger freezes with one finger on the doorbell, often the whole enterprise washes away under waves of fear, fear that nothing can ever really change, that nothing will ever happen, and this has been going on, Jack reckons, for six years, since he came back to L.A. from San Francisco, for six years Jack's been stuck at the portals of a mysterious house, wondering: is this a comedy or is this a tragedy? Nothing answers his agitation. I have been trying to start my life for a whole lifetime, Jack tells Seth, and I still find myself incapable, I'm even incapable of my own distress, like Ophelia, in the worst times Jack envisions himself as the unlucky statistical recipient of ever-more-arcane incurable diseases, secondary infections that will knock his faculties off one by one, *this emptiness*, as he calls it, suggests all kinds of extreme and irrational remedies. *This emptiness* is driving me to something irreversible, he's told Seth, I'm afraid I'll do something terrible that hasn't got anything to do with me that will jump me right out of my life into a world of shit that I've got no control over. And I am already in a world of shit I have no control over.

For a while, to conquer his health fears and rejuvenate a waning sense of usefulness, he volunteered in a clinic, advising people: a weekly procession of men, mainly young men, who didn't know how to abide their onrushing deaths, distracted by the verbal pursuit of an empowering rhetoric, a tonic of defiance and solidarity that sounded like nobody in particular and often had the marmalade cheerfulness of a Hallmark sympathy card, underneath that loaded with fear the way guns are loaded with bullets, discovering in some cases that the longer you live with death the less of a friend it becomes: these stories that shouldn't have been but usually were the same story, a template of premature death as tragic for what it couldn't articulate as for the death itself, leached into his psyche on a daily basis, a large, stinking assortment of wounds, shaman's entrails that were obvious and indecipherable at the same time. Jack's clients still suffered from the normal disorders of nature, from their families and friends and lovers, from bad internal wiring, from wishes that couldn't come true, from regret. After a month or so, Jack realized that their condition didn't interest him. Moved him, like his own condition, but didn't interest him. At first he thought he was feeling compassion, thinks now that maybe he was, but the demand for sympathy they projected as their due stimulated his natural reserves of contempt: Jack himself wasn't asking anyone for sympathy, suspecting there was no one in his life to offer any. His political friends suffered emotional constipation. There was Seth, on the other coast, but Seth's optimism on Jack's behalf somehow betrayed Seth's impatience with other people's tragedies. And Juan, who left. Jack lost his facility for the sincere phrase, the consoling word. He heard himself urging his clients to shape up and face the inevitable with dignity. To view their predicament dialectically. Eventually he suggested to a few really annoying clients that they take the painless way out with a shotgun or sleeping pills before the more debilitating features of the disease set in. These he described with a richness of detail worthy of Jonathan Edwards or Cotton Mather. Several took Jack's advice. A few entered the next world with Jack's assistance. His reputation at the clinic developed a certain unsavory edge. He quit.

On this night of loveless nights, Jack winds up a session on the Internet, disguised as Lisamar704, one of five false identities Jack assumes when he's prowling the external synapses of the terminally lonely. Lisamar704 is twenty years younger than Jack, with fabulous breasts, Uma Thurman's mouth, and an insatiable craving for Afro-American manhood. In the two weeks since Jack's computer purchase gave him ten free hours of service, Lisamar704 has become a cyberslut legend among black, ostensibly heterosexual male users of America Online, who aggregate in a Member Room called BlkM4WF. No sooner does Lisamar704's name show up in the ID box than her screen fills with Instant Messages from hackers calling themselves MANDINGO and HARD4U and BLKBONER, people who may or not be black, may or not be male for that matter, but who seem, at the very least, sincerely naked and stroking their organs while gazing into computer screens, conjuring a fully fleshed white girl sex slave from a series of distractedly improvised porno fragments and the completely fictitious Member Profile Jack has created for Lisamar704. Lisamar704 is a Vassar graduate, an associate producer at Universal, has a white lawyer boyfriend who doesn't satisfy her, and can't get enough black penis. When her online lovers suggest, as they almost always do, that the written word segue into phone sex, Lisamar704 has several readymade excuses why this is impossible. The most stimulating one seems to be that her live-in lover is insanely jealous and listens in on her phone calls. Sometimes Lisamar704 works around to the idea that her boyfriend might go for a real live three-way, that she'd have to build him up to it, and asks if her Internet companion would be willing, if the opportunity presents itself, to fuck her boyfriend in the ass. When the answer's affirmative, Jack notes the subscriber's name and sometimes pays him a later visit under one of his other aliases, tracking the mark through directories of Member Rooms and sending a pointed IM: Any straight black studs 4 service from white boy's hot ass & mouth? On occasion, Jack has artfully demoralized these studs into taking it up the ass themselves.

Jack has his Bugle Boys lowered to his ankles, a towel spread under his ass, and some Vaseline on the hand he isn't typing with. The hand he is typing with is busy pleasuring a supposedly twenty-three-year-old NYU graduate student boytoy with a really cute light-coffee-colored face, a pumped six-foot-two body, and the requisite jumbo jism hose, one Mr 9in.

Mr 9in: Now you want to suck this big cock?

Lisamar704: mmm want to lick that shaft from the balls to the foreskin

Mr 9in: play with your pussy as you suck on the head

Lisamar704: i'm fingering my snatch and loving your throbbing dick head with my lips

Mr 9in: take a little more of it into your mouth

Lisamar704: mmm going down on that delicious hard prong

Mr 9in: I can feel it growing as your hot mouth slides up and down on this dick

Jack checks his watch, applies a bit more urgency to his own dick, and pictures some enormously fat old man three thousand miles away jerking off while munching from a bag of barbecue pork rinds. Jack considers the pale organ wrapped in his fist. His genitals or maybe his thighs give off a gluey smell he doesn't like, a smell that suggests sickness.

Mr 9in: damn, you sure know how to suck a dick

Cigarettes, coffee, and alcohol have so aggravated Jack's gag response over the years that he actually hates sucking dick, even hates pretending to on the Net. But this is one of a million things Mr. 9in will never imagine about him, since Lisamar704 writes a mean blowjob.

Lisamar704: why don't you squat over my face and dip that hard fuck pole deep down my throat

Mr 9in: if you keep this up i'll cum all down your throat!!!!!

Mr 9in's idiotic exclamation points rupture Jack's concentration. Now he pictures Juan in his mind, pretends it is Juan, in faroff San Juan, whacking off to Jack's homemade porn.

Lisamar704: mmm now mash your balls against my lips & let me suck & lap them

Mr 9in: stop for a minute, let me suck that juicy pussy of yours

Even though they're in cyberspace, Jack's annoyed when his partner switches positions on him, making him rearrange his imaginary female body in relation to an imaginary male one. He concentrates on his mental picture of Juan and remembers how Juan used to penetrate him, clenching Jack's ankles in sweaty brown hands.

Lisamar704: while you eat my gash i'm licking out your asshole

Mr 9in: spread your pussy let me wrap my tongue around your little clit

Jack can't remember what a clit looks like or exactly where it is among the orchidaceous folds of a cunt. He pictures his own cyberclit as a little cock-shaped jack-in-the-box that has the subtle ability to turn his discorporated Internet friends into avid cocksuckers.

Lisamar704: my pussy's dripping hot juice

Mr 9in: i'm lapping up the juices with my tongue

Lisamar704: i'm licking and rimming your asshole

Mr 9in: i slide my tongue all the way up your hot cunt

Lisamar704: that feels so right fuck my snatch with that tongue fuck it

Mr 9in: i hear you moan in pleasure

Lisamar704: i'm really gobbling your fuck rod now

Mr 9in: my dick is soooo hard it feel as if it will bust open

Generally speaking, Jack finds it easier to be Lisa than any of his other personalities, some of whom are "gay males" in various stages of congruity to himself. In fact, the closer Jack approaches himself on the Internet the harder it gets to score, just like in real life.

Mr 9in: now i want you to slide up the bed so i can stick this big dick up your hot steaming pussy

Lisamar704: my cunt wants your hot fuck so bad my snatch aches with desire for your prong

Mr 9in: i put just the head in first and you moan in estacy

This is, Jack decides, no twenty-three-year-old graduate student but a filthy old illiterate in a crumbling crackhouse tenement near Columbia University. Tonight, for some reason, Jack's running out of synonyms for penis. He'd like to fire off at least one strange and powerful word, now that Mr 9in has entered the boiling moistness of Lisa704's imaginary gash.

Lisamar704: my cunt lips grab that juicy donghead & i'm pulling your fuck pole into me

Mr 9in: my large black dick sinks deeper and deeper into you love canal

Lisamar704: drive that shaft as far as it will go

Mr 9in: i fill up your pussy with all of my 9 inches

Lisamar704: i need your fuck in my cunt fuck my pussy fuck me fuck my hole

Mr 9in: i fuck you so hard my balls slam up against pretty white ass

Whatever else is lies, cosmetology, verbal rearrangement of DNA, the shaving off of decades and pubic hair, sex reassignment, upward or downward register of income bracket and profession, the longish pauses between call and response can only mark the true pace of lubricity. Jack knows that someone, somewhere, is about to squirt because of him. It's a strange feeling.

Lisamar704: crazy for that love bone pounding inside me

Mr 9in: the sweat pours off of us as we fuck and fuck

Lisamar704: making your balls fill with hot cum riding your black pole my pussy on fire

Mr 9in: oh god, i think i'm going to cum, let me cum in your mouth

Lisamar704: fuck my mouth with your love rod shoot your hot fuck into my mouth

Jack comes in an undramatic spurt, wipes his dick with the towel, and switches off the computer, abruptly disconnecting the Internet. Quickly pulling his pants up, he imagines a blob of overheated flesh at the other end tumbling through dead, inky space, like the astronaut snipped from his lifeline in *2001*, spheres of lifeless semen ejecting from his silver space suit as Mr 9in expires from lack of oxygen. Love 'em and leave 'em, Jack says aloud. For a second he misses Juan as if he's been stabbed.

As he prepares to launch himself into the real night in his real taxi, Jack moves through his house with an air of real purpose, straightening the magazines on the coffee table, switching off lights, washing up cups and glasses in the sink, lip-syncing the last two cuts on a Ministry CD, finally taking a 9-mm Beretta pistol with sound suppressor from a wicker basket full of clothes and memorabilia in his bedroom and laying it on the white Formica floating cooking unit in his kitchen. He does his customary coin flip: heads he takes the gun, tails he leaves it home.

On a deserted stretch of Washington Boulevard in West Adams a stout man wearing a cashmere overcoat and an obvious ginger wig gets out of a Lincoln Town Car, walks to a pay phone nestled between two boarded-up storefronts, clamps a voice-altering gizmo to the receiver, and phones a number in Beverly Glen. Janice Wade, wife of the famous movie star Teddy Wade, picks up the cordless in one of the now-bosky dayrooms of her ranch-style home.

Mrs. Wade? Don't even think about hanging up, the high-pitched, altered voice says. And you better not even think about recording this.

I'm sorry, can you repeat that? says Janice Wade, who's been hearing from this lunatic for some time. It started with obscene greeting cards, one addressed to her daughter from her first marriage, age eight, with a condom in it, followed by letters, claiming to be from a "private detective" named Dave Spacey.

You'll be getting a letter in the mail, the caller tells her, and you better pay attention to every word, and do like it says, or you're gonna be in deep doody, and you're not gonna see Sandy again. I'm sick, Mrs. Wade. I need the money.

What exactly do you want, Janice says.

Fifty thousand in hundreds and fifties. You'll get the instructions later.

How do I know, Janice asks, that you'll stop all this when you get the money?

You'll know because I need the money and I'm sick, the twittering voice tells her.

Well what do I get if I give you the money?

You'll get the photographs. You'll get the tapes. You'll get things that'll blow your mind. I'm hanging up now because I think you're tracing this.

Now wait a minute, says Janice. I'm not sure I understand.

Yeah, well, you will, says the caller, slamming down the receiver.

———

. . . *so when they need money,* JD Owsley tells Bunny Honeypot in the Black Light—not really lowering his voice but thinking he is, having a giggle over gorgeous fuckhead Frankie Lomax and his beautiful loser mom, who are busy at the bar scooping change from their hidden places to pay Deadly Paul, the noxious night bartender, for a set of matching gin and tonics—JD's breaking up, more insane pictures float up in his brain, the jukebox sprays "Piece of My Heart" through the bar, which by a queer trick of Mardi Gras lighting has a throbbing blood-orange color with a black edge behind it like a halo of India ink, *they just go down to the cellar to all their sacks of change. They didn't build cellars in that part of the valley,* Bunny spurts, throwing his wig back, *in 1946—Doesn't that illustrate,* he tells Bunny, *once again, the difference between the east coast and here, I'm positive they put cellars in Levittown, but Frankie and Cassandra have to go to the game room, Mommy rolls the quarters and the kid wraps the dimes—Take another little piece of my heart,* all past thirty, built like linebackers or supermodel tall and ultrathin, the core of usual glamorettes, fringed in various pockets of the room by other, younger, déclassé ones, this being the year of conspicuous new drag queens impersonating not Mae West or Liza Minnelli but absolutely ordinary housewives from the San Fernando Valley, *you know you got it, if it makes you feel good.* Bunny Honeypot of the old, Zsa Zsa Gabor school pounds the divider with a soft meaty fist, the clenched digits ablaze with varicolored plastic rings. *And they take them in the limousine to the Great Western Savings Bank on Sunset*

Bunny's platinum wig looks like a topiary bowling ball, a shimmering replica of the one Marlene Dietrich slipped on after pulling off the gorilla mask in *Blonde Venus.* His or her large, optimistic face is adrool with Egyptian eyeliner and green kohl under the eyelids and spread over its wide open spaces a bold palette of fuck-me colors that are sliding out of alignment in the manner of a Warhol Marilyn, merging in spots with the pentimento of last night's paint job. Bunny's determination to be clever this evening demands a certain patience. JD laughs at Bunny's japes just enough to endorse his company, not to encourage more hilarity. Because, after a point, Bunny isn't really funny. JD tries letting Bunny know in a kind of subliminal way that Bunny isn't quite in JD's mental league but that he, JD, likes him well enough anyway. JD commencing his fifth cocktail, KetelOne with the recommended olive-sized pickled tomato, drinking in the happy chaos of a really choice night of the Black Light, a place that's often empty or merely servicing the chronic clientele: toothless burnouts ravaged by oceans of peach schnapps and Thunderbird, a couple of intricately tattooed ex-cons full of scary criminal energy, and a few overemployed prostitutes of various genders floating off their shifts on Western Avenue and Santa Monica Boulevard. Tonight a bunch of slumming UCLA students shyly attempts merger with a trio of desperately made-up Mexican trannies, everyone out of their minds on crank, vodka doubles, and heroin in the economy package. JD has a few hits of Sierra Mierda heroin wrapped in a waxed packet, in case of boredom. He feels like giving it to Bunny to see what effect it would have. He can see Deadly Paul still counting change, glaring down his scraggly biker beard, eyes beady with disgust, and suddenly Cassandra Lomax's trademark Tallulah Bankhead voice rips the void between record changes: *I told you, darling, our money's no good in here—*

That Cassandra, Bunny says, shaking his jaw, at the same time reaching up and pulling the wig down tighter, plump biceps jiggling, winking at the most uncomfortable-looking male in the student body, who stares back in horror. The Wurlitzer begins playing Sid Vicious's cover of "My Way." JD braces himself for a trannie sing-along.

Cassandra's a caution, JD says, not realizing for a moment what a witty thing he's actually said. It would make a good story for Seth, who always enjoys himself a little too flagrantly in the Black Light and therefore tends to avoid the place (a good time, JD thinks, kicks in with Seth as a paralyzing dose of remorse the following afternoon, remorse that pours back out of him in thinly sugared blame, you knew I had work to do, sweetie, when I tell you I've got things to take care of it would be nice if you'd remind me instead of egging me on): the celebrated wreck ex-television star and her demented stud son, blazing a firebreak of Tanqueray across the city, Laurel and Hardy sleepwalkers, their trail winding through depleted race-edgy piano bars in South-Central and wrinkle rooms in Los Feliz and Silver Lake, crossing East Hollywood like a flame licking spilled gasoline from the asphalt, the car service courtesy of Cassandra's divorce settlement, the limo arriving, somewhere long after dawn, at an unimaginable address in Chino or Pomona, some vale of the living dead, JD forgets which.

The last time anybody saw Cassandra working, she was peddling sacks of oranges beside the 101 off-ramp at Sunset and Wilton, limo and driver parked around the corner on De Longpre. No one could explain how she'd beaten out half the labor force of Tijuana for that particular spot. Of course, as JD says, anybody who's nobody remembers her twelve seasons on *Vampire Cop* with the kind of affection reserved for brilliant geeks who could have made it, geeks with a death wish. So for the brief time she worked the off-ramp, Cassandra's oranges sold briskly. *You won't believe who I bought these oranges from,* hundreds of studio drones told their insignificant others, and it even became a status thing, people who had scored citrus from Ralph's would bring home the bag and claim to have bought it from Cassandra Lomax for months after she'd moved on.

Does she ever get hired for anything? JD doesn't think so. She had one very good year when she did seven movies, all by directors of some reputation, the roles completely unlike each other, that year ended with an Oscar nomination but as she said it came with a curse on it, the parts dried up, she got offered nothing for ten months and finally surrendered to TV. *Vampire Cop* had good numbers for several years until the lead vampire turned up dead in his basement dungeon in Palmdale, strangled by a puppeteer-turned-hustler he'd picked up in the One Way. Weirdly or not, Cassandra actually knew the puppeteer, had met him ten years earlier in Phoenix, where he'd opened for a production of *Blithe Spirits* she was doing at a dinner theater. *My God,* JD once asked, *what was his story?* Cassandra thought about it for a long time with her eyes squinted shut and finally muttered, *His puppets were just awful, darling, awful puppets.*

Vampire Cop ran a couple more seasons, quirky ones, they played with the notoriety for a while, alluding to the absent Officer Varney as a slave to his job, chained to his profession, that sort of thing, losing most of the audience, gaining a cult. *"Embrace my nightmare, you Slavic slob"* is still a fondly remembered Cassandra line from that period. The series folded and Cassandra, who never had been exactly practical, decided to take a year off to get in touch with herself. She discovered that herself liked drinking lots of gin and waking in a bleary daze around 5 P.M., when the demands of the day had blown over, an hour when no phone would ring and only the night's freaky oblivion awaited her. She just let go. Letting go did not feel good all the time but it was a kind of nothing she could meet on its own terms.

Once in a while Cassandra pops up like an incubus in underground theater pieces or cabaret acts, or guesting on cable talk shows, booze-addled and pointlessly hostile, her makeup almost as thick and smeary as Bunny's. Her usual thing is to act like a piece of snarling furniture. Still she does not look too bad. The green Mylar dress she's wearing shows off great legs and operatic cleavage, she hasn't run to fat and her face has an inextinguishable vivacity, the marriage of good bones and habitual narcissism, a beige beret fixed at a cocky angle holding her whitish hair in place.

When Cassandra's around, Frankie wears his consort look, his elegant hardbody sheds its sexual aggressiveness, his face goes sheepish as if a light behind it's been dimmed from blazing magnetism to a fuzzy sort of inadequacy and you see him then as a wayward kid needing rescue. Frankie is nothing like that, he floats independent of everyone and even ditches Cassandra for weeks at a time, but he can, if you aren't paying attention, trick you into taking care of him, feeding him and fucking him, your apartment becomes Frankie's crash pad, your clothes Frankie's wardrobe, your telephone bill Frankie's diary. His calculus never hits a pause. Frankie knows how much can be had with a wink and a smile, how much more with a kiss, and once his penis enters the picture Frankie functions like a dizzyingly rigged taxi meter regardless of who the passenger is. The allure, JD often says, is Frankie's stutter, an actual handicap that he uses like Ted Bundy's fake broken arm, proof of a vulnerability that really isn't there.

The Lomaxes are both high as weather satellites and JD detects an abnormal quiver of excitement keening in that quarter, it might be the unusual crowding in the bar or the buzz of an important presence JD hasn't yet picked up on, it isn't entirely odd to see movie stars or even studio heads in the Black Light during a full moon, Bunny senses it too, he's gotten this wise old seabird look on his face, a surge in the noise level feels like the gathering of a psychic tsunami. A claque of Hell's Angels barrels through the door, greasy Vikings breathless with amphetamine, clanning between the hunched backs on the barstools. Cassandra greets several of them by name. *Big Mac, darling, why not buy me a big drink. If you're nice you can fuck me with your big cock.* Frankie shuffles against the music, drawing the usual hungry looks, but his eyes are fixed on his own feet as if he's rolling some faraway thought through his head, something that brings a cracked smile to his lips.

He could be Sal Mineo's brother, Bunny says, gurgling down the thin icy end of his screwdriver. JD considers the regal Germanic bone structure lurking under Bunny's clown makeup, Bunny's dark blue eyes, Bunny's youth. Bunny could probably have Frankie if he wanted. JD can see them together in Bunny's efficiency at the Ravenswood, one floor below the former Mae West apartment. Frankie loving up the Lucia Bosé lookalike from behind in order to pry loose her Versateller code. What would Mae say?

Or his sister, JD suggests. He pokes the tiny tomato in his drink with his fingernail. Without really wanting to, JD measures his own prospects against Bunny's: not simply with Frankie but with anybody, the thickening of only a few years having made all erotic connections less ethereal, heavier, and harder to negotiate.

Frankie dances. His long urgent body sways slowly, partnering his G&T.

Cassandra screams at a RuPaul clone giving noisy entrance to the bar at large—*Miss Whore, it's really you!*

Sometimes, Bunny says, people will say Dean instead of James Dean and they always say Brando rather than Marlon Brando. But nobody says Mineo without saying Sal Mineo. Like it's one word. Salmineo.

That's not unique, JD says. Most people need two names especially in China where everybody's named Dong or Weng or Chu or Fong. Even their celebrities are Dong this or Fong that, Chow Van Dong, Chu Wang Bong, there's no plain Dong the way there is Madonna. Talking about Sal Mineo gives him a spectral feeling, of living in a city crowded with ghosts. Less and less visible history, but a plethora of ghosts. He knows the exact driveway on Holloway where Mineo bought the farm, gutted by a hustler unknown. You don't hear Grant, he says, you hear Cary Grant. Or Lee Grant.

Or Lou Grant, Bunny says. I once got a thing from him in the mail about Nicaragua.

People say Natalie Wood, not Wood. Never Burr without Raymond. Whereas Garbo you don't need the Greta, Gable works fine without Clark, Crawford you think Joan, not Broderick, though Broderick Crawford did some fine work in the fifties. Now, would you say the Mineo of *Exodus* or the Mineo of *Rebel?*

Rebel, Bunny says, perfect example. Even without *Without a Cause.*

Well, JD says, pertly straightening up on the stool. There's a lot of things we could simplify. Just call it the knoll instead of the grassy knoll, for starters. What other knoll do you know about?

I've always called Edgar Allan Poe Edgar Poe, Bunny says. But that's really just an affectation of mine. I think of myself as a Poe-like figure, Bunny adds confidentially.

Why say the Black Dahlia? JD wants to know. She should just be called the Dahlia.

Except there's *The Blue Dahlia.* Veronica Lake, Alan Ladd. Screenplay by Raymond Chandler. William Bendix, fresh from his role in *Lifeboat.*

Which also featured Walter Slezak, JD adds with irritated pedantry, Hume Cronyn, and Canada Lee, but the Blue Dahlia was actually a nightclub, not a person. In fact, they named the Black Dahlia after the Blue Dahlia. How often do you get a woman named after a nightclub? Somebody had to know, JD muses, one of those sailors she used to go dancing with in Long Beach, had to know that murder was in her karma.

Murder in Her Karma makes a nice title, says Bunny idly, with a flutter of one hand. His eyes have been riveted on Frankie Lomax for a long time, jealously clocking Frankie's flirtations with various she-males.

God, he tells JD, if Frankie wasn't trouble . . .

But you know something, Honey, he sure is. Or so the legend goes. I'd hate to see you end up like the *Dahlia*.

Well I doubt if he's *that* much trouble, Bunny says.

Half after midnight, somebody selects a whole side of the Velvet Underground "banana" album, which Deadly Paul and the afternoon bartender have both threatened to extract from the Wurlitzer's innards because it's "too depressing" and people tend to play the whole thing instead of one or two cuts. As JD relates it, this must be when Cassandra runs out of loose change and, determined to keep drinking, hits on her Bright Idea. JD recalls pushing through the crowd and phoning the Marmont from the pay phone in the jukebox alcove around then: Seth answers on the fifth ring, as quickly as JD can say how are you Seth releases a torrent of not very original obscenities concerning that fucking no-neck cunt-eating cunt. Oh says JD to joke him around, you must mean that fucking pussy-eating pussy. Yeah Seth says that Harvey Wallbanger. That muff-devouring shrew. That snatch-lapping sack of Sapphic shit. That k.d. lang clone. Seth sounds drunk but JD is not the best judge.

You must be referring to everybody's favorite lesbian, JD teases. Why not come out for a restorative cocktail? He fingers a graffiti someone has carved in the wooden molding beside the telephone: it looks like a set of balls, with a straight line carved across their upper circumferences, and another straight line running between them. Something like a logo, or a publisher's colophon.

Uh, Seth says. I'm going to have to think about that.

Cassandra and Frankie stumble outside, where their livery driver slouches on the slick hood of the limo sucking a joint. Calvin is a six-foot-five Rastafarian whose natural elegance makes his driver uniform look like an ironic costume. Which in some measure it is, since Calvin's conviction that being stoned all the time actually sharpens his driving skills is belied by a stash of unpaid parking and speeding tickets in the glove compartment. Western Avenue is a blank expanse of darkness flaked with occasional Korean neon. Tiny grains of sand swirl in gusts of hot wind. Cassandra tells Calvin to drive to the 7-Eleven near Western and Melrose and park around the corner, then rolls up the soundproof partition, unclasps her spangled handbag, and shows Frankie the gun inside.

Fffff-ffff-fuck, Ca ca ca ca si si sandra wha wha wha wha's that f-f-f-for?

Cassandra snaps the bag shut. She shrugs. Fucking Deadly Paul, she says, looking out the smoked window at the street. Tears drool down her face, taking some eyeliner with them. Thinks he can cut me off. She loudly sniffles snot into her throat. I am so sick of living like an animal, she cries, while your sonofabitch father with his fucking tennis court in Malibu Canyon gets a thousand bucks an asshole. That's how sick this world is, a celebrity proctologist gets a pool and a tennis court and a fucking Lamborghini while the ex-wife, a legitimate movie star, has to rummage for change just to get a goddam cocktail. I almost won that fucking Oscar you know.

You you you sh sh should've won it, Frankie tells her earnestly, his fingers busy with a dying Bic that sputters sparks in the darkness. Nuh nuh nuh not Louise Fleh fleh fleh fleh fleh Fletcher.

Tall, saucer-eyed, a face sculpted after some exotic bird, dark auburn hair falling like parentheses ending near the squarish chin, an hourglass figure slightly swollen by booze or chocolates, the dress a simple elegant black, Sabrina Wilcox meets Jack's cab in the gravel driveway of a cliff-hanging apartment complex in Silver Lake and recites an address on the glitzy side of San Vincente, her voice breathy and slow, as if it's a major effort to find language for such trivia.

Don't take the freeway, she warns. In the mirror he sees her slumped in the seat, eyes closed, a pretty rag doll weary of dollhood.

Street noises minimal, tires crunching over the road's scumbly surface, occasional pothole jolts reverberating in the dented driver door. Glenn Gould's recording of "The Well-Tempered Clavier," preludes and figures, at modest volume on the tape player. Jack negotiates the loop of empty streets between Silver Lake Boulevard and Los Feliz. At the top of Vermont Avenue he considers dipping down to Santa Monica and crossing Hollywood that way, then decides to stay on Los Feliz until Western. There is a patch of Los Feliz where magnolias fill the night air, even when the winds are blasting down from the mountains.

Would you mind turning that off, the voice in the backseat says. It's not an order but it's not a question, either. Jack halts the tape with a swift stab of the eject button. This reminds him of the curt finale of his computer rendezvous earlier in the evening. Bands of pale light from streetlamps slice through the taxi. As they move across the woman's face it looks like she's weeping. But it could be her contact lenses watering in the Santa Ana. After several blocks she says:

I'm sorry, go ahead and play the music if you want.

Tell you what, Jack says. I'll leave it off if you don't mind me smoking.

Again a ponderous silence. She either doesn't like talking or it takes a long time for thoughts to reach her verbal center.

It's your cab, she says. Anyway, the window's open.

Much obliged. Technically, he tells her when no answer comes, the passenger has the option of letting the driver smoke or not.

A long silence.

I know that, she says. Actually a little music would be nice. Not a lot of music, but . . .

Jack starts the tape again though he now prefers the silence.

It's Bach, isn't it?

Jack nods, leaving it to chance whether she notices this or not.

I don't know anything about music, she says quickly. But I recognized it, for some reason.

Jack considers telling her that he doesn't know anything about music either, to deflect any impression that he thinks he's too cultured for his job, but that could, he imagines, promote a really tiresome conversation about knowing things or not knowing things. Some passengers are a negative absence and some are a negative presence and then there are those who are just composed and present enough to make the silence of a long drive comfortable, he thinks maybe this woman is one of those, but maybe not.

If you quit smoking, she tells him a mile later, it will add twenty years to your life. She says this almost playfully, bored with the stale landscape and quiet.

I've certainly tried, Jack tells her. He mentally adds twenty years to his impossible life and sees himself creaking across the Fairfax District with the aid of an aluminum walker. I've done the patches, hypnosis, cold turkey, everything. It creeps back. Sooner or later everybody who quits starts again.

I'm the rare exception, the woman says, now leaning forward, pressing her crossed arms into the seat near Jack's head.

Congratulations. You quit when?

Let me think. Six years ago. In fact that's what got me into my present line of work. I've got this shop on Melrose, we sell New Age paraphernalia—well, whatever you think about New Age, we do a lot of motivational tapes, we make tapes for behavioral modification. Overeating, smoking, all kinds of compulsive behaviors.

That's how you quit? With tapes?

The tapes have these subliminal suggestions on them. I would just put them on as background noise and clean the house or whatever, it's not like you really have to listen or pay attention, the message just enters your mind like water entering a sponge. And after about a week I was smoking less and less. I didn't even know I was smoking less and less.

So it's like, you taper off.

Right. Exactly. You taper off and then you quit but it's not a big drama. You don't have to use a lot of willpower.

I've seen you somewhere, Jack says.

Maybe, the woman says, cautiously, fading back into darkness.

I'm trying to think where, Jack continues. But he already knows, it's come to him suddenly. Silence thickens in the car and Jack thinks that will be the end of it, he senses that she knows he knows who she is, but after a long time she clears her throat and says:

I have a cable show where I talk about New Age ideas. A lot of people recognize me from that.

I don't get cable, says Jack, though he does.

The woman sighs and makes a pained noise.

I suppose people talk to you about nothing else, Jack says apologetically.

You have absolutely no idea, she says. I'm moving to Arizona as soon as the trial's over. I can't stand it anymore. People come into the shop to gawk at me like I'm this freak. And it's only going to get worse once I testify.

What made you—? Jack catches himself, regrets having spoken.

It's right up here, the woman says, pointing out a small bungalow with its doorlight peeping through a jungle of eucalyptus trees. Jack pulls up in front of the metal gate, noting the Armed Response plaque fixed to the surrounding fence. She hands him the fare with a small card: Sabrina Wilcox, Incunabula & Biofeedback Systems, an address on Melrose. In the lower left corner of the card, a tiny advertising symbol that registers familiarly, a little trademark of some kind that Jack can't place.

When Bobby met Billy it all seemed to click. They both looked great, they both loved going to nightclubs, Billy was a hungry bottom with no ambitions to become a top, and he didn't have a lot of housewifey hang-ups about Bobby's outcall business or the videos Bobby "acted" in from time to time for a spot of easy cash. Billy understood right away that Bobby had this metabolic restlessness, that he had to fill all his hours with the outside world, that sex for Bobby was a recreational sport like tennis or racquetball, it didn't matter very much who he played with as long as they were good at it. Billy did get obsessed with buying things for the apartment on Franklin, stuff that wasn't in the best taste as far as Bobby was concerned, but he could live with it.

After a few months, though, little conflicts arose, like Billy would fix dinner when Bobby'd decided to visit the baths with a quarter gram of meth and stay there for ten hours and when he got home Billy acted like a slab of granite. Bobby started hearing this *I just don't understand you* shit night and day, it could start over him leaving a dirty sock on the bedroom floor or not helping bag the garbage, before long Bobby realized that Billy was one of these people who wanted to be married, to build a life together, wanted some incomprehensible shit that he'd read about in a gay magazine or what have you.

I'd love it if you'd stop turning tricks, Billy told him. Bobby grunted and said nothing. *We could probably afford for you to go back to school* was another Billyism, after Billy got the manager's job at Cobalt. Bobby occasionally tried to explain that the worst way of getting along with him involved planning the future or asking him to give up anything he happened to be doing, but Billy couldn't hear him and Bobby just hated talking about it anyway. Now he was getting harassment via telephone, behind his work station counter in the middle of the store, in a proscenium of twenty-five-cent bags of Fritos and bar-b-que chips and spicy fried pork rinds, the heavy smell of the revolving frank broiler filling his nostrils, *I really fail to see why you need a minimum-wage night job on top of everything else,* Billy whines as Bobby pops a Certs and chews it. *If you came and worked in the restaurant at least you'd get tips.* Asking Bobby to explain himself is another bad strategy. Everything Billy says rests on false assumptions. Billy wants to sound like somebody in a "relationship," in other words like somebody in a movie.

I don't think that's such a brilliant idea, Bobby says, surveying his domain: the aisles mathematical and vibrantly overlit, shelves crowded with mustard, ketchup, bread, pickles, odd varieties of Campbell's soup, Tabasco sauce, canned olives, Spam, donuts, pretzels, chips, a thousand varieties of grease and fat, the surrounding wall coolers burgeoning with quart beer and six-packs and all varieties of Coke, Pepsi, Dr Pepper, Slice, Sprite, A&W root beer, Canada Dry flavored soda water, sliced American cheese, jumbo eggs in cartons, Jimmy Dean sausage, everything on earth you'd need for insomnia and congestive heart failure, plus, at Bobby's space console, thirty brands of cigarettes, hot dogs, chocolate everything and chewing gum. It would be folly for him to tell Billy that he's always wanted to work the counter in this type of store, because saying it would go to the strange fact that Bobby would like to be anything and everything at least once, that he understands the adventure of his life as a series of quirky marginal roles that an actor might try out in movies or on stage. Billy knows this about him but doesn't comprehend it at all, thinks of it as a sort of retardation on Bobby's part that patient counseling can rectify.

It would be nice to see you once in a while, Billy wheedles, his tone floundering somewhere between petulance and tenderness. Customers enter, Bobby's first in a half hour, the woman in a green Mylar dress who used to be on *Vampire Cop* and the young guy she always comes in with, black Levi's and formfitting undershirt, her lover Bobby thinks, paid lover probably, this nervous dude full of seedy sex appeal like some Cockney ratcatcher or professional snitch whose muscles look genetic rather than gym-built. Billy's yapping away about drapes, what does Bobby think about peach drapes for the living room, peach drapes and those really thin venetian blinds in either an aubergine or eau-du-Nile. Bobby munches another Certs while Morticia and the ratcatcher float through the store snatching up pretzel bags and a box of donuts and two six-packs of 16-oz. Buds from the cooler, a jar of Grey Poupon, a loaf of Wonder bread, ratcatcher picks up the tabloids from the rack near the door, the *Star, World Weekly News, National Enquirer,* Morticia's rooted out a package of olive loaf and some chocolate chip cookie dough, *I want you to be happy with this place,* Billy's saying, *after all it's our home,* they pile their goodies on the counter like misers running their hands through money, Bobby starts skimming the price codes over the laser matrix cradling the phone with his shoulder, *It's not our home,* Bobby says in a genial calm way that he knows drives Billy nuts, Billy would like a lot of drama and Bobby never gives it to him, *it's our apartment.* Vampira sticks a gun in his face, a gun Bobby happens to recognize from using the same model at a practice range in Northridge, a Taurus .357 Magnum with a decorative wooden grip, he also sees that the safety's off which is definitely not a happy sign, the bitch chewing a big wad of bubble gum, the kid making these grimaces he thinks look threatening, and they are, actually, both of them flushed with ugly excitement, Bobby just looks at them and says You've got to be joking.

Just bag this shit and open the register, the woman says. She commences blowing an enormous gum bubble which pops unpleasantly as Bobby stares at her.

Juh juh juh just buh buh buh bag it, the kid echoes.

The blunt lethal presence of the gun sinks in, held as it is in this stiff skinny paw that's probably too nervous and addled not to fire it if that suddenly seems like a good idea, and Bobby starts bagging the crap on the counter, dropping things, barely hearing Billy tell him *I know you're not in love with me, believe it or not Bobby I'm glad you're not in love with me, I'm not trying to be possessive*, the kid swaggers to the glass entrance door and swings it open, sticks his head into the night, prances back to the counter chewing his lip. Muh muh muh microwave me a burrito, he says. The woman keeps poking the gun at him, actressy pokes like improvised stage business, Bobby has some idea that he's not so much in the middle of a robbery as he is in the first act of a piece of theater. The trouble is, he doesn't know his lines and maybe his role calls for a bullet hole somewhere, it unnerves him not to be the main character in something as potentially flattening to his own personal narrative. Bobby drops the Grey Poupon and it rolls off the counter, explodes on the floor in a spray of globby soursmelling gunk, *But if we're going to keep living together I want to make you happy*, Bobby feels this frozen amazement inside, like he's been yanked inside a movie he'd been watching from the safety of a theater seat. Shit, the woman says, grabbing a wad of napkins from the dispenser next to the frank broiler and swobbing mustard off her nylons, keeping one eye and her gun hand in wobbling focus on Bobby's head. He keeps telling himself: I'm going to get through this in one piece, nothing's going to happen. But he doesn't believe himself, knows somewhere in the pit of his stomach this is going to be a near-death experience if not the big D itself, and the thought forms as a complete sentence in his head: *If this is it, I've really been swindled.* You want a beef or a bean burrito, he asks the kid. Buh buh buh buh buh buh beef, the kid says, his features squinching and his head kind of jerking on his neck, he's pissed at Bobby for making him stutter and bangs the counter with his fist. Bobby slaps a frozen burrito with a hard blistered skin like warty papyrus into the microwave, presses the timer buttons, arrests his own gaze of habitual dumb fascination into the oven's hearthlike interior, Billy's voice perky, irritated, *Are you there? Are you still there?* The over-made-up woman's eyes deranged as she chews her gum in a way that excludes him from the particular movie she's in, but he forces himself to stare into them and shoves the pretzels into a plastic bag, Did you want some more mustard? he asks stupidly, hitting the cash register key that ejects the money drawer. Scoops bills from the plastic slots, bunches them into his hand. Bobby figures there's all of ninety bucks.

Look, he says, jamming money into the woman's rattled fingers. She grabs the bills, swaddling the gun in a bouquet of currency. There's no weapon back here, Bobby tells her. The surveillance camera's bogus. There's no reason for you to hurt me.

The woman squints one eye and looks down the barrel of the gun.

Bobby? I feel like I'm talking to myself here, say something.

Kneel, she says, sounding loopy and drunk, motioning at the floor with the gun. Kneel you little fucker, she adds, without much conviction. Bobby drops to a squat, losing the phone receiver, which flies on the suddenly untensed cord, knocking over a metal rack of jalapeño potato chips. The red plastic missile ricochets off the counter and shatters the glass window of the frank broiler, strikes the floor with a hideous thud. Bobby kneels with his arms raised in goofy surrender. His knees are his least resilient body parts and crunch painfully against the linoleum floor. He has, he notices, pissed in his pants.

A loud buzzer, like an alarm, startles everybody into nervous action, Cassandra swinging the gun back and forth and Frankie moving for the door with the groceries, which he drops, then kicks. Bobby stands up, ducks as the gun weaves in his direction.

Your burrito's ready, he says, though they're now running out of the store.

Fuh fuh fuh fuh fuh fuck the burrito, Frankie manages to spit out as he leaves, picking the bag up as a sort of afterthought.

JD is still on the phone to Seth when Frankie and Cassandra reappear in the Black Light, hungry for gin, this time with their Jamaican driver in tow. The Hell's Angels have departed in a great farting roar of motorcycles and the mood has mellowed just a touch. Seth's doing his usual Hamlet number about going out, and JD tells him that if he'd left the hotel at the start of their phone call they'd probably be getting ready to go home by now, Seth says that if he could just beam himself there through the phone line, that would be one thing, but he can't drive in his condition and cabs are so horribly expensive out here and JD says well why don't you get Jack to pick you up Oh Jack would love that, Seth says, Well maybe he would, JD says, Jack likes me, he knows I'm good for a laugh, since he says he hears me all the time on the radio. By the way, I'm doing a call-in on the abuse excuse this week, Oh really, says Seth, that's a funny new term, abuse excuse, does that mean you've already made up your mind about Martinez? Actually, says JD, I have. I've decided I'm on their side. But our angry commuters need to vent from their car phones while they're stuck in traffic. I suppose, Seth says, caving in finally, I need to wash this whole Morgan Talbot experience out of my brain, but I'm not going to bother Jack because I think to get him you have to call a dispatcher in Gardena or something. I'll just get a regular cab but you will buy me a few drinks won't you because if I make the cab stop at a cash machine that's going to cost me extra. JD thinks but doesn't say he's never known Seth to be cheap before but then maybe his money situation is really as bad as he says it is. Promise me, he says, now Seth, don't take this the wrong way, but if you are coming down here, promise me you're not going to blame me for it tomorrow. Don't be ridiculous, says Seth. Well, JD tells him, you have been known on one or two occasions, quite charmingly I might add, but still, to blame me for various headaches, stomach cramps, and difficult bowel movements, I'm not saying you do it all the time or even especially often, it's only when you feel ambivalent in the first place and then decide afterwards you should've done something else.

Teddy Wade, godlike in sunglasses, waves at Seth from across the oval pool. Blue bikini briefs with a red stripe on them, a white scarf, stretched on a chaise of yellow plastic bands. Several other bodies lounge nearby, slick with oil. As Seth goes round the water Teddy bounces to his feet and slips on a fluffy white robe, the kind that is always waiting for the bored, rich homicide victim's mistress in a made-for-TV movie, simultaneously working his toes around yellow flip-flop thongs. His movements are brisk and unstudied. He has a soufflé of tobacco-colored hair on his head, golden hair on his legs, and a smooth, unemphatic torso that is, Seth later notices, shaved. His face has a bland midwestern clarity, all its volumes symmetrical, the eyes dark blue and direct, the nose slightly thicker than it photographs, the mouth broad and as flexible in expression as an adolescent's. Even though Teddy lives less than ten miles from the Chateau, his publicists have booked a suite for him here to meet the press.

It's always been rumored that Teddy is gay, and perhaps in defiance of these rumors his latest role is a gay man dying of AIDS, as if acknowledging the fact that he could be is really further proof that he isn't. Teddy motions for Seth to join him at a round metal table set back in the shade. It's a hot, dry day, the fifth day of Santa Anas, a day when small fires will break out just above Malibu Canyon. A harsh disc of sunlight throws wires of wobbling light along the walls of the pool. The surrounding vegetation rustles continuously, casting a roiling net of shadows. Seth sits down as Teddy bestows a complicated, faintly challenging smile and asks if he wants a drink.

Seth makes a small gesture of uncertainty. He appraises himself through Teddy's eyes. He feels a sort of envy, having always disliked his own looks, in the presence of someone whose face is his fortune. Plus his usual wariness in what Seth calls the journalist situation, a situation weighted with inequality, falseness, pathos: all interviews are stupid, Seth says, because what people choose to say about themselves is always the least interesting thing about them.

Out here, he reflects, what you drink in the afternoon is often considered telling. Plain mineral water or orange juice signals that you are sane and professional and moving ahead in a rational manner, with open hands, so to speak, whereas alcohol could spell inner unhappiness, mental turbulence, incipient breakdown. Unless your relation to alcohol is so reliably uncomplicated that it produces, every time, nothing more dreadful than joie de vivre. Seth cannot be so precise in his own calculations. He wants Teddy to trust him, though he senses that if Teddy could peer into Seth's inner life, he would find all sorts of repulsive and amazing things.

A Calistoga, I think.

Teddy has moved for the house phone at the opposite side of the terrace, turns around, and stands flapping his hand on his robe.

For real? I'm thinking about a Long Island ice tea, he says "cockily." The star, Seth observes, has begun to "act," and will continue "acting" until Seth disappears.

Ha ha, in that case—

Watch yourself, Seth tells himself. Teddy returns, adjusts the canvas umbrella above the table. Seth has planted a small Sony tape recorder with its microphone facing Teddy's chair.

Is that on? Teddy asks, touching the machine with thoughtful fingers.

No. Should I—?

However you want to do it, Teddy says. Let me see if I can get my egomania in gear.

This is, experimentally, a "winning" remark, a show of humility or camaraderie, hinting at the hidden sameness they might experience on the checkout line in a shopping mall.

Seth switches on the recorder.

You probably find it hard to be natural with journalists? he asks, his voice trapped somewhere between the formulation of a question and the residue of what has just been said. He is disturbed to find the anticipation of a drink preempting his interest in the job at hand, turning his attitude light and airy.

Well, says Teddy, pretending to think it over, there's really nothing natural about being interviewed, talking about yourself so your words will be printed up somewhere. A plumber or an air hostess never has to articulate anything. They just do what they do. Some people have to explain what they do, and some never have to explain or even think about what they do. I wonder if there is anything natural about explaining anything. There's nothing natural about acting, as far as that goes. We don't have to put all this in. It's just talk.

Don't worry, Seth says, I'll make you sound good. But I'm curious: you've never had a role that was so close to yourself that you just eased right into it and played yourself?

If it was my own life story, Teddy says, I would still be "playing" myself. The moment you have self-awareness—let's say you're eating dinner in a restaurant, you're talking about whatever, and into the restaurant comes someone you're desperately in love with. Or the publisher of a magazine you want to write for. Or your worst enemy—that's the best example. He sits down, five or six tables away, you think he's got a perfect view of you, but maybe he can't even see you, hasn't even noticed you. Either way, suddenly everything's different. You think you're being observed, okay, by your worst enemy. So you begin to project beyond the person you're with, you start doing things with your face, you use certain words, to project an image to this person across the room. Say, an image more glamorous and much happier than you're feeling, more self-assured. All of a sudden, your whole relation to reality becomes one of triumphant self-control. Or, maybe, intense vulnerability. Because maybe you want to plant the idea that this enemy has been unjust to you, hasn't seen the human side, and so on . . . and you're going to make that person guilty for despising you. You know something, the movie star says, lowering his head and his voice in a sort of incontinent and unsure display of secrets, each and every one of us is guilty of everything.

He pauses, apparently surprised, maybe displeased, at having said this: Seth thinks it's because it means something to him and he's said it too theatrically, coarsened it in some way. Well, he goes on after a pause, I suppose that's neither here nor there.

Okay, says Seth, but just between the two of us—

Two of us, Teddy says, and what, half a million readers? How many readers, out in magazine land? Reading. Obviously I want them to think of me in a certain way. And not think of me in other ways.

In other words it's pointless for me to try to get a detailed picture of your, uh, actual inner life into an interview?

You could get a hint, you could get a fragment. A figment. I'm not the world's most mysterious person. But in a way, the more candid I might come across as being, in reality the more hidden I would be. Don't you think? People retreat further back into themselves, the more they tell about what's supposedly inside them. The more they expose themselves, the more covered up they really are.

On the other hand, says Seth, you might forget yourself in the act of speaking. I mean you might abandon your self-protection.

If I forget myself, says Teddy, I'm still sort of absent, when you think about it. If I tell you anything that comes into my head, I'll maybe lose myself in my own words. And later on I'll wonder: "Do I really think that? Is that really who I am?" I might be in there a little bit. You never know.

The Long Island ice teas arrive.

There, Teddy says, taking a big swig of his. Tastes just like ice tea, doesn't it?

. . . Seth says that on Monday the prosecution pinned up several color photographs of the so-called rumpus room and displayed Peggy's bloody tennis sneakers, as well as a fragment of plastic bracelet apparently blown off Peggy's wrist by one of the shotgun blasts, and then played a tape of Felix talking to the Beverly Hills police, claiming he'd smelled smoke in the so-called rumpus room when they found the bodies, and after that Lester Zabar, the detective on the scene, testified that Carlos and Felix turned up at Woodrow Wilson Drive at five o'clock the morning after the killings to ask for their tennis rackets, at that point Seth says Lauren Nathanson seized the opportunity to quiz Lester Zabar about the ferret shit all over the house but Lester Zabar didn't recall any ferret shit, and then the captain of the *Naked Movie Star* gave his version of the so-called shark-fishing expedition, aside from the drama of nobody speaking to anyone else on the boat it turned out that Felix had caught a small shark and Fidel caught a small shark, no one bothered to ask what happened to the sharks, Seth says, or the ferret for that matter, and later on Monday night one of the networks ran an interview with Fidel Martinez's mother, Carmen Martinez, followed by a little chat with Fawbus Kennedy, who claimed that neither Fidel's mother nor Fidel's two sisters had displayed the slightest emotion during opening arguments when the gruesome carnage of the killings and the charges of sexual molestation were being aired, with the result that on Tuesday, Fidel's sister Thelma held a press conference to call Fawbus Kennedy a liar, claiming that she and her sister Luisa had been choking back tears throughout the opening arguments and that their mother had been "practically in the fetal position," Seth says he isn't sure whether Carmen Martinez actually assumed the fetal position in court but disputes Fawbus Kennedy's allegation that the Martinez women were "emotionless," he was not seated near enough to observe their exact expressions but did sense an emotional emanation coming from that side of the courtroom, admittedly a confused and confusing kind of emotion that nearly everyone with the exception of Fawbus Kennedy felt in the presence of such harsh and bewildering information . . .

. . . and on Tuesday, Seth says, you had the weapons expert Lucky van den Heuvel, who it happens lost one of his legs years ago when a container truck rolled over on his Camaro on the Harbor Freeway, the same Lucky van den Heuvel who lost an eye a few years previous to that when a prostitute he was trying to arrest threw a bottle of anal wart remover in his face, a well-known if not legendary figure in the local law establishment, Seth says, though why on earth they call him Lucky is a puzzle, the morning began with Lucky van den Heuvel demonstrating a twelve-gauge Mossberg shotgun, an ugly metal and plastic affair with a sort of goiter around the barrel that has to be pumped up and down after each shot. Lucky van den Heuvel analyzed the so-called pellet pattern in the death room and the wadding in the buckshot and birdshot cartridges and the number of pellets packed in a round of birdshot and the number of pellets packed in a round of buckshot, after that Detective Smythie who interviewed the boys right after the murders explained that he didn't do a gunpowder test on their fingers because they seemed genuinely upset and grief-stricken at the time and besides that they offered a credible alibi, though Smythie now claims with the benefit of hindsight that his "instincts were prickled" by Felix's statement that he smelled smoke in the so-called rumpus room, since the neighbors heard what they thought were Chinese firecrackers at 10 P.M., and Carlos placed the 911 call at 11:47, a gap of almost two hours for the smoke to dissipate, especially since the glass in the French doors had been blown out by shotgun pellets. Quentin Kojimoto, grinning like a Woolworth's Buddha, asked if Smythie knew that Felix wanted to become an actor, the question propelling Lauren Nathanson out of her chair with an objection, Seth says the actor issue went to sidebar with all the attorneys huddled around the court reporter, who normally dictates into a kind of face mask, which gives her the strange appearance of a medieval plague doctor, and after a quantity of furious palaver involving Marlene Quilty's endlessly bobbing ponytail and Lauren Nathanson's shivering ringlets Judge Tietelbaum allowed the question, Smythie said if he'd known about Felix's theatrical ambitions he might well have brought more skepticism to the interview, Kojimoto gave him an unctuous thank you but according to Seth neither the question nor the answer had much visible impact on the jury . . .

. . . the fact is, Seth says, Detective Smythie and his colleagues are a typical assortment of LAPD flatfoots, if they weren't sufficiently "prickled" by Felix's statement about the smoke to administer a powder trace or a lie detector test one would at least expect them to find something peculiar about two kids whose parents had just been murdered coming back to the crime scene five hours after discovering the bodies to collect their tennis rackets, surely there are few human beings, says Seth, who would think of hitting the courts the next morning after their parents had been blown to smithereens, surely that would seem at least a trifle odd even if the victims were Steffi Graf's parents or John McEnroe's parents, surely even Steffi Graf or John McEnroe would skip practice at least one day after such a grisly discovery, and of course neither Felix nor Carlos intended to play tennis that morning, what they did do was calmly and methodically remove the remaining ammunition from the trunk of Carlos's Trans Am in the carport, right under the noses of Detective Smythie and Detective Zabar and half the Beverly Hills Police Department, a piece of audacity you could claim supports the idea of the Martinez brothers as cold-blooded sociopaths, but might also bolster the defense assertion that the whole thing wasn't planned at all, and that any competent police department would have arrested the Martinez brothers on the spot . . .

. . . another witness on Tuesday was the much-discussed former tennis coach Buzz McIlheney, an extremely fit-looking blond with numinous dental work and a slight overbite, limpid blue eyes that riveted some neutral point in the middle distance, and long restless fingers that fretted the weave of his obviously un-Buzzlike tie, who reported that Carlos phoned him on Sunday afternoon, asking to meet Buzz at quarter after ten at the so-called cheese and wine tasting gala in Santa Monica, wanting, Carlos said, to discuss his imminent return to Princeton and some finer points of his tennis game, that he, Buzz, had waited around for the Martinez brothers for a half hour, tasted some cheese and wine, and then drove home, that when he got home Carlos called again slightly after eleven, this time sounding, Buzz remarked, "kind of jumpy," when asked to explain what he meant by jumpy Buzz McIlheney said "kind of anxious," when asked anxious in what way the witness said "kind of nervous," when asked nervous how Buzz McIlheney said "kind of strange," go on then, Marlene Quilty told him, kind of jumpy, kind of anxious, kind of nervous, kind of strange, Carlos now proposed, according to Buzz McIlheney, that they meet at Cheesecake Charlie's in Century City, Carlos said he was calling from Santa Monica (a claim confirmed by the computer records of Fidel's Sprint calling card) and wanted to drive Felix back to the house on Woodrow Wilson Drive to pick up a fake ID he could drink with, and did you agree, asked Marlene Quilty, to meet them at Cheesecake Charlie's, as usual with place names and street names Marlene Quilty cites the location with such rapacity that it begins sounding evanescent and absurd, Seth says, because you know perfectly well a place called Cheesecake Charlie's is here today gone tomorrow, just another architectural dropping someone will scoop off the sidewalk in three years to make way for a Hamburger Minnie's or a Sushi Con Carne or a Korean Dogmeat Emporium, yet here it will forever be, embedded in the transcript, a tony little outpost of cheesecake where Carlos and Felix Martinez stood Buzz McIlheney up the night they killed their parents.

. . . Marlene Quilty is trying to prove that the Martinez brothers are liars, this is what she tells the press at lunchtime, she seems also to believe it's self-evident that if somebody lies about one thing that means he lies about everything, which runs contrary to most people's experience, Seth says, since most people lie about one thing or another at various times, and it's just as plausible to most people that you might commit murder spontaneously, in an access of rage or paranoia, then lie to cover it up, than that you might plan a murder then lie about planning it, in fact, Seth says, most people can imagine killing someone in the heat of a moment and then casting about for an alibi, it's perfectly normal, and already at this early phase of the trial it's becoming apparent that the statutory issues distinguishing *first-degree murder with special circumstances* from *second-degree murder* and *second-degree murder* from *voluntary manslaughter* and *voluntary manslaughter* from *involuntary man-*

slaughter and *involuntary manslaughter* from *not guilty* will never be decided on a factual basis, since nobody can prove or disprove either side's theory of the case, but rather according to the whims and prejudices of the jurors. It's thought that Carlos has had the luck of the draw because the so-called gold jury is on the whole younger and better educated than the so-called blue jury, which has six cantankerous and intolerant middle-aged men serving on it, who have already formed a sort of proletarian eating club down in the courthouse cafeteria, with a regular Munich Beer Hall Putsch atmosphere emanating from their table, and the pressroom gossip mill claims that Lauren Nathanson has already written off these nattering, vicious, ugly old Republicans, with their Bavarian mustaches and Wilhelmine beards and ill-fitting dentures and bad hairpieces, and will pitch her case exclusively to the remaining six jurors, all women, with the sole aim of obtaining a mistrial . . .

. . . meanwhile the state Board of Psychology has issued a sixteen-page complaint against Dr. Potter Phlegg, citing his illegal taping of his therapy sessions with Carlos and Felix Martinez, his illegal dispensing of two prescription drugs, Xanax and Valium, to two female patients, identified in the complaint as C.G. and S.W., and his sexual relations with the same two patients while they were in therapy, one of whom was also acting at the time as his housekeeper, in contravention of yet another regulation governing the patient-therapist relationship: this was announced at the end of the day by Lauren Nathanson, during a press conference outside the criminal courts building, in the course of which Lauren Nathanson told the reporters she thought they were all biased against her clients, this with a great big smile on her face, a flirtatious smile, and she added, even though you're all so cute, and Seth thought, he says, she really knows how to work these people, apparently not considering for a moment that he was, is, one of the people being worked . . .

You're not tracing this call, are you?

No. Where is this all leading, Mr. Spacey?

I was hired a year ago. To shake you people down. I thought the fat pig who hired me was from Santa Clarita.

The what? The who?

The fat pig. A fat pig that hired me.

A fat pig?

Right, hired me, and I thought she was from Santa Clarita. Or Palmdale. Did she give you a name?

Yeah, but I'm not giving it to you. She gave me a lot of shit about her husband and your husband. A fat clown.

I thought you said a fat pig.

She paid me to find out more, and that's when I started calling you. When you see what I got it's gonna blow your mind.

Why will it blow my mind?

Because you thought I was a fucking put-on and you don't know shit.

Why are you threatening Sandy?

You listen to me, lady. I got bad diabetes, see. They took out one kidney and I'm losing the other one. That's why you didn't hear from me all summer. Listen to me. I'm wearing a diaper.

You're what? Wearing what?

A diaper. I've got a diaper on. My teeth fell out. I weigh almost three hundred pounds. I'm not asking for much from you. Fifty thousand.

. . . Seth says he has no natural feeling for music, which is why he insisted on a tape player in his rental car, sometimes he plays Nirvana and Hole and Nine Inch Nails and Ministry, sometimes he plays *Die Zauberflöte* and Schumann's symphonies, hoping the music will "sink in." The only time in Seth's life when music seemed important was his adolescence and early youth, during certain years in Seth's life the music around him was like the sound track of a movie he had a major part in, one he would look back on as a prolonged era of semiconsciousness (for Seth believes he was formerly much more alien and uncomprehending in this world than he is now, that he has, in many important ways, replaced the unhappiness of delusion with the unhappiness of clarity) and then, not suddenly, but gradually, he listened less and less, the first few years he spent in New York without anything to play music on, never missing it, when he did buy a tape player he found himself getting stupidly fixated on one or two recordings that he played all the time, usually melancholy songs about lost love and hopelessness that became urgent and moving when he got drunk.

In New York, where Seth lives a kind of submerged dreamlike existence, he still almost never plays music, but in Los Angeles he tries to recapture some interest, not in his compulsive favorites, but in things he believes other people are listening to, things he has no feeling for, hoping he'll strike a natural vein of the zeitgeist that will let him feel that everything makes a happier kind of sense than the kind of sense everything makes to him now. He's willing to write off music altogether as something that just isn't him, but not quite yet. He drives his bubble, a Mazda, sealed off from outside, taking a bath in the Top 10 tapes he's grabbed off the shelf in Tower Records on Sunset, unsure what it's hip to like anymore, usually forgetting, after court, to switch on the radio for JD's talk show. When he does remember, he's usually forgotten where JD's show is on the dial, if he remembers the numbers he's then confused whether it's AM or FM, and then, too, the radio that comes with the Mazda features two awkwardly placed oblong scanning buttons rather than a regular dial, in fact there's no way to locate a particular frequency manually, you have to keep pressing the buttons and watching the digital numbers, skinny black strokes on a pallid green rectangle, whir around until the scanner pauses somewhere, and if it pauses where you want it to stop you have to press the button again or else it keeps moving across the spectrum. Since he's forgotten the numbers as well as which band he's looking for, Seth pushes the scanner in search of JD's voice or, on Tuesday, chitchat about parakeets, since he does recall JD telling him that was going to be Tuesday's topic. Seth has trouble recognizing JD's voice over the radio for some reason. On the radio JD engages more palate and sounds crisper than in real life, and of course since it's a talk show it isn't always JD who's talking, so when Seth's radio is scanning, Seth has to decide if it's paused on JD's program or some other talk show, furthermore it isn't easy to drive and fiddle with the radio at the same time, a few times now while searching for JD's show with one hand, Seth's swerved out of his lane on the freeway, nearly colliding with other cars. One driver made a pistol with his fingers and fired a make-believe bullet into Seth's head. On these occasions Seth has experienced irrational anger against JD, a completely unwarranted feeling that JD, by the mere fact of having a drive-time radio show, is trying to kill him.

The winds have grown impossibly hot, like invisible fire, clearing the sky to a slate of milky sapphire. The A/C whooshes frigid microbes through the car as Seth trawls across Echo Park, vaguely disoriented streetwise, catching news of a blaze in Topanga State Park off Mulholland, a drive-by with three deaths in Crenshaw, a high school shooting in Northridge. Pieces of discussion about separating the school districts, since the unified district has brought "them" up from Watts into places like Northridge, along with their guns and switchblades and gang colors. The Echo Park fountain tosses foamy plumes up from the lake, vapor rainbows coloring the spray as it sifts down to the water's surface. Seth composes a "report" on the trial in his head, the words smudging as the radio scanner samples traffic reports and Spanish music.

You're saying, then, that birds are capable of abstract thought, he hears JD say, and frantically presses the button, locking KAW into place.

Well, says another voice—professorial yet seductively masculine, a rich warm tenor—*consider the mental process of migratory birds. From their aerial view, they memorize hundreds, sometimes thousands of miles of landscape, finding their way year after year, according to various landmarks. You could say that isn't abstract thought, but the fact is that often the landscapes have been altered by development or what have you, yet the birds continue to orient themselves in much the same way that we, when we're lost, pick out a familiar building, a road sign, some detail of an altered landscape that fills in the missing whole.*

What you folks out there can't see, says JD, *is that Dr. Whatmough has brought quite an assortment of birds with him to the studio today. We'll meet these birds right after the KAW traffic report.*

Poking holes through Seth's mental outline of the trial are various bills accumulating in his mailbox back east, minimum payments on Visa cards, monthly installments on back taxes to IRS and the state of New York, rent, telephone, ConEdison, three thousand he owes a psychiatrist who got him through the worst of his Mark mania, several festering personal loans, his total debt figuring in his inner landscape like a boulder rooted in a rushing stream, immovable, deforming the entire flow of consciousness, sometimes covered in Rhine maidens or peaked by a brooding dwarf. *We've got an injury accident right now at the edge of the city of Orange on the 22, let's check it out with Rachel Lockridge.* He half expected dinner with Morgan to flush out a second and even a third assignment for the magazine, on the idea that giving him more to do on the West Coast would be "cost-efficient," more bang for Morgan's buck. *On the westbound side of the 22 just before Main Street, an accident blocking a left lane and a center divider, and that's actually backed up the drive onto southbound 55, so that's gonna be a good area for you to avoid right now. We've also got troubles in Anaheim, we were looking at this just a few minutes ago* and he now thinks if he'd laid his cards or lack of them on the table with Morgan she might've been moved to do something for him, though really Morgan is incapable of considering anyone else's distress as a factor in her sempiternal calculations *an accident on east 91 at Kramer-Glassell, none of the mainline lanes are blocked, however a lot of right shoulder activity. A portion of the off-ramp is blocked, however you can still exit the freeway there if you wish to. You cannot exit the east 91 from the Kramer-Glassell on-ramp.* But, then, what can you do. Unenlightened self-interest has pushed out most other forms of human feeling, he thinks, among almost everyone he knows. *That is blocked, in fact you'll be diverted right onto the off-ramp if you try to do that. Eastbound 91 is backed up beyond the 57.*

For Morgan, he thinks, there are winners and there are losers. *Now to L.A. County, similar effect to Orange County on the 405 northbound, looks good from the 605 all the way to Santa Monica Boulevardas you leave West L.A. it's heavy the rest of the way into the Valley, a crash site near the 101*

Oh, Jack, Seth tells him. We were so young.

The Santa Monica Freeway's looking real good right now, if y'need to get downtown, do it now, pretty easy drive all the way out to the beach, that's rare, even the eastbound Santa Monica Freeway's in very good shape

Twenty years ago, yeah, says Jack, instantly tapping into Seth's mood. The grass is always greener on the other side of forty. Where are you?

—*as you approach the Santa Monica Freeway there's the usual, unfortunately, slow and go stop and go toward East L.A.*

I don't know, Seth wails, at the same moment realizing he's two blocks east of Hillcrest, four blocks north of Sunset, and therefore knows precisely where he is. I mean, he corrects himself, I don't know in the larger sense. I'm in the car.

You got a car phone? Jack sounds genuinely impressed, even slightly indignant, as if Seth had won a prize. Now there's something to feel good about, you didn't have a car phone last year. By the way, your friend JD is having some type of bird festival this afternoon.

It's still not my goddam car, says Seth, recovering his composure. I know, I've got it on.

Believe me, says Jack, you don't want your own goddam car. Look at my goddam car. Or, you want a real thrill, become a homeowner. I just paid a thousand dollars to get my septic tank repaired. Those are your choices under capitalism. Either let it go and start leasing a toilet in your neighbor's garage or pay a thousand dollars to take a shit. I've seen that bird guy on television, you think JD is fucking him? I don't think I've ever fucked an ornithologist, have you?

Oh, well, I'm sure I would've heard about it, Seth says. I don't know who JD fucks these days. He flirts. He likes a good flirt.

The bird guy and JD have returned to the airwaves, along with Pretty, a jackdaw with human intelligence. The bird guy describes the nest-repairing skills of weaverbirds and coaxes Pretty into song.

A flirt doesn't hurt, Jack singsongs, trying to sound like Pretty. I hate to hear you sounding so depressed, he adds without conviction.

I'm not really. At least I don't think I am. It has to be a chemical thing, I'll get through the day just fine and then have a wave of it knock me over for no reason I can think of.

It's the winds, Jack says. You can feel them sucking every drop of water out of everything that holds water and all some asshole has to do is throw a cigarette out a car window and it's Mrs. O'Leary's cow time.

The thing is, I hate these mechanistic explanations, Seth says, tossing his own cigarette out the window, I don't find any comfort in them. Just to be a bag full of water at the mercy of brain chemicals, or winds, it's almost worse than if I think it's me, but the thing is, I'll get in the car, I'm driving, and suddenly I'm thinking that I've wasted my entire life and screwed up every chance I ever had to be a little bit happy—

Objectively you know that isn't the case, Jack says, with a certain violence. You know what it is? What I think it is? You come out here and after a few days you start remembering things through a very selective filter. You remember when you could walk into a bar and ten guys would hit on you and you could pick the hottest one and take him home, you remember getting fucked a million times and how your body bounced right back after taking tons of speed and alcohol, but what you filter out is how miserable and lonely you were because you could never talk to those guys about anything real, or get a relationship going, since all anybody was interested in was scoring, in fact I remember you telling me once some guy gave you the best bang of your life and you saw him the following night in the bar where you picked him up and he looked right through you like you weren't there.

I think people still do that, Seth says. Maybe now they do it for political reasons.

Sure they do, says Jack. If they're twenty-one they do. Everyone's just a mammal at that age.

Just for the record, says Seth, I was more of a top than a bottom when I was younger.

Moi aussi, I assure you, says Jack. As *much* a top as a bottom anyway.

And there's the tragedy, with most people it's the reverse, as nature intended. It's a fight for the bottom as you get older, as one old fairy said to the other.

I never could get exactly what I wanted, Seth says. You don't think like with AIDS and gay liberation and *Angels in America* the young aren't more into, you know, meaningful relationships—

Oh please, why put it on gay people, if you're not a cannibal you're dinner in this country, are you listening to this fucking bird?

I'm mad at you, an African gray parrot squawks on the radio.

He means it! JD marvels. Even over the radio JD sounds flirtatious, in a tart, ironic way.

You didn't give Timmy the grape he wanted, you gave him the orange, Dr. Whatmough says.

Seth laughs uncontrollably for the first time in several weeks. JD must be in radio heaven, he cackles, with those birds shitting all over the studio. I can't believe this. I'm right in front of Guinness World of Records. Jack, there's a goddam *mime* on the sidewalk in front of Guinness World of Records.

How are the Brothers Karamazov?

A mime has to be seven years' bad luck. Seven *more*.

How were the Brothers Karamazov today?

Oh. Tense. Attentive. Carlos was wearing a white cable-knit sweater over a pink and white pinstripe shirt, Felix had on a blue sweater and a plain white shirt, both gorgeous, and they just sat there basically. You think because they're like Latino and kind of minority their parents only let them make friends with these hideous WASP 90210 types who got a big thrill from wearing a wire on them?

A power surge obliterates Jack's reply. The street as Seth approaches La Cienega's chewed up by subway construction, wooden enclosures festooned with nets of orange plastic narrow the roadway to one lane. *Have you heard? The brand-new Odyssey minivan from Honda is off the assembly line, it's the revolutionary new minivan from Honda with car-lux performance, call Giant Robertson Honda in North Hollywood, 800-NewHonda.*

—spastic colon, Jack's saying.

Who, Felix? We heard it's a kidney stone. Fawbus Kennedy was telling everybody Felix got beat up in the shower, wishful thinking on his part. They had to postpone the second hearing on notes of the therapy session—

We're switching gears here at traffic time on KAW, in a minute you'll meet author Albert Gilbert, whose controversial new book has the hot poop on the Black Dahlia case, and I mean that literally.

If you wanna have dinner, Jack says.

Tell you what, I'm gonna try to take a nap, I'll phone you in a couple hours. Do you know anything about something called the Order?

It's some Scientology thing, says Jack, some Hollywood rich bitch Scientology thing. The Order of the Agape Lodge. I think it's devoted to the cult worship of Juliette Lewis.

So it's like a fan club?

I think it's a gag that some punk band invented, Jack says. Like on the Internet. They have a home page. Meet the Anti-Christ. I downloaded their logo once.

Huh. Are you on the Net?

Sure am. Latest thing in total alienation, why wouldn't I be?

But I thought it put people in touch with each other. Do me a favor, look it up for me and tell me what's on it, okay?

You could come over and look it up yourself, Jack says. You thinking of joining?

Hardy har har, Seth says. Call me later.

Oh-kay, says Jack, switching off the phone. He almost switches it on again and dials Puerto Rico, but instead lays the handset down on the kitchen Formica and explores the refrigerator, never a sparkling prospect, a minefield of pickle jars and shriveled luncheon meats, spoiling take-out items from the Pioneer Market, finds nothing besides the vodka bottle in the freezer he hoped would disgust him but instead looks like a jovial old friend. Better company than Seth, anyway, dear as he sometimes is.

Elizabeth Short had information, JD's guest tells an astonished world of gridlocked commuters. *Which is why she went to San Diego in the first place. She knew she was in trouble, that she had to lay low.*

Then why did she come back to Los Angeles, JD asks with the usual piquant, aren't-you-a-moron insinuation he applies to guests he's not attracted to.

She probably thought everything had blown over. She had a short attention span. Maybe she thought other people did too. So she drove back with a man only known as Red. Red dropped her off at the Biltmore Hotel. Red told investigators he didn't really believe she was meeting her sister as she claimed. But don't forget, Red was married, with a family in Huntington Beach. He wasn't in any position to help her, beyond giving her the ride.

You say Red never slept with her.

Well, JD, the truth is, nobody ever slept with her in the sense you're getting

at. In the course of the murder investigation several men admitted to receiving
oral sex from the Dahlia. But the autopsy showed that Betty Short could not
have normal intercourse. This was never revealed to the public. It was one of
those details the police withheld because it probably would've been known to
very few people, including her killer.

Now, that was because her vaginal canal—

That's right. Her vaginal canal was undeveloped. It would not accommo-
date a normal penis or indeed any penis.

Jack mixes a screwdriver and mentally replays his blackjack losses from
the previous weekend. If he had folded in time, he would've walked out of the
card club in Bell Gardens with five thousand dollars, instead lost everything
except the change in his pockets and almost threw down the pink slip on his
panel truck. He pictures winning and winning and all the freedom money can
buy, for example a long reprieve to some genetically blessed and economically
ruined Third World country full of "his type."

Another detail that's a real shockeroo, Albert, deals with the rest of the
autopsy report.

It's pretty shocking, JD. For one thing, it seems Betty Short may have been
conscious, though horribly abused and mutilated, right up until the time she
was sliced in half. In other words, she may not have died until that started
happening.

Wow.

Postmortem, strips of flesh peeled from her legs and buttocks were inserted
into her vagina and anus.

But if she had no vaginal canal—

Undeveloped canal, the severed tissue was stuffed in there—

Jack, glugging his drink, transfixed, feels his penis thicken in his Levi's.
An unwanted, disgusting erection. He reviews recent fantasies: of picking up
skanky trade on Santa Monica, bringing them down to the basement, chaining
them with ropes and handcuffs. To pale track-marked skin he applies lighted
cigarettes, the taper of a blowtorch, metal clamps, razors, heated needles.
Kicks their balls to ragged pulp with his Doc Marten boots. The boys're blindfolded and gagged, or have their heads stuffed into leather hoods with zippers
over the eyes and mouths.

By far the worst detail, since these other atrocities occurred postmortem, was
the discovery that Betty Short's stomach was full of human feces.

Even JD can't fashion a snappy comeback to this one, though he's been
trying to think of one all day: he clears his throat.

resentment   65

When you say full, Albert—

There wasn't anything else in her stomach. She had eaten, or been forced to eat, a large quantity of excreta before she was killed.

Jack pictures his naked ass squatting over the open mouth of a teen victim, slowly disgorging a substantial turd. He gets the giggles. Yes, it makes sense, if somebody would chop a woman in half he might find some aesthetic pleasure in making her eat shit. In days of old, if he remembers the Goncourt diaries, a well-rounded Parisian hooker was expected to cultivate the art of coprophagia. Why should things be different in Hollywood, where everybody eats shit in one form or another all day?

He drifts to more benign fantasies. He'd like to enjoy brutality more, tenderness less. He considers that the only thing worse than that thing in Proust about being obsessed all your life by someone who isn't your type is to find out your type isn't really your type, either. Maybe just something memorably sordid. The thought flashes to phone a 900 hard-core line he jotted down from the pages of *Frontiers*, where dozens of nightcrawlers deposit their solicitations, some of them way further out than Jack would ever dream of going. *I'm out here on Larrabee and I'm still looking for that snuff scene,* one recent subscriber beckoned. *So if you're ready to bring me through that final door* . . . If Seth craps out on dinner, which Jack suspects he will, maybe he'll microwave something and snort up a line of crystal afterwards, troll the phone lines for company.

Seth turns off Hollywood just before Nichols Canyon Drive, down Genesse to Sunset, up Marmont Lane and into the hotel garage. Fat droplets of rain spatter the windshield. The wrong time of year for rain, he thinks. He later says that this sudden burst of rain slickened the tile slope of the driveway enough that when he hit his brakes the car slithered back and forth for a scary moment, reminding him of the mishap twenty years ago, on the Harbor Freeway, that catapulted him out of his dreary workaday existence and out of Los Angeles altogether, a mishap that Seth has related over the years with increasing refinement, in some retellings Seth claims the car swerved out of control in the underpass under the Hollywood Freeway and flew up the embankment and rolled over *three* times, in others he says it rolled over *four* times, in still others it rolled over *five* times, landing upside down a mere foot from the road surface, *had the car turned over once again,* Seth says, *it would have landed in the dead center of a blind curve,* the fact that it stopped rolling only inches from the curb Seth took as a sign, he says, a *get out of Los Angeles before it's too late* sign, adding that he crawled out of the car through the window, the door being jammed, and then crawled up the embankment and over a fence and hobbled across the Hollywood Freeway and climbed another fence, all the time spewing blood from a gash in his forehead, his arms and legs livid with ripening bruises, his clothes ripped as if he'd been blasted with shrapnel, guided by the muzzy idea of getting back to his hotel apartment and reporting the accident after sleeping off all the gin he'd drunk out in Venice with the nonunion projectionist from the movie theater where he'd been working behind the concession counter, Seth always illustrates this story with an array of squirming motions and pained faces, at any rate, when the car slipped out of control in the Marmont driveway it almost slammed into a white Geo Prism turning into the garage, he says, piloted by none other than Fawbus Kennedy, who turned and stopped and stepped out of the car shooting Seth a dark inquiring look as he handed the Prism over to the valet, Fawbus Kennedy in a pinstripe yellow shirt and impeccable gray slacks and what looked like Gucci loafers, his silver hair swept back, his big black eyes bugging out under sagging tents of eyelid flesh, and then as luck had it Seth found Fawbus Kennedy still awaiting the elevator when he got to it. Seth says he attempted to glare at Fawbus Kennedy through his dark glasses in the cramped elevator cage but instead returned the saurian smile Fawbus Kennedy aimed at him, the smile of a celebrity who's been recognized by someone too polite to ask for an autograph. *I had an overwhelming urge*, Seth says, to kick his stupid ass, and I hate that feeling of helpless violent loathing, one ought to have some devastating ice-cold phrase ready, or maybe just a rag soaked in chloroform. Seth stepped off the elevator feeling unpleasantly compromised, short-circuited, unable to project his disgust in any meaningful way, molested, he later says, by that iguana smile, that ingratiating crease in that third-rate middlebrow mug, old.

On a typical night during those early days of the Martinez trial the players and nonplayers orbiting the black chunk of myth at its radiant, empty center are each locked up in his respective cell, as the hot winds flutter down the canyons, Seth in the oversized corporate suite a few yards up from the Strip, Jack in his monkishly small bedroom swilling the last of the Stolichnaya with someone who describes himself as a "middle-aged sex pig" slobbering into his ear via mobile phone. Carlos Martinez lies on the narrow bunk in his actual cell in the celebrity lockup downtown, in his orange prison jumpsuit, legs crossed at the ankles, admiring his own elegant bare feet while reciting, for the amusement of his currently favorite phone mate, one Doris Spree of the Spree Rubbish Removal Service of North Hollywood, some of the mantras drilled into him by Fidel Martinez, culled from a slender inspirational volume called *The World's Greatest Salesman*, beginning with *I am nature's greatest miracle. Since the beginning of time,* Carlos tells Doris with a humorous wink she obviously can't see, his hand rubbing an oval of glabrous bald scalp she has never seen, *never,* he says, *has there been another with my mind, my heart, my eyes, my ears, my hands, my hair* (Carlos pats the glossy fringe around his baldness), *my mouth.* Doris, who weighs three hundred pounds and has recently filed for divorce from her philandering spouse and rubbish removal partner Teddy Spree, is taping all her gabfests with Carlos Martinez on the vigilant advice of Fawbus Kennedy, who has also introduced her to a literary agent, laughs along with Carlos, laughs at his imitation of Fidel, *If I feel depressed I will sing, If I feel sad I will laugh, If I feel ill I will double my labor,* Carlos renders these bromides in a lisping airheaded Spanish accent, guiltily, remembering that Fidel had actually devoted years to painfully expunging the smallest whisper of spic from his English, Doris laughs uproariously and massages her labia at the same time, having "befriended" Carlos in the first place as an aid to masturbation, establishing contact by means of a torrid, improvised saga of childhood abuse, a richly imagined affair with her father that may well, Doris muses with a fatalistic sigh, account for her compulsive overeating, further representing herself as honorary chairperson of a Simi Valley organization devoted to "recovering memories" of sexual molestation in childhood, gamely hurtling past the obstacle of Carlos's skeptical lawyer and patching herself directly into Carlos's jailhouse telephone scam, her three hundred pounds of trash-clearing flesh tingling from top to ungainly toe with fantasies of Carlos's big Cuban pecker churning the fetid swamps of her capacious honeypot, its moist walls of muscle slackened from years of self-abuse of the very type alleged against Fidel Martinez by Felix Martinez's lawyer, that is, from the insertion of myriad household objects, in Doris's case implausibly large ones which have, over the years, stretched her Temple of Venus into a permanently yawning Gothic basilica. The prospect of betraying Carlos heightens the thrill of imagining his ample Cuban manhood thrusting and prodding inside her, as she envisions, at the same time, herself as a featured guest and inspirational speaker on morning talk shows, promoting her tell-all book about Carlos. At forty-three and three hundred pounds, Doris Spree plans to finally be somebody, and she figures to have the divorce finalized well ahead of the event, the glamour, the money. Doris mistakenly believes that she will turn into a raving beauty, on the order of Cindy Crawford or Linda Evangelista, after shedding Teddy Spree and a hundred and seventy pounds, a transformation that awaits her advance from Random House and promises to become the readymade subject of her second book. A line of Doris Spree fitness products and healthy frozen meals hovers on the distant but discernible horizon, the inevitable second act of a fairly standard American life.

Janice Wade has received three more letters: two from "Dave Spacey," and one from a "Theresa Novelli," supposedly the woman who hired Spacey in the first place, to follow her husband around. Novelli writes that she made "a major mistake," not realizing until too late that Spacey "has his own agenda." Spacey's letter included a gay oral sex picture, by the look of it photocopied from a porn magazine.

I know you don't think this picture is of Teddy, the letter says. But it's him. Tom Novelli's hand is in Marty's hair and Marty's gobbling his wad. I've got two others where Marty's taking it up the ass.

Spacey's second letter came taped to a package wrapped in plain manila paper. You stupid lousy cunt, it reads. I'm going back to Santa Cruz. You better hope I die because if I don't you'll wish you were dead. You better kiss Sandy good night every night.

Under the wrapping paper was a square blue Tiffany box, full of crinkly tissue paper enclosing a large human turd. It is just about time, Janice thinks, to call in Anthony Pellicano.

JD is almost certainly at Taylor's Steak House on Eighth Street near Normandie, drinking vodka with Dylan Whatmough, the ornithologist, at the padded bar. JD is developing a willful crush, a kind of "as if" crush, on the comely bird lover and Krishnamurti disciple, whose menagerie has been whisked back to the Valley by a cryptic-looking Sikh assistant whose eau-du-Nile turban resembled a plushy bird's nest. Since the recent demolition of the Nickodell (another Los Angeles landmark callously razed, its site obliterated by soaring privet hedges that look like they've stood there for decades, obscuring, as the Nickodell had, the main gate of Paramount Pictures) Taylor's has become JD's postshow cocktail lounge of choice, an oasis of glistening dark wood and maroon banquettes in the welcoming thirties style of Musso's or Boardner's, redolent of a slower, more elegant moment when a good meal was a steak and potato swilled down with six martinis, when restaurant paintings were moonlit seascapes in seamless silvery oil paint or whimsical portraits of cigar-chewing bulldogs in plaid sweaters and tartan caps. Taylor's features all of this and more. Yellowing press clips under glass, mementos of long-forgotten celebrity patrons, here and there visual allusions to sport, racehorses of yesteryear, football teams that have died of old age, faded newspaper columns of ancient jock chat.

JD imagines the full arc of a love affair with Dylan (a lovable fellow if his treatment of birds is anything to go by, thinks JD, which it probably isn't), who reminds him of boys he longed for when he viewed himself as a tragic figure in need of rescue. Someone different enough, removed from the small world of JD's immediate worries, that getting involved could in some mysterious manner correct the lens he sees everything through. JD no longer adheres to this salvational notion of love. JD pictures his consciousness as a round, milky iris: objects in it are at once closer and farther away than they appear, especially ones he desires. His projection: Dylan falls in love with him. At first they can't get enough of each other. When the physical passions subside, their romance deepens into authentic feeling. They move in together. Before long, JD's caustic tongue has become a problem. JD's drinking has become another problem. One night, hardly aware of what he is doing, JD attacks Dylan's character at epic length, probably in a roomful of friends, and drives him out of the house. JD tries to imagine a different outcome. Even if he subtracts the booze factor, he knows there's some genie or demon bottled up in his brain, an incubus of resentment with its own uncontrollable agenda, namely human sacrifice. JD believes that unless certain changes occur in his life, he will feed this demon whatever meal is handy, lover or (less certainly) friend.

He notices that Dylan holds a martini glass with unpracticed, boyish bravado, if not unpracticed exactly then unstudied. Dylan is a tall lanky thing with a floppy mop of surfer-blond hair, not ungraceful but, what is the word (JD rummages for it), unstylized. A practical person, used to dealing with concrete problems, those birds and their habits, testing their IQs, keeping track of their development, the main thing, thinks JD, is that Dylan doesn't flounder around in intangibles, he has a real object in front of him flapping its wings, whereas he, JD, traffics in ephemera, in unquantifiable segments of radio noise that have god knows what effect or meaning in the invisible world of the listening brain, and this ephemera can be shaped any which way as long as it sells Hondas, Immodium D, and the other products currently on offer during his hour on KAW. Dylan's work is all measured, Dylan's results can be verified, whereas my work, JD thinks, has no measure and no value. Dylan is grounded in certainties. He's not afraid of anything.

Dylan drives wildly, at high speeds, with a scary contempt for other drivers.

JD watches the rim of Dylan's glass hover at Dylan's mouth. Dylan's mouth, large and expressive, has an overdrawn quality JD associates with Australians, which Dylan isn't. When he glances at Dylan's pale, heavy-lidded blue eyes, his first thought is that he, JD, seldom notices what color people's eyes are. They've been yakking about movies. JD hears himself satirizing the dumb, pretentious, inept films he's recently seen. Dylan offers opinions blandly, though his opinions aren't bland, and when a mildly negative judgment comes out of his mouth he gazes down at the bar for a second and then says I know I'm probably being too harsh. Dylan is playful and open as a puppy, it seems. JD's sarcasm reads on Dylan's face as entertainment but there's a shadow of reserve there, JD suspects, perhaps Dylan's thinking that a little of JD goes a long way, maybe Dylan's telling himself that his own easygoing niceness really must be the superior way to get along, since JD's wit and conversational agility obviously haven't made him a happy person. JD is afraid. JD has begun to feel, in Dylan's presence, a lightheaded pleasure. He's afraid that all but the most contrived and self-conscious manifestations of himself will destroy this pleasure bit by slow bit, that the more he reveals of himself the darker this shadow of reserve will grow, a slow fade to pitch-black. Yet there's no immediate evidence of this. Dylan politely asks if JD would like another martini. He sure could use one, he says.

I was really jumpy in the studio, he says.

Funny, I was just thinking you didn't seem nervous at all. JD feels like he's pacing the backstage area of his mind's théâtre de luxe. It's this waiting, this preliminary getting-to-know-you crap, that always spills over the border of spontaneity into the kingdom of game-playing, JD's never been good at it, and on the few occasions when he was, he hated himself.

I don't know how you go in there with all these different people and improvise the way you do, says Dylan, admiringly. That's impressive. I'm one of these people who gets along better with animals. You have this way of drawing people out.

Well, I write out questions even if I don't use them, says JD. If a program starts running away from me I always have some words in front of me to steer it back with.

Do you, are you planning to stay, doing radio? Dylan has trouble formulating this question, because he doesn't know what to call what JD does. He's also unsure how JD pictures his radio thing in the grand scheme of JD's life. Most people whose lives involve public presentation have world domination as their inner theme, this much he knows, it's only the scale of JD's wishes that Dylan hasn't measured.

Uhm. Hard to say. You know, you sit in this little room with a technician every day, it's the same radio station wherever you go. It's still interesting of course when there's guests that're fun to talk to, like you. But, I thought I would have a more active sort of existence. I don't know about settling into this as a career. JD says this with a smile that says: I'm not the monster you take me for. But I am a monster, just like everybody else.

Well, what would you—

I don't know really I think I might put all this aside and become a lounge comic. Or open a travel agency. Cheap air tickets, you know.

JD doesn't feel like telling Dylan about the afternoon talk show he's been negotiating, in a desultory way, with Fox TV for the past year and a half: everything could still go awry, and with Dylan, he thinks, there could be some advantage in presenting himself as directionless, open to the cosmos, a seeker, even a potential Theosophist.

Have you traveled a lot?

No. And you?

I spent a year in India. And Nepal, Thailand, Japan. I've been to Peru because of the macaws, and the Galápagos, which I guess is part of Ecuador. I didn't really see Ecuador. It's mostly been bird-related. I worked for a while in the Jain Bird Hospital in New Delhi. When I first worked there, they would only treat birds that were vegetarians. Then somebody brought in a hawk who'd been shot at, and I said look, religion or no religion, we've got to help this bird—

Dylan laughs a breathy unemphatic laugh as he tells the story. The story isn't very long. JD considers that the conversational ball keeps bouncing back into his court and that he, JD, tends not to volley it back before sitting on it for a long time.

So, says JD, you've had a pretty rangy life for somebody what, twenty-six? twenty-seven? Peru, India, you worked in the Jane Fonda Bird Hospital, you saved a hawk, you're an author—JD pauses, angles his neck—what's not to love? And for emphasis he gives Dylan's thigh a little squeeze through Dylan's chocolate-brown corduroy slacks, solid muscle, Dylan's hand drops down for a second, JD shivers, thinking Dylan'll knock his hand away, or, worse, remove it "diplomatically" with a friendly but firm grip, JD is imprinted with an encyclopedia of other people's rejection strategies, but instead Dylan's fingertips brush the back of JD's digits, an ambiguous move, he gives JD's palm a sweaty stroke, an unambiguous one, and suddenly they're plugged in, electromagnetized, talking on another plane where words are difficult and basically irrelevant yet still have the ability to turn everything ugly and impossible. Which JD feels certain they will, and, as if to make sure, waves his hand for another vodka.

In a gay bar, he supposes, they would already have their tongues down each other's throat. In Taylor's this would precipitate something just awful. A lot of cheesy loose talk passes for conversation in Taylor's but most of it is straight and none of it accompanies any action, a furtive feel under a banquette table maybe, Taylor's is always full of lawyers for some reason, lawyers and courthouse secretaries, and besides, JD wants to preserve his excellent relations with Luis, the soulful Mexican bartender, who invariably undercharges him and is generous with bar snacks—a bowl of little sirloin nuggets usually, a meal in itself when JD's broke, which he often is because of a tax lien on his salary.

They leave Taylor's at eleven. They drive through Hancock Park on a wobbling course to Western Avenue. The hissing of summer lawns reminds JD fondly of the Manson family. Dylan's midnight-blue Mercedes, with its spacey control panel glowing in the dark like a constellation of quasars, is the kind of car JD would drive if he (a) drove, and (b) could afford it. The interior smells new. The only personal objects in the car, on the rear seat, are a 1991 *Thomas Brothers Guide,* a pair of sunglasses, and an orange book JD recognizes in the dark as Paul Celan's *Collected Poems.* On the crummy street beside the Black Light, Dylan parks in a blunt way, shuts the car off, and kisses JD on the mouth. They trade saliva long enough for JD to get a crick in his neck. Dylan's a good kisser. JD can tell because he doesn't kiss much and doesn't like it as a general rule because he hardly ever feels anything when he kisses and thinks that he should. The bar's empty. Deadly Paul, expansive from his usual late brunch of crystal methedrine, brings JD up to speed on his, Deadly Paul's, new romance, a woman in her forties who wandered in one night and sat at the bar emitting too much personality, JD's seen her a half dozen times since then and thinks her a dangerous mess, a skankier version of Cassandra Lomax without the looks or the residual brains: for some reason, Deadly Paul's gone nuts for this "foxy lady" (as he insists on describing her), Lorraine— probably, JD thinks, because Deadly Paul isn't any prize himself. He's had dinner with the creature again, he tells JD—at her house, he adds suggestively, and it's obvious the horny old goat wants to describe what they did in nauseating detail, and he's only slightly inhibited because that might diminish what he calls Lorraine's "classiness," a word Deadly Paul produces while slapping his palms on his potbelly through his Led Zeppelin T-shirt, a veritable cartoon of satiated swinishness. Dylan politely spaces out on the recitation.

I told you dint I about Monica? Lorraine's kid? Fourteen years old, already she's wearing the shorts cut up to here and the halter tops and the makeup. I told Lorraine, you better keep an eye out, kids that age, I says to her, you gotta reel them in on a tight leash, they don't even know how to work the oven yet, you don't control 'em they'll have a cake baking in it.

Not only does he make a good drink, JD tells Dylan, Paul's also master of the metaphor.

Remarks of this type flash across Deadly Paul's sensorium like dazzling lights on a hovering spaceship. Paul has a dim mind, thinks JD, stuffed with received ideas. Instead of intelligence, thinks JD, Paul has a low peasant cunning that is actually more useful than intelligence. Paul's only good quality, to JD's thinking, is his lack of real malevolence, despite a personality one would expect to be filled with it. And even that seems more the product of lethargy than of any actual virtue. Paul resumes swobbing glasses with a yellow starburst sponge on a long plastic handle. Dylan's switched to Bacardi Coke. He fishes out the lime wedge, gnaws on it, puts it on the paper napkin. He looks bemused, if that's the word, his face placid, torso hunched over the curved lip of the bar counter, one large Reebok planted on the floor, the other leg wrapped around a tine of the barstool. All the libido fizzing between them in the car has suddenly gone flat.

JD thinks it's the second or third time Paul's mentioned Lorraine's daughter lately, and that Paul's the exact type of hillbilly loser who'd get into a "relationship" with a slut like Lorraine out of a secret and probably unconscious lust for her fourteen-year-old. It also occurs to JD that half the people he's friendly with are people he wouldn't want in his apartment.

Frankie Lomax shuffles in, dressed in loose denim pants and open denim jacket, with a string of green, glow-in-the-dark plastic pearls hanging on his smooth bare chest, his white feet in what look like regulation California prison sandals. He pauses in the doorway intending to strike an extravagant pose for the room, abandons it as he looks around, shambles up to the bar behind JD's back, drums his fingers on the bar with stoned bravado and orders himself a gi-gi-gi-gi-gi-gin and t-t-t-t-tonic, JD hears the sandals scuffing over to the jukebox while Deadly Paul clatters around mixing the drink. Dylan has been talking about fear: Krishnamurti says we don't know how to live with fear, Dylan says, he asks us to look at what we're afraid of, for instance the fear of disease, without invoking the word that animates our fear, without saying "death" to ourselves, he asks us to look at fear without trying to solve the fear problem, without letting our inner voices run away with our fear and turning it into something else, without starting a bonfire of anxiety, JD struggles to understand what Dylan's telling him, because it's actually of great interest to him, even though he hears "vanity" instead of "anxiety" and doesn't grasp how the fear of death would connect with being vain. As soon as the jukebox goes on, *Ground Control to Major Tom,* he starts losing bits of Dylan's voice, starts talking louder himself, Dylan's saying now he hopes JD doesn't think he's some type of spiritual fanatic. A few young people drift into the bar and take over the stools at the wooden divider.

commencing countdown, engines on Frankie looks at the ten and six ones crushed up in his disintegrating billfold. This is what's left from the twenty his stepmother handed over in the doorway of the house in Malibu Canyon, making a disgusted face, like the kid had leprosy or something, first the maid wouldn't let him in and then Gloria came to the door in a terry-cloth robe, hair wrapped in a yellow towel, face (which Frankie can never remember anyway) an opisthognathous fright mask of mint-green facial mud, Your father's at the office, she said, and this really isn't such a great time, I'm expecting people. She looked over his shoulder at the steep, empty road. *I'm stepping through the door* Frankie stared at the lines of unspackled skin where her eyebrows extruded like centipedes in aspic.

She really startled him. Gloria's never been openly hostile before, and Frankie's never been prevented from entering the house, though there have always been signals that he isn't entirely welcome there. His father's always let him use the pool and, if he needs to, sleep in his old room, whenever they change the security code his father calls to give him the combination, but his father phones him less and less often lately, when Frankie calls at the office his father's always occupied with somebody's asshole. *I'm feeling very scared* That Gloria could do this while looking so ridiculous herself seemed to mark a new stage in his estrangement from the old man. He knew if he said anything it would come out gibberish: his stutter thickened when anything upset him, it only really went away when he either felt entirely calm, or had worked himself into a complete rage. *And I think my spaceship knows* I suppose you need money, she speculated, practically spitting. It was a perfect afternoon up there in the canyons, except for the winds, and Gloria could always jump in the pool, so why her green face was so twisted with ugly feelings he really couldn't figure. *Planet Earth is blue, and there's nothing I can do.* Some flakes fluttered from Gloria's nose, revealing a reddened patch of skin. She said other things like: If your mother sobered up for a change you people wouldn't be broke all the time, and: I don't see what's preventing you from getting a job, and then, a little less harshly, she reminded him that his father had offered to pay for speech therapy if Frankie would only stick with it. *Floating in a tin can* Frankie cowered inside, and maybe outside, too. He felt a kind of lethal embarrassment burning all over his skin. It was often a stupid idea to see his father, who usually acted like a kindly but disapproving distant relative, and even stupider to see Gloria, who'd dropped a set of twins right after she married his father, as if to establish a greater claim to his money than the single child from the marriage before. Fucking precocious girl twins they'd named Amber and Amethyst, which made them sound like cleaning ladies from Inglewood, Frankie thought. Gloria told him to wait and closed the door in his face and came back a minute later with the twenty-dollar bill and said This is all I can give you, we're not doing so well these days ourselves. And now he does feel the deafening anger he should've felt this afternoon, instead of leaving Gloria in the full effulgence of her shittiness and walking all the way to PCH and getting the bus into Hollywood, where he cruised Santa Monica around La Jolla for three hours with no luck, ate an Astroburger, and let some fag from Lakewood buy him four drinks in the Gold Coast. He would've done the guy, who seemed to decide in the end that there was something ominous about Frankie he couldn't risk finding out about.

Frankie feels: restless, impatient, pissed off, mildly curious about the conversation that JD (whose name he forgets, even though he hears him on the radio all the time, and then remembers, and a few seconds later forgets again) is having with his tall friend, which goes something like: It's only a west coast tour, they're sending me to San Francisco, Portland and Seattle, Portland's a nice town, something hotel in Portland, Gus Van Sant, what about that serial killer they had up there, Oh all the serial killers come from Portland or Seattle, If you have a day or two you should take the ferry to Orcas Island, something Cafe, of course the seafood, fresh clams, oysters, hepatitis, Frankie keeps wanting to join this conversation, pipe up with some interesting comment, and why shouldn't he, Deadly Paul puts his two cents in every time he makes his sweep of the bar, but Frankie can't imagine what he could say or why anybody would be interested, he's never been to Portland or Seattle, he's never even been to Mexico which is really a lot closer, he wishes he could tell these people that it isn't his fault that he's never been anywhere, that he only seems conniving and maybe even evil to people who know him from the Black Light because he's smart and he sounds dumb because of his stutter, that he can't get out the nice polished sentences that run through his head like an LED sign lit up in red letters, it's as if a thick glass sheet separated him from their busy words, he has to let his body talk for him, and naturally his body only speaks one limited, pornographic dialect that everyone associates with dumb animal desire.

When he strolls back outside (quickly, as if he's stepping out to look at the street, at this time of year the difference between outside and inside isn't so dramatic), Frankie doesn't know if he's headed for one of the bars around Ivar, or simply craves the hungry looks of passing drivers, but his steps take him only as far as La Mirada Ave, a squalid stretch of bughouse apartment bunkers, where the blue Mercedes glistens in the darkness, anomalous and vulnerable, beckoning like a child's piggy bank. He isn't quite drunk, but pissed enough that he notices he isn't walking straight. Frankie's suddenly so flushed with hope and despair of an utterly inchoate nature, so filled with a cosmic appreciation of the spinning universe that he staggers up to the Mercedes, braces himself on the hood, then lurches across the street to the cyclone fence where he clutches the metal latticework and stares down the embankment at the unbelievable ribbons of headlights and taillights whizzing through the city's nervous system. He doesn't hear steps growing louder and quicker behind him, the first blow to his head might as well be a beam or a brick tumbling down from nirvana. When he doubles over, the tennis sneaker that slams into his stomach registers as a tennis sneaker, but he's in too much pain and not quick enough to dodge the second and third and fourth kicks, which land on his neck and his face and his back, he curls like a fetus on the shoulder dirt and hears some gross canine howl coming out his throat as a strangled gasp for air. In the dim stellar residue of a streetlight he sees a watery face, or a face rippled by the water in his eyes, vaguely recognizes the tall guy from the 7-Eleven last week, who's unzipped his fly and stands over Frankie's face with his legs spread apart, ejecting a thick stream of urine, hosing Frankie from his hair to his sandals. As a garden of pain blossoms all over, Frankie understands that he has to lie there and take it unless he wants more kicks, having some incoming vibe that this is a not normally violent person venting an unwanted rage, not a fellow psycho having fun. The guy says nothing, doesn't even laugh, just sprays him all over with a gallon of hot piss, soaking his jacket and shorts. Frankie feels it drooling down his bare chest, tastes piss that's shot up his nostrils coursing into his throat, mixed with a bloody salt taste. He wonders about his ribs because that's where the most pain is. When the piss finally peters out, Frankie whimpers impressively to show what terrific agony he's in, thinking in fact he's got off pretty easy, though he isn't really sure he can move his arms and legs. Another kick, straight to his balls, puts him on a whole different planet of sensation where he doesn't have any thoughts or even any breath. His innards brace for more blows, endorphins pump into his pain centers. Maybe it'll go on until he's dead: Frankie gets a purchase on that one single thought, which isn't a thought but a gut feeling, in his guts, guts he's now aware of in a whole new way. But the kicking stops. He believes he hears the guy moving off across the street and down the sidewalk, hard to tell, his eyes are on fire and blind from piss trickling through his eyebrows. Frankie lifts his face from the dirt. The plastic beads from his necklace glow in the dark all around like the dowry of a ravished bride, and he can't help laughing, even though it hurts.

An eruption of violence ratchets Bobby's allure up to an excruciating radiance. The encounter hasn't ruffled his newly trimmed, spiderish black hair, or creased his pale green sports jacket (silk), he doesn't even have any telltale blood on his size 12 Nikes. The sole effect of kicking the shit out of Frankie is a roseate bloom in his magnificent cheeks. He strides into the Black Light where his magazine-cover comeliness sets off interference patterns in the magnetic field between JD and Dylan, who cruise him as an involuntary reflex, at sufficient length to throw the whole evening's previous development into disarray, not that either of them would, on this occasion, venture the slightest feeler in Bobby's direction, but to each is revealed the passive feminine drift in the other, the incorrigible bottom rising to the top in the presence of emphatic virility, Bobby being the most rarefied and well-hung flower of Colombia (the country), hybridized with a strand of Sicilian DNA, a thing of appalling beauty from every angle: JD and Dylan become, not briefly enough, two Valley girls checking out the talent at the Tarzana Mall, a moment whose logical extension would be a flurry of home permanents and mutual pedicures. Fortunately, the bar has filled up a bit, other bodies and other voices dilute the Bobby effect into a light libidinal mist. It doesn't take long to forget that one is not the other's image of perfection, though such knowledge is never perfectly forgotten and usually returns like a bad penny on a clear day. Bobby slogs down a beer and slips over to the phone, where he discreetly consults the digits on his beeper, the standard seven followed by a room number. Hotel client. When the voice comes Bobby reels off his statistics in reverse order of magnitude, quotes a fee fifty dollars above his usual, and says he can be there in fifteen minutes, twenty tops. The voice's about to say more but Bobby puts the receiver down, feeling sudden vertigo, and leaves the bar as if pushing himself through the gelatinous medium of a dream.

Describing his evening the following day, Seth is anxious to recount, in a calculated way—that is, with the precise degree of circumspection required to transmit some as-yet-unassimilated piece of fortune without also conveying various suddenly activated character flaws—that Teddy Wade, the movie star, phoned him at eight-thirty, gushing compliments over the collection of Seth's magazine pieces Teddy claims he bought at Book Soup. Seth says Teddy told him what a good writer he was, that Teddy even went into detail about it, Seth doesn't go so far as to claim that anything Teddy said was especially prescient or intelligent, merely that it wasn't stupid, even if it didn't prove that Teddy had actually read any of his book, You know, Seth says, he made the type of remarks you'd expect from a movie star, Teddy talks the way actors talk (Teddy has become a first-name-only person for Seth on the strength of this telephone call), well, Seth says, he invited me to some sort of party at his house later this month, I wonder if I should go, this is Seth's way of hinting that he isn't all that impressed or flattered by the attentions of movie stars, when he's clearly tickled pink by them, on the other hand Teddy inhabits a sphere of fame so much larger than Seth's little specialized patch of celebrity that Teddy's interest or pretended interest actually does make him edgy, Seth is neither so old nor so mired in obscurity that he doesn't plan on stretching the modest bustier of his persona in the near or middle future, and he detests walking into places where he turns out to be the least-known person in the room, which is, he tells me, certain to be the case chez Teddy. I can just imagine, Seth says, a mixture of Hollywood types ranging from stars to agents and working actresses or what have you, every one of whom inhabits a higher rung on the evolutionary ladder than I do, in his or her chosen profession, especially since none of these people read and if they did read it wouldn't be anything I wrote, but of course, Seth continues, I probably will go, just for a glimpse of everything I can't have, a house I couldn't dream of living in, cars I could never hope to drive, Seth says all this out of superstition, the way he'll sometimes say Oh I've probably got AIDS or Let's face it I'll be dead in ten years, Seth thinks if he says these things they can't ever come to pass, if he says he'll never get success and money they will come to him sooner than later, and even though Seth's a grown-up, and knows better, some roped-off VIP room of his psyche's funky mansion still believes, sometimes, that aneurysms and neoplasms and failure and death only pay their fatal calls on other people.

. . . On Wednesday a terrific fracas broke out in the pressroom in the criminal courts building, Seth says it started when the CBS correspondent, Roddy Severnick, dumped a camera and a lot of gear on the ABC desk while getting his makeup on for the three-thirty feed to the east coast six-thirty news, the whole day was consumed by motions, Seth says, motions to suppress, motions to dismiss, motions mainly remarkable for their utter lack of motion, plus preliminary questioning of Poppy Pignatelli, Felix Martinez's former best friend, most of it concerning the so-called screenplay Felix and Poppy wrote in 1988 at the Pignatelli family's weekend cabin near Sequoia National Park, Poppy of course wore a wire for the BHPD in an attempt to get Felix to repeat the confession he supposedly made to Poppy a couple weeks after the slayings on Woodrow Wilson Drive, Poppy had not been able to extract any damning statements out of Felix while wearing the wire, but claims Felix told him all about the killings, in the version Poppy tells, repeating his grand jury testimony, but changing it a little as it turns out, Carlos fetched both of the Mossberg shotguns a few minutes before the killings and after the brothers burst into the so-called rumpus room told Felix to "Get Mom," Judge Tietelbaum's holding off on ruling vis-à-vis the admissibility of certain bits of the so-called Felix Martinez confession to Poppy Pignatelli, the same applies to the so-called screenplay, *Buddies,* which Fawbus Kennedy, in a mini-interview during the morning break with Lips McKendry of Court TV, claimed he'd already read, further fanning the already considerable antipathy most of the press corps feels toward Fawbus Kennedy, who is not a legitimate newsperson but has some entirely honorary job arrangement with an obscure local media outlet, which provides a purely technical legitimacy to the state marshal's assignment of a permanent daily seat for Fawbus Kennedy, who mainly writes a lot of unsubstantiated gossip in what Seth calls that putrid magazine and once every year or two produces a Jackie Collins type roman à clef about family scandals of the rich and famous, though compared to Fawbus Kennedy, as Seth puts it, Jackie Collins writes like Michelet, in the pressroom, Seth says, Fawbus Kennedy's known as Judith Krantz in pants, there's a general feeling, says Seth, that Fawbus Kennedy epitomizes pompous mediocrity of a type unprecedented and decidedly unwelcome in this kind of grave proceeding (though there was, he qualifies, Walter Winchell, another pernicious gasbag, at the Bruno Hauptmann trial), it would be one thing if it were Norman Mailer or Truman Capote descending on a death penalty murder case, full of pretentions and noblesse oblige, but a third-rate middlebrow Depends ad like Fawbus Kennedy is another kettle of fish altogether. This nattering, brainless old turd, says Seth, with his shelf of worthless drugstore novels, who merely feeds the public back its own prejudices and clichéd opinions, isn't morally or literarily qualified to read the bones of this particular sacrifice, and lately, of course, Seth says, Fawbus Kennedy, in his dull-minded dispatches for that putrid magazine, has started italicizing the kind of extraneous but supposedly telling cocktail chatter or dinner conversation his sister-in-law features so prominently in her essays and novels (to infinitely wittier effect, it must be added, Seth adds), the coy little anecdote designed to drop famous names as the author's intimates, as if the dreary cocktail chatter or dinner conversation of bored Hollywood sophisticates imparted some special insight into the vagaries of the judicial system, should in fact determine who should live and who should die, always the same sorts of fatuous pseudoprofundities from C-list actors like Edward James Olmos or one of the Hearst brats or what have you, what irritates the press corps, Seth says, is Fawbus Kennedy's assumption that because he writes these so-called works of fiction he's free to lie about things and invent rumors and report them as facts in that putrid magazine, a Norman Mailer or a Truman Capote makes an effort to understand why events occur whereas Fawbus Kennedy's only interest lies in brainless editorializing, he hates the Martinez brothers and therefore his thoughts about them have absolutely no enlightening dimension, and of course in his so-called novels people routinely kill other people for money, it's the kind of one-dimensional psychology Fawbus Kennedy provides to air travelers and people sprawled on summer beaches, and of course, Seth says, behind all this is a grotesquely misdirected rage over his first wife's murder, Fawbus Kennedy believes if he shows up at every first-degree murder trial as the grieving Cassandra people will come to accept the idea that his deep personal loss makes him something more exalted than the hack that he is, a deeper and more thoughtful writer than the craven mess everyone knows Fawbus Kennedy to be, and the worst part, Seth says, is that Fawbus Kennedy's rage over his first wife's murder has become indistinguishable from Fawbus Kennedy's jealousy of the good literary fortunes of his brother and his sister-in-law, who are taken seriously by the *New York Review of Books* and similar publications where a writer like Fawbus Kennedy is considered a bad joke. Only if Condé Nast ever acquires the *New York Review of Books* and appoints some jumped-up British hyena to turn it into garbage will Fawbus Kennedy ever be allowed to publish his so-called writing in the *New York Review of Books*, says Seth, not that the *New York Review of Books* is any better than it should be, but it's still too good for Fawbus Kennedy, says Seth, and thank God, he adds, that there has always been and always will be at least one place too good for the likes of Fawbus Kennedy, though the Fawbus Kennedys of the world make it their business to corrupt and destroy such a place, to transform such a place into a literary toilet where the stale droppings of themselves and their friends can be flushed out into the public, proclaiming such a toilet, after its utter editorial devastation by some spiritual pygmy, as the best magazine in the world.

I realize, Seth goes on, that Truman Capote called the *New York Review of Books* a *snotrag,* and that James Purdy once remarked that everyone who writes for the *New York Review of Books* should be *lined up against a wall and shot,* but that was before every other publication in the world had been turned into meretricious pig shit by that evil stoat *whose father was the best friend of Roy Cohn.* Actually, says Seth, I have no idea why I'm defending the *New York Review of Books,* or why I've been on about Fawbus Kennedy, who really signifies less than nothing in the long run, but he's the kind of nothing this whole culture has been moving toward for decades, a sort of aggravated and insatiable zero, and frankly he's the kind of nothing these proceedings, things being what they are, fit like a glove some psychopath would use to fistfuck his mother, and like the alibi he'd use to deny it afterwards, the quintessence of a no-fault attitude of the nonincarcerated toward the people behind bars, the powerful toward the powerless, the fortunate toward the losers. And isn't that what America is all about?

Seth says that tensions ran high all day on Wednesday, not least because Fawbus Kennedy had managed or claimed to have managed to examine the Felix Martinez/Poppy Pignatelli screenplay, which seemed to indicate that the prosecution was feeding information to the press on a selective basis. In the hearing outside the presence of the jury Marlene Quilty argued that *Buddies* describes a young man very similar to Felix Martinez who discovers a will in his father's desk, a will bequeathing Felix Martinez or rather a young man very similar to Felix Martinez an estate of ninety million dollars, whereupon the character, whose name is Brett Ashley Montague IV, takes a shotgun from the hall closet and shoots both his parents, furthermore, Marlene Quilty said, Seth says, this screenplay, which is a virtual blueprint of the actual slayings of Fidel and Peggy Martinez, was written months before the real-life killings, clear evidence of premeditation, whereas Lauren Nathanson dismissed the similarity of the screenplay to the real-life killings and said the screenplay was nothing more than a puerile adolescent effort, one which Peggy Martinez herself apparently typed up for Felix Martinez and Poppy Pignatelli "without hearing any alarm bells," Lauren Nathanson further argued that Peggy Martinez told Felix Martinez his screenplay was "dumb and stupid," "the worst thing she'd ever read," and "dopey," the only significant thing about the screenplay, according to Lauren Nathanson, was the fact that here again one of the Martinez parents used an admittedly puerile creative attempt by Felix Martinez as an occasion to demean and diminish him, furthermore, under questioning by Lauren Nathanson, Poppy Pignatelli admitted it could have been himself rather than Felix Martinez who came up with the fictional murder idea. The second matter taken up at the hearing was the admissibility of the so-called Hidden Hills burglaries committed by Felix and Carlos Martinez a year before the grisly killings on Woodrow Wilson Drive, it's the prosecution's hope that these burglaries can somehow work their way in as evidence because it was after the so-called Hidden Hills burglaries that Fidel Martinez, ordered by juvenile court to seek psychological counseling for Felix Martinez, contacted Dr. Potter Phlegg, and it's also a fact that the Martinez family moved from Hidden Hills to Woodrow Wilson Drive as a direct consequence of the burglaries, Lauren Nathanson of course asserts that admitting the burglaries in one or both of the Martinez brothers' cases will prejudice the jury or juries. She further typifies the Hidden Hills burglaries as the types of gratuitous crimes committed by affluent disturbed children as a cry for help, a claim bolstered by the fact that Carlos Martinez actually attempted to return the stolen property before the Martinez brothers got caught, in fact, Lauren Nathanson points out, the only reason they got caught was that Carlos Martinez returned too much jewelry to one house and not enough jewelry to the other, having only participated in the second robbery and thus having been unsure which jewelry belonged to which house, this kind of absurd screwup, Lauren Nathanson says with a tight determined grin, belies the prosecution's attempt to portray the Martinez brothers as hardened criminals. We see instead,

Lauren Nathanson says, two inept, traumatized children who were acting out the drama of their own horrendous abuse at the hands of two monstrous parents, one a dishrag of complicity, the other a raging authoritarian monster whose only reproach regarding the burglaries, it turns out, was to ridicule both sons for fucking up a simple burglary, implying that he, Fidel Martinez, if so minded, would have masterminded a completely successful and much more epic burglary. In other words, queries Lauren Nathanson, what message did Fidel Martinez send his two sons on this occasion, if not the message that it was perfectly all right to break the law but unforgivable to get caught?

. . . Seth's version of the disturbance in the pressroom has it that Roddy Severnick from CBS believed from day one that the ABC desk was some sort of communal property, for weeks now, Seth tells me, Roddy Severnick has been using the phone assigned to ABC and leaving his personal things on the ABC desk when he has to run up to the courtroom lobby or down to the plaza for a press conference, despite the fact that CBS has its own desk. It so happens there's a shortage of phones in the pressroom, and a shortage of desks, and those of us working for the smaller media outlets all have to share desks and share phones whereas the network correspondents have desks assigned, they've paid for the desks and the phones, and Chris O'Dowell from ABC went into a rage, finally, having dealt with Roddy Severnick in a diplomatic fashion for weeks, suddenly out of nowhere this violent rage came pouring out of him and the CBS minicam went flying across the pressroom, crashing into a case of water cooler refills, ditto the CBS lights, there was also a struggle that would've turned into a fistfight if Roddy Severnick and Chris O'Dowell hadn't been separated by various interlopers. This would have been bad enough if Fawbus Kennedy hadn't entered the pressroom in the middle of this fracas and instantly started taking notes, whereupon Marvin Payton from the *Sacramento Bee* threw a punch at Fawbus Kennedy, on general principles as he later said, unfortunately knocking off Fawbus Kennedy's expensive eyeglasses, and now there's talk of assault charges. Fawbus Kennedy's lawyer has already sent an investigator over to the courthouse who's asking for witnesses and depositions. So far, Seth says, everyone including me has told the investigator we didn't actually see Marvin Payton hit Fawbus Kennedy, although we all did, since the general feeling is that Fawbus Kennedy hasn't any business being in the pressroom, since he's basically an advocate for the prosecution and has said as much in his magazine diary, not that sentiments among the press run especially high in favor of the defense, it's simply a question of balance and fairness to both sides . . .

. . . this altercation, Seth says, is being reported as an *outbreak of passions* between pro-Martinez reporters and pro-prosecution reporters, even though ABC and CBS have both issued disclaimers, it appears that Lips McKendry got this *outbreak of passions* idea from the *Los Angeles Times* reporter, who walked in after the whole thing had settled down and simply assumed from the muddled zap of gossip that everybody's passions were inflamed by the Poppy Pignatelli hearing, when the very opposite was true, if anything the Poppy Pignatelli hearing had put most of us to sleep, Seth says it's quite easy to fall asleep in the courtroom and in fact unavoidable at times, the only real passions involved in this pressroom rumpus, Seth says, were Chris O'Dowell's passion to have his desk surface clear and Marvin Payton's passion to pop Fawbus Kennedy in the face, neither passion had any relation to any sympathies for or hostilities against the Martinez brothers per se, and even the term "passion" grossly exaggerates the type of feeling rampant in the pressroom on Wednesday afternoon. Irritation, Seth says, would be a closer term, ravening bored irritation of a high degree instilled by sitting for hours and hours in the mortuary dank of that courtroom, and then the hours and hours of every particular detail's inescapable regurgitation. The precise smell and texture of this paralyzing boredom is utterly lost on the home viewer, says Seth, who can always flip stations or shut the TV off or leave the room, whereas for those of us with our asses nailed to the courtroom benches all day a feeling of slow strangulation and suffocating tedium is scarcely relieved by the various bombshells dropped by the various witnesses, quite often the effect of these supposed bombshells can't be felt until we leave the courtroom and the outside world revives us, there is often strenuous and difficult debate in the courthouse corridors over whether or not a particular bit of testimony was indeed a bombshell or instead a fizzled incendiary device of no significance, it's one's natural tendency, Seth says, to resist what one hears in the courtroom, just as one resists what one hears in a schoolroom or a church, even though what one hears in these places is supposedly of great importance. The fact is, says Seth, the greater the importance claimed for what is heard in a courtroom or a schoolroom or a church, the greater our resistance to it, since it invariably issues from absurd individuals, wrapped in the ridiculous mantle of authority, like Judge Tietelbaum, Seth says, whose celebrated sense of humor is really that of a cackling hen in a Protestant barnyard, and whose so-called *impartial decisions,* far from reflecting judicial wisdom, actually suggest the *arbitrariness of desperation,* it's Judge Tietelbaum's incompetence and flagrant bias, Seth claims, that set the prison guards free in the first prison guard beating trial, and kept the infamous Ventura County sewage treatment kickback trial running for four years after the charges were exposed as a frame-up, in virtually every case where Judge Tietelbaum has presided, says Seth, the innocent have been found guilty and the guilty have been set free, every conviction obtained in one of Judge Tietelbaum's trials has been overturned on appeal, despite the notorious reluctance of the state appeals court to overturn convictions, and of course in the prison guard beating trial it was necessary to file federal charges against the acquitted defendants to reverse the miscarriage of justice achieved by Judge Tietelbaum's incompetence . . .

Could Seth, or anyone else looking in, imagine this stout, plodding Tietelbaum (who is, by the way, widely considered to be at least as competent as any other judge in Los Angeles County) as a creature of mystery? The owner of a rich and dangerous fantasy life? As a man who believes himself, sometimes, to be the final avatar of the Lord Maitreya, the consort, in a former existence, of an earlier incarnation of Janice Wade, whose trust fund he administers at the behest of Janice Wade's late mother, Buffy Singer Oldham Vandermoeler Patterson? Dedicated mystic, Very Illustrious Most Puissant Grand Commander of the Order of the Agape Lodge of Former Scientology, a secret cartel of venture capitalists who plan to do for a hitherto desiccated, empty sliver of Ventura County what Kaufman and Broad did for Antelope Valley? Implausible, perhaps, that Rupert Tietelbaum is an enterprising collector of other people's secrets, sometimes an avid broker of clandestine knowledge, or that his own secrets include an alter ego named Dave Spacey, a three-hundred-pound private dick with a mouth as vulgar as a sewer, or that he sometimes spirits himself from chambers to a pay phone in Chinatown, where he incarnates Dave Spacey in order to throw a little terror into Janice Wade's youngish life, during lunch breaks in the Martinez trial. Yet every human being has at least one important secret, why shouldn't somebody as connected as Rupert Tietelbaum have several? For another example: an obsessive-compulsive disorder that makes him spread the papers on his desk in a particular pattern, with the edges of the paper clips lined up just so, and whenever he receives motions or other items from the attorneys he must take them with his left hand, bringing them into his "sphere of communication," as he thinks of it, with a specially inflected motion, and arranges them in a special configuration, because if he doesn't do all these things exactly so the universe will crack open and he will die. Even Tietelbaum-Spacey, when mailing off his obscene letters and greeting cards, has sometimes had to drive all over the city before finding the single possible mailbox to drop them in.

Events are moving swiftly in the prosecution case, though they seem to unfold in an endless dilation of verbiage. On Thursday the so-called murder scenario screenplay is ruled to have no useful probative value in the matter at hand, a mere repository for the stray thought of family homicide, a thought so everyday and American and Greek, too, that few of us can claim never to have entertained it, and Poppy Pignatelli, Georgio Armanified for the benefit of the blue jury, shows up at court with two blond babes from Beverly Hills High School, he's Tenaxed his strawberry hair to resemble Sean Penn's, with a defiant upward sweep in front, and on the witness stand his gaping unbeautiful face with its small malignant green eyes and its too-red pursy little swollen lips and its dinky pointed nose marooned amid too much uninflected freckled flesh appears to impersonate Sean Penn, to the infinite dismay of the prosecutors. There is something unpleasantly self-assured in Poppy Pignatelli's manner, an attempt at sophistication that exposes his immaturity, an off-putting air of obvious pleasure in his temporary status as the cynosure of all eyes, and at the same time Poppy has the shrugging, grudging testimonial reflexes of someone who's been hauled into court on a capital felony charge of his own, a disreputable, slinking youthfulness that gives the civic-minded betrayal he's committing the bilious flavor any snitch leaves in people's mouths, it doesn't help that Poppy Pignatelli looks even more like Pinocchio than he does like Sean Penn, on account of his pointed nose. On the witness stand he avoids meeting Felix's gaze, whenever his eyes stray into Felix's ambit Poppy flushes and has to pause, a trickle of sweat migrates from his swept-up hairline across his squarish forehead and down the white space between his spooky eyes, spreads out along the left slope of his nose, he recounts Felix's so-called confession of September 1, 1989, swiping at the spreading droplet with his fingers, he describes himself and Felix walking from the guesthouse on Woodrow Wilson Drive to the main house on Woodrow Wilson Drive, past the tennis court and the swimming pool, he says Felix asked him out of the blue whether he, Poppy, wanted to know how it really happened, how the killings were done, he says Felix then told him that Felix and Carlos came home from the movies to fetch a fake ID Felix used to get into nightclubs, that Felix had gone inside and up to his room and when he came outside Carlos was standing beside the Trans Am holding both of the shotguns and said, Let's do it, he says Felix went on to say that they loaded the shotguns and crept to the side of the house burst through the so-called French windows, that Peggy and Fidel were both sitting on the couch and both sprang up as the brothers burst in, that Fidel shouted No, no, or words to that general effect, as Carlos fired his shotgun, that Felix immediately fired his shotgun at Peggy, that they both continued firing their shotguns until the parents were a bloody pulp of gristle and bone. Felix, for the first time anyone remembers, stares at the witness the whole time as if daring him to make eye contact, and this surely impresses the blue jury, since Felix usually looks dazed from the copious doses of Prozac and Valium he's fed all the time in jail, and the heat of his unmet stare pumps cascades of moisture out of Poppy Pignatelli's forehead, the sweat of a born liar by the look of it, and it looks that way because Poppy's so pleased with himself, so unconflicted, so Pinocchio and Sean Penn, whereas each juror, even those who already detest these defendants—and of course on the blue jury, as opposed to the gold jury, you have those stubby, awful middle-aged men, whom Seth calls The Burghers of Calais—can picture himself or herself keeping their mouths shut if a worthier person than Carlos or Felix, lifelong intimate or retarded cousin, murdered in heat and then spilled his conscience into the juror's ear.

Lauren Nathanson sets about ripping Poppy Pignatelli to shreds on cross-examination, bringing out that Poppy told police that Felix confessed to him in October, on the same day the computer expert came to the house on Woodrow Wilson Drive to erase the computer data, and that the police had then pointed out to Poppy that the computer expert came to the house on September 1, whereupon Poppy revised his story, placing the confession a month back in time. Lauren Nathanson also gets Poppy to admit that he gave a different version of Felix's confession that November to the grand jury, that Poppy told the police and repeated to the grand jury that Felix told him that Carlos had shot both parents, and that he, Felix, shot Peggy twice but only after she was dead, or after Felix thought she was dead. Poppy says he didn't know if Felix was telling the truth, also that he didn't want to be the one who turned the brothers in.

But you agreed to wear a wire, Lauren Nathanson accuses. You were willing to get your best friend arrested, weren't you.

Poppy squirms. He finds himself decorated with a beauty contestant's silk sash that has the word fink scrawled across it in silver glitter. Even in the realm of Judge Tietelbaum, it lacks glamour. I didn't want to, he tells the court, suddenly ruminative and scriptless, depleted from all the attention he's getting and knackered by the late-dawning realization that Lauren Nathanson is quite a lot smarter than he is, what choice did I have? It was a hard thing for me, that my best friend killed his parents.

You never asked Felix why he did it, did you.

Everybody brings that up. I know. No, I didn't ask him.

You and Felix liked playing mind games with each other, didn't you. Did it cross your mind that Felix might have been playing a mind game with you when he confessed?

That's why I told the police it might have happened, not that it did happen, I didn't know if he was telling the truth.

But you agreed to wear a wire, didn't you?

Objection Your Honor already established says Quentin Kojimoto, startling Judge Tietelbaum from a surreptitious nap.

Goes to state of mind, Your Honor, says Lauren Nathanson.

Overruled, says Judge Tietelbaum, clearly intending to sustain the objection, but too drowsy to correct himself. Proceed, Counsel.

And you went with Felix to Happy Talk Seafood for dinner, Lauren Nathanson says, and you brought up the killings to Felix, and what did Felix tell you?

Felix said he didn't want to talk about it, says Poppy. He opens his mouth again to elaborate, but Lauren Nathanson cuts him off with a well-timed toss of her ringlets.

Didn't Felix actually say, says Lauren Nathanson, that you didn't know anything about it and you didn't know what you were talking about?

He said that, yes—

Isn't it true, says Lauren Nathanson, that nothing Felix said to you at Happy Talk Seafood, nothing that's recorded on that tape, gives any indication that Felix told you anything about the killings at any time?

No, says Poppy, I mean yes, but—

No further questions, says Lauren Nathanson, her voice dripping with disgust.

Seth says a whole different atmosphere prevailed after Poppy Pignatelli left the stand, though only for a few minutes, mainly because the cranky, polarized blue jury retired from the courtroom and the more buoyant and better-edu-cated gold jury came in, an almost festive group of attentive well-dressed types, Seth says you wouldn't mind encountering most of the gold jury in a social setting, whereas half of the blue jury belongs to that netherworld of graceless, sullen tract house inhabitants one only sees in supermarket parking lots, the kind of squat and mentally deficient gun owners and lawn waterers Seth calls the human radio sets, bits of gene pool bacteria that drifted west from Oklahoma, bitterness stamped on their faces like the seal on a trade school diploma, bitterness against the Martinez brothers for being rich and young and good-looking, bitterness against Lauren Nathanson for being smart and female and Jewish, Seth says the brainless portions of the blue jury haven't had much opportunity to resent Sarah Johnson so far, Sarah Johnson's quiet schoolteacher's style intimidates them too much, reminds them perhaps of some patient grade school teacher they had who taught them whatever primitive reading and writing skills they possess, Sarah Johnson, Seth says, no doubt is the very type of person who, once upon a time, instilled in these appalling blue jurors the modicum of civility and restraint that has kept these appalling blue jurors out of the state penitentiary themselves, restrained them from lynching niggers and clubbing faggots to death with baseball bats, though it probably hasn't prevented them from knocking their wives around and bat-tering their children, whenever the so-called Burghers of Calais leave the courtroom there's a general feeling of relief, says Seth, and whenever the so-called gold jury enters a wave of optimism washes over the proceedings.

Seth says they'd all been looking forward to Jocko Phelan's testimony, the press having picked up a rumor that morning that one of the so-called authors doing a book, this Tippy Crenshaw person whom everyone likes quite a bit more than Fawbus Kennedy or the two tubby farts from the *Houston Chronicle* (McPulsive and McPugnant, as they're known around the pressroom), had gone to the defense the weekend previous with tapes he'd made of Jocko Phelan, but before they could get to Jocko Phelan some issue was brought up to sidebar, and after the sidebar Judge Tietelbaum sent the so-called gold jury back out, and next there was a hearing wherein Marlene Quilty asked Jocko Phelan if Carlos Martinez had ever told him that he'd been molested by Fidel Martinez, and Jocko Phelan said no Carlos never had said anything of the sort, even when he, Jocko Phelan, had confided to Carlos Martinez, at a teary late-night heart-to-heart in the bar at Cantor's on Fairfax Avenue, the secret of his own abuse, by his uncle Lionel on his mother's side, a confession Jocko Phe-lan had found embarrassing and difficult to make. Carlos Martinez, Jocko

Phelan said, Seth says, had made a lot of sympathetic remarks on that occasion, but nothing to suggest that anything similar had ever occurred in his own life, even though Carlos often complained that his father was "ragging his ass," or "chewing his ass out," by which he did not mean—and Jocko Phelan felt quite certain on this point—that Fidel Martinez literally had made oral contact with Carlos Martinez's buttocks or anus, but rather that Fidel Martinez had been giving his son a hard time, for example pushing Carlos beyond his endurance at tennis practice, deciding which girlfriends Carlos could continue to see and which ones he had to drop, weeding out "losers" from among Carlos's friends. Marlene Quilty further brought out that Fidel Martinez initially approved of Carlos's friendship with Jocko Phelan because Jocko Phelan could write Carlos's school papers for him at Princeton, something Fidel and Peggy Martinez had habitually done for Carlos at Beverly Hills High School, but could no longer do so easily now that Carlos was at Princeton. At first, Jocko Phelan testified, Fidel Martinez had continued doing Carlos Martinez's schoolwork and sent the papers he wrote for Carlos via fax machine, but after the year's suspension Carlos got for cheating, Fidel decided it would be more convincing for Jocko Phelan to do the schoolwork. Later, however, for various reasons, Fidel Martinez's attitude toward Jocko Phelan changed. Fidel, Jocko said, decided that Jocko was a "loser," and ordered Carlos to kick Jocko out of the dormitory room they were sharing. And that was how Jocko Phelan lost his wallet, dropping it or somehow forgetting it when he moved out, and of course the wallet contained the driver's license that Felix Martinez later used as ID to purchase the Mossberg shotguns in San Diego. On cross-exam Sarah Johnson asked Are you quite sure Carlos Martinez never told you he'd been abused by his father? When Jocko Phelan said yes Sarah Johnson said Why is it then that a writer who interviewed you for a book on this case claims that you told him that Carlos Martinez told you his father had abused him? Jocko Phelan said I don't remember telling him anything like that and I'm quite sure I didn't, but even if I did, I don't remember it. We all knew then, Seth says, that he had said something, just imagine, says Seth, if every witness in the case turns out to be a liar, one by one they are making mistakes, tripping themselves up, and for no reason at all, Seth says, since no one can prove or disprove that the Martinez brothers were molested, the most that can be proved or disproved is whether or not they said they were molested, said it before the murders to someone, and if they're liars such as the prosecution claims, and let's face it they have told a lot of lies, perhaps they'd make up such a story for who knows what reasons besides the one of giving some excuse for shooting their parents. What if everyone is lying, or stretching things just a little, moving conversations and events backward and forward in time, suppressing important facts, inventing others, and thinking they're doing the right thing because Carlos and Felix are lying, too, what if everyone's fighting one lie with another lie? After Jocko Phelan got off the stand Marlene Quilty called the writer Tippy Crenshaw and asked Tippy Crenshaw for the tapes of his interviews with Jocko Phelan. Tippy Crenshaw then cited a state law protecting journalists from having to produce unpublished material. Judge Tietelbaum said that the law Tippy Crenshaw was talking about only applied to newspaper journalists and radio and TV reporters and not to so-called book authors, ordering Tippy Crenshaw to surrender his tapes the next day. So you had the blue jury going out and the gold jury coming in and the gold jury going out again, and after the hearing the blue jury was called in, right after that the gold jury was called in, and of course this meant that some journalists had to leave the courtroom, since the blue jury has to vacate the jury box and sit in the left aisle of spectator seats whenever the gold jury is seated, and of course the blue jurors hadn't been told that the gold jurors were also coming in, so had settled themselves in the jury box, and now had to move to the spectator seats, displacing fifteen of the journalists, since there are three so-called alternates sitting with the blue jury, Seth says that fortunately he's still juggling his courtroom pass with the woman from Pacifica Radio and the TV reporter from the San Bernardino cable station and the usually absent reporter from the *Miami Herald* and therefore wasn't sitting in the section reserved for the blue jury and the blue jury alternates, but some reporters who were seated there decided to dispute the pass system with the State Marshal's Office, circulating a petition during the lunch hour to get Fawbus Kennedy's daily pass revoked, along with the passes of McPulsive and McPugnant, throwing in Tippy Crenshaw's pass for good measure, claiming that these book authors have no pressing need to attend every day of the trial since they aren't even journalists according to Judge Tietelbaum and don't meet the First Amendment criteria of informing the public. While these excluded reporters were fulminating downstairs and drafting their petition Marlene Quilty called the so-called bodyguard Sturfan Levindowski, a large square-headed enforcer type with lard-white skin and beady black eyes whose hair and mustache were cropped, Seth says, to resemble the President of Poland's. This Sturfan Levindowski person testified that Carlos Martinez hired him right after the murders and claimed that his life was in imminent danger from members of the Mafia who had probably murdered his parents. Levindowski described the twenty-four-hour protection service provided by himself and his partner, which included a so-called bulletproof limousine followed by a so-called crash vehicle or armored backup vehicle, at that time, Levindowski said, Carlos Martinez was living at the John O'Hara Motor Inn outside of Princeton, but decided suddenly to move from the John O'Hara Motor Inn to the posher and more centrally located Hotel Carol Oates. When Carlos moved out of the John O'Hara, Levindowski said, he left behind a whole closetful of expensive clothes, saying that the clothes reminded him of the tragic deaths of his parents, that he wanted to buy new clothes, furthermore he did buy new clothes, which Levindowski helped him select, from the Gianni Versace outlet in Princeton, Levindowski also accompanied Carlos to test-drive the infamous Porsche, which Carlos test-drove, Levindowski added parenthetically, Seth says, with total disregard for the local speed limit, Levindowski also claimed that Carlos at various times told Levindowski that the burly Pole "reminded Carlos of his father," and quizzed Levindowski for his opinions not only regarding the designer clothes that soon filled his room at the Hotel Carol Oates, but also his opinion of the so-called buffalo chicken wing recipe used at the bistro or brasserie Carlos frequented (and later purchased), the so-called Marquand Avenue Cafe (which Carlos later renamed Carlos's Marquand Avenue Cafe), according to Levindowski Carlos spent much of his time in the days just following the murders of his parents asking Levindowski and his partner, a Mr. Henny, the driver of the so-called crash vehicle or armored backup vehicle, to sample these buffalo chicken wings and rate their various qualities, Levindowski said that on more than one occasion Carlos Martinez sent Levindowski or Mr. Henny to the Marquand Avenue Cafe for a so-called take-out tub of buffalo chicken wings and had them convey it to Carlos's room at the Carol Oates. Carlos would then invite both Levindowski and Mr. Henny into his room and offer them some of the chicken wings, he would ask them, Levindowski said, to sit on the sofa in the so-called conversation area and empty their minds of all distracting thoughts, instructing them, Levindowski said, to grade the chicken wings on a scale from 1 to 5, according to what Carlos called their personal standards of tastiness and "snackability."

Can you tell us, Mr. Levindowski, Marlene Quilty asked, on how many occasions during the ten days when you were employed by Mr. Martinez, did Mr. Martinez ask yourself and Mr. Henny to give your opinions about the chicken wings?

Irrelevant, Your Honor, said Sarah Johnson.

Overruled, said Judge Tietelbaum. Witness will answer the question.

At least six or seven occasions, said Levindowski.

And what would Mr. Martinez tell you, asked Marlene Quilty, was the reason for all these so-called taste tests?

Hearsay, Your Honor, said Sarah Johnson.

Rephrase the question, Counselor, said Judge Tietelbaum.

Didn't Mr. Martinez seem more concerned about his chicken wings than the supposed threat to his life from the so-called Mafia, Mr. Levindowski?

Objection, Your Honor, said Sarah Johnson with restrained irritation, calls for a conclusion on the part of the witness.

More emotional about his chicken wings, pressed Marlene Quilty, ignoring the objection, than about his dead parents?

Your Honor, shrilled Sarah Johnson, as Judge Tietelbaum tapped his gavel.

I'll withdraw the question, Marlene Quilty said with a contented smirk, mugging for the jury. How were these so-called taste tests conducted, Mr. Levindowski, in your own words, please.

Well, Levindowski said, the Marquand Avenue Cafe has five kinds of buffalo chicken wings, and Mr. Martinez wanted us to try each kind.

Can you name for us the five different kinds of wings, asked Marlene Quilty.

Gosh, said Mr. Levindowski, I'm not sure if I can. I know there's one called Fiery, that's the hottest kind, that you dip in this blue cheese dressing, then let's see, there's Hot and Spicy, I believe there's one variety they call Mild But Crispy, there's a sweet kind also, that has like a duck sauce that comes with it, that's maybe called Sweet and Crusty, and then there's the non-buffalo wings which are cooked differently.

Would those be the so-called Broasted Wings, Mr. Levindowski?

That's right.

And the so-called Broasted Wings are cooked without batter?

They're plain. You have a choice of dipping sauces on the side.

Go on.

Well, Mr. Martinez would have us eat the wings one by one, and he'd have us take a little bite, and ask us to concentrate on how tangy the sauce was. Not the dipping sauce but the sauce on the chicken itself. For instance he would ask if it was too tangy, or not quite tangy enough, and if the tangy flavor overwhelmed the basic chickeny flavor. And the same thing with crispy. He used to say that if the skin was too crispy all you tasted was the skin, but if it wasn't crispy enough the wing would have a soggy texture. We'd have to eat our way through the whole bucket or tub, grading some of the wings on tanginess and others on crispiness, also on chewiness and the evenness of the cooking, in other words, if the wings were crispy all over or only partially crispy, whether the taste and the texture was consistent all through the wing, and consistent all through the tub.

And Mr. Martinez's parents had been murdered about ten days before you and Mr. Henny began tasting these chicken wings for Mr. Martinez?

I think it was more like two weeks.

Is it a fact, Mr. Levindowski, Marlene Quilty said, that two weeks after his parents died, Mr. Martinez blindfolded you and Mr. Henny and asked you to compare the chicken wings served at the Marquand Avenue Cafe with wings from another establishment?

If it please the Court, the form of the question—

Sit down, Mrs. Johnson, overruled.

Please answer the question, Mr. Levindowski.

Carlos, Mr. Martinez, said that he wanted a really objective test because he was planning to buy the Marquand Avenue Cafe and couldn't decide whether to hire a new cook or keep the one they had.

Objection, Your Honor, assumes facts not in evidence—

Your Honor, what the State seeks to establish here is that Carlos Martinez was looking into investment opportunities in Princeton, and the State will show, Your Honor, that Mr. Martinez had already inquired about the asking price of the Marquand Avenue Cafe before Fidel and Peggy Martinez were killed—

Your Honor this is irrelevant and absurd, said Sarah Johnson. Lacks foundation and calls for conclusions on the part of the witness.

The witness, said Judge Tietelbaum, will confine his answers to the contents of the question. Mr. Levindowski, just answer yes or no without getting into these collateral areas of why the defendant wanted you to do this or that.

Did anything unusual happen, Mr. Levindowski, said Marlene Quilty, while you and Mr. Henny were blindfolded by the defendant?

I don't know what you mean by unusual, said Levindowski.

Did something rather strange happen, said Marlene Quilty.

It depends what you mean by strange, said Levindowski.

Anything funny, said Marlene Quilty. Anything you didn't expect.

Well, said Levindowski, emitting a little laugh that clogged in his throat like a little burp, it wasn't that funny to us, but Mr. Martinez put the blindfolds on us and started giving us the chicken wings, and we were eating them, and at one point Mr. Martinez handed me a chicken wing that felt kind of cold and not very crispy, and when I started eating it it tasted just awful, and I heard Mr. Henny go, Yech, what kind of chicken wing is this?

Tell us, Mr. Levindowski, if you know, why that chicken wing tasted so terrible.

Because he gave us these rubber chicken wings he bought from a novelty shop, Levindowski said, there we are, thinking we're helping him with this important business decision and there he is, laughing his head off. At first though Mr. Martinez, he kind of stifled his laughter, so it sounded almost as though he might've been crying rather than laughing, and I thought maybe it suddenly hit him about his father and mother, and how probably it was a good thing me and Mr. Henny was blindfolded because Mr. Martinez wouldn't have wanted us to see him crying. We kept chewing and chewing like these were real wings, and Mr. Martinez says, Levindowski said, and I can tell from his voice he's been laughing rather than crying, he says, I might as well tell you, what you're eating is from our competitors.

So two weeks after his parents were killed, Mr. Martinez was laughing and playing practical jokes with rubber chicken wings?

Your Honor—

I'll withdraw the question, Your Honor.

A cleaner, Seth reads into the phone to Jack, *who has taken in clothes for cleaning or mending can bring an action if they are stolen from him,* this is a Roman dry cleaner in the *Digest of Justinian,* Seth tells Jack, *provided he is solvent because he is responsible in his contract for their safekeeping. But if he is not solvent, the right to sue for theft passes to the owner of the clothes, for there can be nothing at risk for a man who already has nothing more to lose. But an action in theft is not available to one who possesses things in bad faith, even though it is in his interest that they should not be stolen; for no one can acquire a right of action by his own dishonesty—and also the law gives such a right only to someone who possesses property in good faith.*

Good old bad faith, Jack says, listening fitfully. Red numbers flicker by on his cable box. A sleek new telescope stands poised, three-legged, with its shiny eye trained at a clapboard hovel across the canyon. At last, he thinks, the material for his screenplay may swim into view all unsuspecting, like, if any of his neighbors ever do anything interesting.

Seth puts his book aside and clears a batch of interview printout off his

bed in the Marmont suite, a pile of Teddy Wade's ipsissima verba he's whit-
tling down into formula. What interests him, always, are the digressions, the
flutters, the flights of idle verbiage that swoop off the subject, and these, of
course, are the very bits that have to be trimmed away, leaving only the lean
boring meat of that season's mania.

Did I ever tell you, he asks, about the time, this was years ago, when I
said something about bad faith to Nathan Greenglass? Seth's eye wanders over
his printout to the phrase *guilty of everything,* and he feels himself treading
dangerous ground, recalling that Jack, who doesn't know Nathan, somewhat
admires Seth's friendship with the well-known artist.

Jack's attention is arrested by the bright saffron logo of *Celebrity Buddhist,*
the so-called spiritual quiz show on VH1. He jacks up the volume.

What about bad faith? he says.

Tonight's contestants, a euphonious voice, accompanied by the faint tinkling of chimes, murmurs over the sound of muted chanting, *composer Philip
Glass!*

I don't remember the context, Seth says. But Nathan said, in that way he
has, which is meant to terminate if not annihilate the whole subject, he said "I
don't understand what that's supposed to mean, when people talk about bad
faith."

Actor Richard Gere!

And it wasn't like he was drawing a line in the philosophical sand—

Oh, says Jack, I don't know him of course but it sounds like he was—

Well, maybe, I guess, he could've been saying an action is what it is
regardless of what someone's intentions are—

Poet Allen Ginsberg!

—but I mean it was as if he literally didn't understand the concept, or
thought it was a *corny* concept. You know. A *loser* concept. I mean, *I* understand bad faith.

You should, Jack drawls.

Thank you and fuck you.

Filmmaker Oliver Stone!

No, I mean, anybody does, I think it was extremely disingenuous of Nathan Greenglass, if he said it the way you say he said it—

*Our first round is cerebral categories elucidated in texts a thousand years
old. First question: Mind, thought, consciousness, and discernment are different
names for what?*

Take my word for it Jack he said it exactly like that, says Seth with sudden violence, it's always the same thing with him, that imperious dismissive Jewish thing, like, get real, you'd have to be a *loser* to worry about bad faith—look, I'll be the first to admit, the contrast between what Nathan Greenglass has managed to reap with his AIDS paintings and the rest of that glorified kitsch and the puny glory I get as a writer is never what you'd call invisible to me, but I'm *glad* he's done well, Jack, the trouble is Nathan doesn't like it that way, he prefers to think I envy him—

For one thousand karmic points. Richard Gere?

I'll say "mental activities."

Mental activities is correct! Now for the second part of the question: In what sacred text is this concept of mental activities found?

Well you mentioned your relationship with him had changed a lot, Jack ventures neutrally, weighing the allure of Buddhism with part of his mind.

I can't say, says Seth, whether I'm the envy-ridden creature Nathan takes me for, after all, he says, he's known me for thirteen years, I don't believe I reacted with envy on the many occasions when Nathan scored some kind of triumph with his paintings of sarcomas and tombstones and imperial crowns and little red ribbons and his other various artworks about his condition as a, you know, AIDS-menaced homosexual, Seth says, all of which have made him an extremely well-off and comfortable AIDS-menaced homosexual, which he was anyway, he was born with everything except fame, so naturally he was miserable until he became famous, and now that he's famous he's insufferable.

I'll pass.

It's a pass from Richard Gere! Allen Ginsberg?

That would be the Mahayana.

Correct for two thousand karmic points!

Ever think about becoming a Buddhist? Jack asks as he lights a cigarette.

Oh God, says Seth. It's nothing but narcissism raised to a cosmic principle. People like you and me don't need religion, Jack. And religion definitely doesn't need us. Especially these esoteric snob religions from the mystic East. Speaking of which, I don't suppose you looked that stuff up for me. The Lodge of the Sacred Grouse home page or whatever it is.

I'm going to, though, Jack says. Anti-Christ dot com. Think how comforting believing in something must be though. Even with Marx I used to feel a kind of warm certainty.

What exactly does that mean, "believing in something"? You have to believe in reality the best way you can.

Yes but you have to analyze reality to know what reality really is.

Whatever. Anyway, I was telling you, I don't recall ever once referring to Nathan, as so many have, as a rich dilettante milking a social issue with a teeny-weeny talent, a vapid socialite, a whining parasitical creep who surrounds himself with the worst sorts of craven social climbers and brainless celebrities, or a pathetically shallow, feckless, phony queen. On the contrary, Seth continues, for thirteen years I have invariably behaved in a respectful if not downright obsequious manner vis-à-vis Nathan and his so-called artwork, even when in the privacy of my own mind I wondered how he managed to constantly replenish his volcanic sense of loss in the face of owning four quite enviable properties, a BMW and a Mercedes, and several million dollars' worth of his own and other people's paintings, I've just chalked it up to the miracle of creativity, all the while wondering how he managed to convey a more heartfelt, more depthful, more genuine concern for the suffering of others than anybody else in his immediate vicinity, while his portfolio of Microsoft shares expanded every quarter on the advice of his broker. Furthermore, Seth says, the minute Nathan Greenglass realized he could get a fatal disease from getting fucked up the ass, he started fucking women again, he came out of the closet at the same time he went back to fucking women, he even fainted at the proctologist's when the doctor put his finger up there, in fact, Seth says, that's where the inspiration for all those drippy sentimental paintings came from, fainting at the proctologist's office, and believe me, says Seth, it wasn't any generalizing humanitarian fear for other people's health and safety he was thinking of, far from it. I suppose it is some kind of social progress, says Seth, when someone can push their career further by posing as a homosexual than they can by being queer and in the closet, but there still seems something defective in that formula, frankly. I mean we already had that with, uh, *Ziggy Stardust*, didn't we? A quarter of a century ago? Why would we need somebody with a face like a boiled turnip to do that now? I realize, says Seth, that in his own mind Nathan wrestles with his high and mighty situation and flagellates himself once or twice a year for being so much better off than his former friends, and prefers in fact to maintain the fiction that his former friends are still his "real" friends, but with these former friends, such as myself, says Seth, Nathan has steadily reduced his relationships to once- or twice-yearly meetings, usually at his house in Montauk, the much-touted holiday weekend in Montauk has become Nathan's annual sop to his conscience over his ex-friends. During these supposedly festive weekends, which generally amount to nothing more than a charity barbecue full of Nathan's odious celebrity gargoyles and a thousand bloodsucking hangers-on, Nathan makes a lot of rueful noises about how infrequently he sees his "real" friends, whom he no longer really considers his friends at all.

Jesus, says Jack, let it *go*. What is all this? You talked to him?

Yes I talked to him, says Seth. He invited me to Montauk. Well, enough about you.

I think I'm going to Reno for the weekend, Jack says. It's not the same, I realize—

Oh Jack, Seth dutifully sighs. *Don't.*

I know, I *know*. Believe me, if anybody knows, *I* know. But I'm only taking two thousand dollars. And it's two thousand dollars I made selling drugs, so it's not even real money.

Since when are you selling drugs, says Seth, feeling left out of a possible bargain.

I'm not really selling drugs, says Jack. But I did sort of inherit some methedrine from this friend of mine who was dying and wanted to get rid of it.

You wouldn't happen to have any left, would you?

Sorry, says Jack, sounding just the opposite, it's all gone.

Funny there's no drug angle in the Martinez case, says Seth.

It's a nice clean double homicide, Jack says.

Yeah, right.

Incidentally, Seth, when are you coming over here?

Oh. You know I'm trying to milk a few more days out of the magazine. Because after that I'm on my own financially. I told you about seeing Morgan Talbot.

Several times.

Speaking of Nathan Greenglass's friends. God what a monster.

You know you can come whenever you like. But if you can give me a day or two notice.

I'm sure it won't be until next week. And thank you by the way. I'm sure I can get them to pay another four days. This suite costs them nothing, you know. They do an ad trade. You'd think Stanley Bard bought the Marmont, they're even trading art for rooms now, too bad I'm not an artist. I mean especially too bad I'm not a bad artist. They're decorating this whole hotel with really lousy out-of-focus photographs. That school of pathetic subjectivity that's all the rage. Money's so tight, Jack. I've really ruined myself. All those dinners with Mark. I'd be embarrassed to tell you how degrading it was with him.

You did tell me.

I didn't tell you everything. I mean the lengths I went to. For what, I'd now like to know.

It couldn't be any worse than my thing with Juan, Jack says.

Oh yes it was, Seth insists. At least with Juan you got laid. Which reminds me of another thing about Nathan's AIDS period, it happened right after his thing with Michael Waldheim, who was this absolutely gorgeous young painter, Nathan's assistant, I believe.

He has a career, Jack interjects. I've heard of him.

That doesn't mean he has a career, says Seth, but yeah. Michael Waldheim was everything Nathan wasn't except rich: tall, beautiful in this patrician way, supposedly hung like a bull, young, and with a full head of hair. Nathan wanted that kid to the point of absolute mania, and eventually started giving him these ultimatums, like if Michael didn't put out, Nathan would destroy him in the art world, all sorts of rinky-tink emotional blackmail that would put anybody's back up, Nathan would call me every day and give me a blow-by-blow, at one point he'd gotten Michael to agree to leave his girlfriend and move in with Nathan, I remember, "He's leaving her tonight! He's taking her to dinner and telling her it's all over!" And then, get this, supposedly Michael takes the girlfriend to dinner, tells her he's leaving, walks her back to the apartment to pack his things, they walk in and the place has been burglarized. Vandalized, burglarized, and one of the burglars even took a shit on the living room floor. So naturally the girlfriend is hysterical and terrified, and Michael ends up agreeing to stay with her at least until she moves somewhere else, and even though Nathan doesn't cop to it at the time, that's the end of that. Of course it was all a complete fabrication, Michael Waldheim never had any intention of turning fag for Nathan Greenglass, and nobody dropped any turd on Michael Waldheim's carpet, either. I really have to give him points for improvisation. He never even put out for Nathan Greenglass, although Nathan then told everybody that he had. And right after that Nathan picks up a skanky piece of meat somewhere, the guy attacks him in Nathan's apartment with a knife, Nathan picks up a two-by-four and clobbers the guy on the head, then chases him out of the building and all the way through TriBeCa to the Canal Street subway, where he loses him. Then after getting himself stitched up at St. Vincent's he tells everybody it was some total stranger lurking in his vestibule.

Well, he doesn't have to worry about things like that anymore, Jack says restlessly, now he can chase male supermodels down the street waving money.

He always could have, says Seth. Except he never wanted to be a repulsive baldheaded nobody from the Five Towns waving money. He wanted to be a repulsive baldheaded important artist waving money. I have to hand it to him, he hasn't had any work done.

You saw him? When did you have time to see him?

No. I mean he's in New York, isn't he. He's the Montauk junior don of the Velvet Mafia. But he was sort of audibly lacking a chin, nose, and ear job. I guess he got hair plugs, but that's not as bad as doing your face over. He still looks bald, anyway, so I'm told. No, I had to call him. I didn't want to call him, what happened was, this journalist called me. To confirm some quote Nathan gave him about me. I mean a quote about Nathan someone gave the journalist that was also about me, that Nathan then supposedly was quoted on. To the effect, you know, that Nathan gave me money to write that profile of him in *Vogue*. So I had to like confront him. Because Nathan was completely willing to sell me out to the worst type of journalistic scum, confirming a story that really wasn't true the way it was told, after all I did for him out of the brainless goodness of my heart. Which was like confronting a warm stick of margarine, frankly. It's not bad enough that he's a stale artist and a public joke, he has to be spineless into the bargain. I can't talk about it. It's stupid.

JD says that none of the Frankie Lomax drama that went down would've happened if JD hadn't decided to prey on Dylan's weakness and wheedle him into a toot of Deadly Paul's methedrine. Sometimes meth grafts you onto your barstool but sometimes it makes you hyperactive, and suddenly Dylan wanted to leave. Then they ran into Frankie staggering around near the car and took him to the hospital, and not just one hospital as it turned out, because the first one they took him to had closed its emergency services, because of the widely publicized county budget cuts. JD and Dylan had talked about a nightcap at the Detour but they suddenly had Frankie on their hands, blood all over himself and this awful ragged gash in his face, luckily he didn't have anything broken. At the second hospital they sewed a few stitches over his eye where the guy'd kicked his forehead open. And Frankie stutters, JD says, he can barely spit out a sentence in less than an hour, and these emergency room types expected him to file a police report, which JD could see would be a major verbal event for Frankie, plus he didn't want them to phone his mother, as he'd been staying in a crack squat off Santa Monica to avoid Cassandra's latest manias. Against his own judgment JD told Frankie he could stay at his place overnight, but then he didn't trust the situation, didn't trust Frankie in his place and didn't trust himself with Frankie, JD says guys like Frankie look even better beaten up, so that led to inviting Dylan to spend the night too, and once again Dylan hesitated, like he really shouldn't but he really wanted to, JD says they could've left Frankie at Hollywood Presbyterian but that would've looked a little seedy, and that led to the three of them finishing JD's scotch at five in the morning and watching this movie with Harvey Keitel and Romy Schneider set in the north of Scotland, where Harvey Keitel has these cameras implanted in his eyes, it's supposedly this future world where people no longer die of natural causes, or something like that, they missed the beginning, but Romy Schneider was, atypically for this future world, dying of cancer or something so the national television network wants to follow her around during her last days, she runs away to escape these television people but then they get Harvey Keitel on her trail and his eyes transmit what he sees directly into the television, so they're alone in this primal wilderness up in the Shetland Islands or what have you, experiencing all these turgid interpersonal dramas in various abandoned buildings and remote cottages, but the whole country is watching them on television. Frankie, who startled them both with the idle, accurate guess that Max von Sydow would show up by the end of the movie, had scored a lot of painkillers so they did some of those . . .

. . . opening his eyes nine hours later to this cryptic seminaked configuration in his bed, the $3,000 brass bed with debutante canopy he'd madly acquired in the svelte days before the IRS came after him, with Frankie wedged at an expressive angle between him and Dylan, one of Dylan's long legs thrust out of the covers and wrapped across Frankie's hips, Frankie's cotton briefs pressing their sleep-hard lump against JD's thigh, JD's calico Jinx intently crouched near JD's nostrils, preparing to grip the spur of his nose between her teeth, as is her morning wont. Where is Scavullo when you need him, says JD. He had planned to put Frankie to bed on the couch, that obviously hadn't worked out but he was quite certain nothing irreversible had happened anyway. And then, right after he got his robe on, Angela and Terry from downstairs rapping on the door with the handle of a clay oven Angela borrowed a few days earlier. Angela a pert and slightly chubby red-haired punkette and trainee shiatsu therapist, wrapped in a tight short something or other resembling a black-dyed surgical bandage, scads of plastic jewelry flashing on her neck and fingers, Terry her formerly surfer-beautiful fashion photographer boyfriend, recently gone fat as a house on burritos and jug wine, him in cutoffs and an expressively ripped olive T-shirt, wanting to know if JD felt like catching *American Heart* at the Los Feliz, which led to coffee and a long discussion of *American Heart* and whether they all really liked Jeff Bridges or really hated Jeff Bridges and whether or not they would like the movie, Dylan stomping out of the bedroom with the wings of his pinstripe shirt flapping over his underpants, his fingers busy at his mouth as birdcalls warbled and cooed from his thorax, and then, what the hell, a little communion breakfast with the rest of Deadly Paul's foil packet, which JD fishes from his flannel bathrobe with a faggy admonition, As you know, I hardly ever do drugs, a sentiment each of them echoes before sculpting off a line with JD's metal nail file. JD had the rest of the week off because it was Pledge Week at KAW, which he refuses to do because it's not in his contract, JD says they whip up the crummiest scripts imaginable for Pledge Week and when you do Pledge Week you have to go on air with all these losers who used to be well-known movie stars and television personalities and pretend that they're still well known and even legendary, since these are the only so-called celebrities who offer their services for Pledge Week. They did land Alec Baldwin once but that was a fluke, it's mainly losers lining up to beg for those contributions, not because they have any slobbering affection for partially listener-supported KAW but because it's their one chance all year for public attention, so, JD says, I had all this time on my hands, when I have free time I tend to dissipate, that is if I'm full of anxiety, or, on the other hand, when things seem to be going too well, those are the two danger areas, says JD, feeling horrible and feeling very good, the area in between I can manage with a certain grace. JD says that Frankie eventually limped into the dining room, bare-chested and barefoot and bruise-mottled like some sleek injured leopard, his pants stiff from bloodstains, logy from downers, of course he knows Terry and Angela by sight from the Black Light, reels into the living room for his denim jacket and his Percodan, in the dining room it's more coffee and more speed, JD clearing bales of paperwork off the table, Angela whips up something like a giant Spanish omelette that nobody can eat, then Terry runs down to the corner for a couple of six-packs, and Dylan suggests they all drive out to the Bird Ranch. Dylan lives on this ranch at the Calabasas end of Malibu Creek State Park, there's an aviary and horses and riding trails up and down the mountains and these little guest cabins, a regular home on the range, fifty acres of wilderness and pure mountain air, campfires and great dope, the nature trip in its most unsullied form. At first, JD says, we all felt that familiar horror of spontaneity, followed by a completely bogus "love of adventure" thing. Naturally Frankie feels like the fifth wheel, which he is, so everyone breaks into an elaborate song and dance to convince him that he isn't. And since it's this crystal fest we can't budge an eyelash until Terry dashes out on another beer run, coming back this time with vodka and Kahlúa and a bag of limes, plus chips and pretzels that he's already stuffing his face with when he walks in the door, by this time we're all rapping nonsense a mile a minute, JD says, the Cranberries on the CD player and the Martinez trial on the TV, Frankie's sprawled on the carpet and Angela's massaging his feet, to stimulate his natural painkilling endorphins according to her, and then as I recall, JD says, Terry began massaging Frankie's scalp, probably so that Angela doing his feet would be less of a sexual thing and more of a New Age thing. Meanwhile Dylan's pacing all over the apartment putting on his clothes and talking into the telephone, giving instructions to his bird feeders and ranch hands and what have you, JD was on his second vodka when the Martinez trial recessed for the day, and then they had this epic debate about either seeing *American Heart* or going to the Bird Ranch, or seeing *American Heart* and going to the Bird Ranch, or canceling the Bird Ranch idea, going to *American Heart,* and then going to the Black Light, or going to the Black Light instead of going to *American Heart,* or going to H.M.S. Bounty instead of going to the Black Light, or going to Taylor's instead of H.M.S. Bounty, and then it came back to a general enthusiasm for going to the Bird Ranch, and that was settled by Dylan saying if they didn't go then to the Bird Ranch he wouldn't be able to drive to the Bird Ranch unless he took a nap, this gave everything a focus, everyone suddenly perceived the importance of going to the Bird Ranch, and then it became a question whether all five should go in Dylan's car, or if Angela and Terry should follow Dylan's car in their own car, and what they should do if the cars got separated in traffic, this inspired Dylan to draw a map on a piece of legal paper, a rather detailed map reflecting Dylan's intimate knowledge of the area, then Terry said that maybe the others should go on ahead to the Bird Ranch while he and Angela ran some errands, since they could get to the Bird Ranch by following the map, then Angela said it was too late in the day for them to run their errands, though maybe she would like to change her clothes, then Dylan said come to think of it he needed to take a shower, and Frankie asked if JD had any fresh clothes he could borrow since his own clothes were full of bloodstains, he thought he'd like to take a shower also, so then we decided, JD says, we should all freshen up before leaving for the Bird Ranch, that took another hour and a half, and then we needed a bracing cocktail, and it looked for a while like we might end up at *American Heart* after all, when Angela said quite forcefully, The rest of you can do what you want, but I'm going to the Bird Ranch, and Dylan said, Well, everybody's welcome, but I have to go to the Bird Ranch, and that settled it.

On direct by Marlene Quilty, Jocko Phelan testifies that Carlos Martinez told him during a flight from Los Angeles to Princeton that he, Carlos, had been seeing a therapist, that the therapist had tapes of their conversations, that if the police ever got hold of the tapes he and Felix would be "fucked." That Carlos always wanted a Porsche, and always referred to his Alfa Romeo as "a piece of shit." That Carlos wore a gold Rolex all through that fall following the killings. That Carlos fired the bodyguards claiming that one of his uncles with mob connections had ascertained that the Martinez brothers were "no longer in danger" from the Mafia. That Carlos made a $400,000 down payment on the Marquand Avenue Cafe, and that Carlos paid him, Jocko Phelan, $500 a week to supervise the renovations, and later hired him as the restaurant manager.

On cross by Sarah Johnson, Jocko Phelan admits that his memory isn't foolproof, that he's made inconsistent prior statements to the grand jury, and that he embezzled thousands of dollars from the Marquand Avenue Cafe while acting as its manager. Jocko Phelan also admits that most of the items on his current job résumé are invented, that he was not the valedictorian of his high school as the résumé claims, that he did not win a writing award from the Princeton literary magazine, and that he has not held five of the seven previous jobs listed on the résumé. Jocko Phelan further admits that he told the grand jury he never accepted anything from Carlos Martinez, whereas he did, in fact, accept cash, a down payment on a car, a rent-free apartment in Princeton, plane tickets, hotels, and a Rolex watch, in other words several thousand dollars' worth of gifts from Carlos Martinez, at the same time that he acted as a police informant in the Martinez case. Jocko Phelan states that there are many things he would do for a friend, but covering up a homicide isn't one of them, a line that sounds rehearsed and, coming as it does from a confessed thief and liar, a little bit ironic, too.

Jack doesn't believe that these people really exist, with their dazed faces, their piles of five-dollar chips, their ineluctable air of failure and crippling optimism, churning swizzle sticks in beakers of whiskey and melting ice. He doesn't believe that the magenta lip gloss on a black woman with hair ratted up like the high note of a show tune has really been applied to the mouth of a sentient being, that a white-haired gentleman Jack thinks of as the Old Colonel, gnashing a ten-inch cigar between loose-fitting plastic teeth, can really be wearing the white buckskin jacket and matching Stetson he has on. The big and tall Chippendale number in the lilac suit, radioactively blond, whose sinister, Nordic, blue-eyed mug has been stapled into place at least three times by somebody expensive in Rio cannot, Jack thinks, have come from anywhere besides Central Casting, but which Central Casting is it? His? Theirs? They are perfect, like waxworks, like a tableau confected by a team of ethnologists, the woman's beaded dress, the faggot's pectoral span and fussy onyx cuff links, the miniature set of longhorns on the Colonel's string tie. A blackjack dealer in his white shirtsleeves and ruffled black bow, virtually faceless, a human smudge: this is a creature you find in your dreams, impalpable, vaguely reptilian, shape-shifting at will. Everything framed in a mayhem of colored lights, as if an amusement park's whirling around them, but in a movie with minimal sound effects and no voices, though the Old Colonel emits a garrulous hum from time to time and grunts when he lays out a bad hand. The fag keeps flashing a big smile at his cards, and Jack notices a gold-encrusted, obsidian pinkie ring with an ugly little diamond in its center. Jack feels like a gaffer or some craft services person who's wandered into their shot. They look him over from time to time, interestedly, sometimes with a smile, clocking his bets. He is trying to count cards. He's had a certain success at this in single-deck games in Gardena, it requires a quality of attention usually unavailable to him but he sometimes believes his brain's secret resources are awesome and uncanny. He knows the dealer has already thought of asking him to leave the table, the house policy on card counters being posted, but changed his mind after Jack lost a couple hands and continued losing. It's a four-deck game. Jack keeps getting dealt soft 17s, instead of standing he asks for cards because by his count most of the low numbers are still in the deck, and he keeps getting hit with 10 cards. He doesn't mind being out of his depth. Everything is there to teach him something, he thinks. He remembers that Linda Kasabian said the same thing at the Manson trial.

Somewhere in the night a new person joins the group, a short creature spreading delicately at the waist, in a pale, rumpled jacket and poinsettia-red shirt, the face a pitted alcoholic slab, hairpiece the color of liverwurst. He reminds Jack of an actor who had an abbreviated heyday in his twenties and a revival in character roles in his late fifties, after AA and several ruined marriages. The hair goes back, the neck and the waist and the buttocks expand,

and if you're lucky you come out the other side of that as a somewhat intact personality instead of a slice of pathos. The new arrival spurs a rearrangement of psychic forces. Jack feels himself absorbed into the group already at the table: now the new player becomes the suspect intruder, and Jack eyes his fingers on the baize, his pattern of play, exactly as the others studied Jack. Jack doesn't think the addition or subtraction of players much affects one's fortunes at twenty-one when the shoe holds four decks. Still he recognizes his fleeting resentment of the newcomer as part of his nature no effort of will or moral understanding can ever eliminate or even bring under control in a way that satisfies his better ideas of himself. That's the perception of a moment, he can easily throw it away, but not before thinking the next person to land at his table will assimilate this one into the club of first arrivals, the founders of tonight's particular lake of ruin in the desert, and that it could go on like that in an endless mathematical sequence.

By four in the morning he's down twenty-two hundred dollars, two hundred over his stake, the danger zone, and they've all become friends in some horrible unspoken way. He has an impression of large women hovering with festive cocktails, their coked cheerfulness wearing thin, of the Colonel pinching a waitress's ass, of great piles of red and blue chips stacking up all over the table while his own hoard is scraped away by the dealer, of himself floating out of the Cal-Neva and down Virginia Street to the Nevada Club and noticing this dark brown object on the sidewalk, snapping it up unhesitantly as if he's dropped it, shoving it in his pocket, hailing a cab, climbing out at the Lucky 7 Motel, fanning out fifty hundred-dollar bills from the wallet on his chlorine-blue bedspread. He comes back to himself in one of the Cal-Neva lounges, where a band dressed as the Carpenters is performing a medley of easy listening pop from 1975. The room has the dead glare of a nightclub at noon, the air conditioned to the temperature of an ice cube. The blond fag from the blackjack table lights a Kool with a noisy metal lighter.

So, it was bye bye Lee after that, the fag says, releasing a plume of blue-white smoke that scatters in the arctic atmosphere. Then I got my real estate license, and Eric and I closed on the condo in Tahoe. And the rest you could say is history.

Who the fuck is Lee? Who is Eric? Soap bubbles in a bad brain. Jack studies his new friend, rummaging garbled circuits for the transition between the blackjack table and the lounge, can't find it. Ever since his HIV diagnosis, his reactions to alcohol have become unpredictable, and less and less is required to produce little sunspots of amnesia or abrupt mood switches. His doctor says this has nothing to do with HIV but Jack feels pretty sure it does. From the rapt theatrical morphology of the face before him, he suddenly understands that the fag is attracted to him, and has already taken Jack's availability for granted. Jack veils his revulsion behind a boozy glaze. The man exudes a former time when overmuscled blonds with ageless prep school faces came with certain houses in Los Angeles, ranch-style homes off Mulholland owned by antique dealers and retired child stars. Parts of the houses were often leased for porn sets, and the fags that came with them usually doubled as live models. His name, Jack thinks, will be Brad, or Troy, and before Tahoe it was Palm Springs, Key West, and Fire Island. Maybe. The obscure, complicated histories of his tribe always remind him that it isn't really his tribe, that encounters with people supposedly like himself simply require him to wear a snugger mask. The true name, it turns out, is Philip.

It was really on accounta Lee I fell in love with Nevada, Philip says. Not Vegas, not the showbiz glitter, but the landscape. Lee would do his shows down in Vegas and I'd drive up here, up around Tahoe, and groove out on the landscape. It was no picnic being with Lee, I'll tell you. Of course there were the good times, hey, I wouldn't trade them for anything, but talk about a prima donna.

Jack gulps his drink. He suddenly gets that Philip is referring to Liberace. This is better than he expected. The only better thing, he thinks, would be if this new information is the sort of lie that would be considered a useful card to play in Philip's world. Jack cannot imagine what such a world would look like, if not the bleak metallic lounge they're sitting in.

Incidentally, Philip adds, I've tested negative for ten years. A lot of people, you tell them you used to be with Lee, they suddenly just assume.

The manner in which he brings this out tells Jack several things he doesn't want to know. For instance, that this man views his negative antibodies as a triumph of personal shrewdness, that he thinks of people who're positive as losers, types who didn't play their cards right, and of course, Jack thinks, it's also possible that Philip's lying, that Philip, in his own eyes, is an undeserved loser bluffing his way into bed with what he sees as an undeserving winner. He doesn't seem to expect his own revelation to prompt another in kind, as people usually do.

The world grows old around him. Jack is spilling quite far down the minus scale, into the polar regions of his thanatosis. He somehow makes conversation, grudgingly (which looks thoughtful), though everything this person says drives Jack further away from himself into a make-believe identity that gives him some slight advantage. He claims to be a screenwriter, with an address several miles west and slightly south of Mt. Washington. He gives himself a lover named Peter whose foibles and endearing habits he renders in some detail, until Philip feels comfortable referring to Peter like someone he knows and doesn't mind deceiving. Philip's Eric is no less familiar to Jack by the time they finish their second cocktail in the lounge, and for all Jack knows no less imaginary, though he suspects Eric exists and the negative lab report exists and the only embroidered details of Philip's story have to do with Philip's current fortunes in the real estate game. Telling the truth gives him more malicious pleasure than lying, Jack can tell. This is a person who considers his crummy life enviable. Maybe it is. Jack notices that Philip's hands are much older than Philip's face, and he imagines that Philip's body, well maintained as it might be, would also yield various archaeological markings.

Over the third drink—his seventh of the night—a horrible desire seizes him. It isn't a desire for Philip's hideous person but a blunt desire for power over him, using no greater blandishment than his, Jack's, flabby, repellent body, which Philip's need, he realizes, has already transformed into something wonderful. The casino gurgles around them like a mortally wounded machine. It's the magic hour when everything hits its nadir and then switches over to daytime energy, when the pit bosses and croupiers change shifts and the morning cocktail waitresses apply their makeup.

I'm at the Nugget over in Sparks, Philip says.

I'm in a shithole near the train station, Jack says. It's closer.

In the motel room the heavy curtains and noisy breath of the air conditioner keep the night going. Jack waddles out for a tub of machine ice and when he comes back Philip has expressively stripped to his underpants. His body is much larger than Jack's, its pentimento of pumped muscle and faded tan sprawled across the bed with the backside on view, the legs spread, everything big and masculine about him grotesquely askew and absurdly submissive. Jack stands near his face cradling the ice bucket as Philip fumbles with his belt and zipper and fastens his big wet mouth to Jack's penis, which hardens despite his unfavorable visual inventory of the thing sucking him. Philip groans and moans like some wildebeest tucking into a slain hyena, it has nothing whatever to do with Jack, who pulls away from him finally and puts down the bucket and switches off the room lights and turns on CNN without the sound, undresses in the dim TV light while Philip squirms about on the bed striking expectant poses, in some trance of consumption that makes

Jack's planned offer of a drink superfluous. He takes a folder of condoms and a K-Y tube from his overnight bag and sets them on the lampstand. Philip rolls off his underpants and his face becomes an enthralled question mark: where should he put his ass? Jack squeezes some K-Y into his hand and slides onto the bed, pumping his cock.

It's all up to you, he thinks, as Philip balances on the balls of his feet to squat over him.

The other way around, Jack instructs him, and the big looming weight shifts instantly, happy to be ordered around. Philip lowers his ass, pulling apart his white cheeks at first to display his hole, then reaches under it to guide Jack's erection. Jack always has a moment's surprise and disbelief when they do it themselves. He never forces the question, it's been forced on him from time to time but with him the damage is already done. Jack feels his cock enveloped by slick warm rectum, tighter than he expected. It isn't clean. He smells shit in the air but it doesn't get more emphatic, thank God. In the glow of the TV he watches a thin shiny band where his prick catches the light slosh in and out of slippery darkness, he thinks a guy like this probably wants variety and feels relieved when it settles into a contented rhythm, Philip doing all the work while Jack peers around his ass to watch the television. He hates the thought of feces leaking out of Philip's hole all over him and pictures the hot shower he will take to get it off. He slaps the ass a few times to show interest. There are pictures of Bosnia on the screen and then some pictures of the Martinez brothers in court. Philip jerks himself off as his ass toggles up and down on Jack's rod and when Jack thinks Philip might be getting close he blows a fat wad of infected fuck straight up Philip's shitty bum. Second-degree murder, he thinks, and then he thinks no, depraved indifference, the both of them.

Dylan bought the ranch off a horse trainer who used to lease it out for Westerns. There's a stable and a renovated farmhouse and trails running out through the locust trees and a fenced-off aviary and down behind the main house a wooded slope where a thin dirt car track shears the side of the canyon, with some clapboard cabins at the bottom, there are other little houses hidden in the woods because the staff lives in them, these Sikhs Dylan hires to care for the birds and look after the horses. There's a housekeeper, too, Dylan said, JD says, but she had the night off. The main house has a swimming pool and a picnic table and Christmas lights strung through the trees. Whenever he sees Christmas lights in California, JD says, he thinks of Cielo Drive. The aviary lights were off so Dylan walked them through the barn and showed them the horses and Angela said they should ride out into the night. Terry said he wasn't getting on any horse but Dylan thought it was a good idea. He said they could ride into the state park and back and then cook the lobsters they bought at Chalet Gourmet and Terry said he'd stay at the house and cook dinner if Dylan showed him around the kitchen. Frankie started saddling the horses. He didn't say a word, just began fetching moth-eaten horse blankets from a pile and hoisting bridles down from pegs in the horse stalls and Dylan came back and they went from stall to stall in the dim stable light draping blankets and saddles from a weary-looking stack onto the horses' backs and looping girths around the horses' ribby stomachs. JD says it shouldn't've surprised him that Frankie knew about horses because even if Cassandra was a television burnout Frankie was still a Hollywood brat. He looked an improvement over the previous evening. The swelling around his stitches looked awful but he wasn't staggering and once he got on his horse he slid off his sandals and cantered out of the building with his bare feet joggling in the stirrups, brightly confident, whereas Angela whooped and giggled and jiggled fatly as if she were going to slide off. Dylan rode out in front of the others down a dirt path where they still had a row of Wild West facades near the ranch gates, Angela and JD and Frankie clopping along behind him and out a side gate into pitch-black canyon.

Can horses see okay in the dark, Angela kept asking.

No but they smell rill accurate, Dylan told her. They can smell their way anywhere around here.

There was a ranger at the park entrance who waved a battery torch across their faces. Dylan told him something that got him laughing but JD was too far behind to hear it. The horses resumed moving, at this point into really thick dark, picking their way over rocks and soft fissures in the trail, but there was a big lemon moon, you could roughly see ahead of you, trees and rocks, Dylan picked out a trail that ran almost flat for a while and then plunged way down the slope of a ravine, the trailbed rough and stonepitted, the horses lumbering down it nervously, sometimes indignantly halting and refusing to move, even trying to circle backward. Frankie barely stuttered, JD noticed: his voice always had a pulling quality, and some elongated sounds, but sometimes words came fast and undistorted. Frankie asked where the trails went and Dylan explained the intricacies of the park trails and said it was impossible to get lost even in the dark. JD felt confident that he could get lost. He had a touch of night blindness in his left eye and no real sense of direction. He thought he smelled juniper berries, a ginny smell. He could see shapes of horses and people on them as they traveled deeper down the trail, sometimes where the woods thinned out the maroon acetate thing Angela wore caught the pale faraway light or he made out a patch of the lime-green pants he'd lent Frankie, or Dylan's shirt. When a horse galloped on ahead he supposed it was Dylan until Dylan yelled Frankie's name, there was a fearsome racket of hooves fading into the dark and Dylan stopped his horse and steered it around and came up beside JD and yelled again into the dark.

I wish he wouldn't do that, he said.

He could get his neck broke, Angela said in a fake redneck accent.

No but he could scare the horse, Dylan said. They don't like it here at night particularly.

It's kind of creepy, Angela said. I mean it's really beautiful with all the stars and so forth but it's kind of creepy, too. It's got that helter skelter vibe.

Yeah, Dylan said, Spahn Ranch is just a couple hills over. But it's really safe, there's no, like, middle-aged creepy-crawlies hanging around. Maybe some snakes. Charlie doesn't live here anymore.

Well, said JD, divining something careless in Dylan's attitude, realistically he could get his neck broken, let's face it, you can't see a foot in front of you. But as he said it Frankie came back and trotted ahead of them in the opposite direction. The horses picked up speed moving back up the ravine. Dylan told them to rein in the horses when they reached level ground because the animals would throw them going home otherwise, and as they climbed the horses moved apart until JD couldn't locate the others by sight. He felt a slight panic because the trail forked in a few places and what if his horse took the wrong one. He heard Frankie and Angela laughing and called out and gave the horse a little kick, and suddenly the ton of muscle between his legs roared up the incline in a trance of speed, churning up gouts of mud. JD yanked at the bridle and bounced up and his shoe slid off the stirrup for a second and he pictured his brains splattering against a tree, but then the horse settled into a monotonous canter. JD worked his foot back into the stirrup and came up level with Dylan, who told him to pull the reins just a little and not tug. I hope you're hungry, Dylan said, I'm starving. Then he said, I'm thinking maybe this is a little complicated for a first date. He was apologizing, it seemed, or complaining, JD thought. Maybe what had sounded like a good idea in the city wasn't working out and now he wanted to pull the plug. He felt a familiar detachment, a protective indifference growing inside him like a weed.

It's a little long for a first date, he said, but that sounded bad, I don't mean long per se, he amended, it's just a little crowded.

Look, Dylan said, why don't I put them down in the cabins tonight and we'll sleep in the house.

JD wondered if the next thought would be: why don't you all go home.

So this is like, a date, JD said.

I don't know if I even know what a date is, Dylan said, but yeah, why not?

Okay, JD agrees, it's a date with a few hairs in it.

There were definitely vibes. JD wasn't sure at first whose vibes were going where. He was getting used to the idea that Dylan was rich, and trying to puzzle out how rich. Too rich he didn't know how to deal with, but he supposed a little rich was okay. On the other hand, as his mind shaped everything from the night before to now into a story he would tell someone who understood him, all the pieces glittered like bits of colored glass in some arrangement that did not include him. He half wished he were home with his cat.

Quite a spread here, ain it, Angela said as they walked away from the stable. She was wondering how rich, too. Frankie and Dylan stayed behind getting the saddles down. JD flashed on Dylan's leg on the bedspread earlier in the day, Dylan's leg on top of Frankie's leg, and he thought it had been a mistake not to leave Frankie at the hospital. Then he thought the real mistake had been snorting the speed. He detested Angela, suddenly. Her trashy lack of restraint.

Terry had opened several bottles of Médoc "to breathe," and was making Spanish rice. He had on a pair of striped shorts and a Betty Boop T-shirt, Doc Martens with thick white socks. His legs, JD noticed, were hairless, and less chubby than the rest of his body, as if fat refused to travel below his buttocks. The kitchen had that *Martha Stewart Living* look, all clean bright surfaces and a sultan's ransom in cookware, overhanging implements for every possible gourmet whim. An array of vegetables was ranged on the sideboard.

That looks good, JD told him. He didn't want to see the lobsters in the sink, their claws rubber-banded shut.

You know, I used to think Frankie was what's her name's boyfriend, Terry said.

Must have had him young, said JD. He felt his resentment of Angela spreading to swallow her companion. He moved decisively for the fridge and found the antidote in the freezer. Stolichnaya, pale mother, he thought, pouring.

I wouldn't rule it out anyway, said Angela, pouring herself some wine. I don't mean because of the way he is, but she's fucking weird. She gazed at the lobsters. You poor little fuckers, she told them. Who beat him up?

He says he didn't know the guy, JD said. The vodka attacked a wave of annihilating sarcasm gathering inside him, reducing it to bland unhappiness.

Think he did? Terry said.

I really don't know, said JD, lighting a Marlboro Light. He waved at the smoke as if waving Frankie out of the area. He refilled his glass. We just sort of found him.

You don't sound ultrathrilled about it, Angela said. I'll do the tomatoes.

Who knows if what he says is true, said JD, or it's what he thinks you want to hear.

But you didn't see the guy, right? Angela persisted. She was smoking and slicing tomatoes at the same time.

Funny thing is, JD said, swallowing emphatically, I'm pretty sure we did, because Frankie thinks the guy could've gone into the Black Light afterwards.

Was he like thug of the year or what, Angela said. She brought a tomato slice to her mouth.

JD looked at the vegetables on the cutting board. He looked at Terry's ridiculous calves shuffling in front of the stove. He looked at the rime of liquefying frost on the vodka bottle. He was in California again and these were his friends. Not his best friends, perhaps, but that hardly mattered now.

You know that South American that works in the 7-Eleven on Western? he said.

Oh God, said Angela, chewing. Not the one with the horse dick who wears those Speedos to work sometimes—

I'm not saying it was him, JD said, brightening, but he came in right before we left. Those ones with the vines attached are the only things that taste like tomatoes anymore. A lot of people came in but he's the only one I remember coming in alone.

It is so rare, said Terry, to cook in a well-thought-out kitchen. You've seen ours. It's like yours only we have that rangetop thing. These are good tomatoes. So why would that guy do it?

Some kind of dope thing? Or sex thing? JD was, if he thought so himself, positively elfin.

Israeli tomatoes, Angela munched.

He has a little beeper. The 7-Eleven guy. I mean he doesn't wear it but he has it on him, JD said. I never cook anything but Stouffer's. I did ask them to put in that rangetop when I moved into the building, and I'm still waiting.

You cook, Angela accused. You made those caramelized onion things.

Well, yeah, onions, JD said.

But that clay oven chicken, said Angela. The best. So moist. You think Frankie owed him dope money?

Terry made a face. I hate that word, *moist,* he said. Angela ignored him.

It's possible, said JD. Listen, said the vodka, if you guys are so fond of him, you're welcome to borrow him for the night. Or the rest of the year, be my guest.

I was giving that some thought, chortled Angela. I forgot my poppers, though.

Some looks shot back and forth between Angela and Terry as they potted around making salad. JD stood near the screen door listening for Dylan, swirling vodka in his glass.

Dylan's showing him . . . stuff, Angela told Terry, who thought about this for a moment, wiped his hands on a paper towel, and lit a joint. He sucked a big hit and passed it.

Horse stuff, Angela clarified.

I think he'd like us to eat on that picnic table, Terry said. He started getting down plates from an overhead cabinet.

A midnight swim, Angela said insistently. Lobsters and a nice swim.

JD sucked on the joint.

Dylan's cool, Angela told him briskly, moving past him with the plates. Her eyes were dilated. JD nodded, holding in smoke. Cooler than you, he thought, his malice reviving. While she was outside Terry peered into his rice pot and said, I hope everything's cool about everything. He looked at JD and shrugged. He looked, JD thought, small and desperate.

You know, Terry said, she says it as a joke but she means it. She goes for scary dick, what can I tell you.

They were stoned enough to verbalize.

I imagine he would dig another shiatsu demonstration, JD exhaled. I mean don't let me stop you.

Terry held up a green ear of corn and began shucking it.

Hey, he said, you know me. Any scene in a storm.

JD considered that he did not know Terry all that well, but figured he probably knew him as well as he ever would. Angela had met Frankie and

Dylan out by the pool. He heard their voices, squiggles of incoherence. The key in this situation, he thought, was not to exhibit any disappointment if things worked out funnier than they were supposed to. It would not be cool to spell things out further, so to stay cool he had to guess whether other people were more clued in than he was.

Dylan killed the lobsters, as he was good at killing things. With a quick knife blow to the brain instead of boiling them alive. They set candles out on the picnic table. The Christmas lights twinkled in the trees. Beethoven piano trios merged with insect noises in the backyard. There was corn on the cob with cayenne and lime juice, the rice, and the salad, everything yummy and, except for the drawn butter for the lobsters, low-fat, though JD supposed the butter erased the good health benefits of everything else. He raced through eating, not being hungry, urgently refilling his wine and vodka glasses, both, but he talked about the food incessantly, how good it was, until Terry, seeing that he wasn't really eating, made worried faces and waved away the bottles JD pointed at him. Angela sat beside Dylan arguing spiritual points about Krishnamurti and karma, the seven chakras, and stimulating kundalini through massage, with Frankie across the table straining to find an entrance into their conversation. Frankie didn't know from chakras and thought they meant American Indians when they talked about Indians, but Dylan helpfully said that the Incas also had this concept of chakras, only their chakras moved from the top of the skull down to the groin instead of the other way around. JD worked it out that he and Dylan were seven or eight years older than Angela and Terry, and Frankie was maybe five years younger than them, two complete generation gaps, and if you paid close attention you found that the quality of information declined steeply from one to the other. It wasn't just a question of vocabulary. When you got down to Frankie you were dealing with people who lived in a world of appearances, random visual impressions.

He really liked Dylan when Dylan talked about his birds, but when he got on his Krishnamurti thing it seemed to always go into this fear stuff, overcoming fear, looking fear in the eye, JD thought that maybe Dylan had different words for things than JD's words for the same things. Angela could talk the talk because she'd been to the ashram in Vancouver or wherever they all went, the Krishnamurti people. They had levels of enlightenment they were going for in a supposedly disciplined way, and names for the various levels, and whenever JD was around that sort of thing he reflected that self-improvement and snobbery were indistinguishable in certain people. The world held no real secrets from them and everything that happened fell into a category. The truth, he supposed, was that their false certainty allowed them to do good things for the wrong reasons: it was good that Angela studied shiatsu, and Dylan had his bird studies, it gave them an income and something to do. But their brains sounded crowded with the kind of psychotic bric-a-brac piled up in Hindu temples. They imagined themselves wired to benevolent cosmic forces that would rearrange their molecules into something appropriate after death. Not just a handful of dust, but a real special handful of dust.

Jew ever get into the Order, any of that stuff? Angela wanted to know.

Nah, it's too wiggy, Dylan said. Scientology, it's all—

Wait, though, I thought it was based on the Agapemone, and all that Madame Blavatsky stuff, they have a special language called Senzar. They believe Jesus was only the avatar of Adam and Noah and then there were dozens of avatars afterwards right up until the present day. Crowley was an avatar supposedly. They have the Dark Knowledge.

Yeah, well, Crowley, Dylan said. The Order people are buying up, like, massive real estate out in the desert. Out by Palmdale, with all these irrigation deals. You run the water for two weeks and roll out a readymade white-flight community.

That's what I call the Dark Knowledge, said JD. Frankie laughed; otherwise he might have spoken to himself.

You see their symbol all over the place, Angela said. It looks like a cock and balls.

It's supposed to be initials, Terry said. OTO. They're weird. It's like the Masons, with robes and candles and shit. Their thing is to call up the Whore of Babylon.

They worship Satan, Dylan said.

Who doesn't, said JD.

Angela stripped and jumped in the pool. Frankie shed his clothes shyly, but then peeled off his underpants and went in naked. Terry took his drink to a chaise lounge and began unlacing his boots. JD registered these events with great excitement, as the start of some new, racier scene, then dimly interpreted them as people fleeing from him. He stayed at the table, drunk, feeling stolidly removed from ordinary life but somehow keenly implicated in an unspoken horror, one turn of an inner spiral away from vomiting and vertigo. Dylan cleared plates away and put R.E.M. on the CD player and sat down again and lit a cigarette. JD sensed more than saw Dylan hunching forward on his elbows and tried to line him up in a wavering gaze. By closing one eye he managed to isolate two Dylans in a relatively small space. Smoke threaded from quadruple lips. *I think you should lie down,* the lips were saying. JD thought the Dylans had said this a few times already. He wondered how much of what had been going through his mind had also escaped through his mouth, if maybe he had already gonged the note of irreversible offense. He didn't care. Some words passed between them that vanished from JD's memory as they were spoken. Then they were staggering through the dark rooms of the house and crashing into furniture, on the stairs Dylan tripped on top of him and JD smooched him on the mouth and gagged, then he felt his deadweight dragged up the stairs by one arm, two arms, he closed his eyes and let himself be pulled across a stubbly carpet and next his face was in a toilet and everything came up, his stomach jackknifed, the whole wine-dark Aegean gushed up his throat, with bits of lobster in it, until his head went cold and he dropped facedown on a duvet that tumbled down a chasm.

He woke in a dark room he made no effort to comprehend, heard Dylan snoring beside him, Dylan under the sheets and JD over them. He tucked his hands under a pillow and let himself glide off again. He was less drunk when he woke again, his stomach keening with bilious residue, but it was still dark. Dylan's body had shifted a little. His snores were louder, aggressive, shielding his dreams with their stertorous monologue. JD searched the immediate area with numb fingers, and felt a night table and a squashed pack of cigarettes with no matches, so turned over on his back and held a scrunched cigarette in his fingers, plumping the wrinkled paper until the tobacco fell out, the furniture shapes in the room growing clearer and more ordinary. Guilt crawled on his skin. Provisional guilt, since he didn't remember if he'd said or done anything hideous and, even if he had, it was unsure that anyone else would remember it either. But he was pretty certain that he had, and they would. Losing control did not, in itself, make him guilty, only careless, exposing a defect he'd have to work on, a weakness he liked too much to completely eradicate. It was his only real fun. He put the emptied cigarette paper down on the table. He closed his eyes. From far away he heard a muffled throbbing noise come louder and sharper, the noise of a horse galloping on soft ground.

Outside the presence of the gold jury and the blue jury Dr. Potter Phlegg testifies on Friday about the so-called Hidden Hills burglaries, and the fact that Fidel Martinez sought him out when juvenile court ordered a hundred hours of psychological counseling for Felix and Carlos Martinez after Fidel Martinez turned them in to the Hidden Hills police for the 1988 house burglaries, which the prosecution has inflated into a haul of over a hundred thousand dollars' worth of jewelry, VCRs, home computers and a Nautilus machine, and which the defense has correspondingly deflated to a mere twelve thousand worth of cheap electronics equipment and paste baubles. Seth says it's the first time some of them have gleaned a real-life close-up of the much-discussed so-called clinical psychologist, viewed by millions a few nights ago in a comically earnest tête-à-tête with Diane Sawyer, Potter Phlegg who Lauren Nathanson reminded everybody at a morning press conference will probably have his license revoked for illegally dispensing Xanax and Valium to the so-called mystery witness Sabrina Wilcox, who told part of her gnarly, often impenetrable, truly mysterious story last night to Jane Pauley.

Potter Phlegg's hair is going back, says Seth, and his suit makes him look academic, so do his gold-rimmed glasses, Potter Phlegg is a California smoothie, not a bad-looking smoothie of the elbow patch and briar pipe variety, no major beauty either, genetically favored, perhaps, since at forty-eight he isn't collapsing into mush around the middle, though he has those unfortunate wiry wisps, wisps of "sandy" hair swept athwart a parabola of fallow scalp in a frizzy convoluted wave, he has ink-blue eyes that bulge a tad, a pale, sanctimonious, reptilian mouth that's pointy in the middle, and a clear, even voice, and his personality, says Seth, is braced, measured, professional, he's smart and scared enough not to use all his quack jargon on the witness stand, not to become the cocky, effusive, egocentric control freak Sabrina Wilcox says he is, he's never at a loss for an answer and never too quick or direct with one either, he says the brothers said the murders were planned, he says the brothers said they got turned on by planning the murders, he says he wrote up his therapy sessions with the brothers and then read his therapy notes into a tape recorder and then destroyed the notes, he says that they said that once they had the murders planned they couldn't change the plan because the plan was perfect, he says they said the idea was to kill the father, because the father controlled them, the father made them feel inadequate, but once they decided to kill the father they also had to kill the mother, since the mother would necessarily be a witness and they couldn't leave any witnesses alive, furthermore their perception was, he says, that Peggy Martinez had been suicidal and unhappy, alcoholic and miserable, that she would not know how to go on living without Fidel Martinez, that killing her would really be like euthanasia, like mercy killing, he says that Felix Martinez said that a few days before the killings Felix Martinez noticed that his parents were locking their bedroom door at night, he says that Felix told him that Peggy Martinez looked as if she sensed something dreadful, something ominous about to happen, he says the brothers seemed in his words pleased with the excitement of pulling off the murders without getting caught. Seth says that Judge Tietelbaum is wearing a new tie with a wacky abstract pattern, sort of sporty, only the topknot and an inch or two visible above the pleated neck of his so-called judicial robes, while Lauren Nathanson has opted for a checkered jacket in muted olive and brown, Carlos has on his white cable-knit sweater that sets off his dark eyes, Felix's sweater is a soft blue, Mrs. Quilty wears a white jacket with dramatic black border and white skirt, as far as Seth can tell Carlos shoots a disbelieving look as he glares at Potter Phlegg, he's not well positioned in court, Seth that is, though today his seat's closer to the defense table and he has a better than usual POV of Felix, whose features are so finely sculpted and pale that he resembles an anemic Hispanic faun, and Felix's delicate hands dart back and forth between the defense table and his yellow legal pad, his yellow legal pad and his chin and his nose and his ears and his glasses, Felix puts his glasses on now and then to peer at Potter Phlegg, Felix takes them off and rubs his eyes and lays the glasses down in a way that Seth finds strangely affecting, Felix's way of handling objects, Seth says, is very considered, very sure, Felix knows that he exists, knows that objects exist, whether he's being watched or not his relationship to the objects doesn't change, and the rare gestures he makes in court are beautiful, Seth says, spontaneous yet graceful and contained, whereas Carlos hams it up, Carlos scowls, Carlos exaggerates and acts out emotions even when he's only tapping his felt pen against his yellow pad, and Carlos's fingers are stubby at the tips and unrefined, Carlos always tries to look as if he's on top of things, Seth says, steering the course of events, whereas Felix plainly knows nothing all that good can happen here whatever the outcome, that the future is full of variable degrees of badness, Felix has no expression, he's pensive, Seth doesn't know what Felix is thinking about, Seth thinks that in prison people probably think a lot about what they're going to eat on any given day, as he studies Felix he wonders how many times a night Felix jacks off in prison and what or who Felix thinks about while he's jacking off, does he jack off into a sweatstiff sock or a wad of toilet paper, or pump it straight into the toilet bowl, Cynthia Farrell the auxiliary Felix lawyer perches between Lauren Nathanson and Felix, a larger, younger version of Sarah Johnson, and Sarah Johnson, whose outfit today is salmon pink, is wedged between Felix and Carlos, and on the other side of Carlos, Peter Fagin, the auxiliary Carlos lawyer, gaunt and dignified and barely there, stares impassively at Potter Phlegg like a gray-eyed

entomologist observing a specimen of great peacock moth or a clump of cater-
pillar larvae, everybody busy with their notepads, everyone scribbling as Potter Phlegg talks, every word of Potter Phlegg is important, every utterance of
Potter Phlegg has lethal consequences, Potter Phlegg is the great white whale
that may very well sink the good ship *Martinez* even after the attorneys har-
poon him, dragging it under the waves by the sheer bulk of his slaughtered
carcass. The defense side of court is full of Martinez relatives, and as Potter
Phlegg goes on about the perfect murder and all these so-called perfect murder plans, his long neck strangely craning his bland face toward the gold jury,
Carlos turns around and shakes his head and flashes a complicit frown at his
aunts and uncles and cousins and grandmother. Seth believes the Martinez
relatives favor Carlos because he's so much like his father.

Judge Tietelbaum plucks through the suet of Potter Phlegg's testimony,
deeming what's admissible, what's inadmissible, Lauren Nathanson argues
that the Hidden Hills burglaries are ambiguous, that Fidel Martinez's reaction
to the Hidden Hills burglaries was highly unusual and morally confusing to
Felix and Carlos Martinez, Lauren Nathanson also wants to know where the
boundaries of the privilege issue lie, how much of the therapist-patient confidentiality can be breached without opening the floodgates, between
Tietelbaum and Nathanson the tension is palpable and heavy, the feeling is
that Tietelbaum will rule against Nathanson whenever he can do so without
creating appellate issues, and yet we hear, Seth says, that Tietelbaum and
Nathanson are friends, that Tietelbaum and Nathanson often dine together
when they aren't thrown together in a trial, in other words this tension and
antipathy are part of the game, the trial itself is a game, and when the players
move off the court they buy each other dinner, the same way Carlos and Felix
used to drink with their opponents after tennis matches, though it's doubtful
that Marlene Quilty and Lauren Nathanson will break bread together anytime
soon, since Marlene Quilty referred to Lauren Nathanson this morning as a
piece-of-shit attorney, responding to Lauren Nathanson's remark of yesterday
that Marlene Quilty is a sneering ignoramus. On the other hand, says Seth, it's
easy to imagine the soft-spoken Sarah Johnson having a beer with the laid-
back Quentin Kojimoto, and of course, he adds, it's odd that Quilty is pitted
against Johnson, that Kojimoto is matched against Nathanson, these temperamental opposites would be peculiar in a mixed doubles match, the shrill
Quilty pounding the ball with her powerful backhand, the supple Johnson
lobbing it back just over the net, the sly Kojimoto diving for the ball, Nathanson moving in on it as it feebly blips across the net, slamming it past Quilty's

head and landing it just on the outer edge of the line, where Tietelbaum declares it out more often than in. So it goes this morning, when Tietelbaum gives the prosecution almost everything it wants except the hearsay declaration by Carlos and Felix, "we're sociopaths," having already ruled against use of that terminology in the trial. Tietelbaum says that sociopath is a buzzword, but apart from this buzzword he'll allow the avalanche of Potter Phlegg's hearsay testimony because it is highly relevant, and of course it is well known that most of what Potter Phlegg's hearsay alleges comes from a tape recording currently marooned in appeals court, a tape the defense is scrambling to keep out of evidence, on which the actual voices of Carlos and Felix Martinez can be heard.

Seth eats lunch on Friday, alone, at a place inside the arcade in Little Tokyo, shabu-shabu with cellophane noodles, tofu, cabbage, scallions, mushrooms, and paper-thin beef slices, served beside a ceramic casserole of boiling water on a hot plate, he also drinks a large bottle of Kirin beer, he says he made a mistake and put on The Suit this morning, in such awful heat, he hates wearing The Suit, his one and only Armani, not the jacket so much as the pants, Seth says he's been wearing jeans for so many years that any other trousers feel like he's going to Mass, and besides that, he says, he's already excavated a numbing daily rut for himself after such a short time in California, when the whole point of coming out here was to feel more alive, the disease of habit has already colonized his existence, there's the trial first of all, and putting his car in the same parking lot every day, even going for the same space in the same parking lot every day, and this lunchtime walk to Little Tokyo, where he buys the *Los Angeles Times* from the same coin-operated dispenser, which often rejects his coins or swallows them without opening, and goes to the same generic restaurant full of orange paper lanterns and slatted wooden screens, and eats the same cook-it-yourself shabu-shabu and drinks the same large slightly oversweet Kirin beer, and what's even sicker, he says, is when I don't have a dinner engagement, I drive to Los Feliz on my way back to Hollywood and eat two pulled-beef tacos at that taco shack on Hillhurst next to the liquor store, two regular daily meals of beef, knowing perfectly well that beef is heart attack food, and then at the Marmont, Seth says, I realize I haven't had any greens, except for the blanched greens that come with the shabu-shabu, so I order a salad that I can't eat, because the Marmont's salad's horrible.

He reads about the fires raging out of control up in Malibu Canyon, several homes and dozens of acres so far consumed in the blaze, unaccounted-for homeowners suspected dead, origin unknown, the Santa Anas pushing the fire in a southwesterly direction, birds and wildlife fleeing into human neighborhoods. Rattlesnakes have invaded the Malibu colony and all sorts of unusual roadkill's squashed along Pacific Coast Highway. A funnel of blue-black smoke hangs over the area like the Shroud of Turin. Los Angeles and catastrophe, Seth thinks, eternal soulmates, endlessly restaging the primal collision of man with nature. He feels tiny and lost in the vastness. The odd thing about the human metastasis, the metal and glass hives humanity spins in its ceaseless ruin of space, is how few people die in earthquakes, tornadoes, floods, fires, and volcanic eruptions, a recent 6.8 tremor in Japan only claimed four lives, even when the epicenter is right where people live nature only bags a handful, never enough to make a dent. Seth believes it would be in the world's best interest for natural disasters to wipe out at least half and maybe three-fourths of the human race, starting in the most built-up and treacherous human clusters—get rid of half of us and there might be a future, he thinks, and suddenly Mark springs into his mind like an ectoplasm inhaled with the vinegary steam from the shabu-shabu. Mark has been waiting to ambush his thoughts all morning, a spectral nimbus of ungraspable cockteasing youth, with years to burn before his perfection crumbles. Seth knows he will never possess this boy, who seemed for a while so open to Seth's attentions. But today, for the first time, Mark's features refuse to form themselves inside his head. He's become an assortment of receding moments, a smudge or erasure across pictures where he once appeared, and what Seth glimpses instead are the zinc bar counter in the restaurant where Mark worked and the stiff waiter's shirts he wore, and a set of shiny plastic Rollerblades he had hanging from his shoulder the last time Seth saw him. Seth feels Mark turning into a fiery node of regret inside him, a bald patch of murdered possibility with no face attached, in some strange way Felix inhabits the same place as Mark, Felix forever inaccessible because of history and Mark because of history, too. It's not that Seth wants Felix as he wanted Mark, exactly, but that both of them have moved beyond the door, this is what he tells himself, the door, the pale, whatever. The State will kill Felix and Seth is killing Mark, rubbing him away, replacing him with scar tissue.

Salt water on the tennis court. Gray marble and annealing asphalt, thin clouds, blue sky stuffed between buildings, the unforgiving architecture of purgatory. *The Lord will cause you to be defeated before your enemies,* he remembers. *You shall go out one way against them, and flee seven ways before them; and you shall be a horror to all the kingdoms of the earth.* The jaundiced white hulk of the contemporary museum, a flag-patterned pentimento of whitewashed mural on one block-long wall. The courts rising leviathanlike from the sloping barrens of Temple Street. *And your dead body shall be food for all birds of the air, and for the beasts of the earth; and there shall be no one to frighten them away.* The gaudy faux-fiesta micromexico of Olvera Street a few meters from the jail, bougainvillea gushing from marble escarpments above the sidewalk, jasmine bushes scenting the entrance. Withered royal palms around Union Station scissoring the wind. *The Lord will smite you with the boils of Egypt, and with the ulcers and the scurvy and the itch, of which you cannot be healed.* Everything lies insensibly in the sun like the debris of a plane crash scattered across the desert.

A landscape where the soft machine of the brain squishes between the iron gears of law, expelling a substance closer to bile or jelly than blood. *The Lord will smite you with madness and blindness and confusion of mind; and you shall grope at noonday, as the blind grope in darkness, and you shall not prosper in your ways; and you shall be only oppressed and robbed continually, and there shall be no one to help you.* The cavernous courthouse lobby like the barrel of a cannon, frigid as gunmetal. *You shall betroth a wife, and another man shall lie with her; you shall build a house, and you shall not dwell in it; you shall plant a vineyard, and you shall not use the fruit of it. The Lord will bring you, and your king whom you set over you, to a nation that neither you nor your fathers have known; and there you shall serve other gods, of wood and stone.* People betray their slots in the pecking order through their clothing, and the condition of their nerves. Armies of losers swarm over the floor's starburst pattern of pink and obsidian marble. Defendants in small, bailable criminal suits. Central Americans trapped in interminable INS hearings. Jailhouse lawyers with faulty hairpieces, bondsmen in poorly cut suits, aggrieved persons with no money whatsoever dressed in the national prole style of faded plaid and sagging denim and ugly twenty-dollar shoes. Hysterics coping on Prozac. *And you shall become a horror, a proverb, and a byword, among all the peoples where the Lord will lead you away.* People driven half-mad and bankrupt by small, malignant lesions in the social contract, some wandering in voluble argument with invisible adversaries. Natty attorneys, photogenic reporters, judges oozing gravity from their pores, none as glossy or well groomed in close-up as they appear from a distance. Secretaries, records clerks, licensing personnel, marshals, security guards, creatures of marginal competence and soporific mien on life support from the State of California, imbibing its soft dusty bureaucratic oxygen by day and at night bathing miscellaneous brain matter in the effusions of cathode tubes. *And you shall eat the offspring of your own body, the flesh of your sons and daughters, whom the Lord has given you, in the siege and distress with which your enemies shall distress you.*

People fall into this system and never come out. The Martinez brothers, unconvicted, have been inside for three and a half years, in the slablike panopticon down the street, Carlos in isolation, Felix in the celebrity hospital ward, amid the largest incarcerated population in the country. An overwhelming number of their immediate neighbors are young black males hauled up on crack cocaine charges. The jail can be considered an annex of the state university system in which they, like graduates of the more conventional business schools, learn to tackle larger and more desperate crimes upon release. The truly accomplished felon is considered a member of the teaching staff. And then there are the big-time eccentrics who conjure extraordinary fear and a wide berth. A former trusty who served meals to the brothers told CNN this morning that "nobody messed with the Martinez brothers," on the theory that "anybody who'd do his parents would do anybody," that the brothers are considered "crazy."

The daily postlunch stampede into the elevators and onto the eighth floor jams up in the corridor in front of the metal detectors. Keys, rings, watches, change, drop into gray plastic bowls. Sometimes belt buckles, eyeglasses, hearing aids, and metal-reinforced footwear set off the alarms. Fawbus Kennedy's diamond cuff links, Rolex watch, and thin gold tie clip plop into the bowl. A liver-spotted hand scoops them out a few seconds later. Fawbus Kennedy's liver spots are pale and scattered over his skin like tiny garnets in a veil. Seth notices you can lay a jacket on the screening table and retrieve it on the other side without having the pockets rifled: presumably a gun or a switchblade would lend the garment suspicious weight, but the guards usually don't touch the thing and let you slide it across without inspection.

The rest of Friday's witnesses fill up hours on the clock over the bailiff's head like some excruciating algebra problem holding up the weekend: there's the first computer expert, the little Jewish guy, that Carlos hired a few days after the police cleared the crime scene and all the blood and brain matter had been scrubbed off the rumpus room furniture—Seth wonders how, exactly, you go about getting all that blood and tissue out of expensive fabrics, and whether the police department sends a cleaning lady or the survivors have to do it themselves; the first expert erased the hard drive with the so-called Norton's

Wipe Utility, and the next day another expert scanned the hard drive for data residue, the second expert testifies he could tell stuff had been wiped, but couldn't tell what or how much. Seth says that both experts were anxious to lay their little eggs of evidence and slither off the stand. The first expert said the visit to Woodrow Wilson Drive made his spine crawl, which isn't the correct phrase, but something you'd expect from a computer expert, who would picture his spine crawling free of his exoskeleton into creepy hyperspace. He goes over there, says Seth, on an absolutely mundane mechanical job, and thinks he's in an X-Men adventure comic, he noodles around with a household appliance and imagines himself in a David Cronenberg movie . . .

. . . which carried over into Monday, the weekend a blur of depression, according to Seth, who ate dinner Saturday with some lawyers he knows and on Sunday met with a producer friend of a friend at the Farmer's Market for late breakfast. The producer wanted to know, Seth says, if Seth's considered writing a screenplay about the trial, of course they're already casting two TV movies about the Martinez brothers, knocked out by enterprising hacks who have garbled all the details of the case, Now that you've published a book, the producer told him, you're ready to write screenplays. People don't read books, the producer added with a certain zest. Why are you telling me this? Seth asked. Because I like you, the producer replied without irony. When his meal came the producer clasped his hands together and recited the Lord's Prayer, and not just under his breath, Seth says, but exuberantly, which terrified Seth in ways that eating dinner with Morgan Talbot never could, and later in the meal the producer claimed he'd been cured of incurable lymphoma by prayer, as soon as I went back to the church, the producer told him, my cancer went into remission. Seth says he's afraid of Hollywood, afraid of the movie business, afraid of being sucked into years of wasted buck-chasing futility, My moment for Hollywood would've been twenty years ago, Seth says, twenty years ago I could have wasted ten years without noticing it, he cites a former friend who left New York in 1980 and now has two horrible movies to her credit, one a miserable failure, the other a huge commercial success, two pieces of unabashed shit and scads of uncredited rewrite assignments and, snout's up, a few million in the bank, but never mind that, Seth says, I'm scared of it and that's all there is to it, having to talk and deal with these people, people who pray over yolkless omelettes in the Farmer's Market, people with healing crystals concealed on their person, as if I took them seriously, but what am I going to do, Seth wants to know, I haven't prepared myself to live this long, I haven't planned, I'm this late-blooming underachiever, the only assets I have are two dinky little paintings by Nathan Greenglass. Here I am putting down Hollywood, he says, while scamming a few extra days out of Condé Nast at the Marmont, Seth tells me he phoned Morgan Talbot's office on Friday and claimed he needed a second interview session with Teddy Wade, which he told them he'd already scheduled for Thursday, giving him another ten or eleven days of free room service and privacy before shipping himself over to Mt. Washington, whereas he's already got Teddy's interview edited and ready for print, the magazine kept him on pins through the weekend and then said okay, and on Monday, he says, the prosecution brought on this unpleasant woman from Bosnian Serb Jewelers on Rodeo Drive who sold Carlos and Felix three Rolex watches and some money clips three days after the murders, more evidence of the wild spending spree, then Tuesday they brought on the Deputy Medical Examiner, a skinny weirdo who looked like some elongated Chinese vegetable pickled in formaldehyde, who pinned up a lot of autopsy photos that Seth couldn't see from where he was sitting, people sitting closer told him that one showed Peggy nude, with big meaty gashes in her face and torso, another showed Fidel's head where the top of his skull had been blasted into tripes, finally on Wednesday the formal testimony of Potter Phlegg began in front of the two juries.

Carlos never understood why Felix went sobbing to the quack when he had his so-called attack of conscience, since neither of them trusted Pot, as Carlos called him, in the first place, Pot short for toilet where you dropped your shit, Carlos says, even when Fidel and Peggy were around the brothers had been circumspect, because Pot and Fidel had some deal where Pot told Fidel whatever Carlos and Felix told him, not everything but anything important, anything clinically significant, which is one reason Felix never told Pot about these feelings he gets about other boys, or the BJs he and Poppy gave each other, or stuff him and Carlos did a few times years ago, Fidel would've hit the ceiling even though Fidel had those feelings himself obviously and furthermore acted on them with his own children, and just forget telling Pot about Fidel, this whole idea the prosecution keeps putting forward, that they would've naturally told the therapist about the abuse if it really happened, shows how little Marlene Quilty and Quentin Kojimoto understand or care about the whole phenomenon of incest, which is really insulting to the entire abuse community, where the whole point is how the family keeps it secret, it's not like the molester leaves a record for other people to find although there are those peculiar snapshots Fidel took of both of them on Felix's birthday, stroke of fucking luck those turned up, Carlos naked with his head cropped out of the picture standing beside the pink bathtub, another one with Felix in the tub, shot so you can see his itty-bitty willy poking out of a bubble bath, Carlos wonders now, as he tells Doris on the phone, if Fidel went down on them both just before that birthday party, which is what's on the rest of the roll of photographs, Felix's seventh- or eighth-birthday party, cone hats and crepe streamers and confetti, a big chocolate cake with candy violets and Happy Birthday Felix scripted in pink icing, they were living in Kalamazoo and Carlos thinks Fidel must've started diddling Felix around then, Carlos had his own abuse completely locked away in his brain until thank God he finally got therapy in prison, Felix had kind of wiped it out too even though with Felix it went on for years and years, Fidel making him do Knees and Nice Sex and Rough Sex really right up until that fatal night or anyway just a few days before, which simply shows how traumatic that type of abuse is, you go right into denial the minute after it happens. I mean we consciously knew it happened, says Carlos, that's why we were afraid of them, that's why I confronted my dad about Felix, but at the same time we were in denial all the time pretending it didn't happen. Even afterwards when Felix spilled about the shootings, we were not about to tell Pot a single thing about the abuse, no way. Carlos tells Doris that the worst part is, Pot's lying even about what they did tell him, this so-called perfect crime idea, and killing Peggy as a mercy killing type of thing, which isn't what they told him at all, that was all Pot's hypothetical scenario which he and Felix signed on to in order to shut Pot up and keep him happy. That he would have this so-called confession tape in his safe for the lawyers to discover if anything weird happened to Pot. The way he worded it, says Carlos, *if I should die or mysteriously disappear,* like we were the only weird thing that could possibly happen to him. When all he'd need would be one patient a little more loosely wired than Sabrina Wilcox with access to a lethal weapon.

The sick part, which is what Lauren Nathanson's bringing out now in cross, is Potter buying three heavy-gauge shotguns himself at the same place Felix and Carlos bought theirs, supposedly to defend himself and anyone else in what Potter refers to as the sphere of danger, and then trying to get that Sabrina Wilcox lunatic to phone his wife, disguising her voice as Felix's, threatening her, of course Potter and his wife never even learned how to load or fire the shotguns which shows you how much danger he actually thought they were in, instead he has his wife and kids go stay with a neighbor and moves in with Sabrina Fucking Wilcox, making her all paranoid about the Martinez brothers bumping her off for what earthly reason Carlos would like to know since he and Felix didn't even know she existed though now it turns out Potter had her sitting in the waiting room when Felix was spilling his guts. First she said she overheard the whole so-called confession but now she says Potter brainwashed her, no superhuman feat obviously, Carlos tells Doris, telling her stuff and programming her to believe she overheard it. Of course she's a nut case but wait till you hear these love poems he wrote to her claiming all this time she was stalking him and making his life impossible terrorizing his family, we even have him singing "Love Me Tender" into her answering machine, she saved all these tapes by accident she says, she says she made them by accident too the machine has a mind of its own and just tapes things when it isn't supposed to, so she has like two hundred hours of calls we can prove he made to her, not the other way around, besides that she's already filed a rape charge, plus Pot has another patient who says she's been raped by Pot as well, plus there's this other case where Pot took goods for services getting some long-term phobia patient to do all his gardening for a year. That's against the code of professional ethics in California. Potter has a whole garbage bag full of love letters from his patients, Carlos says, it turns out he's been banging every female that wandered into his office, and then, says Carlos, he's got all these queer little businesses on the side, little scams, for instance these motivation tapes, how-to-get-over-phobia tapes, evidently that's how he met Sabrina Wilcox, she has some tape duplication service besides the occult store she runs down on Melrose, she's also got this bizarro program on channel 18 where she shares her thoughts about the universe and shows off her titties, she was going to dupe and maybe help market Potter's motivation and get-over-phobia tapes, sell them on her cable show maybe, I think he even passes himself off as an investment counselor, anyway he's got about six different business cards unrelated to this so-called psychotherapy.

By day five, Carlos claims that Potter's been demolished in front of both juries. Doris isn't convinced. She's followed most of it on Court TV and agrees that Potter looks ridiculous, he used the excitement of Felix's confession to mobilize a little drama in his personal life, his professional dignity's blown to hell, but Lauren Nathanson hasn't been able to budge him on the key points of his testimony, which really boil down to whether you believe him or believe the two brothers, that they planned or didn't plan the killings, that they were or weren't afraid of Fidel and Peggy, of course the defense still has Sabrina

Wilcox up its sleeve, the nymphet on a golden steed with eyes of lapis lazuli as Potter Phlegg describes her in one of the poems Lauren Nathanson forced him to read in front of Felix's jury, causing great hilarity in the courtroom, not just from the defense table but from the prosecutors and Judge Tietelbaum and even Potter Phlegg as well, Doris meanwhile labels her microcassettes of her Carlos conversations while working the Thighmaster she ordered from Suzanne Somers's 800 number, a device she's not totally thrilled with, feeling her usual ambivalence about Carlos, who never asks her how she's feeling or what her life is like, just complains complains and complains about the various lockdowns and confiscations taking place in the jailhouse, expecting Doris to haul her cumbersome poundage downtown every time he needs a writing pen or thermal underwear, granted these visits will make colorful chapters in the book she's writing with the guy from the *Enquirer* if and when the deal goes through, but she resents the way Carlos takes her for granted, as if he were some big celebrity she's lucky to have anything to do with, always mentioning her weight problem and recommending diets he's read about in magazines as if she's never gone on a diet before, hinting that she just doesn't try, when the agony she's endured getting off even five pounds would test the patience of Job since it's really a genetic problem and she's fighting her own DNA with these Healthy Choice and Weight Watchers frozen meals that she ends up gobbling five at a time without even obtaining a full feeling, because these low-calorie meals are like methadone to a junkie, you don't get the rush you get from eating good old-fashioned fat, anyway Orson Welles was obese, a lot of really brilliant people have been heavy, look where having a perfect tennis body's gotten Carlos, who's never labored for a dime, when she's spent fifteen years clearing rubbish off properties all over Los Angeles and Orange Counties, every time she gets off the phone with Carlos she has to remind herself that she's a good person, a caring person, and a worthwhile person who deserves love, and that those who treat her like a blubber doormat cannot expect her loyalty and generosity forever, but will have to pay much more than they bargained for in the fullness of time.

Rain hangs in the air the day the prosecution rests, the gathering clouds staining the sidewalk, and on the drive back to the Marmont the radio is abuzz with weather, the parched condition of the hills where the blazes around Malibu have only yesterday subsided is spoken of with awe as the next big danger to life and property. Seth can smell the rain, and wonders if it's really necessary to ferry JD out to Venice before driving up to Teddy's party near the reservoir. Norma Woolcoate, the so-called punk novelist, plans on reading her latest drivel at Beyond Baroque at seven, and Seth's agreed to deposit JD there, and Jack's agreed to drive him back to Hollywood, where JD and Jack plan on attending the ritual crucifixion of Marvin Paley, the transgressive performance artist. In a knot of traffic at Santa Monica and Vermont, Seth feels a brand-new pain in his body, a tugging ache in an area he believes to be his left kidney. He wonders if his internal organs have suddenly grown responsive to weather. Or if various problems that beset his parents' innards late in life will strike him early because of some acceleration of genetic weaknesses. Do things work that way? He phones the hotel from the cell phone and asks for his messages. There aren't any. He turns down Vermont, where a long-standing mess of resurfacing has closed the northbound lanes and turned the southbound ones into two-way traffic. Nothing registers in his eyes or his ears besides brake lights and car horns and the drone of Reverend Samuel Clayton Fuller on Christian Promise Radio, a station which has, among its many splendors, first-rate weather coverage. He follows Vermont to Wilshire, heads west on Wilshire, the mellifluous tones of the evangelist warming the immediate area of the dashboard. *And the generation to come, your children who rise up after you, and the foreigner who comes from a far land, would say, when they see the afflictions of that land and the sicknesses with which the Lord has made it sick—the whole land brimstone and salt, and a burnt-out waste, unsown, and growing nothing, where no grass can sprout, an overthrow like that of Sodom and Gomorrah, Admah and Zeboi'im, which the Lord overthrew in his anger and wrath.* Seth reflects on the unsown, burnt-out waste he is passing through, noting that the May Company has closed its doors for good. He feels like a boatman steering his ruddy craft along the swift currents of a mighty river, seeking the cool shore of a sympathetic port. I will head up to Hollywood before reaching Bob's Big Boy, Seth biblically promises himself, dreading the nether reaches of Wilshire, its agoraphobic asphalt plains, its onrush of stately untouchable affluence at the threshold of Beverly Hills. With a click of directionals he turns onto Western Avenue, a wilderness of polychrome signage and colorless buildings, the distant hills darkening, the Hollywood letters ranged across them like the loosened teeth of a prizefighter.

Exactly why he parks the car on Selma and walks up Ivar to the Hollywood Spa he couldn't say. Some thought of popping into Boardner's, or even the public library, of proximity to a carnival shank of Hollywood Boulevard, attracts him. Next he has the (for him) daring inspiration to do the baths. It's the very worst hour for sex, the free condom and lube packet he gets with his towel and cabin key look like sorry promises, and inside, the glass and metal cavern echoes like the hull of a ghost ship. There is too much aqueous light leaking in from the day, seeping over wine-red carpets through a decorative wall of glass bricks. High above him toweled waists dart along balconies at a speed too swift and definite for cruising, the bodies pale and imperfect even from a distance. Seth's cubicle, near the end of a row of wide-open doors, seems miles from whatever action is going on. He dims the cabin light to a muddy pall, undresses, spreads his towel on the thin plastic mattress. Alone with his body, he considers his defects—the slightly bulbous calves, each with a single thick livid vein too close to the skin, the udder of wayward flab at his navel—and ideal postures for dissembling them. He gauges the desirable amount of space to leave the door ajar, arranges himself with his naked back to the rear wall, legs sticking forward, decides this looks too "active," tries lying on his stomach with his face near the door, this is somehow too supine, finally he sits up, back to the sidewall, with his knees drawn up, and lights a cigarette. The silence of the corridor excites him, the thought of hungry bodies prowling for the thin provender of late afternoon—for surely Seth looks better, even with his flaws, than much of the aged or bloated meat on view in other stalls.

At least ten minutes pass before anyone ventures past his cabin. An eternity in bath time. He snags a rousing glimpse of chocolate flesh, a muscled body, sleekness. But the eyes skip over Seth's milky form without pause. Next a fat, pallid old horror whose pace slows meaningfully for a moment, who moves on when Seth turns his head to avoid eye contact. It's like some mating dance of geese or chickens, wordless, barely perceptible, fantastically cruel. Traffic is slow, unhopeful, the rejections firm and immediate. Men wandering the halls, naked under their towels, vanish for long spells and later reconnoiter this stretch of cabins, memorizing their contents, searching for the optimum body while clocking a hierarchy of lesser bodies, in case. Seth, too, rates the passing apparitions as more or less repellent, sizes up the available or unavailable goods, adjusts his desire to the range visible from his little dungeon.

The scenario, the trope, as he thinks of it, is "all wrong": because Seth's picture of himself in L.A. is all business and quick gratification, and even though this picture is patently askew with the large pockets of nothing that polka-dot his time here, he almost never risks, in L.A., possible sexual disappointment, favoring instead the services of a monstrously reliable Trinidadian hustler he's been using for years. He hadn't fully imagined himself squirming in a black cell, swallowing the indifference of other men. Hadn't cast the picture for himself before coming in. Seth has mechanisms at his bidding, of course, emotional endorphins that coat all this late afternoon abjection with an oil of sardonic resignation. But his bowels feel clotted with self-pity after a half hour. He knows that a fart in this crypto-utopian twilight would carry the stench of a Third World lavatory drain, an odor of impacted toxins, of meat spoiling in the gut. Something lanky with spidery hair too long for its weak face pauses in the doorway. Seth equivocates, venturing a quarter-glance that might be read as a twitch. As he decides that the imperfect ectoplasm hovering there would not be the worst thing that's ever fucked him, the vision returns his gelid appraisal and moves on. Seth has been in enough baths to know that this specter will return, full of tasteless self-assurance the second time. But the sex will feel nasty from the initial encounter, sex ambitious with revenge. Excitingly unpleasant, or unpleasantly exciting—all wrong, it strikes him with sudden vehemence, because if I'm relieving the same need it's for quite different reasons. Seth has always hated the generic institutions of the gay world: gay bars, gay political groups, gay magazines, and gay sexual rituals like cruising. He never even entered a bath house until such places had become anathema to many gay people, had become once again the most furtive and at the same time most direct venues for anonymous sex—in militant rhetoric, incubators of disease and emporiums of "self-contempt." Well, he does see that what he's likely to get in such a place, at this hour anyway, is someone as ill at ease with himself as Seth is, and that the relaxed, impersonal intimacies he sometimes enjoys for a daunting fee with professionals has spoiled him for this kind of random bottom-feeding. He throws on his pants as if the building's on fire, and a few minutes later whips past his prospective suitor in the corridor, flashing him a weird smile. He hands in his cabin key, grabs his wallet from the safe-deposit, and strolls out onto Ivar con brio, like a man escaped.

This little light of mine, warbles JD to the convex mirror on his dining room wall, a joke replica of the one in the Parmigiano painting, *I'm gonna let it shine!* JD enjoys belting out songs he detests, in an Oakie accent, such stupidities empty his mind, like a sorbet between courses of thought. His bulbous, straining reflection breaks into the Triassic smile of an extinct herbivore. At least I am tall, JD thinks, at least I have a good body, my face is vivid if not handsome, and of course my rich voice is known to all Los Angeles. He wonders why he painted so many of his apartment's surfaces peach, recalls himself in white overalls running a roller of peach latex up and down the dining room walls, spattering gray tarps bunched stiffly on the floor, at that time picturing the fuzzy nimbuses of scented candles in a smoky twilight of peach, yes I do look good, by God, and I haven't had a drink in four days, but what was it, he wonders, grasping in his mind for the missing bit of emotional memory, that once led him to believe the color peach announced something piquant and unexpected about his personality?

The door buzzer wrenches him free of the mirror, in which he catches his fisheyed face organizing itself into the bemused mask Seth brings out on its surface, a mask that loosens in a physiognomic drawl in the course of an evening, after many drinks and hurtled inhibitions. This isn't the face he wears for Dylan, which in turn has no resemblance to the one his radio guests see, or the one his cat sees—and suddenly Seth is there, in baggy jeans and gray Armani jacket, his own face wrestling itself, wrestling "hungrily," it seems to JD, though he couldn't say what about it suggests a churning rumination, aside from a wad of Chiclets Seth's masticating with his left molars.

I've never been in this apartment, Seth announces with a trace of accusation.

Yes, you have, says JD with asperity. Between them there can never be criticism of any kind, only an occasional wheedling to prolong the time they spend together: this has become a fixed rule, its occasional breach leading to spans of brittle hostility that run their course in a sort of radio silence and are never discussed afterwards.

I mean since you did it over, says Seth, backing down.

Well, says JD. In an access of nostalgia for his flat's earlier days, he describes his efforts with its four large rooms, marching Seth down the hall, in and out of the bedroom, back through the living room, the dining room, the kitchen, points out the gardening he's been attempting on the grounds, regales him with little stories about the neighborhood, recent shootings in the neighborhood, the holdup in the Korean market on the corner that ended so badly, gouts of blood from the grocer's brain still staining the decayed Deco linoleum, an unusual northerly drive-by down the block, and the dismaying influx, into this very apartment complex, of two Salvadoran families, not simply families but entire kinship systems illegally festering in single-family units, filling the catwalks with the smell of fried who knows what and the howling of infants, monopolizing the laundry room, bringing down the generally hip tone of the building, turning the place into a barrio.

I doubt very much, JD says, that these are what you would call political refugees, I don't think they're having guerrilla briefings down in the laundry— I hate all the anti-immigrant backlash that's going on and at the same time it's obvious these people multiply themselves senselessly like rabbits, or lemmings, their fucking rug rats trample all over my flower beds, they're not supposed to have eight or ten people crammed into these places, and you know not one of those babies they bring into the banquet of life has the slightest chance to develop, especially now that they're cutting public assistance, the girls will be pregnant at fourteen and their brothers will be knocking off convenience stores, once they get into a building like this unfortunately you either have to flush them out or give up and move, because the next thing you know it's salsa parties with their countrymen and people pissing off the balconies. I wish it wasn't like that but it is.

Seth sits at the long dining table where JD plans his radio shows. JD fusses around the room, picking things up, putting things down, moving little objects around as if to restore some idyllic order. The table piled high with books, files, loose papers sliding out of folders. JD's flat is pleasant, light and airy. Like so many houses and flats Seth's spent time in in L.A., JD's has this one room that doesn't look like a page in *Architectural Digest*, where work is flung on a great daunting slag heap on a broad oak table. As if the rest of the house were a seldom-used weekend retreat. Seth sits with his left foot tucked under his right thigh, his arms crossed on the table, the fingers of one hand nervously fondling and stroking bits of scattered paper. He idly digs out a publicity glossy of JD in which the latter looks like Andy Warhol, struggles with a cigarette lighter as he stares at it.

God, he says. This is another piece of brainlessness. He pauses artfully, giving JD a second of mild paranoia before elaborating: The childproof cigarette lighter. They've actually passed a law, they all have to have this nasty little flap, you can't even buy a normal lighter anymore.

Why would you want children, says JD, all blasé again, who couldn't light your cigarettes for you?

JD circles the table, looking around, forgetting something—he rummages through papers, picks up various small items on a bookshelf, puts them down.

Or kids so stupid they couldn't figure out a childproof lighter. How are things going with that—Seth drags thoughtfully on his cigarette.

With what? JD locates a cough lozenge tin, pries open the lid, selects a longish roach from an assortment.

That—exhale—guy with all the birds.

Uh. He's up north promoting his book. JD lights the roach as Jinx comes padding into the dining room. Sucks on it, holds it out for Seth, who shakes his head.

There's precious, Seth says, bending down over the chair arm, trying to attract the cat with his fingers. Yeth sthweetie, ithn't the a prethious.

Dylan hasn't phoned me or anything. You know how it is. I think I'm maybe a little over the top for him.

As long as you don't have to *be* a top for him, Seth says, his head near the floor. Sweetie sweet—

Really not, says JD. Dylan's a real homo erectus. He's not even versatile. But he's got that seeker-of-wisdom thing going on, it's hard to know what he's really looking for. Emotionally. If anything. Anyhow he's been busy since the fires. They didn't get any fire damage up there but he realized how hard it would be to get the birds out, so he got obsessed with figuring out an evacuation procedure. You know something, I actually know somebody whose father got killed in those fires.

Eeesh, says Seth, sitting up so abruptly it makes him dizzy. That's got to be the most horrible of all deaths, fire. Fire is not your friend. It's freaky that people couldn't get out.

That doctor and his family, JD says, pacing about as he puffs on his joint. Trapped like rats. The house went up like cardboard. Everybody was sleeping. Him, his wife, two little twin girls.

The news said a *proctologist*, Seth says half-satirically, lucky for your friend he wasn't home.

No, he doesn't live there, it was his father's second family. In fact by complete coincidence he was out at the ranch with us. I mean it's ironic because the fire started right across the state park or at least that's what they think, and we'd been horse riding in the park that same night.

There but for fortune, says Seth, barely listening, brazenly rummaging through JD's office files. Maybe the people never woke up, they could've died of smoke inhalation.

You know there was a guy in Glendale setting fires, JD says. All up and down California, in department stores. You only have to put a lit cigarette in a folder of matches and stick it inside some flammable material. He would go right to home furnishings and put his little device in some pillows. San Luis Obispo, that type of place. He left a trail of fire.

Sick, says Seth. Some people are so sick.

It turned out, says JD, the guy was the Glendale Fire Department's arson expert. You know how they found out? He'd written a novel about an arsonist and sent it to some publisher.

I wonder what kind of advance they gave him, Seth yawns. Every town has a firebug, he muses. Every town has a murderer, a retard, and a firebug.

And a novelist, JD adds.

Right. And a novelist. Even if the town is only the size of a trailer park. You got Grace Metalious in her fifty-footer over the Whistlin' Pines Trailer Park and Jeffrey Dahmer down the road in that RV with the blue awning and then you got Flem Snopes settin' fire to a barn up behind the Baptist cemetery. Seth laughs. Help me out, JD, who's a famous retard?

Who isn't? says JD.

He notices that JD has gone to some trouble to look sportif. His usual jeans and a pink shirt, but everything new and crisp. His face also pink from whatever scientific skin-peeling regimen he's lately discovered. In the car, they smoke and chatter like magpies, setting off on surface roads because JD is the only person who doesn't get annoyed by Seth's freeway phobia. It's a special point of mutual understanding, though Seth has forgotten ever telling JD about the accident twenty years ago and would be surprised to learn its significance in JD's notion of how Seth is put together. Seth uses the freeway, hiding his panic, when he thinks his passengers will think he's crazy for avoiding the freeway—his lawyer friends, for instance, who attack all practical daily matters with a brash absence of idiosyncrasy, though these lawyer friends also have their peculiarities, and in some cases have completely deformed their lives by constructing them around certain phobias and quirks, settling, for example, in impossible neighborhoods where no sane person would choose to live and where certainly no lawyer needs to live, in one instance by filling her house with dozens of temperamental and sickly cats, Seth even knows a lawyer whose houseplants require such specific, elaborate attention that she hasn't taken a vacation in fifteen years, unwilling to entrust the jungle of her home to another person. Yet all these various lawyers take the freeway for granted.

They pull in at the 7-Eleven on Western and Melrose for cigarettes. While Seth runs into the store, JD rubs a little leftover speed on his gums and thinks some more about the kind of person he was when he painted the apartment. Naive despite his intelligence, emotionally naive, hopeful in a stupid way, he thinks, aware that he still lacks an intelligent way to be hopeful. He's embarrassed to recall that he painted the walls peach and haunted swap meets for months, stick by stick filling out the rooms with Mission furniture, Arts and

Crafts Movement sconces, and that sort of signature SoCal thing, so his dwelling would convey a certain maturity, rootedness and éclat to a hypothetical partner. It had never been terribly clear in his mind where this partner would come from, though he did, he recalls with deeper embarrassment, imagine himself throwing parties quickened by available men, imagined himself dressing for these parties in sleek white parachute pants and matching cashmere pullovers from Maria Sartini, and fretting with pensive fountain pen over his guest lists, Merle Oberon of the Wilshire District. The gloomy weather brings his mind around to Dylan and the unnervingly formal tone Dylan took the last time JD called him. He'd called to tell him about Frankie's father and to remark on the irony of the fire happening so close to the ranch on the same night they all got so drunk, and Dylan said, Well, you certainly were drunk, and JD apologized for what felt like the fiftieth time, and Dylan said neutrally, Oh, we don't have to talk about it. His voice wasn't mean, not even unfriendly, but it wasn't welcoming or tender, either, more like a voice that would give you a second chance against its better judgment if you absolutely insisted on it. Inside the store, Seth and the South American guy who probably beat Frankie up look like they're having an involved conversation. From the car it appears that they know each other and JD thinks, How odd. Seth's body has that rubbery laughing jointlessness it gets when he's talking to someone he knows or someone he likes, he's talking longer than you'd talk to a store clerk you didn't know, or that's how it seems. JD pushes in a cassette sticking out of the tape player. The blast from the speakers makes him jump. Speed. *So ladies we just ain't talkin' 'bout you* Between the windshield glass and the store entrance the linear breakage of space glitters under the speed, the concrete ingots and crumbling yellow lines of the parking spaces suggest Incan schemes of human traffic. *Cause some of your niggers are bitches too.* Speed propels JD into realms of primordial residue. Los Angeles becomes all mountains and blocky architecture, its soft parts friable as incandescent thread. He can't be sure if he's reading the scene inside correctly, for the drug deforms his sense of time as well as facial cues and body language, mines the surroundings with auditory hallucinations and tricks of peripheral vision. *So if you wonderin' why we lookin' at you funny it's because* A drug that makes silence and solitude scary, and what's keeping Seth, and why didn't Seth invite him to Teddy Wade's party? Afraid he'd get drunk and do something horrible? JD, all mental munificence, forgives him. Seth's probably afraid of drinking too much himself out of nerves and decanting his own demons in front of strangers. *Some of you niggers are bitches too.* The 7-Eleven clerk is

Seth's type, maybe Seth saw the beeper on his belt and assumed it's a hustler beeper instead of a dealer beeper. JD doesn't really know if the 7-Eleven clerk is a dealer or a hustler, in fact so many young people have beepers now that the only safe bet is that he isn't a doctor or a limo driver. Right after Frankie heard about his father he said: Gee, I wonder if my muh muh muh mom will have to give up the limo. He left Angela's place after sleeping there one night and moved back to Pomona or wherever with Cassandra. *Yes I was born in America true does South-Central look like America to you?* Surprisingly, Angela went with them to the funeral and later said that Frankie'd had to say a few words at the service. And then Angela did a vicious imitation of Frankie stuttering his little eulogy, which was either out of character for Angela or revealed an unpleasant facet of her personality, JD wasn't sure which and didn't much care. He sees Seth kissing the 7-Eleven clerk right on the mouth. *Straight up nigger.* Very strange. *The ultimate male supreme white women's dream big dick straight up nigger.* As Seth comes out of the store JD flicks off the tape and makes busy with his Filofax, as if he didn't see the kiss or anything else.

God what a small world, Seth sighs happily as he climbs into the car.

Not if you have to clean it, JD says. It's an old line, but they both laugh.

In the car (which is, by the way, propelling them through several patches of Santa Monica Boulevard where, for unaccountable reasons, some of Seth's bleakest memories have taken residence, like wood lice, in the landscape—something to do with a long-vanished Mazda dealership, but he can't remember what), Seth, avid from a microscopic lick of speed, says:

I can't believe Marvin Paley's really going to crucify himself and I'm going to miss it.

He's done it before, JD yawns, he'll do it again.

I remember when Marvin was just sticking needles in himself.

Everyone has to grow as an artist.

Speaking of which, what's happening with your TV thing?

Fox? It's not clear.

Yeah but they want you, right?

They want me, but my agent thinks they want some other show to fail first. They're trying to get a read on my demographic.

What *is* your demographic, JD?

Well, that's what they're trying to figure out. Am I more appealing to people who're driving at five in the afternoon, or people who're sitting home watching television?

What's the difference?

People driving are employed, generally.

You do a lot of book author stuff, no?

Not a *lot*. Some. Issue and sidebar topic oriented author stuff more than, you know, literary.

They probably won't want that on TV.

No, they want a slightly more elevated geek show than the Montel, Jerry Springer type of thing. But lots of audience participation, JD says, shivering with horror.

God, Seth says, shuddering in sympathy.

Hey, says JD brightly. I'll be the best goddam cow they ever had.

You like Jack okay, don't you?

Let's see, says JD, holding up fingers for counting. What's not to like.

I mean I'm sorry I have to go to this thing and I'm probably stupid to go anyway with this weather.

It's fine.

Listen, I would've asked you to go to Teddy's but I don't even know these people really, I just hope you don't find Jack, you know, boring—

He's not boring. Didactic, abrasive, judgmental, but not boring.

To me he's actually improved a lot. But then I've known him a lot longer. When I first met him he was kind of an aesthete, but then he got into that political head, everything is politics sort of thing. He had that way of making you feel like you were living in a sappy little dream because you didn't apply a rigorous political analysis to every teeny little action. Jack really believed there would be this violent revolution in the seventies.

I saw a poster on a wall near the station the other day, JD says. It said, "The seventies sucked then and they suck now."

Yeah, but they start to look good, the older you get, right?

I was only born in 1964, JD reminds him. They still look pretty runny to me.

I'm so old, Seth says. So old, and I still feel I have to go to these Norma Woolcoate events. I still have to see Norma, I still have to worry about money, I still haven't budged myself—

Does Norma know you're here? She might not, you know. You could just drop me off. I mean she doesn't know me from a hole in the wall. She wouldn't think because I'm there that you're here.

She certainly does know you, you're on the fucking radio. Someone would have told her I was out here, for sure. People we know in common just love fanning this feud or whatever it is. It's better if I stay for her reading. If I don't it looks like I'm avoiding her. Believe me, with my luck, if I just dropped you off she'd see me in the parking lot or something. I'm always locked into some terrible drama with Norma. I'll never understand it. We were close for such a short time, so long ago. There are people I was much more involved with than Norma, that if I saw them today it would be like I never met them.

You've never really told me anything about you and Norma Woolcoate. Or you and Jack, for that matter.

I was a completely different person then. Not completely different but, I don't know, I was in the dark about so many things. It's so tangled, when you're young all this stuff happens for who knows what reasons and then you spend the rest of your life trying to figure out what it means. Norma . . . Norma is really mentally ill. I'm not saying I'm *not*, but she's been in bad need of a shrink for the past fifteen years. I mean she has this psychotic need to present herself as a personage, some great important figure, and the people around her are always just dream matter. Like little dolls she plays with.

You were a doll.

Exactly, I was a doll. And I am a doll whenever I somehow stray into Norma's orbit. I inhabit some special dungeon in her doll house. What I hate is that you can't have any other relationship with Norma. Either you're a doll, in which case you don't exist, or you're the enemy, and you still don't exist.

At least an enemy represents something, says JD.

So does a doll, but either way, it isn't *you* that it represents. It's some primal trauma in Norma's brain. I'll tell you something, she grew up on Park Avenue with a lot of money, and one time she told me that when she was a kid, she had to fight with her mother's dogs every night to get a hamburger off the dinner table. She really believes all they ever ate were hamburgers and these dogs were fighting her for her food every night. Tell me that isn't crazy.

Maybe it's true! The rich are different from us.

Norma has probably forgotten ever telling me that dog story. What she does remember, is this crazy idea that we're supposed to be close to each other, and we just aren't. I mean some part of me does feel close to Norma, but it's a part that buys into sentimental myths and sort of enables other people's lies, if you see what I mean. My God, you'd think we'd been married or something. JD, that's it, I've just figured this out. Not to compare them or anything, but with Jack, there really *was* something. We really had that something a long time ago, we lived it, we finished it, and it doesn't haunt either one of us. But with Norma it's all about something that never happened. It's a myth she carries around, and because she does, somehow I do, too, only because I know that she does. God, Seth adds, noticing a well-built piece of talent standing at a bus stop, I need to get laid.

After they drop this subject for more frivolous ones, the thought worms into Seth's mind that "really something" with Jack wasn't really much of anything, either: two months of deluded adolescent romance in a past so remote it would require a forensic archaeologist to reconstruct the mise-en-scène. At Beyond Baroque, his composure crumbles as a familiar crowd of artists absorbs them, the mood of the place colored by impending weather, and there word has it that Norma hasn't shown, that as usual she plans to keep her fans waiting while she consumes and then vomits up a large Japanese meal somewhere in Brentwood. It's said that this human anaconda is in the thick of one of her crazes, one of her endearing follies, having a reckless, violent affair with a trainer of aquatic mammals. Even Jack has a little Norma gossip to offer, detaching himself from a Seattle poet with problem skin. He's wearing mirrored sunglasses, an assertive look for Jack. People Seth barely knows come up to remind him who they are. Word has spread that Seth spends his days in the Martinez courtroom, so everyone has an opinion about the Martinez trial, or a favorite Martinez brother, or some pronounced disdain for the death penalty, based neither on morality nor squeamishness but on a feeling that the death penalty is not hip and that killing your parents is cool—but Jack, astonishingly, has actually had Sabrina Wilcox in his taxi, and Seth's able to deflect these draining conversations into Jack's zone of piquant trivia. Seth is a minor east coast curiosity in this crowd. JD, whom everyone knows rather well, has lots of people clinging to him, competing for his favor: JD is radio, and radio is important in L.A.

The swelling size of Norma's audience gives Seth an obscure pang. Because he notes with displeasure an ignominious wish (tonight only, suddenly) to play the part Norma usually casts him in, so that his own importance will manifest itself in the throng of Norma's followers. It irks and irritates to feel as unimportant here as Jack either pretends to feel or really does, though Sabrina Wilcox is presently lending allure to Jack's ego. Seth sometimes forgets that Jack's one published book of poetry made no impression on this particular regional elite, and when he remembers it, Seth thinks that Jack let himself get done in by their indifference. They were not bad poems, Seth thinks, just a bit overdeclarative and lacking that ineffable quality that makes something a poem rather than an irregularly laid-out piece of prose. But most of the poets jammed into this hallway lack weight, or resonance, or some other essential ingredient of high seriousness, and Jack at least prowls the nocturnal streets with a gun tucked under the driver's seat, capable at any moment of an awesome gratuitous act. Maybe. Seth murmurs in Jack's ear:

I'll be sorry to miss that crucifixion.

He looks at his own face bent out of shape by Jack's sunglasses.

Who knows? Jack says. Maybe they'll have one where you're going, too.

Norma does materialize, whether arriving in the hall before or after most have settled in the raked seats, Seth doesn't know. He hustles Jack and JD to the least conspicuous row, as he thinks, Jack pulling off his mirror specs en route, revealing a seriously bloodshot right eye, impatience, extreme fatigue. Seth squeezes Jack's sleeve, strokes his neck reassuringly when he sits down. Jack looks surprised, maybe grateful, and confused by the gesture.

Seth imagines Felix Martinez, magically free, anonymous, dropping into Beyond Baroque for a little alternative L.A. culture. This world would be terra incognita to Felix, who wants to be a writer according to courthouse gossip, but has probably never heard about writers who don't make money. Seth falls into a trance, the audience breaking down into colors, colors and haircuts, like geological strata, veins of crystal and amethyst in rock croppings, spattered by vegetation, draped with exposed roots, stained by patches of impacted dirt, fifty or sixty, he guesses, but in Seth's mind all breathing in unison, expanding and contracting like a stomach, the air in the auditorium smelling of school, chalk, disinfectant, cloying like a classroom, all clotted together in a shared suspension of disbelief, like the audience of a long tedious opera, sustaining an illusion of cryptic depths and shimmering meanings lost to the outsider but present and palpable to them. At first he waits in dread for Norma to appear, disdainful of Norma, intimidated by Norma, resentful of the smirking anticipation on certain faces, particularly those of the overdecorated, in some cases obscenely attractive young, reflecting that Norma Woolcoate's unsurpassed narcissism acts like a candle to the mothwing narcissisms of far younger people, for whom Norma Woolcoate's scatologies and gynocological fantasias represent something radical and subversive. Norma Woolcoate ropes in scads of disaffected literary theorists and emotionally damaged art students who pay, like Norma, an unseemly portion of their time on their physical appearance, which of course does make an undeniable impression.

As Seth ponders this, noticing how many in the audience have bits of metal riveted into various parts of their faces, something resembling a Hindu deity, swathed in weirdly draped billows of a gossamerlike white fabric, with the sheen of a black undergarment flashing in its interstices, a narrow, compacted, Kabuki-faced entity, sweeps grandly into the room, with an air of flushing everything from its path by some reverse suction of its grandeur. It is Norma. In the years he's known her, Norma has remained depressingly the same, yet her visual evolution has been prodigious, from waif to leather queen, from diminutive supermodel to what now looks alarmingly like Mothra. Her white face with its coal-black eyes scrapes across the audience, though Seth suspects that Norma sees and hears nothing, is blinded and deafened by the rush of adulation. He hopes, at any rate, that she doesn't see him, but of course it will be worse if she doesn't, and if she does, it will be worse still if he doesn't stick around to goose her ego after the reading.

I have spent this entire day squirming, Seth thinks. Norma is explaining the peregrinations of her world-swallowing mind, setting up the passages she will read from her novel-in-progress. Seth, who has heard Norma read at least a dozen times in as many years, can never distinguish one of these novels-in-progress from the other novels-in-progress, since they are all written in a language peculiar to Norma, a language which, in Norma's words, is meant to "be something" rather than "mean something." To be, he supposes, an object, some Mallarméan artifact, or perhaps even something more banal, like a toilet plunger, or a key ring. Seth has never read any of Norma's books, though he feels he's read all of them, not only the many she's written, but all the books Norma will ever write, and it now crosses his mind that each of Norma's books must be a vivid and distinct experience for Norma, while for him each of Norma's books is exactly the same book as Norma's other books. Norma's attachment to her own books can be measured by the fact that Norma not only writes these books and reads these books, but also memorizes these books. Norma's peculiarity as a reader is that she barely glances at these books while reciting them, in fact she is reciting now, in a strange new manner, a kind of Mother Goose manner, flapping the swelling sleeves of her modified nun's habit, as if ensorcelling a room full of preschoolers, in a singsong, strident little-girl's voice, a manner in which some coy novelty of defiance is operating, Seth can't exactly identify what this defiance consists of, but it's something to do with the intoxicating awfulness of Norma's writing, a shotgun wedding of the infantile and the obscene, and the fact that Norma happens to be a lot smarter than her writing—a kind of obdurate stupidity in Norma's writing serves as a wall between Norma and her audience, and the wall itself has become a sacred artifact in the realms of Norma.

Another gnawing thought nibbles the fringe of his gray matter. This while Norma declares that she is a female dolphin named Dido swimming in a school of dolphins somewhere near Madagascar. Dido is not a happy mammal. Like her antic, lovable fellow dolphins she scours the reefs and shoals of East Africa, devouring brilliantly colored fish, her dolphin consciousness transmitting her watery thoughts to earth scientists, but the disturbed nature of Dido's cosmic mind causes her to regurgitate most of her meals. She has some sort of dim cetaceous memory of abuse by her dolphin father. Norma has rendered the dolphins' speech as a sequence of vowel-laden grunts, cries, calls, warnings, and so forth. Dido's adventures include the discovery of a sunken freighter, quite possibly the ill-fated *Mary Celeste*, a battle with a great white shark, and many interspecies sexcapades with Wotan, a Hun biologist. Meanwhile, Bobby swims into Seth's cogitations, a charmed, ingenious fuck from three years ago, reincarnated in a 7-Eleven three thousand miles away from the site of their last coupling. He pictures Bobby in a marine setting, with fins, sluicing through the vomit-murky waters Dido has clouded with her bulimia, his sleek ten-inch dong torpedoing between Seth's open legs. As Norma's throbbing but hard-to-reach, gray-pink dolphin pussy wetly gyrates in the vicinity of Wotan's inflamed earth-member, Seth damply recalls Bobby's similarly heroic phallus embedded deeply inside him, and audibly sighs at the knowledge that this prize will once again be his, in all likelihood later this very evening.

After myriad adventures at sea, Dido assumes earth form, becoming an anarchist hooker named Dolores in Manhattan. At a decaying S&M brothel, Dolores and her skanky confederates plan the overthrow of the federal government. Though they are whores, they dedicate themselves to a world without men, extracting the sperm they need for reproduction via painful mechanical methods, and seize control of one of the prison ships on the Hudson River. Dolores's connection to the ocean, the tidal flow of her menstrual cycle, inspires several monologues about the moon, female astronauts, Georges Bataille, Jacques Derrida, Jacques Lacan, Dr. Jekyll and Mr. Hyde, and the conquest of outer space. Norma's audience, despite its collective affectation of enchantment, becomes restive as Norma brings her word magic to bear on various echoes of seventies feminism, perking up slightly when Norma describes the battle aboard the prison ship, a confusion of flashing cutlasses and decapitations, some of which has been cribbed from Aphra Benn. The convicts become the whores' slaves and sperm suppliers. Seth can almost feel Bobby penetrating him, Seth kneeling over an arm of the sitting room couch, Bobby ardently pumping away behind him. Seth has a vast repertoire of sex memories of Bobby, positions, expressions, improvisations, stuff with dildos, handcuffs, thongs, poppers, there was never any desultory or bored sex between them, and Bobby, as far as Seth could tell, seemed up for anything again, had even suggested locking the store and knocking off a quick one in the storage room, which Seth would have done if JD hadn't been waiting in the car.

JD and Jack throw impatient looks Seth's way, for Seth's amusement. Perhaps even for his comfort. Confirming that his opinion of Norma's work is so well known that his friends believe their scorn will give him pleasure. There's something too mean, too public about it. He would actually like to enjoy Norma's writing, has often tried. But similar looks flare among the audience, among the older, less readily awed witnesses, Norma's hard-core fans, all college age, strain against a general torpor to recover their enthusiasm. Seth notices various eyes raised to a clock on the far wall. It's as if almost everyone, at the same moment, has realized that Norma, who ought to be winding down about now, sounds like she's just getting started.

The quality of attention in the room starts to fray. Seth's noticed that people usually have a twenty-minute threshold at this type of gathering and Norma, now clocking in at close to an hour, has delighted everyone quite enough for one evening. The room becomes less careful about noise, coughs and whispers and the tinny rattle of shifting chair legs create a lowering change in acoustics. Seth, embarrassed, colors as if it were him and not Norma Woolcoate losing control of the auditorium. He feels a familiar, spontaneous protectiveness toward Norma, whose skill at mobilizing this feeling has not gone unremarked among her friends. Norma drones on, at first oblivious, then darting sharp looks at people sneaking away from their seats, then interrupts herself to say she has a few more pages, I can see some people are getting tired, she says without humor, but I just want to finish this because it makes sense of some of the earlier text, Yeah, sure, Jack whispers, causing a snort-suppressed fit of giggles to snuffle through JD's nostrils. Norma's announcement quiets about half the audience, but the other half, if not in open mutiny, continues to scrape and shift and murmur, Norma's recitation having hit a patch of such baffling opacity that no one has any idea what she's saying, and to make matters worse she suddenly resumes speaking in dolphin language, mooing out long Icelandic-sounding verbal squiggles, seal barks, throaty vowel arabesques, churning the diaphanous sleeves of her tunic in mimicry of porpoise flippers . . . yet, with a kind of showbiz surrender to her own absurdity, Norma sustains this really bad animal impersonation with such uninhibited zest that she actually wins back the feckless listeners who haven't already fled the place, some arrested in flight, truly startled by the incredible weirdness of what Norma's doing, her demonic abandonment of all dignity and imperiousness, groveling for their attention by any means available. As a finale, Norma releases a squalling, desperate, foghorn bellow from the pit of her diaphragm, a sound prickly with terror and madness, a genuine feat of vocalization which, unlike what preceded it, is something people in Norma's audience probably could not easily do themselves, in recognition of which their closing applause echoes like thunder through the building.

Now the complicated part, he thinks, as everybody he's already had to talk to pools into the lobby, surging around Norma, but instead it turns out to be the simple part, because Norma stares right through him when she sees him coming toward her, cutting him dead. Before he gets close enough to deliver his all-purpose line for this kind of aftermath—*Norma, you've done it again*—anticipating the forgiving hug, Norma's gelid expression spins him around in the other direction and pushes him out to the entrance arch, where a dozen people mill around gaping at the rain. The talk is all about Marvin Paley's crucifixion, scheduled in less than an hour from now, and JD, who wants Marvin on his show, is insisting to anyone who'll listen that *of course Marvin won't cancel his own crucifixion for a little rain, it was highlighted in the* Weekly.

Seth blames his adventures later that night on the speed hit JD gave him in the car, but in reality he drank much more than he realized (he confesses as much) at Teddy Wade's party, an event he describes in the darkest possible terms, starting always with the rainstorm churning the streets in Beverly Glen into dark erratic rivers, skidding at intersections, losing his way on unlit roads that snake into each other in confusing patterns, and it's true the downpour that night tops up the local reservoirs instead of missing them as usual, sends mudslides foaming through Malibu Canyon, right through houses, knocking homes off hillsides and devastating the areas scorched by the recent fires, besides causing an appalling number of freeway collisions. It keeps many of Teddy Wade's guests at home, and one reason Seth says he drinks too much there is that when he arrives, having driven straight past Teddy Wade's gate no fewer than six times because of some lacuna in his written directions (twice touring so far afield that he ends up in Benedict Canyon and passes the bottom of Cielo Drive, prompting him to hit the door lock control, ka-chunk, speed makes paranoid), he discovers that the only people who've braved the ugly weather, the only people keen or socially desperate enough to hazard the flood-maze of hills and spillways around Teddy Wade's sprawling house, are nonmovie people Teddy Wade and his wife have evidently culled from the B phone book. Brokers and entertainment lawyers, some actors from a local theater group, an assortment of museum curators, two Fox radio reporters Seth sometimes sees at the courthouse, several chubby children in baseball caps and Royal Hawaiian Hotel T-shirts, and a tight, forbidding claque of New Yorkers who put Seth's back up from across the living room before he even recognizes them.

The house has endless insides, what Teddy Wade probably calls "eclectic," Seth thinks, the front area mainly Southwest Industrial: distressed-steel furniture, sculpted floor lamps, Navajo rugs, sideboards with pottery, painted clay urns lurking in corners, humble-looking, priceless wooden tables, vanda orchids bursting from Chihuly vases, children's drawings framed beside Picasso lithographs, the rooms bloated, with cavernous ceilings, adobe-warm colors on the walls, yawning spaces Teddy's guests meander through like whirring particles. A perky assistant named Susan emits a practiced, thrilled noise when Seth identifies himself at the door:

Sporting of you to make it through this muck, she says, with warm insincerity, and waves him down a wide hall, past a vast room full of people and furniture, into a vast kitchen where uniformed waiters bus trays of champagne and beluga caviar. Teddy Wade stands near a tiled kitchen counter roughly the length of Versailles.

Yo yo yo, he greets, holding a large slice of turkey to his world-famous mouth. He pops it in, chews, and moves toward a lanky woman who fusses over chafing dishes on a Mario Bellini table. The woman looks up from a congealing expanse of croustades aux crevettes, an expression of frazzled welcome passing briefly over her stunning features. Teddy Wade hugs her like a vase.

This is my wife Janice, says Teddy Wade. Janice Wade licks sauce from her finger. She punches Teddy Wade in the stomach.

Go ahead, he tells her, breathless, throwing out the arms of his aubergine silk jacket. Shoot your best shot. These abs are like tempered steel.

You are strong, man of steel, says Janice Wade in an awed robotic voice. They begin tickling and grabbing each other, limbs darting and flailing defensively. Teddy pretends to dig in his nose for a booger and wields it like wolfbane. Janice straightens and coughs in a dignified manner. Welcome to our home, she says.

Seth wonders if their adorableness is something they work at in public, if it's natural or an exaggerated image that a Hollywood person would recognize as flagrant showbiz. They are so beautiful they could belong to another species.

Have something, Teddy tells him, marching out of the room behind a waiter. There's three tons of food.

Janice Wade snatches a champagne glass from a passing tray and hands it to Seth, watching intently as he sips it, like a movie poisoner. She's wearing an elongated black blazer striped in silver dots, matching flared crepe trousers, and a pair of orthopedic-looking white shoes, and she looks, Seth thinks, a little like Tuesday Weld, the same high glabrous forehead and flashing eyes and wide feline mouth, blond beatnik hair flowing across her shoulders.

There's food for forty people, she says a little sadly. A miscalculation, like the weather. Are you hungry?

Well, Seth admits, no, to tell you the truth.

Neither is anyone else. But of course it's early and they're trapped here. You interviewed Teddy? Was he incredibly pompous?

Oh no, not at all.

Well, that's a relief. We had a lot of whirling dervishes staying here last week. We're only now getting back to normal. Incense and anything whirling give me headaches and the house was full of it.

The perfection of the room's every detail and the perfection of Janice Wade belong to a level of endless wealth where life becomes punishing theater. Each awkward moment enlarges itself into existential monstrosity. And for this moment, it feels that the preceding high-spirited moments are about to crash down into queasy silence. Janice smiles, cryptically. She lifts lids from various chafing dishes and peers into them as if she expects to find her next line written in the food.

Come look at the house, she says at last, clattering a final lid. She leads him through a narrow hall at the north end of the kitchen, into a startling room containing two gigantic bamboo sofas, festooned with gigantic white pillows, a glass table mounted on a hundred-pound chunk of malachite, wicker chairs in bentwood frames, a putty-colored marble floor, and three altarlike teak panels, intricately carved, fretted, and perforated, inset with door-sized mirrors, running along the walls. On strips of sisal carpet more gigantic pillows are arranged in stiff symmetry, like seating for a Zen ceremony. A wall of this room is an immense glass sheet, offering a spattered black nonview of the mounting deluge outside.

All this is from Bali, Janice informs him, flipping a switch that lights up torrents of rain flooding the swimming pool. They pause uncomfortably for the appropriate long look. The ceiling is alang-alang, which is some type of reed. It's a pavilion ceiling copied from a Balinese puppet theater and the way it joins the old roof of the original house is quite remarkable when you see it from outside. That's a Gauguin, she adds unnecessarily, and in this case here is a Joseph Beuys . . . something or other, some scribbles of his, kind of pretty, don't you think?

There is no way of telling there's a party elsewhere in the house. The rooms are huge and go on forever, and have lots of smaller rooms clustered off them, rooms crammed with period chairs and settees and paintings and clocks and carpets and tapestries. The decor grows thicker and heavier as the rooms pass, Janice Wade pointing and naming things like a somnambulist, and it occurs to Seth that this walking tour may be Janice's way of escaping the party, or even some form of habitual inventory in preparation for a divorce.

This is really an incredible house, Seth finally says, for lack of something else to say, as Janice shows him a perfect little screening room tucked away like a jewel box. In the screening room are a black and silver Warhol Marilyn, two Cindy Sherman photographs, and a small painting by Cy Twombly.

It's what people do out here, Janice yawns. Fill houses. The more house you have, the more stuff you need to fill it. I wish you could see the garden. That's where I reign supreme among my catalpas and so on. I know, let's look at Teddy's bugs.

Teddy's bugs?

Yes, right down here. She flicks a light in a long narrow room. Walls are covered by lacquered trays of butterflies under glass, and along the walls run numerous glass vitrines of insects mounted on pins. Janice turns suddenly animated.

Look at these grasshoppers, she invites, they love to fester in meadows. Teddy catches them on Long Island. This species vomits on its enemies. I wish we could all do that. You can't find them out here. These yellow-green ones live in marshes.

Teddy collects these himself? He doesn't just buy them?

Oh no why would he he loves the thrill of the hunt. Which is why I tell him he can never be an authentic Buddhist. I read that certain Buddhists wear bells to warn the smallest ground-crawling creatures so they don't step on a soul, even the worms. But can worms hear bells I wonder? There are so many things in nature I don't understand. Teddy thinks people are like bugs. There are so many millions of different kinds but they're really all just rooting around for food, killing and eating other bugs. I mean we're more refined about it aren't we. It would be interesting if we all looked as different from each other as these things do, according to what type of bastards we are. Teddy and I are like dung beetles rolling all these objects into our lair. Here's a critter you don't see every day.

God. What is that.

Death's-head cock-a-roach, Janice says excitedly, native only to Key West. Then we have desert roaches. Creeeeepy. Note the hairy femora. Teddy finds them in Texas. They live in the nests of wood rats. Aren't these bizarre? Spotted water beetles? Such pests beetles but quite pretty. And this is the hairy bear beetle, with this reddish brown hair, and this metal-green head? What sort of deity would cook up something like that? Here's a skunk beetle, this black one, I'll bet you anything the soul of William Randolph Hearst migrated directly into something like this. Silver twig weevils, and these of course are moths. Moths are so extraordinary. I think they're subtler and prettier than butterflies really you wouldn't guess there were so many varieties. My god I've been keeping you from the party all this time.

No, this is fascinating. Thank you for showing me.

Janice urges him out of the room anyway, down through the endless house as if she has shown him something more intimate than insects. Seth finds her very odd.

Teddy never mentioned bugs in our interview, he says.

But you do like them, Janice queries nervously.

Oh, he says. What's not to like?

Now they're standing in the hall before the big open archway of the living room, about to go in. Seth is distracted by the appearance of a large, dressy object he recognizes, with horror, as Sheraton Pyle, a New York writer he was briefly friendly with eight or nine years earlier. Sheraton enters the hall like an idling bulldozer.

I knew I saw you come in, Sheraton gripes, wagging a fat reproachful finger, his manner obsequious and condescending at the same time. Sheraton is a massive black man whose girth, encircled in a light gray suit and black silk shirt, suggests a fortuitously even distribution of baby fat. His face is strangely genderless, and always makes Seth think of unbaptized baby souls trapped forever in Limbo. Sheraton's eyes obtrude unnervingly from tight, narrow sockets. His incessant grin, with an indecent length of pink tongue wedged between sparkling teeth, conveys a coy malevolence. His face looks like something carved from brazilwood to scare children.

Oh hiiiii, Sheraton, Seth dilates, willing a forced smile not to crumble, and attempts to air-kiss the vicinity of Sheraton's cheek. Sheraton's repoussé middle region obstructs him, and before he can recoil, Seth finds his face being crushed against Sheraton's soft, repulsive breast. Sheraton holds the embrace much longer than necessary, presumably to give Janice the impression that they are very close friends. She, however, has moved into the crowd.

What a small world, Seth hears for the second time that night.

Sheraton immediately begins digging around to discover what Seth is doing in Los Angeles, how Seth happens to know Teddy Wade, what kind of car Seth is driving, who Seth is sleeping with, where Seth is staying, and who Seth's L.A. friends are: for this type of grilling, Sheraton assumes a visage of utter surprise and naiveté, of real delight at seeing Seth, whom he hates, and who hates him. Seth resents Sheraton's *oh, the Marmont, I always love staying at the Marmont,* it conjures a horrible picture of Sheraton checking into the hotel and asking for *his usual room.* Sheraton offers that he himself is staying with Babe Sklar in Malibu, Babe Sklar being Sheraton's current meal ticket, a universally dreaded multimillionairess with significant Hollywood bloodlines and a fondness for leftist causes. Babe Sklar, Seth thinks, has sliced the balls off far better men than Sheraton Pyle with her breakfast butter knife, turned far better people into lapdogs and carriage blankets and little furry muffs with a wave of her magic checkbook. Thinking this, he feels slightly sorry for Sheraton.

He regrets this twinge of sympathy before he even knows why. It relaxes him enough to tell Sheraton what he's actually doing in Los Angeles. A fatal misstep. The workings of Sheraton's mind are sufficiently visible that Seth observes a sly pause in its gearworks as it absorbs a significant morsel of news. What possible value it could have for Sheraton, Seth can't guess, but that it has some, he plainly sees.

Are you, um, writing something about the trial? Sheraton's casualness is distinctly false. But really, Seth thinks, what possible harm could there be in talking about it?

I don't know, he says.

Sheraton makes a skeptical noise through his nostrils.

I really *don't* know, Seth shrugs, I just like going to trials. He wonders how he'd reply if Sheraton suddenly said: When did you ever have the money to just go to one and not write anything. He remembers that Sheraton can never accept a straight answer, that Sheraton's calculating brain always assumes some delicious secret lurking behind everything.

Again the pink tongue, the blazing teeth, the idiotic grin.

You and those trials, clucks Sheraton in a comic darky accent, as if Seth were a "character" defined by a handful of lovable foibles. Everything Sheraton says is a bid for some clammy, false intimacy. Is it hard to get in?

I have a press credential, says Seth, too quickly, forgetting for a pleasant moment that Sheraton Pyle has ranged all over the journalistic world in the years since their friendship, and would not be daunted or amazed by the words "press credential."

It's a very tiny courtroom, Seth fumbles. There's a few seats for the public but they get grabbed up at five in the morning.

How did you get a credential? presses Sheraton. Something is blossoming in his brain, its first little buds popping free of their embryonic goo.

Seth explains the Marshal's Office and the morning lottery, feeling with every word that he's relinquishing control of a mysterious, volatile substance. It's uncanny how perilous casual talk becomes around people like Sheraton Pyle, who has some blunt, efficient use for everything, like a battlefield chef. They wander into the party, where Seth wriggles free, joining the fringes of a conversation Teddy Wade's having with some actors from the theater group, who are in rehearsals for a play.

This is Mike, this is Cyrinda, this is David, Teddy says, this is Seth a wonderful writer from New York, Seth maybe you've heard of Howl Theater I'm on their board frankly David if every movie company in town can do it there's no reason you can't do a sniping for this play all those hoardings and construction sites where stuff was burned in the riot and that huge corner on Beverly it's always completely blitzed with concert posters maybe it's technically illegal but when did you hear of any prosecutions for that kind of thing.

They fine you plenty, another actor says. They are all talking at once, like kids clamoring for the teacher's attention.

I'm Imelda Marcos, a stout woman wearing too much eyeliner tells Seth, gobbling some vegetables from a plate she's holding.

You are?

In the play, Imelda Marcos explains.

Great, Seth says. That's great. He smiles. He hates theater plays. Imelda

Marcos grabs a short good-looking man who grins at Seth as he devours something that resembles veal or fish.

This is Ferdinand Marcos, Imelda says.

Sheraton hovers nearby, stuffing himself from a tall mess of salad, talking to two women who are talking about a German artist, Seth catches a bit of the dialogue and recognizes the story, an artist who sings Nazi songs in restaurants when he's drunk. The women can't seem to agree which of four or five well-known artists they're talking about, and Sheraton speculates that perhaps all four or five have the same unfortunate tendency.

We might bring *Life of Doris* to New York in the spring, Ferdinand Marcos, whose real name is William, tells Seth.

William has something of Teddy's mesmeric actor beauty, an aspect of soft clay molding itself into the shape of other people's desire. He gnaws his food as if eating pussy in front of an audience. Imelda Marcos darts worshipful looks at Teddy while nodding and grinning at Seth, her face running through a morphology of craven expressions like an electronic billboard in Times Square.

That's great, Seth replies, a little uncertain about how many people he's talking to.

It's really a great play, William says, as Sheraton, standing some feet behind him, catches Seth's eye and winks familiarly.

What's it about, Seth asks, vaguely agitated by Sheraton's movements.

Teddy hasn't told you? I'm surprised, he talks it up to everybody. It's a chamber piece about the last years in the life of Doris Duke. But actually there are flashbacks within the play, we have different actresses playing Young Doris, Middle-Aged Doris, and Old Doris, Cyrinda there is Middle-Aged Doris. It takes place in Hawaii where Old Doris adopts Chandi Heffner, who poses as a socialite but is actually a follower of some swami, and then Imelda and Ferdinand Marcos arrive. Imelda borrows five million dollars from Doris to pay Gerry Spence to defend her in court and there's a lesbian cabal sort of thing between Chandi and Imelda.

I'm also Barbara Hutton, Imelda Marcos interjects. Doris's chief social and love rival.

Look, says William, that old guy over there used to play tennis with Samuel Beckett. I'm Porfirio Rubirosa in some of the flashbacks.

Do you have to wear padding? Seth asks, but William isn't listening. As he looks around the room he has the sensation that the air has been replaced by a denser, less easily breathed medium. That the space between people is turning gelatinous. That the people themselves are strangely out of scale with each other—some tiny and evanescent, others enormous, like elephants. Voices clot in this atmosphere, becoming a variegated drone.

Seth passes from conversation to conversation, plucking champagne flutes from passing trays and draining them with no attention to how many he's had or what they're doing to him. Wherever he goes, Sheraton angles himself into his sight lines. People are drinking a lot, which isn't usual for this kind of party. The speed keeps him zipping along. At some point he traps himself in a cul-de-sac consisting of Sheraton, Babe Sklar, and Unguentina Carribou, the latter, weirdly enough, being the only other black person besides Sheraton whom Seth truly loathes. While it's hardly implausible to find them together, finding them together here strikes Seth as a grotesque statistical unlikelihood. In different regions of the middle past, they both used him viciously. Unguentina Carribou married early into an incredibly prestigious white publishing family, securing for her slender, rage-inflected memoirs of an entirely invented Caribbean girlhood the kind of inflated adulation Sheraton himself hopes to win for an ever-unfinished but often-announced first novel entitled *Mammy*. It is odd to see Sheraton flanked by the living embodiments of his ambition, especially when they're physically so much tinier than he is.

Babe Sklar is like a miniature pony. She wears a look of permanent surprise achieved by too many face-lifts. She never appears to speak, but rather to gasp in reaction to other people. She does speak, though, in a raspy voice that rustles with the secret life of money. She says things like Oh boy and What do you think? and Gosh, a perfected withholding acquired in the School of Warhol. She smiles at everything, as if beaming down from a planet of mildly drugged debutantes. Seth believes that if he suddenly confessed to serial murder, Babe Sklar would smile her toothy smile and say Gosh that's interesting. Her presence is like a ninety-pound tumor of gold bullion. In contrast, Unguentina Carribou has the kind of menacing changeability associated with African military dictators. She is a surpassingly ugly woman with lumpy features and a wardrobe of frilly faded dresses worn to evoke the gentility and dignified oppression of her island forebears. Tonight she resembles a faded cabinet photo, in a lace-collared sepia frock and a rope of seed pearls that look piqued at not being larger.

This whole Martinez business is so fascinating, Babe Sklar says brightly, plunging right in. Do you believe they were really sexually abused?

Unguentina Carribou rolls her huge eyes. It's a case of two monsters, she declares, killing two other monsters. You can imagine what would happen if two black children from the South Bronx were on trial for the same thing. The cries for blood! The outrage!

South-Central, chimes Sheraton, all soulbrotherly.

People seem reluctant to believe them, says Seth, simply because they're rich. He aims this at Babe Sklar, as if they are both rich. He dimly senses that he really says it because they are both white. Babe Sklar, however, isn't about to enlarge on the disadvantages of being rich or white.

One hears such odd things, she says.

Really odd things, Sheraton growls.

The whole Scientology angle, says Babe.

What is it about these sad unhappy white people, opines Unguentina, in a voice suitable for an off-off-Broadway stage, born with everything yet vulgar and resentful and finally murderous, cursed by their very blessings, I believe all their well-born luxury drives them to cannibalism, most particularly here in California. First the Manson family, now the Martinez family. Always seeming to involve a family, a twisted family of sad unhappy white people.

Actually they're Cuban, says Seth. Probably sad unhappy neighbors of yours I should think.

Cuba is a far cry from Montserrat, Unguentina snaps imperiously. Her precise island of origin has changed several times over the years. Sheraton, who was born in New Jersey, moved his own birthplace to Barbados the year he selected Unguentina as a role model.

Well what Scientology angle are you talking about, Seth demands.

Supposedly there's some involvement, Sheraton says vaguely. In certain aspects of the case.

Of course these sad white people are too rich to worry about the death penalty, Unguentina sighs with disgust. One doesn't find in these prisons built by the white man yet peopled by the black man any rich white people on death row.

And they ain't any rich black people to put on death row, says Sheraton blackly.

That's so true, Babe whispers, nodding.

There's always Michael Jackson, Seth suggests.

Why aren't you people eating, Janice Wade wants to know.

I'm stuffed, Sheraton says truly, drumming his belly.

Oh Janice, Babe says. That Twombly.

I know, says Janice. Isn't it?

This has been lovely, Janice, says Babe in a summarizing way.

Yes lovely, echoes Unguentina.

You're not going? Please, Janice says, visibly alarmed, waving at the room, stay, it's pouring outside, it's early.

Well we would, says Babe.

I have an early flight, says Unguentina.

Sheraton stays. He has his own car. A while later Seth finds himself alone with Sheraton once again, in a study where a Magritte hangs over the fireplace.

Holy mackerel, Sheraton says in his faux-darky voice, how much is that worth?

A million five, says Seth, who pretends to know about such things. What's all this alleged inside poop about Scientology?

Well I didn't say anything in front of Janice, says Sheraton, because I mean, you know, they're in the Order.

Why do I keep hearing this? It's like the Hollywood version of the blood libel. You can't even find it in the phone book but supposedly everybody on earth is in the Order. Kurt Cobain, River Phoenix, Margaux Hemingway—

Supposedly, says Sheraton, that judge in the Martinez case is.

Huh. Seth has to admit, though only to himself, that this really is an intriguing idea. I have a hard time picturing Rupert Tietelbaum, he says, in some Druid costume prancing around a satanic pentangle.

Why not, he wears those robes in court all the time, supposedly they—

What exactly do they do in this Order, has anybody ever gone into that? I am really curious, Sheraton, do they eat babies? Blow up nuclear plants? Litter indiscriminately?

I think it's more economic, Sheraton says, less sure of himself. Like the Masons or the Knights Templar or something. They control certain businesses. Video porn and I don't know what all. An economic conspiracy. See, what Babe heard, was that the Martinez father was in the Order too.

I can't avoid the feeling, Seth says, that this is horse shit.

Sheraton gazes covetously at the Magritte, which depicts a shotgun with a bleeding foot growing out of its butt.

Heather Locklear, he darkly japes. I've heard Heather Locklear, too.

Seth wonders as he leaves Teddy Wade's house if he is one of the faceless ones, a guest acquired for such affairs because he is available and temporary and easily pleased, invited as insurance, in his case, against an unlikely negative slant in his Condé Nast interview. Or if he has disappointed some pale hope they entertained after skimming his book, that he would turn out to be their sort of person. True, the Wades were nice to him, but Teddy's attention all evening was perfunctory, almost distracted. Babe Sklar is rich beyond avarice, Sheraton Pyle an amusing sycophant, Unguentina Carribou a classy gargoyle—and the others are, in various layers, the Wades' friends, associates, employees. But what, who is *he*? In their world, practically nothing, a stray mote from the middle rungs of the New York media ladder. Insignificant even at a party where nobody really important showed up.

Sprinting through the rain again, he feels a surge of drunken spite, a strangely consoling anger at his puniness in the place where he finds himself. Although his coordination is absurdly shot, the car keys slipping through his fingers as he squints in search of the door lock, the twisted quality of this anger is apparent to him, like the rage he felt against Mark whenever his, Seth's, bizarre behavior had driven Mark further away from him. *You need to decide what you're really guilty of, if anything,* the therapist said. He would try, then, conceiving of his self-contempt as a baroque penitentiary that some-one truly worthy of its prisoner would have the wit and strength to storm. *I think you're pooling all your little problems together to make one enormous problem too big to deal with.* He squats beside the Mazda's front wheel, grop-ing the wet gravel of the driveway. *Try to subtract your emotions from what's actually happened.* Now, that would be lovely: losing his keys, having to phone a cab or beg a ride from somebody, making nice with the dregs of the party while his clothes drip all over the sisal carpets. Even that little bit of distress would show everyone how drunk he was. *Ask yourself what it is that's making you think this way.*

He finds the keys under the car, the yellow plastic Hertz tag winking in watery blackness like a sentient evil totem, wrestles the door open while across the drive through a drizzle of willow boughs someone steps into the wan entry light from inside the house. Vague figures in the rain, voices splashing across the lawn, the wind tossing tree branches back and forth in the cool clean air. Headlights shatter across the glassy ripples scudding down his rear window as his tires crunch past the gate, way down at the bottom of the drive. It could be Sheraton Pyle's car, he thinks, Sheraton Pyle on his way to Malibu, or, who knows, maybe Sheraton Pyle thinks it's cute to trail him, with the storm beating up again, lashing the frantic wipers, the slick black road dis-solving between strokes.

He believes he knows the way back to a main road. He instructs himself to drive with extra caution, moderato cantabile, and is slow to notice that unless he shuts one eye the road splits into two ectoplasmic ribbons, with a third more solid one running below them, maybe it's stupid to poke the ejected cassette into the tape player but he thinks it'll perk him up, now with one eye closed he seems to be driving okay, it's weird how sober he feels with one eye squeezed tight and how trashed he is when he opens it. The lights behind him brighten, glare on the rearview mirror, and the pounding rap from the speakers with its lumbering refrain of *niggah niggah* creates the impression that the car right behind him probably is Sheraton Pyle's car, that Sheraton is tonight's wicked messenger, and it feels like the fumes of intoxication are burning off in the night air, leaving him lucid and powerful, pressing his shoe on the gas to soar off away from his pursuer, a little scarily because he knows, he can feel straight through the car's purring metal intestines that the brakes won't catch right on the inundated road, that a hard stop will send it flying sideways, but he's not afraid, the road being wide and untraveled, he simply wants to scare Sheraton motherfucking Pyle, throw a little terror into that miserable excuse for a life, show him how easily Seth takes chances, how at home Seth is on Los Angeles streets, in Los Angeles weather, the headlights surge up in the rain-slick rear window, ebb as he picks up speed, sneak up again, Seth imagines the driver nerving himself repeatedly against all caution, one mile, another mile, another mile of slithery blacktop, imagines him shitting razor blades as the needle climbs to seventy then eighty and the tires toss up scalloped troughs of water, Seth raps along with the music now, tries to, scrambling the words, he feels cool and stupid at the same time, abruptly eases up on the accelerator because the road in the mirror now is empty and black with steam or fog swirling off it, and to his sodden brain the suddenly vacant reflecting oblong is a mystery, a trick of vision, like the sudden jerking movement in his windshield, the running body lit up in a flash by his headlights that smashes the grille of his car with a hideous thud as loud and unexpected as a sonic boom, a noise with the snapping and crunching of bones in it.

In Dead Zone, an annually rechristened punk club off Ivar, Marvin Paley is dragged onto the main floor from an improvised dressing room by two tall blacks who look like basketball giants, the wrists of his outstretched arms lashed to a thick wooden plank, his crossed ankles roped to a second plank nailed perpendicularly to the first, while the drummer from Cunt, the band that's just played, beats out a frenetic, monotonous rhythm. The drums conjure a primal world, of mud below and an angry deity above, of ritual and abandon. The cross is laid on the grimy cement floor. Throngs of young people form a semicircle.

Marvin Paley is five foot seven, stocky, muscular, shaved bald, his sharply carved features immobile in a stoic mask, and much of his visible flesh is decorated in tattoo work. He's naked but for a Japanese loincloth, a kind of broad-pleated diaper. His assistants, also in white loincloths, alternately insert long needles into his body, with lugubrious ceremony: under his scalp, through his nipples, across his shoulder blades. It looks like precision work. His punctures commence weeping blood. Blood trickles over his skin like crimson ink.

The drums are deafening, hostile. The ritual does not need the audience. It draws its energy from itself, like sex. Marvin Paley winces, bites his lips as the long needles probe beneath his skin. But these expressions are "for" himself, involuntary, somehow hermetic. This is all the more menacing because Marvin's blood, infected with HIV, has an almost supernatural potency in the packed room, the rivulets dripping down his white flesh could just as well be rattlesnakes. At the same time, it would be completely uncool for anyone to show fear. The truly cool press closer and closer to Marvin's space, observing an invisible perimeter, but sort of testing its edges. Marvin, prone, stares at the ceiling, his mouth hanging open. Way in back JD struggles through gaps in the crowd. He's not interested in getting too close to Marvin—blood sprays— but he can't see anything. A few bodies behind him, Jack has just bought Frankie Lomax a tangy and refreshing Bloody Mary. They're both moving forward with caution. In the fifteen minutes since JD irritatedly introduced them, Jack has been trying, with limited success, to make himself interesting. Physically, Frankie reminds him of Juan. He also finds Frankie's speech defect incredibly attractive, a kind of penalty for beauty that makes Frankie mortal and vulnerable. Better still, Frankie can't pay for his own drinks and probably needs a ride somewhere.

Marvin's basketball studs, armed with new-looking hammers, position spikes against Marvin's wrists. There's a technique to driving the spikes through without hitting veins and little bones, JD read about it somewhere, but the visual is horrendous, the first nail tearing into squishy flesh sends up a big collective groan and a tall GQ type slumming near the front of the crowd faints and falls over. A major commotion as the guy's friends carry him out. JD wants to witness this, but it's grossing him out. He's hit the place in his speed high where each sip of his gin and tonic challenges his vomit reflex and all this blood everywhere isn't helping things.

Without thinking—well, he is thinking, it's obvious to him later on how fast and efficiently he thinks when he can't breathe for animal panic (grinds the transmission into park, jumps out into the rain, runs behind the car, catches a look at the blood-soaked T-shirt and chino pants, the battered head, runs back, reaches into the car to kill the lights, flicks off the tape player, and next thing drags the guy off the road by the flaccid arms, like a sack of potatoes), his brain's full of words like *hard time, vehicular manslaughter, CHP, California penal system,* and this is not something that can happen to him, this is not the next installment of his tarot hand, *this didn't happen* is what his mind tells his mind as he rolls the body over the lip of a shallow, springy culvert where it lands with a dull splash and watches it settle facedown in the muddy runoff. The world is silent again except for the seething rain and the hollow sound of the wind ripping through it, like a sheet flapping on a clothesline, and the Babylonian chatter in his head. He staggers back to the car, vibrant with fear, weightless, sits behind the wheel for a moment without doing anything, soaked to the skin, breath labored, heart hammering, incapable of reckoning, switches on the headlights, slams the door shut, decides that his adrenaline-drenched sobriety would never fool a breatholator, throws the Mazda into gear and drives away. He's pretty sure he's on Beverly Glen, pretty sure the next major intersection will be Sunset, and pretty sure he can get away with this, that if he gets caught he'll be sober when that happens. The seriousness of the charges dropping in direct proportion to his blood alcohol level. He'll stop somewhere far away, somewhere safe, and check the car. If there's damage he'll have it fixed at some discreet garage—Jack will know a place, cabdrivers have accidents they need to cover up to keep their medallion. He'll tell Jack he hit a cement post in some parking lot. Or something.

Marvin Paley is completely crucified. Sweat and blood roll down his body as his assistants, their chestnut flesh oiled with sweat, hoist the cross at an angle that displays the nailed body to dramatic advantage without shifting its entire weight to the spikes holding it in place. Marvin looks less like Christ than like a stout, vaguely Aryan avatar of Vishnu, covered as he is in tattoos of barbed wire, ferocious green dragons spitting flames, and Chinese idiograms. Harsh spotlights and popping flashbulbs give a solarized look to Marvin's ensemble, the look of a hallucinated autopsy, flesh become quivering yet dead thing. The club smells of damp cement, since all the doors and windows are open to the rain, and JD thinks of Marvin as an offering to the Storm God, as well as one amazing exhibitionist. He dislikes this mortification of the flesh stuff but it's the kind of thing his drive-hour audience can't get enough of. He can already hear the call-ins, from pain freaks all over the county, enraged Christians, curious housewives and know-it-all psychiatrists. JD feels a rating surge coming on.

Out on Selma, in the creepy darkness of a row of rotting bungalows, Frankie and Jack do 69 in the cab of Jack's panel truck, rain throbbing on the roof. Jack is marveling at his unexpected fortune, willing his gag reflex to go away, a little paranoid about the random-killing neighborhood, while Frankie, who finds Jack's average organ easy to accommodate, debates the wisdom of lifting Jack's wallet from the jeans bunched around Jack's legs. 69 confuses Frankie, as it scrambles the priorities. As far as he's concerned it's better to receive than to give, and though he senses that Jack's a big giver, an over-the-hill type who knows he must give plenty for something as young and desirable as Frankie, Frankie can also tell he's the type that demands something back, that Frankie's usual I'll-lay-back-and-let-you-worship-me posture doesn't quite meet the occasion, especially in these damp clothes. So he starts sucking with some attention to nuance, though this makes his own penis go numb, thankfully still good and hard but barely sensible of Jack's efforts to pleasure it. 69 confuses Jack, who, as a point of fastidious safety, has decided not to ejaculate, so concentrates on Frankie's penis instead of his own.

The only light in the television room is the nighttown glow of the hotel's neon sign. Susan Hayward sits up suddenly in her slip, tossing her hair in a honky-tonk imitation of Rita Hayworth, lights a cigarette, hands it over her shoulder to the trick lying beside her. With a grunt of animal satiety, restless fingers handjiving to the bebop coming in from the street, she slithers out of bed, pulling the sheet down, her body prowling the room—this girl has to move, has to dance—as Seth lies in the dark, a pain that feels like brain damage stabbing behind his right eye. In fresh jeans, fresh socks, fresh T-shirt. Ten minutes under icy shower wearing his wet clothes, rinsing out possible forensics. He thinks: mud on dress shoes I bought in Chicago and only wore tonight for maybe third time. He thinks: soil sample on rubber mat under floor pedals. He thinks: dumpster in parking lot of liquor store on Hillhurst. He thinks: car wash on Third Street. She looks at the guy's open wallet on the dresser, the picture of the wife and kids in the glassine pocket. The rattle of a key in the door: the fat vice cop seen a few minutes earlier lumbering into the jazz club. He thinks: who, running in a rainstorm, in Beverly Glen—? He thinks: I don't even know what he looked like. Skinny. Dark. Young. Pictures: photo of victim pushed across table in interrogation room. I've never seen this person in my life. Susan Hayward locks herself in the bathroom. The vice cop bursts in, the squat essence of every piss-smelling plainclothes J. Edgar Hoover wannabe of the 1950s in crumpled trenchcoat and snap-brim hat. *Hey, what is this?* says the trick. *Come on, get out of here, where's the girl? What girl? All right, come out. You heard me I said come out.* Behind the door, Susan Hayward flushes the toilet. Comes out, dressed. Flippant. *Trick: Let's not make a federal case— Cop: It is a federal case, ever hear of the Mann Act?* Bobby's soft knock on the sitting room door.

Barbara Graham: *Just a minute, copper. Did you and your runny-nose witnesses check on who was gonna pay for the room? Me!*

Seth: Hi baby. *Oh god. Long-lost penis. I've actually killed somebody.*

Bobby: Hey. *Looks like shit and all freaked out as usual and I'm hard already, go figure.*

Seth practically drags him into the dark sitting room and begins fooling with Bobby's complicated belt. Bobby squeezes Seth's ass, still nice and firm thank Christ, sucks his mouth. Seth feels Bobby's huge erection through his jeans.

Cop: *Know what you're saying? What you'll be charged with?*

Barbara Graham: *Yeah I know and it's a misdemeanor, no federal rap. I've been there before.*

Bobby: You look kind of—*like you got your head all scrambled up like the song says if he gets complicated & starts raving like he used to I'll squat on his mouth & make him eat it.*

Cop: *All right. Come on.*

Seth: Yeah, I—*because it didn't happen, misdemeanor vehicular homicide it was his fault anyway oh man that bone he can rip me open & kill me, fine, leaving the scene of a two-to-five-year felony & what if they find the charge sheet from '75 previous record never indicted what happened to my fucking eye if it didn't happen in my head it didn't happen, maybe, they say a true socio-path can pass a polygraph they don't feel any guilt.*

Bobby: Rough night, huh? *showing his age why doesn't he stay off the juice how he keeps his hole so tight with all the stuff he puts up there he'll like it if I toe-fuck him afterwards or fist him without a glove no cuts on my fingers fuck-ing toenails though so what maybe that floor lamp or the TV remote.*

Seth: Oh man I can't even tell you. *if he doesn't put a rubber on I won't stop him but I should stop him I shouldn't kill people either but there it is get the carpeting shampooed in the car the rubber mats are glued down get a sponge and something heavy-duty like Drāno, rubber gloves, stick the shoes in that dumpster.*

Bobby: Let me get comfortable—

He pulls off his shoes, yanks the belt off, his pants drop to the floor.

Barbara Graham: Get your paws off. I soil easily.

Seth kneels at the plump scrotum. Pulls at the taut seam of Bobby's bikini briefs. Licks a salty bulb of testicle.

Bobby: That garage is open all night, isn't it? I forgot to ask.

Bobby pulls him up to his mouth, sticks his finger between Seth's lips. Reaches under Seth's crotch and squeezes the finger into his asshole, twisting it in up to the knuckle.

Bobby: How d'ya like that new R.E.M.?

Trick: Life is funny, isn't it.

Barbara Graham: Compared to what?

PART TWO

—————

quake

Toward the end, when his father had his thing in him, Felix pretended it was Pete Sampras or the guy from Duran Duran, Sampras right after that first pro final in Philadelphia against Gomez, if he was going to get fucked hard, if he had to hear *aww that's right take that big hard dick,* he had to imagine somebody closer his own age, who might be a real animal in bed but gentle and kind of innocent afterwards, somebody whose rutting sweat would have the smell of sharp young funk instead of aging pituitary glands, wrinkled balls and Vaseline, Pete Sampras would do him with a degree of tenderness, he thought, whereas Fidel made him feel like what he now recognizes as a bitch, somebody's bitch in a prison, and when he thinks about his room in the house on Woodrow Wilson Drive he thinks of it as a prison cell, thinks of Fidel as the prison warden and Peggy as the prison matron, though Peggy was really just as trapped there as he was, locked up in a dreamworld with her Valium and highballs, an inmate with keys to the medication cabinet, he thought maybe Peggy never sucked Fidel or let him fuck her in the asshole and that was why he had the mistress in New York and Leona Finkelstein at the office and why he did Felix too though it was more than that, because Fidel growled things during the act like this pussy hole is mine and this fuck hole belongs to me and sometimes to prove it he'd shove most of his hand in or stick things up there, the handle of Peggy's hairbrush or the base of the Water Pik, and make Felix march around the room with half of whatever it was dangling out of his rectum, toward the end Fidel started calling that giving Dad a little fashion show sometimes slapping Felix's buttocks as he awkwardly paraded past, this was after Fidel found out God knew how that Felix had had a bunch of pictures taken for a modeling portfolio, he now guessed Peggy'd heard something about it from tapping his telephone, strut that moneymaker, Felix, give your old man who fucks that good-for-nothing faggot fuck hole a little fashion show, real sarcastic, like no way could Felix even be a good model, as he got older Felix had to wonder about his father's father and his father's mother but he just couldn't picture his grandparents doing stuff like this, the way everybody in the family told it Fidel had been the golden boy down there in Havana before Castro that godless bastard came down the mountains and took over everything, nobody ever raised a hand to Fidel, sometimes Felix pictured his dad getting ass-fucked by Castro while Castro puffed a big cigar but of course nothing like that ever could have happened. His father was a man. You were still a man, even more of a man, when you fucked another man. When a man fucked you, then you were a maricón. That maricón Castro has got no balls, his father said. His father said that when they moved to Florida, when Felix and Carlos finished college, or maybe even before then, they would live in a big walled compound just like the no-balls bastard Kennedys, his father would run for the Senate from Florida and build a huge base of support and then finish Castro off for good. They would get the Martinez houses and the confiscated Martinez bank accounts back when that lousy faggot Castro was swinging from a lamppost just like Mussolini. Felix believed that his father could kill Castro, there wouldn't be any Bay of Pigs fiasco with his father in charge, *I will never consider defeat,* Fidel made them say it ten times a day, *I will remove from my vocabulary such words and phrases as quit, cannot, unable, impossible, out of the question, improbable, failure, unworkable, hopeless, and retreat, for these are the words of fools.* Fidel would win. Fidel would always win. A winning attitude was everything in life. Felix remembers the sex with his father turned really ugly when Fidel decided Felix had not a winning but a losing attitude, a weak sensitive attitude like Peggy, that Felix was not a Spartan warrior but a sissy loser and a faggot. In Sparta the love between man and boy had been a noble practice that prepared a youth for manhood, it was different than a man fucking a maricón, you fucked a youth to make him manly but you fucked a maricón to humiliate him.

It feels like they've been in court for twenty years. Strangely enough he only feels halfway normal and safe in his cell, because here he sits the way Lauren tells him and looks the way he's been told to look and the jurors are watching him for signs, they can consider your demeanor as part of their deliberations, if you looked guilty or moved or contrite or what have you, and a lot of his energy every day is burned up trying to stay awake, working some appropriate human expressions into his face, fighting off the torpid slackjawed incontinent idiot gaze the drugs would otherwise settle there, and Felix thinks if this nightmare ever really does end he will write an essay about defendant lethargy in capital cases, revealing that besides flight or fight in the face of deadly peril the human mammal has the third option of falling asleep when the danger is infinitely prolonged, the threat wrapped in weird procedural jargon like insulation around electrical wires. But it's never going to end. Felix knows this. Lauren thinks his jury's going to hang and the D.A., who looks like he's rotting inside from some wasting moral disease, has his reelection at stake in nailing them. And Tietelbaum has been bought and sold so many times by the dark Republican powers that be, look at the prisonguard beating trial and the Ventura County sewer fiasco. Carlos is still absurdly confident, planning his Oscar performance on the stand, it hasn't really sunk in with Carlos yet that he might never walk around outside again, never drive a car again, never do anything again except eat and shit and sleep and maybe get stabbed by some enterprising inmate, Carlos talks about good odds, odds on manslaughter, odds on acquittal, 5–7 odds on a hung jury, and he's blabbing a lot to that tub of lard Doris the garbage woman with her stupid newsletter for losers, Lauren's paranoid about all these phone calls Carlos makes from the jail, she says his big mouth will come back to haunt them in a retrial, and that Doris, says Lauren, I mean, could she be a little fatter? Cousin Bette is on the stand, no size 3 herself, recalling the summer she stayed with them in Mugdale, a time Felix barely remembers: he must have been ten or eleven, when he and Carlos jumped her on the living room couch, Carlos stuck his hand up her shirt and squeezed her tits and told Felix to finger her pussy but Felix just hugged her leg and rubbed his crotch there like a dog, it didn't really excite him that much, it scared him, and anyway Bette pushed them right off, she says now when she told Peggy that Peggy blamed her for running around in shorts with her blouse flapping open, Bette says what stands out that summer besides this couch episode is Peggy driving them around the country-side at seventy dead drunk, Peggy ripping up the lawn with the station wagon, plus Fidel's history and current events quizzes at dinner, that if Carlos or Felix didn't answer the quiz questions correctly Fidel sent them off to look it up in the encyclopedia or what have you right in the middle of dinner, plus Fidel whipping off his belt and smashing it down on the dining room table when someone was going to be punished, plus the way Fidel marched Felix off to his room and disappeared in there for hours at a time and how nobody could use the bathroom at that end of the hall during these mysterious punishment sessions, plus all the weird stuff with Peggy's ferret, and how Bette once found a turd in a Tupperware bowl under Felix's bed, hearing Bette testify about it makes Felix see how weird their lives really were, how twisted and sour and shabby they all looked to the few outsiders that spent a lot of time with them, how pathetic spending all day doing laps in the pool was, and later on the 5 A.M. tennis practice, and Fidel's so-called boxing lessons, and the mealtime drills, pathetic because all this pointless exercise and so-called intellectual training never added up to anything, it never made them any different than what they really were, Carlos was never a real person and Felix never added up to a real person either, they were so desperate to satisfy their father and keep their mother from sliding into her insane rages or some sodden suicidal depression that they grew up like dolls, dolls that would say whatever Fidel and Peggy wanted them to say, dolls that did whatever Fidel and Peggy wanted them to do, with no real will or personality. And how weird it was when anybody did visit, if Carlos brought a friend home or relatives came the family closed ranks around its secrets and playacted the script of a more normal family, Peggy would say things and Fidel would say things that were just plain lies, lies about little things for instance how everybody spent his day, the kinds of activities they had as a family, the grades he and Carlos were getting in school, but it was mainly this overwhelming feeling that you had to put up a front and look different, look happy, and never allude in any way to the sad things that happened all the time. If people came for a long visit the craziness eventually spilled out everywhere, Felix can see this now a lot more clearly than he did when they lived in Mugdale or Kalamazoo. For example Peggy's fits, which no one could ever predict, though if he thinks about it now he's pretty sure these fits came on when his father called from the office and told her he'd be spending the night in New York, she'd wait until the kids came in from school before smashing all the plates and glasses in the house, sometimes a whole stack of plates or a whole shelf of glasses, muttering dark things to herself, and she would tell them, in the blind drunk voice of some-body unsure about who exactly she was talking to, that her life had been ruined once by Fidel Martinez and ruined again by giving birth to them, and sometimes when they begged and pleaded she pretended to calm down, let her children lead her out of the mangle of crockery and broken glass, would settle her fat ass at the dining room table, smiling stupidly at her own annihilating thoughts, and then all calm and almost sober-sounding mention that she was thinking of burning the house down, what was their opinion on that, or maybe, just maybe, when their father got home she might take the shotgun they kept in the hall closet for protection and end her troubles then and there, either by shooting Fidel or shooting herself, it didn't matter which. What he remembers most clearly is that he and Carlos didn't figure at all in these monologues, what would happen to them if the house burned down or Peggy shot herself never got articulated in her zonked calculations. Marlene Quilty doesn't want all this testimony getting in, but Tietelbaum says the prosecution should've litigated all these witnesses in pretrial, the horses are out of the barn. Aunt Thelma for instance who lived across the road from them in Pennington, out-side of Pennington, tells how three-year-old Felix wandered out of the house and across the road without Peggy even knowing, that's how much attention Peggy paid, Felix could've been squashed in passing traffic, and once he got to Aunt Thelma's he never wanted to go back. Peggy drank, Aunt Thelma tells the court, She wanted to go to nightclubs. Fidel was the first one out of Cuba, always the first in everything. He always told the story about burning down the dance floor at the country club down there, how they'd covered the swimming pool to make a dance floor for some big event and Fidel set fire to it with a liter of gasoline he'd siphoned out of the family Buick, how the family paid ten thousand dollars cash for the damage and Fidel never even got a lecture for it. Fidel always told that story to show how bold and unusual he'd been at an early age, in contrast to the two pale shadows he'd gotten for sons. It was mainly to prove he could do something just as ballsy as Fidel that Felix did the robberies in Hidden Hills, but in Fidel's mind the two things were totally different, all the stuff Fidel did and got away with happened in Cuba, where no one could honestly say what a crime was since the country was run by criminals. And in case Felix had some smart-ass thing to say about that, Batista was a criminal too, as a matter of fact they had welcomed Castro in the beginning, imagining that he would usher in democracy.

You did not show emotion in the Martinez house—Cousin Vincent now, who heard the beatings with Fidel's belt, witnessed Peggy's fits, when Felix was he forgets how old Vincent stayed for the summer, and the summer after, a cousin on Peggy's side, Vincent had been diddled too by Peggy's brother Felix thought but maybe it was a swimming teacher or some friend of the family, Felix remembers playing with Vincent's cock, he remembers the field behind the house and how big and blue the sky was, and the sound of the wind shirring through the tall weeds, they lived in Michigan the summer Carlos made Felix lie on the ground and pushed a crooked twig up his bum, Vincent says Peggy locked him in his bedroom at night and he used to pee out the window, all these little details Felix never even knew about, or if he did he's forgotten them, bruises on Peggy's face, sounds of blows behind his parents' door, what Felix remembers and Carlos really doesn't is the stuff with the car keys, yet Carlos would be sitting right there every time it happened. Peggy would be drunk, not just drunk but losing her coordination because she'd taken pills on top of the liquor, yelling at Fidel, that he never took her any-where, she wanted to go dancing, or wanted to drink at the country club, she was sick of sitting on her ass in the goddam house, Fidel yelling back for a time until he saw nothing was getting through to her, this was always in the kitchen or the dining room and Peggy predictably lurched off into the bath-room and disappeared in there and Fidel then rummaged through her purse, took out the car keys and hid them somewhere, always in front of Carlos and Felix, he'd stick the keys on a shelf or somewhere in the cabinets under the sink or the clutter of cookware under the stove or slide them under the cush-ion of Peggy's favorite chair, when they heard the toilet flushing Fidel ordered them to sit up and talk to her, listen to her stories, keep her talking, not in his usual braying field marshal's voice but with the whispering suggestive unction of conspirator and prankster, this was always torture because Peggy would talk to them normally for a few minutes, seemingly happy to be paid attention to, and then her anger would flow up into her face and her fist smacked the table and she screamed out accusations, incoherent threats, slurry maledictions that poured from her throat like some corrosive industrial solvent, at those times Peggy looked like a monster flailing around in an invisible tempest, until her contorted face dropped into her arms and she passed out, but never for more than a few minutes, slowly the head would rouse and the glassy eyes blink and the mouth open she would start to tell them a story, sometimes it was the story of losing Felix and Carlos in the shopping mall, which had actually happened many times but collapsed into one interminable anecdote in Peggy's synapses, and halfway into the story she'd lose her way, her mind clouded over and she started the story again, she said the same thing over and over until the raging part of her brain foamed over and the screams came up, sometimes they sat there for hours watching this madwoman and smiling and begging her to tell the story again, both of them miserable and terrified, as not far from the dining room table or the kitchen table was the hall closet where the shotgun was, and Peggy often talked about the shotgun, or even without mentioning the shotgun made the presence of the shotgun somehow conspicuous in their minds, and when at last after two or three or four hours of dirgelike reminiscence and raving Peggy roused herself from her sitting position, looked for the car keys in her purse, and dimly realized Fidel had once again hidden the keys, when Peggy commenced poking into the cabinets and peering under the cushions and snuffling around the house, Fidel usually hovering just out of sight, or sometimes shut up in their bedroom with the door locked, emerging at hourly intervals to monitor the family comedy, as Peggy staggered about pulling open drawers and making things crash she wobbled meaningfully toward the hall closet many times in the course of her peregrinations, never actually opening it or if she did open it gazing stupidly into it pointedly ignoring the shotgun, and Felix knew though he didn't know that this was all deliberate, all contrived to put the fear of the shotgun into their little hearts, since after a time it had dawned on both brothers, though they couldn't have put it into words, that if Peggy never mentioned them when she talked about shooting Fidel, it was because she would just naturally take them down at the same time.

And he remembers something else, something that now seems more important than the rest of it: sometimes, instead of exhausting herself and passing out, Peggy found the hiding place, gleefully brandished the keys, and headed for the front door. And at the same moment, no matter where he had been in the house a second before, Fidel appeared beside her, and struggled with her—as far as Felix can recall, Fidel always managed to slip the keys out of Peggy's grasp and distract her somehow and hide them again, until she finally lumbered off to bed, or passed out, as she often did, sitting on the toilet, sometimes clutching one of the stuffed ferrets from the mantelpiece in a fierce maternal hug. But Felix remembers one particular night, one particular struggle over the car keys, when he and Carlos, aghast, sat watching from across the dining room, that in the heaviest part of that violent tangle of hands and fingers and faces and voices Peggy stopped suddenly, froze like a statue, and Fidel froze exactly the same way, that they both looked down that long room at their petrified children, giggled, then looked at each other and burst out laughing, like actors in a play who'd wrought the intended effect on their audience.

Portia Van Sustern reminds herself that if she gets on the 210 going home, that turns into the 110, and, given her photographic memory for surface roads, she can probably find the Trader Joe's in Glendale and redeem herself for this awful masochistic trip to Altadena, where the ugly streets and uglier homes are a powerful reminder of everything she's managed to avoid in California since her days as a secretary at CAA. With this same retention for little nuances in ghostly stretches of fallow lawns, twisted tricycles rusting on hopeless porches, fire hydrants, minimalls, gas stations, and strangely angled intersections, she's able to radar in on Cass Lomax's dreadful neighborhood while tapping numbers into her cell phone and booking callbacks for twelve people on her client list, mentally rolling a shopping cart through the always busy aisles of Trader Joe's, reflecting too that saving the hundred or so dollars she'd otherwise spend in Westwood is also a form of masochism, since being able to pay West Side prices for everything is what it's all about, but then again, Portia sighs to herself, I am a masochist, why else would I be here? She parks her black BMW in the empty driveway—there is no garage, just the driveway—and, armed with the blue-bound script, cell phone, and a pack of Carletons, marches to the back of the squat stucco house, passing under a rotting trellis with some sort of desiccated kudzu fibers dangling from its joints. She pauses to survey the swimming pool, its surface a veil of yellowed eucalyptus leaves, the sad aluminum lawn chairs, the unclipped hedges that've engulfed the cyclone fence.

Through her own wan reflection on the sliding glass doors, Portia makes out Cassandra's gloomy bedroom, a huge bed afroth with rumpled sheets and blankets and myriad embroidered throw pillows, facing a 36-inch flat-screened Sony on which Carlos Martinez, in an ecru sweater and light blue shirt, testifies in the famous murder trial. And in the bed, sitting up, dressed in a varicolored muumuu made of some unpleasant fabric, Cassandra herself, looking every inch the alcoholic reprobate. The room itself makes no concession to aesthetics. It looks vaguely like a porno set. Portia slides open one end of the door and pops into the room, feeling very imperious and professionally thin in her olive pants suit. This causes no reaction from Cassandra, who, on closer inspection, turns out to be asleep. The only sounds in the room are the metronome voices of Carlos Martinez and Sarah Johnson. *Did you want to do something to help your brother? Yes. And did you have an idea how you were going to handle this?* Portia shakes her roughly. Cassandra opens her eyes, focuses, screams.

Cass, it's me! Portia assures her, as Cassandra cowers, arms akimbo, fingers clenched in a pose remembered from a Joan Crawford poster, and attempts to slither off the bed.

Just to tell my dad the same thing that I had done before, it obviously didn't work, but I'd been able to talk to him about it—

Who are you, Cassandra gasps in a terror-stricken voice, the one she used to such camp effect in *Satanic High School* (1988).

I told my brother I could sit down with Dad when he came back, and essentially, we held all the cards, and if I needed to, I could threaten to tell people—

It's Portia, PVS croons soothingly, drawing upon six long-ago months as a psychiatric nurse's aide. I'm your agent.

Cass, crouching now on the floor as if preparing to bolt for the depths of the house, squints skeptically at this pale, skinny apparition.

What are you doing here? she rasps, echoing the pediatrician/stalking victim she portrayed in *Nightmare Nursery* (1985).

I got up and said Dad, I'm only going to tell people if you don't stop touching Felix, and he just looked at me and said you're going to tell people anyway.

Oh for pity's sake, says Portia girlishly, helplessly lapsing into the cheery cadences of Serena, the nubile apprentice vampire who costarred with Cass on *Vampire Cop*. Three of the four Serenas the show had cast over the years were Portia Van Sustern clients. How is anybody supposed to reach you with your phone disconnected?

I paid the goddam bill, Cass whines furiously, punching the bed. She lunges suddenly for the blue script folder. Portia tugs it back.

It was a disaster. I'd just made it a hundred times worse.

Cahill Dunleavy weren't sure you'd want to work so soon after your recent tragedy, Portia tells her with a soupçon of menace.

What did you think was going to happen?

Which tragedy, Cass grumbles.

I thought we were in danger, that he would kill us.

The tragedy of Gus getting fried like rice in that fire, Portia tells her, remembering expository characters in Dario Argento films. The tragedy of losing your alimony payments and the tragedy of Frankie being left out of the will. That tragedy. Look, I've got you reading for this in three days, and if you get it, it's nice money and a serious treatment of a contemporary issue, namely this trial you're watching right now on your television—

For a moment they both gape at the TV.

I realized that my dad at some point sort of coming forward in my direction and then I remember firing directly at him. There were things shattering, and the noise was phenomenal, Carlos Martinez is saying.

I wasn't watching it, Cass says with dignity, composing herself. They want me to play that lawyer with the hair?

The mother, Portia says, with ardor. The mother that these boys are painting as a monster, except that in *Dark Blood*, Cass, this mother is a victim, a well-meaning woman on a downward spiral, trapped in a *loveless marriage*—plus, they're shooting this soon, they might be able to air it before the trial's over. I won't lie to you, you weren't their first choice, and they definitely want to test you. But. The guy they signed for the father checked into Betty Ford and he's being replaced by Teddy Wade.

I'm old enough to be Teddy Wade's grandmother, Cass moans, groping under the bed for a bottle of Stoli she's sure was on the night table.

See, Portia chirps, that's one of the tensions in the marriage, her being a few years older than him. Teddy's playing him old, so it's not a mega difference, eight years. They've also got Matt O'Reilley from *The Adorables*—big hit Spelling series, Cassandra, I'm sure you haven't seen it—playing one of the boys. A breakout role for Matt. And a great comeback project for you, Cass.

The Martinez trial is all anybody talks about in this town. And, get this, they're using *the actual death house* in the movie. The minute I read this I told Cahill Dunleavy, Cassandra Lomax is Peggy Martinez.

Yeah, *dead*, says Cassandra. Since when does Teddy Wade do television?

Don't tell me you missed him in *An Ordinary Heart*, Portia clucks, reminding herself, a shade uncomfortably, of Cassandra's portrayal of the fast-talking theatrical agent in *Glitter and Goldfarb* (1979), her last really prestige project. People are talking Emmy.

People are talking homo, is what I heard, says Cassandra. Triumphantly her fingers lock on what is certainly the neck of a large bottle.

Portia is already speed-dialing her office on the cell phone.

I think I'll just send someone over and get your phone bill taken care of, she says.

Carlos Martinez remembers entering the darkened room, the so-called rumpus room, where Fidel and Peggy Martinez were supposedly eating ice cream and watching *It's a Wonderful Life*, with his shotgun held forward, the butt resting against the shoulder of his cardigan, an aqua cardigan he later disposed of in the trash Dumpster of the Laurel Canyon Pick 'n Save, he recalls firing the first round of buckshot *at the dark shape of my father*, who may or may not have had time to say "no, no," upon noticing the dark shape of Carlos, neither Carlos nor his brother could remember afterwards if Fidel had actually shouted "no, no," but they are both certain that Peggy didn't scream, didn't say anything, according to Carlos it was too dark to see anything clearly, it's his own impression that both Peggy and Fidel were standing rather than sitting, menacing dark shapes in the dark coming forward, and the smoke from the first and second rounds of buckshot obscured everything even more, Carlos claims that Felix didn't fire his own shotgun as he was supposed to, that Peggy jumped away and began scrambling toward the hallway leading into the depths of the darkened house, which was when Carlos turned his shotgun away from his father and fired at his mother's back, the blast knocking her sideways against the so-called souvenir shelf, dislodging several items, including a large bronze tennis trophy won by Felix in the South Covina Tennis Tournament the previous winter, according to Carlos the South Covina Tennis Tournament trophy struck Peggy on the head, without however rendering her unconscious, immediately after the blow from the South Covina Tennis Tournament trophy, Carlos says, Peggy began crawling around aimlessly, which caused

Carlos to step across *what I guess was my father* and to fire another round of buckshot into his mother, this time hitting her in the leg, whereupon he remembers spinning around and firing again into his father, and by this time Felix had gotten over his fright and started pumping rounds from his own shotgun into his mother and father, though exactly where Felix fired from Carlos cannot say with any certainty . . .

John Wayne Bobbitt and John Wayne Gacy: sound alarming? Today on Drive Time, *meet some parents who named their children after John Wayne and the strange stories they have to tell. We'll also meet director Lucas Spelvin whose new movie on the Martinez murder case the defense attorneys don't want you to see. Join me, JD Owsley, today at four on* Drive Time.

On the StairMaster. At the Sports Center. A busy chunk of Santa Monica and La Cienega spread out below like an old-fashioned child's puzzle, in harsh yellow light, the sky smeary and toxic-looking. Jack, determined to shear off the porky roll where his T-shirt meets the ribbed waist of his red nylon gym shorts, tries to focus on Isaac Deutscher's *The Prophet Armed: Trotsky 1879– 1921,* the book he's wedged into the black metal groove under the StairMaster controls, but like the other twenty or so people using the new StairMasters and treadmills, he's watching Carlos Martinez on his individual monitor, hypnotized by the fixed frame, the sweater, the ruffled hair, the sagging shoulders, and the face, comely from the angle of the camera, but sometimes slipping out of definition when Carlos moves his neck, suggesting a tendency to fat, to Oriental plumpness, to frogginess, there's something impossible about this face and the things it's saying, an impossible pressure holding it together, *things shattering, we fired lots of, many many times, there was just glass and could hear things breaking and could hear ringing noises from the booms and smoke from the guns and it was, basically, just chaos, and I really didn't know who was firing,* on Jack's right and Jack's left and behind Jack across the room, bodies in spandex, climbing in place, staring into screens, *Rural Russia, vast, illiterate, boiling over with revolt and revenge,* clutching the tubular metal rails, his body feels like a creaking, rusted assortment of gears and levers squooshed into soft, fallible organs, he's on Lunar Landing with six or seven minutes to go on the high-intensity part of the program, he wants to get off, but he refuses to get off, if he keeps moving and actually finishes his half hour his heart will grow stronger, endorphins will launch themselves through his noggin, and though it is only the first step in an agonizing turnaround, the bare beginnings of sobriety and health and a new way of being, Jack believes he really can put the brakes on the backward-speeding chariot of his muddled gestalt, throw it into drive, and move forward into a better tomorrow.

He can become a better person. Or, if not a better person, a different one, with a different body.

Of course he's dying. But he could die slower and be prettier. All these people are dying, he reminds himself, slogging up and down, thinking they're shaking the cancers out of themselves, you never know what can happen. He sees his mother dead in the ICU, hardly older than Jack is now. A life of perpetual worry that things would not work out, and surprise, they didn't. His mother's father suddenly had cancer of the colon, and his mother out of simple prudence—but not so simple, only after endless lobbying by Jack's father—had gone in for a checkup. They found a tumor as big as the Ritz. Funny thing was, Jack's grandfather survived the surgery and chemo and everything else, but his mother had metastasized all over the place. The chemo scorched the veins in her arms, her hands, which stood out in eerie charcoal gray. She was convinced that the checkup had itself somehow "triggered" the cancer, and on some level beneath thought Jack must have believed it too, because in dark moments he blames his HIV infection on the blood test. Don't go there. Thirty minutes of daily exercise will boost his immune system, fructify his T cells, pare off his inner tube and make him attractive again, because he'll feel good about himself, and when you feel good about yourself you attract people. For example, Frankie. Who he managed to attract even with the inner tube and the haggard mug he gets from drinking, so the potential is there for greater attractiveness. Okay, Frankie asked for forty dollars afterwards, but shyly, suggesting they see each other again and asking Jack for his address and phone number, Jack really didn't feel used. The next time he sees Frankie, Jack will look better and feel better. First thing tomorrow, or maybe the day after, he'll start the nicotine patches and buy those motivation tapes and reverse twenty years of lung abuse, unclogging all the arteries and smaller tributaries, rushing blood to his brain, his skin, his fingertips and toes.

For the sake of the person he's becoming he hopes this Martinez psychodrama ends soon. The longer it lumbers on the longer Seth stays in his basement, though Seth now says maybe he'll go back to New York for a while, after the brothers testify, Jack doesn't trust himself to stick to his regimen with Seth around, Seth is a classical enabler, though Seth, too, seems like he's collided with a harsh self-appraisal and claims he wants nothing besides peace and quiet, and so far, in fact, they've had several peaceful, quiet meals together in the house, Seth getting in from court an hour or so before Jack leaves for work, mostly prepared foods from the Pioneer Market, fried chicken and baked okra and Hawaiian treats and what have you, accompanied by, at most, one 16-oz. Budweiser apiece. But there's something wrong with the general picture, some element Jack can't identify, an aura of embarrassment and shame around Seth, an uncharacteristic jumpiness, a suggestion of rising panic, all sorts of volatile vibrations leaking out of him, and zero concentration, totally scatterbrained, Jack thinks maybe it's some massive midlife crisis that's about to segue into semicatatonic depression, the kind of thing where the depressed person shuffles around the house all day in pajamas, in a state of chronic apology for his very existence. Something bordering on outright psychosis. Which would really interfere with Jack's reinvention of himself. He has always felt slightly vulnerable, slightly inadequate beside the person Seth's become since their twenties, has often wished that Seth would weaken, fail, experience a derailment of whatever that automatic mechanism is that keeps him productive through his worst calamities, but now that this wish appears to be coming true, Jack feels he may be harboring a contagious form of mental ruin in his bottom floor, that Seth could somehow transfer all the icky things in his head into Jack's head, becoming stronger as Jack grows weak, the pajamas migrating upstairs, and how would that be, Jack wonders, what would that be, would it conceivably be a cosmic payback for that time more than twenty years ago, when Seth was desperately in love with Jack, and Jack treated him worse than shit? Jack barely recalls any of the details, and the ones Seth remembers are different details. He remembers dry-humping Seth in the pitch-dark toilet at the old Spike (the grilled window framing perfectly the silhouette of a single palm tree) and refusing to have sex with Seth after bringing him home and stripping in front of him, but the only thing Seth calls up is Jack sodomizing him with a Snickers bar, which Jack ate. There just isn't enough there for payback, it's ancient history. Anyway, why is he losing himself in these ratmaze circuits of unhappiness, when he's just decided to improve himself?

Okay Daria this is the incident we discussed on the phone. Ill get right to the point & after reading this when you feel youre familiar with it I want you to destroy it. Destroy it right away so you dont forget. Basically there is one incident that may seem irrelevant to my case but believe me itll be very helpful. I can explain why later but for now Ill just lay it out. Ive thought about this and I feel you can do it however if youd rather not just tell me. You were at our Beverly Hills house about to have dinner with me my parents & Felix. We will decide later on what date this occurred. It was a weekend for sure. You and I had spent the afternoon together. Mrs. Martinez cooked dinner and we ate in the dining room. Everyone was sitting except Mrs. Martinez who was still bringing dishes in from the kitchen, you were beside me with your back to the kitchen door. Felix was across from us. Behind Mr. Martinez were the double doors to the foyer. Finally all the food was out. You dont remember what we ate but suddenly Mr. Martinez said in a stern voice to Mrs. Martinez who was standing behind you, "what have you done to this food"!!! Then after a very long silence Mr. Martinez shoved his plate aside knocking over silverware and glasses. He stood up and said "go outside and wait in the car, we're going to a restaurant" or something like that. I got up and said "come on Daria" and we walked out to the foyer with Felix. You got your purse and jacket. We stood outside in front of the Mercedes. Felix and I were discussing something in whispers, you just stood there embarrassed and confused by all this. Then Mr. Martinez stormed out of the house very upset. Either Felix or I (you dont remember which one) said to him "Dad, you think she tried something?" As Mr. Martinez got in the front seat he said "I dont know, I dont trust her." We all got in, you & me in the back & drove off, & we ended up eating at the Source. At dinner suddenly everything was normal and Mr. Martinez was charming. What you remember is how he was completely different after we left the house. He paid the check. We drove home. You and I stayed out front making out. You didnt feel right asking about what had happened earlier. You drove away in your car. It was still early. You didnt see Mrs. Martinez again because you didnt come back in the house. (It was just getting dark when we left for the Source.) You were confused driving home about the incident in the dining room but got the strong impression Mr. Martinez thought Mrs. Martinez was poisoning the food. You were really curious about it but just couldnt ask me about it. OK, thats it & you dont need more detail than what Ive provided. It was a long time ago so you wouldnt remember too much detail but you do remember the statements above very clearly, who said what. You dont recall insignificant conversation like at dinner. Its obvious why you remember what you do remember because it scared you . . .

Seth says when he left the Marmont some aspects of the accident became less real in his mind, that he began to really doubt that it happened the way he remembered it, for one thing he didn't remember it at all the following day, woke with an inky black hole in his memory, and at first only recalled having sex with Bobby, blurry sex, blurry recall, like actions and body parts mirrored in spattered blobs of mercury, and the day passed in one of those low-burning failure-hounded funks that a great deal of alcohol in the system will bring on, that he drove to Larchmont Village early in the afternoon to buy tea tree oil for an incipient cold sore and ran into Zorah Thornton, one of his lawyer friends, in the pharmacy, as Seth remembers it Zorah was buying *Vanity Fair* and sanitary napkins, they went across the street for coffee, Seth feeling starved for oxygen, as if a black cloud occupied his forehead, and somehow the subject of the Sunnydale Preschool trial came up, because one of Zorah and Seth's mutual friends was a reporter who broke the original Sunnydale story, and Zorah told Seth that despite the acquittals in the Sunnydale Preschool case, acquittals that came after seven years of criminal litigation, the children's allegations had all been true, not just the sexual molestation but the really bizarre allegations, the owners of the preschool really had taken children up in helicopters and sacrificed horses and rabbits, far-fetched as it all seemed there were scads of evidence defense lawyers had cleverly kept out of trial, evidence of satanic rituals, decapitated turtles, people in black robes, candles, weird symbols written in blood, and Zorah went on to say that in *Martinez*, the real story would never be known, that Carlos Martinez had been the mastermind, had planned everything meticulously at Princeton and come home that fatal week for the sole purpose of killing his parents, that Felix Martinez had been the weak link in this chain of events, Zorah paused to swallow a pill, Seth remembered that Zorah was a narcoleptic and took an amphetamine pill every few hours, which gave her a certain avid quality, the real story, Zorah continued, is that Felix is gay, his father suspected he was gay and beat him up all the time and ridiculed him, and the older brother, Zorah said, started working on the younger brother's mind, started filling him with this idea that the parents were going to get rid of him, but they can't go with that story, Zorah said, there are some big-time homophobes on those juries, and even though the cases are sort of separated with the two different juries the Martinez brothers have to pitch essentially the same story, since they're both sitting there, and a lot of the evidence comes in with both juries present, all the while Zorah chattered Seth found his attention slipping, he says he kept flashing on unconnected images, of the rainstorm Friday night and the thing thumping against the headlights and rolling the body into the culvert, and Zorah would pause and look at him strangely, and later, on the sidewalk, while Zorah climbed into her Jeep, the whole accident slashed into him spreading a wicked freezing cold all over his body, followed by a burning feverish rush, first cold, then hot, then cold again, that he weaved on the sidewalk and had to steady himself against a parking meter, and still later at the hotel, after vomiting up the coffee and passing out beside the toilet, he studied every page of the newspaper, thinking it might be in the late edition, but there was nothing that day and nothing Sunday and still nothing Monday, by Sunday night he'd remembered to clean the car and dispose of the clothes he'd worn Friday night, on Monday Carlos Martinez began testifying, on Tuesday Seth checked out of the hotel in a blur of paranoia and moved into Jack's, and at first, Seth says, he expected at any time the knock on the door from the LAPD, or the LAPD breaking the door down without knocking, was so convinced of its inevitability that he couldn't concentrate, in Jack's house he was always listening for the knock, or the splintering of the door frame, or the whirring lights and chopper twitter of a SWAT team, jumped at any sudden noise, his mind kept clouding over with pictures of himself in jail, himself in handcuffs, himself on trial, it was like doing something wrong at school and knowing that your parents were going to be notified, that awful period before they found out what you'd done, when you tried extra hard to remind them how much and why they loved you, in those first days Seth was almost unctuously flattering to Jack, continually giving him unsolicited pep talks about writing his screenplay, and Jack, who normally would have loved this attention, was too bewildered by Seth's other behavior to really get the benefit of it, Seth's habit of drifting out to buy beer or cigarettes or what have you and returning an hour later empty-handed, having driven aimlessly all over the neighborhood, and with Jack, Seth says, it was a case of knowing something's wrong without fully registering that something's wrong, the way you know when someone lies to you, not because you consciously think you're hearing a lie, but because there's something off, some interruption of the scanning pattern, a lie might not register as a lie, Seth says, but when you try making sense of things your mind doesn't accept the lie, it sort of closes up around the lie the way bees will isolate a foreign object in a beehive by sealing it up in wax, Seth says he rehearsed his confession many times, if the police came he wouldn't bother denying anything, except the drunk part, and of course they would question people at Teddy Wade's party, people at Teddy Wade's party would remember or not remember how much Seth had drunk at the party, of course Sheraton Pyle flopped into his mind then, like a great brown sea cow heaving itself onto an ice floe, Sheraton Pyle would be only too eager to say that Seth had been very drunk, or else—and this was even worse—Sheraton might cover for him, Sheraton might lie and tell them Seth had hardly touched a drop, might even cook up a story about Seth telling him that he wasn't drinking, that this detail "stuck in his mind" for some reason, maybe to make it interesting and a little dicey Sheraton would tell the police that Seth had formerly been a heavy drinker and therefore Sheraton had noticed how little Seth was drinking, who knew how Sheraton might embellish it, when Seth thought about it he realized that Sheraton would not be inhibited by any moral imperative to tell the truth, would say whatever he thought would benefit himself, that covering up the condition Seth had been in would create an ever-unpayable, lifelong debt, give Sheraton a real hold on Seth, the grisly, guilty fact of what had happened naturally felt unbearably heavy but this other thing, Seth says, had more immediate substance, was somehow even more appalling than the accident itself, Seth's mind was stuffed with the most insupportably awful scenarios, and it did not surprise him that one morning walking into court he saw Sheraton pacing around by the elevators, Sheraton in an XL dark blue suit, pink shirt, and Gucci tie, and those awful wing-tip shoes on his big fat feet, that Sheraton's face lit up in its customary shiteating grin, that Sheraton flashed him the special yellow visitor's badge for one of the seats reserved by the Court for VIPs, which gave him a seat right beside Fawbus Kennedy as it turned out, it was the day Carlos testified about confronting his father about Felix's abuse, about driving to the Gun-O-Rama and driving to the E-Z Mart, about Felix telling Carlos in the car all the sick details of the sexual abuse, about which store carried handguns and which had rifles and where the various weapons were displayed in what store, a day when the tension in the courtroom reached an unbelievable pitch, yet in spite of the almost apocalyptic feeling in the room, a feeling as though Carlos Martinez were wobbling on a tightrope suspended high above their heads, every word of testimony another perilous step, Seth was desperately wondering the whole time how to make himself agreeable to Sheraton Pyle, planning to ingratiate himself with Sheraton Pyle during the luncheon break, to helpfully answer any questions Sheraton had about the trial, and whenever he looked in Sheraton's direction, Seth says, it seemed that whenever Sheraton wasn't trying to make himself alluring to Fawbus Kennedy he was looking right back at Seth, studying Seth, thinking about Seth, Seth queasily felt, Seth says, that Sheraton knew, moreover there was even something vaguely sexual, some quiver of sexual arrogance emanating from Sheraton Pyle, some predatory wanker's will to power beaming forth from Sheraton's bulging eyes, and this all brought back memories, the kind of icky memories you just can't reckon with, Seth says, of years and years ago, when Seth first met Sheraton Pyle, that before they became, briefly, "friends," there had been a demure type of sexual overture, some fishing from that quarter, including a desultory attempt at blackmail, of the you-won't-sleep-with-me-because-I'm-black variety, which put Seth in the charmless position of explaining that he actually preferred black men as sexual partners and that Sheraton simply wasn't his type, Seth remembers how badly he handled that moment and now reflects that Sheraton must have needed something else from him because he'd continued trying to get closer to Seth as a "friend," did get closer in fact but never really close the way Seth's friends were close, Seth's idea of a friend is someone without an agenda and Sheraton transparently had an agenda several miles long. And now, says Seth, smiling across the courtroom at Sheraton Pyle, I suddenly have an agenda, too.

I just leaned over and shot her close, Carlos told the court, on one of those days, for that one day was destined not to be Sheraton's last day at the Martinez trial, Seth says, far from it, he had to cope with Sheraton Pyle for many days, in addition to having his mental circuits tangled up in what Carlos Martinez was testifying, for there were times, Seth says, when Seth pictured himself on the witness stand, I left the party at about eleven-fifteen, he heard himself saying, and Marlene Quilty would ask, And how much would you say you had had to drink that evening, Maybe a glass and a half of champagne, Seth replied, Oh, come on, Quilty badgered, you've heard other witnesses testify that there was an unusual amount of drinking going on, Yes, said Seth, but I was making a conscious effort to keep my drinking to a minimum, And why is that, said Quilty, No special reason, said Seth, Isn't it a fact, said Quilty, that you have a drinking problem? I don't think I do, Seth said, In 1976, snapped Quilty, you had a drunk driving accident on the Harbor Freeway, did you not? Objection, Sarah Johnson or Lauren Nathanson would shrill, lacks foundation, or prejudicial, Goes to credibility, Your Honor, Marlene Quilty would argue, Remoteness in time, Johnson or Nathanson would counter, We had decided before, said Carlos Martinez, that we wouldn't confess, What did you tell the police when they arrived to question you at the address in Mt. Washington, Marlene Quilty asked, I said I didn't know anything about this accident, Seth told the Court, And you were lying, weren't you, Quilty grilled, I was scared, Seth said, I asked if you were lying, Quilty pressed, Yes, Seth admitted, And when you say you only had two glasses of champagne, Quilty continued, moving in for the kill, you are also lying, aren't you?

I like you, JD, Dylan told him at dinner, at a new Japanese place on La Brea, but I knew right away we were way too different. I don't mean too different for a friendship, he hastened to add.

Aren't you being a little hasty? JD vainly asked, I mean, he said, we had all that unexpected stuff happen, we did crystal, we were drinking, we had all those people around—believe me, that's not what I'm like most of the time.

Dylan's hair was disheveled. He looked as if he'd put on weight in Seattle. JD attempted a light tone, nothing morose, but it sounded pleading all the same, and JD wasn't about to plead, so he stopped. He sensed that the curtain had come down decisively, and nothing would move this relationship along any further, it had barely gotten started and was already over.

Listen, Dylan said, the last thing I want to do is hurt your feelings. I mean it's really not like we're involved or something like that, am I right? You're a really bright guy, I really admire what you do, and I really hope you get that TV gig, it's not like I hold it against you that everything got out of control that time, it's just that—

What? JD fiddled with an orange chunk of fatty tuna. He'd let himself imagine things, but he hadn't really fallen in love, he thought. Almost, or almost got interested enough to begin to entertain the possibility, but now it was becoming irritating to contemplate his own near-vulnerability. In some sense, he could see, Dylan had taken the possibility more seriously than he had (but maybe Dylan was looking more avidly for things, and with a stronger conviction that he deserved them), and felt swindled by his own disappointment. Dylan was the kind of person who would feel JD "deserved to hear the truth," felt honorable about meeting things head-on instead of simply fading into the woodwork. Fading would be kinder, JD thought, but people like Dylan get their own back with gentle stabbing that only sounds like kindness to the people they tell about it afterwards.

You have a really negative, pessimistic aura, Dylan said with obvious difficulty, tapping a livid gnarl of butchered octopus with his chopsticks. I mean in the time we've spent together I've been able to see that's an integral part of who you are. I'm not making a value judgment, I respect that that's you. And hey, the world is a horrible place. I know I blind myself to a lot of things.

Maybe I need my blindness just to function every day. The fact is I would probably fall apart if I looked at things as unsparingly as you do.

It was not a restaurant to get emotional in. The tables were too close together. By some miracle JD got through the rest of the meal without hitting back, without saying: Look here, who do you think you're fooling. They said almost nothing to each other until the check came. Dylan was exasperated, he expected to make small talk after dropping his bomb. I'm sorry, he murmured abjectly, several times. Don't be, JD hissed. He grabbed the check with a certain violence and insisted on paying. There was a problem with his credit card, and a bad moment when they almost had to break the brittle mood because of the bill, but JD dug out cash before Dylan could open his wallet again. He felt exposed and humiliated on the drive home, ran from the car without saying goodbye. In the house he mixed a large vodka and orange juice and smoked ten cigarettes while he drank it, then poured another. He tried focusing on a rerun of *Law and Order,* an episode based on the Baby M case. Then he called Seth.

I just got the kiss-off, he announced in an ambiguously despairing voice.

I have to talk to you, Seth told him.

The worst thing—hard to tell what the worst thing was, JD kept changing his mind about it, but at one point, anyway, the worst thing was having his worldview trashed by someone who believed in reincarnation and the seven chakras or however many there were—they were in Numbers, the hustler bar on Sunset, an elaborately mirrored place with pale gray banquettes that managed to be dank and overlit at the same time, with a sequence of fancily dressed porn extras and their customers, even fancier older men with fabulously tight bodies, passing their banquette at a cruising speed considerably slower than that of less pricey whorehouses, like guests in a carpeted living room inspecting spotlit objets d'art (themselves, in fact, in mirrors running behind the banquettes)—and Seth, who had no use for anything mystical or otherworldly, agreed that it was pretty thick, but figured maybe JD himself had sensed from the beginning a basic incompatibility, Somewhere, Seth said, even unconsciously you must have known this wasn't for you, so you decided to show him your worst qualities right at the beginning. That's exactly what I did with Mark, he empathized. It's something about me, JD flagellated miserably, Dylan was so open when I met him, I think if I had done anything besides what I did there could have been something. Yeah, said Seth, I told myself that for months afterwards with Mark, he was so open, so interested in me, and I got so excited at the idea that something different was about to happen, I couldn't stop throwing myself at him, which apparently scared the shit out of him, and every time I saw him I got so anxious that I'd lose him, not even that, I was so scared of my own feelings I'd get unbelievably trashed on Xanax or something and act like a raving maniac. And it got worse every time. More psychotic, more grandiose, more insane. I knew I was driving him as far away as he could go. But you know something, JD, looking back, I think I knew what would eventually not work out with that person the second I laid eyes on him. This wasn't the big love of my life, JD minimized, waving for a waiter, but it makes me believe I'm compelled to screw up anything, simply because this wasn't a case of some neurotic fucked-up drugged-out asshole of the type I'm usually attracted to. Another screwdriver and a scotch on the rocks. You know what I'm saying. Okay, Seth expatiated, slapping the air near his heart with his open hand, Maybe we're both too fucked up for anything, but leaving that question aside, all I'm saying is, okay, if I think about Mark, right now, and mind you I haven't so much as seen him in six or eight months, first of all it was the same thing, everybody that I'd been with for a long time before that was a fucked-up mess, and here's this kid, really bright, really funny, good-hearted, not a drunk, not a drug addict, a quiet guy with his gyroscope balanced or what have you—Seemingly, said JD. Seemingly, said Seth, or maybe for real, what do I know? I never said *he* was the big love of *my* life, either. But a major, minor figure in the ongoing drama that is me. I didn't really know Mark. Not really. There was an immediate intimacy between us that was based on us both being clever, I suppose. I met him in a restaurant. Where I'd taken refuge from an obnoxious dinner situation by chatting up the staff on my way to the men's room. Waiters notice everything, you know. He saw I was having a miserable time with these dull people. That's a whole story in itself, another time . . . And Mark was the brightest one of the waiters. The youngest, the quickest. He was so wide-awake and full of life. There was something about me that he liked and something about him that I liked. But. What you liked about him wasn't what he liked about you, JD finished for him. Seth heaved a sigh, thinking that the whole subject was wildly irrelevant. There's that, he agreed. But maybe also there was something about him that I didn't like, something I registered about him way down deep in my psyche without even knowing it (Seth paused for a long swallow of scotch), something that told me (here he raised one finger dramatically) that no matter how fucked up I was and however normal and unneurotic he was, there was something processed and inauthentic about him. Something callow and conforming and mentally cheesy. Something I resented because of the pain I was in. I sensed that he had no demons. That he wasn't ripped up inside by everything that can go wrong in your life. Which I was. Inside he was like a clean bright room with a little brass bed and a comforter his grandmother quilted and a Gladys Goose lamp on the night table, and right next to the lamp, Seth said, a copy of *Bartlett's Quotations* or the complete works of David Leavitt. JD puffed a cigarette. Krishnamurti, JD corrected. It's a drag, anyway, Seth said. These clean unsullied people. They probably are better people than we are, but I can't quite believe it. I think they've just been lucky to avoid certain disappointments.

Seth leaned closer and dropped his voice. He looked at his scotch as if it had a worm in it. Something terrible happened last weekend, he said. JD scooted closer on the banquette. With Condé Nast? he wildly guessed. Seth shook his head. If I tell you you have to promise never ever to tell anyone, he said. Okay, JD said. A hustler who could have been Brad Pitt's stunt double hovered near the table. Seth swigged his beverage and glared at him until he went away. This is what's left from the Church, Seth thinks: confession, and the demand for absolution. I was driving too fast on Beverly Glen, he said. That night it rained. In the middle of nowhere coming back from that party. I don't know what he was doing out there but this guy ran in front of the car. Oh wow, JD said. Oh shit, he amplified. I was drunk, Seth said. You know they send you to prison in a case like that. Because of these Mothers Against Drunk Driving and everything. You know I wouldn't last a week in a California prison. A long moment passed in which a bevy of surfer-blond boys in leather jackets frothed grandly down the entrance stairs and ramp-walked over to the bar. You're saying you took off, JD murmured. I didn't see what else I could do, Seth pleaded. The deed was done. Oh man, JD said. Did you at least, um, call the cops, I mean anonymously? Seth chewed his lip. He shut his eyes. Yeah, he said, I did, I called them from a pay phone. At the Virgin Megastore. He was surprised to find the room intact when he opened his eyes. The monstrosity of it all washed over him again as he noted his compulsion to obscure this last part, as though it were the only unforgivable part. JD sank back against the soft convex pleats of the gray-blue leatherette. He somberly swirled his vodka and orange juice. Seth lit a Marlboro Light and studied wet spots on the table. He began linking the spots with his fingers. Skid marks, JD said thoughtfully. I don't think the car skidded, Seth said. His hand trembled. It went right over him and then I just stopped. It was raining, JD said. Heavily, said Seth. Still, if the police got there right away—JD left the thought hanging. Oh fuck, JD, Seth said, I didn't call the police. Oh, said JD. He thought about it some more. Gosh, he added.

Sabrina Wilcox is about to enter history, or at least enter a protracted footnote of the judicial history of the era, if not by name then generically, and she is also becoming a character in a screenplay by Jack, which he's writing with the help of a book called *Creating Unforgettable Characters.* "Characters need to be consistent," it advises. "This does not mean that they are predictable or stereotypical." Yet real characters must also contain an element of paradox. "They do things that surprise us, startle us, change all our preconceived ideas about them." On the one occasion that Jack drove Sabrina Wilcox from Silver Lake to Brentwood, he gleaned what is known as the germ of her character, but to supplement this germ, or rather, to cultivate this germ into a full-blown infection, he has subsequently watched her weekly cable show, *Metaphysical Me,* a program whose production values, even for cable, are distractingly shabby. Most episodes (if that's what they're called) consist of fixed medium shots of Sabrina Wilcox in velvet dresses or gypsy-hippie attire, her generous bosom festooned with cabalistic amulets, usually poised before a velvet-draped altar or multilayered table that's bedecked with talismans, lingams, quartz chunks, statuettes of the Virgin Mary, stuffed owls and snakes, penta-grams and the like. During the show, Sabrina, her angular features frozen in contemplation of some distant light, free-associates, in a voice soft as cotton batting, on a myriad of occult themes, weaving in her reflections on war, politicians, environmental decay, and the salubrious effects of vegetarianism. We are all, Sabrina says, mere atoms of one great organism, blinded by super-ficial phenomena, just as the humans were all blinded by the phosphorescent green, blue, and red comets in *The Day of the Triffids.* Like them we stumble sightless through life, prey to the deadly nightshade of cynicism and hatred. Since these notions seem, not only consistent, but predictable or stereotypical as well, Jack has twice visited Sabrina's New Age head shop on Melrose hoping to ferret out her element of paradox, but on both occasions was in-formed by the salesclerk that Sabrina had "taken a leave of absence." He had his tarot read by the assistant store manager. He was told that he would soon have "an earthshaking experience" involving a Youth. He was urged to buy a desk-sized marble obelisk for its potent energy field. He bought a set of sub-liminal tapes. To his own surprise, Jack's trimmed off five pounds and kicked the cigarette habit without the egregious discomfort and uncontrollable appetite he expected. He misses smoking, sure, but feels so much better without it he wishes he'd quit years ago. And he's cut out alcohol, and the weekend poker games in Bell Gardens, too. Shedding all these supposedly defining habits leads Jack to wonder about his own viability as an unforgettable character, a creature of wants and needs, a vessel of paradox.

What does Sabrina Wilcox want? In Jack's screenplay, so far, she wants the love of a disreputable clinical psychologist who involves her in a dark scheme to shake down two rich brothers who've killed their parents and confessed under the seal of confidentiality. At the same time she wants release from this nightmare relationship and the peace of mind that doing the right thing will give her. Is this enough to want? Doesn't she need more? The real facts are so screwy that Sabrina Wilcox is almost implausible, but Jack isn't sure what to add or take away.

The shorter drive from Mt. Washington is also more convoluted, there are more ways to get stuck in traffic or miss a turn, and all across the radio spectrum it's Martinez, Martinez, Martinez, with call-ins from all points of a wilderness of pain. The temperature is almost always eighty or eighty-five degrees, the morning skies soft and clear as Handi-Wrap. The voices enraged, or confused on points of law, or convinced that even darker things than have already been revealed lurk beyond the pale of admissible evidence. Seth counts bumper stickers that say, I BELIEVE CARLOS AND FELIX. The voices fill the sour cocoon of the rental car with competing theories about how we all should just get along.

Carlos has committed a major gaffe during cross-examination. Describing the shootings in close but strange detail, as if the occupants of the rumpus room on Woodrow Wilson Drive were not so clearly his parents but dark shapes he supposed were his parents, as if he had fired his shotgun without really thinking he was killing his parents, reliving those five or six minutes, Carlos says that "someone" was still moving after the ten blasts. Who was this someone, Marlene Quilty demanded. My mother, Carlos admitted. What was your mother doing? In my mind, Carlos said, she was sneaking around the side of the couch.

Sheraton Pyle rolled his eyes for Seth's benefit. Seth tried imagining the moment when someone's mother becomes a half-dead piece of sneaking meat on the floor. He could not see Felix or Lauren Nathanson. Sheraton had a much better seat that day. Sheraton explained during an afternoon recess that Fawbus Kennedy had fixed his seating with the bailiff. So they were now tight, Sheraton and Fawbus, Fawbus and Sheraton, black and white evil twins, in Seth's mind, one old, dropsical, the other young, fat, shrewd. Fawbus could suck youth from Sheraton, Sheraton would make new friends through Fawbus. For Seth they represented the same thing, a world of social forms from which he was, by some indefinable quirk in his nature, firmly excluded. It was a world he had no wish to enter, but the fact that he could not sometimes brought him craven pain. He could see them in all sorts of palmy settings— opera box, charity ball, Wimbledon—not together, necessarily, but equally at home, social climbing with the easy agility of chimpanzees scaling a baobab tree. Seth dreaded meeting Fawbus Kennedy, but after a few days he realized that Sheraton was still tacky enough not to introduce him, hadn't yet acquired the polish to present someone and negate his existence in the same breath. By then Seth had also absorbed the idea that he would never be caught. JD had made some discreet inquiries, as he called them, and learned that a great percentage of hit-and-run incidents were never solved, and, in this city of several million cars, seldom even pursued with any diligence. Given the heavy rain and the absence of visible damage to the car, the lack of witnesses, and the fact that nothing turned up in the newspaper (indicating, JD said, that the victim either wasn't identified, or belonged to some marginal group, possibly an undocumented alien) the whole episode seemed unlikely to carry any repercussions. Of course Seth can envision an implacable detective, methodically matching microscopic fibers or flakes of auto paint, somehow tracing these things to the rental car, even tire imprints on the body, but as the days pass the accident seems more and more chimerical, a blank patch of chemical memory Seth has filled in with something that might have happened rather than something that definitely did.

Because, he thinks, it's even easy for hypothetical memories to seem real. As Carlos testifies about his father molesting him, Seth reviews memories of his own father, always in fragments, and the years of his childhood, which are like a flutter of meaningless snapshots or snippets of old movies embedded in silence and darkness, with no legible narrative flow connecting them, and at times, Seth says, he can picture something charged and secret occurring in that darkness, constructing his father's naked body from disparate images the way a dinosaur skeleton might be assembled from scattered bones. The invented scenes he comes up with seem at least as believable as events he knows happened but can't fully bring into focus. It can be as hard to prove the reality of something real as something dreamed up. When he and Jack sort over the faraway past there are always discrepancies, odd-shaped pieces in one person's head that don't fit the other's puzzle.

I believe we talked yesterday about the fact that you and your brother had a conversation after you left Dr. Phlegg's office on October the 31st, correct?

Correct.

During that time you were concerned because you wanted to know what your brother had told Dr. Phlegg, correct?

That was one reason, yes.

And you wanted to know just how much your brother had told Dr. Phlegg, correct?

Yes.

You wanted to know if he merely said he was involved or if he gave details of his involvement, correct?

I wanted to know if he'd given details as to what was going on and as far as the arguments and issues and the crisis and basically the things that would explain what had happened and he said he had not, he had just said a few specifics of like firing the guns and a few things afterwards but no details about the issues, he said he hadn't told him why.

Now, why was it you felt that if your brother had talked about the sexual abuse, that was something you should get angry with your brother about?

A lot of my anger was that I felt he'd gone to Dr. Phlegg instead of coming to me. And it was more that I was hurt by that and I was feeling like Why did he do that, if he's suicidal, how come I don't know, and he didn't even come to me, and feeling very caught completely off guard by the fact that he had now told somebody who I did not trust, and the whole thing was very upsetting and confusing and frightening.

So you were angry because you thought your brother might have told Dr. Phlegg about something that would mitigate the crime, is that correct?

No, there are a lot of reasons, I just said all the reasons, but the reason was basically that he told him we were involved at all. I wasn't thinking there were things that mitigated that, we were both feeling bad about what happened, the only large thing in my mind was that we had killed our parents, there was nothing you could say about it that was good.

JD even thinks it's possible that what Seth hit was a large dog, a sheepdog or some other sort of outsized breed, an event one would naturally feel bad about, that maybe the amphetamine Seth took that night was a bad batch, it certainly had affected JD strangely, or so he claimed, possibly cut with strych-nine or another hallucinatory poison, maybe by dumping a lot of booze on top of it you had some type of psychotic episode, JD suggested, and thought you'd run over a person, when in reality it was this big dog, it could even have been a coyote, he said, I mean, what would anybody be doing running around in a part of Beverly Glen where there aren't even any houses in the middle of a rainstorm, But I dragged him off the road and rolled him into a ditch, Seth said, But what if you really were in a psychotic state, JD said, and just halluci-nated that a big dead dog was a human body, it could happen, especially if that speed was cut with angel dust, JD said with an air of great conviction, It certainly felt like angel dust to me, he said, I didn't wake up until about seven the next night and when I did I felt like I'd been nailed to the bed. And I did hallucinate, he insisted, at Marvin Paley's crucifixion, what with the drums and all, I kept seeing these faces of people who weren't really there, at the dark edges of the crowd, for all we know, JD continued excitedly, there could've been acid in that speed, it's been known to happen—

Now when you talked to Dr. Phlegg on November the 2nd, did you say anything about the crimes being perfect?

No.

So when Dr. Phlegg testified to that in front of the jury, he was lying, is that your testimony?

That's right.

I believe you testified, though, that there were many things Dr. Phlegg testified to that were actually either said by you or said by him.

Right.

And one thing you repeated here yesterday was the fact that Dr. Phlegg told you he felt you were menacing.

Yes.

Did you by any chance tell Dr. Phlegg about your father's theory about the Russian Revolution and how he would have handled it?

Yes.

So when Dr. Phlegg said that here in court, he was telling the truth, correct?

Right.

Dr. Phlegg repeated for the jury what you told him, which was that it wasn't done for money, correct?

Right.

And that is your assertion, correct?

Right.

So when Dr. Phlegg said that, that information would be helpful to you, he was telling the truth, correct?

I'm not sure he said anything helpful to me, but he was telling the truth about that.

It's possible, in the way that anything is possible, and in fact Seth has precious little sense-memory of the accident, aside from a few murky images, the suction of drenched clothes against his skin, the vegetal smell of the woods the road ran through, the noisy, bright traffic that met him on Sunset when he left Beverly Hills. His eyes wander from Carlos to the Martinez relatives, ranged in the seats behind the defense, the aunts and cousins and ancient Cuban grandmother, three generations of Martinezes and—what was Peggy's maiden name?—Richardson. Most of them have testified, vehemently, to the chronic ill-treatment of the brothers by Fidel and Peggy. It's said that only one family member, a brother of Peggy's, plans to appear for the prosecution, during the rebuttal phase. What do these people honestly remember? Have they exaggerated the horrors of the Martinez household? Do they figure, as pro-prosecution people are always claiming, that they can't do anything for Fidel and Peggy, so they might as well lie to save Carlos and Felix? If what they've said is true, did they suspect that the rough treatment they saw was only a mild taste of what really went on? They've spoken about slaps, kicks, punches, verbal abuse, sadistic games Fidel played to "toughen up" Carlos and Felix. Catching Felix three times when he jumped from an elevation, letting him hit the floor the fourth time. Punching Carlos in the stomach when he talked back, hard enough to knock him over. Making Felix hang by his hands from a pipe near the ceiling, ignoring his tears and screams. Pushing four-year-old Felix down a curved cul-de-sac on a bicycle without training wheels, letting go, letting him crash and skin his arms and legs repeatedly, refusing to bandage his cuts until he rode the bike correctly.

I believe you indicated during your direct examination that Dr. Phlegg repeated something that you said wasn't true, Dr. Phlegg said that your father told you, "You can kill me if you want to, but you won't get anything." And you indicated that, "I would be in a hospital if I had intimated that I would kill him." Do you remember saying that?

Well, so would anybody else, I would think.

All right, then on the night of August 17th, the night your father came home from his trip, and you had this conversation with him, you indicated to the jury that you threatened him after you felt your plan hadn't worked, correct?

Right.

And your father didn't put you in the hospital, did he?

No, he was going to kill me instead.

Okay, but—

But I didn't threaten his life, I certainly could never make a statement like that, even from the little bit Dr. Phlegg probably knew about my dad, he knows when he makes that statement it just isn't possible. It's ridiculous. My father isn't the type of person to say "You won't get the money," if somebody was that disrespectful to him, he just goes off.

Yet when you told your father you were going to expose him to the world as a child molester, he didn't put you in the hospital that night, did he?

No.

In fact he didn't put you in the hospital at all between the 17th and the 20th of August, did he?

No.

One of the Carlos jurors, half-awake, glances up from her steno pad, rubs her eyelids under a pair of thick glasses. The judge slumps against the high padding of his throne. The courtroom is always cold, maybe to keep everyone awake: even so, a couple of jurors look like they're nodding off. Seth pictures running over a big sheepdog. Time is standing still and shuddering forward all at once. Marlene Quilty sniping crisply, Carlos Martinez responding in his unexcited monotone, back and forth, back and forth, the bailiff discreetly scratching his balls with the hand in his pants pocket. In a trial every possible secret, every possible hidden corner of your life comes out. They would find Bobby, no doubt: And this encounter took place on the night of the accident, at the defendant's hotel, correct? Correct. You got to the defendant's room at what time, Mr. whatever Bobby's name was. About one-thirty in the morning. And the defendant was intoxicated? My impression was that he was pretty wasted. And you had sex with the defendant, is that correct? Correct. They could even call Mark, god. During the winter of 1993, did you meet the defendant? Yes. Where did you meet the defendant? At the restaurant where I was working. Did the defendant ask you to go out with him shortly after that first meeting? He did. And did you go out with him? Yes, on several occasions. When you went out with the defendant the first time, what was his demeanor? Well, I thought he was very nice at first. But as the evening went on, he kept ordering drinks, and I had the impression he was on some kind of drug. Objection. Sustained. Did the defendant tell you he'd taken pills of some kind? Objection, hearsay. Overruled. He said he was on Xanax. Did you happen to comment on the dangers involved in drinking alcohol in combination with a drug like Xanax? I tried to, but he told me he'd been taking drugs all his life and knew what he was doing. Objection. Sustained. Strike the witness's last answer. Did the defendant indicate to you that he had used drugs many times? Objection. Overruled. Yes, he did. Did the defendant make a sexual overture to you the first time you went out with him? Yes. How did you respond? I told him I had just been in a relationship and wasn't ready to get intimate with a new person yet. And how did the defendant react to that? He said he understood, but then he came on to me again the next time I saw him.

Dr. Phlegg was the only person who could turn you in to the police, correct?

That's correct.

And you had an interest in making him understand why you did this, so he wouldn't turn you in to the police as a cold-blooded, threatening killer, but rather as a victim. You had an interest in making sure you were pictured in the best possible light to Dr. Phlegg, isn't that so?

Right. And at that point he said he could be helpful in a trial, and it was clear he did not feel threatened. He was in a better mood, trying to piece what had happened together, he seemed interested in doing hypnosis with us later on, he wasn't afraid.

So during the November 2nd session, Dr. Phlegg talked about abuse as a defense, correct?

No, he talked about piecing together a family constellation, the dynamics in the family, the emotions that might have made this happen.

Dr. Phlegg is the one who planted the idea of using abuse as a defense, isn't that true?

No.

Seth thinks: if I knew how to draw, I could sketch this whole courtroom with my eyes closed. He thinks: someone, somewhere, right now, is feeling all the things I felt when I was young. He thinks: some person not far from here is hiding a shotgun in his room, waiting for his parents to push him over the edge. Quilty slides into her chair beside Quentin Kojimoto. The flat plane of Kojimoto's haircut intersects the line of the witness box railing, above the line is the robin's-egg blue of Carlos's sweater. Sarah Johnson walks behind Felix and Lauren and stands at the lectern, adjusts the little microphone, opens a folder of notes. Someone coughs across the room. Someone blows his nose. Seth remembers feeling trapped in the house with his parents, no escape from their craziness, their eternal antagonism. Running away and knowing there was nothing to run away to. Thinking: if I could just kill my father.

In your years of living in the same house with your parents, did you find it was important to try to guess what was going to happen next?

Objection.

Sustained.

Did you sometimes have to make decisions or read signals?

All the time. With regard to my parents, because of the way they were, just, my mom's facial expressions and tone of voice, or the way she moved, and my dad for sure, my dad controlled people with hand signals, but it was more than that, you could read his face, and whatever he did, if he changed into tennis clothes right away, or if he stayed in his business suit, or if he went over and watched TV, the atmosphere changed very significantly and very suddenly, all the time. So I was constantly aware of that. It's been very frustrating trying to describe what they were like, and what it was like, and why I felt the way I did that weekend, and I've felt frustrated through this whole thing, not being able to express that in a way that's the same as it was.

Why was it necessary for you to pick up cues in the atmosphere or read signals? Why did you do that as a child?

Because there was not a lot of normal communication. It was a very unpredictable place, my home.

Were you trying to read signals that last week?

Yes.

And did you talk to your brother about what various things meant?

Yes.

And did he also seem to be reading signals?

Yes.

And based on all the things you learned about your parents in your life, about their behavior, when you saw the things they did that last week, did you believe they were going to kill you?

I believed that they were. Yes.

Marlene Quilty again.

Mr. Martinez, what hand signals did your father give you when you put the gun to his head?

He didn't give me any.

What signal was your mother giving you as she was sneaking around the sofa before you went out and reloaded?

We've just heard a bit of live testimony from the downtown courtroom where the Martinez murder trial is in its seventy-sixth day, Carlos Martinez, the older of the two defendants on the witness stand, and my guest for this segment is Judge Aubrey Vanowen a retired Superior Court judge we've had many times on the program welcome again Pleased to be here, We're taking your calls Judy from Hawaiian Gardens go ahead please you're on the air Hi I love your show JD Thank you I have to disagree with the criticism that the prosecutor's style has been really low-key, I think she's very snotty, I think he's holding up tremendously but perhaps it's going unfavorably for him it's almost he's caught in between, if he's too composed it looks like he's the ruthless character that they've painted yet she's being so sarcastic and nasty the stuff about the mother sneaking around anyway my question is did they have previous attorneys Yes there was it gets confusing, someone represented the family when the brothers were first arrested but your question on prosecution style let me go to the judge, it's my understanding when you have defendants alleging they've been victims of child abuse you don't really want to attack them do you because that can make the jury turn against you Yes it's a difficult matter cross-examining someone with that defense you don't want the jury antagonistic but in this case you want to show that this is a fabricated defense, that's why Mrs. Quilty is using this disdainful antagonistic cross-examination trying to convey that she doesn't believe the testimony and the jury shouldn't believe it, maybe she's not being successful Yes well it's worth mentioning that the term sneaky initially came out of Carlos's mouth, thank you so much let's talk to Brenda in Ladera Heights hello Brenda Hello you want my statement I feel Carlos Martinez is lying and they killed their parents for the money, if there was abuse they could've gone to the police Now here we've got Brenda who's not buying any of it Well it shows you have two reasonable people coming to a different conclusion, this points out the uncertainty of any kind of jury trial, and this emphasizes that the most crucial thing will be the jury instructions, Absolutely thank you Brenda let's go to Rod in Santa Monica Hi my question is it seems like these Martinez brothers are putting their parents on trial making them look like the bad people without any corroborating evidence Well we don't know what further corroborating evidence may come in Tina you're our next caller you're on the air Hi I want to tell

*you JD that you're my favorite commentator on the air, I'm a nurse and I look a
lot at body language, there's been a lot of studies done that when you're lying
your nose itches and I noticed Carlos Martinez for several days was constantly
scratching his nose and then all of a sudden he stopped doing that, I wonder if
someone else noticed that and pointed it out to him Well I don't know we
certainly didn't have that information but I guess everybody will be looking now
but remember he was out a few days last week because he was ill if his nose
suddenly grew a few inches that might be a better indication Well I kept watching and he kept scratching his nose All right thank you let's go to Martha Myers
in Burbank JD? Yes I'm a law student and I kept looking at I guess in California it's an affirmative defense, self-defense, in other states you have to prove that
by a preponderance of the evidence, if that's so this allegation of sexual abuse is
the core of their defense, what does the judge think the jury instructions might
be I don't think they've proved it, also, I went to college with a lot of rich
students some came from very dysfunctional families and the threat to cut them
off from their support was a very common way to control these kids and very
much resented a lot of them had low self-esteem, poor academic records, they
had no work experience and they really really resented this control at the same
time they recognized their dependency and it created a lot of antagonism between them and their families so I think it's a very relevant aspect of motive here
Okay let's bring it back to those instructions Earlier I spoke about the perfect
self-defense and imperfect self-defense, what I've seen so far I don't think the
judge will give an instruction on perfect self-defense, which means a reasonable
person believing they were in imminent fear of harm and death so as to justify
completely the killings all the judge needs to give the instruction is to find
there's some evidence of that defense presented from which a jury could come to
a conclusion that this defense has been made, I don't think that's happened, but
I do think there's some evidence we've seen to the imperfect defense, a subjective
standard, that the defendants here had some reason to believe they were in fear
of death and he'll probably give an instruction on that based on the battered
child or battered spouse syndrome so you can expect that kind of instruction and
an instruction on who has the burden of proof and the degree of proof that has
to be sustained, then it will be up to the jury.*

I still have the turd, Janice Wade tells Bates, the investigator. And all the
postcards.

Bates squats on his heels to stay level with Janice, whose espaliered roses surround them in the backyard, a rococo effulgence of velvety petals in every conceivable pink, crimson, and scarlet variety, some soft-edged, some spiky, some simple as tulips, some intricate as cabbage hearts, their rich fragrances mixing in a nauseating way with the fumes from a Folgers coffee can full of kerosene. Numerous Japanese beetles wriggle helplessly in the kerosene.

These are Empress Josephines, Janice tells him. Those are Chlorises, those very bright ones are Gloire des Rosomanes and the dark almost purple ones there are Tuscanys.

Her yellow rubber gloves pick over the foliage, which casts a complicated mesh of light and shadow on her soil-stained khaki gardening trousers and hyacinth T-shirt and lightly tanned skin.

Would you like to see it? she asks, plucking a bright green beetle off a saw-edged leaf and dropping it into the writhing syrup. The turd, I mean.

Maybe not right now, Bates says. He is a tall young man, with angular features, very full lips, heavy eyebrows. His suit is pale green linen, and so wrinkled that Janice decides it's a deliberate look. But hold on to it, he cautions, it's evidence.

Janice rises to explore higher thickets of her vegetation. Bates springs to his feet, swiping at his trouser knees with his fingers. Across the yard, whirling sprinklers dampen the ground cover with a fizzing, delicate splatter.

I'm convinced it's Rupert, Janice says, peering into dense leafage. He's always had a big crush on me and he just hated the idea of my marrying Teddy. He tried forever to talk me out of it. Everybody knows Teddy Wade is a big fag, Janice, you're marrying a goddam paaansy, he used to say. Rupert loves to drag that word out, paaaansy, *Would Buffy have left you the house in Palm Springs and all those IBM shares Janice if she knew you'd marry a paaansy,* of course the only reason Buffy had anything to leave was that she married two pansies one right after the other after Daddy died. And I was the one who introduced her to Max Palevsky, so . . . You know my father was one of the very rare people killed by lightning every year. On the golf course in Huntington Beach. Rupert tried molesting me once when I was twelve but I smacked him in the ankle with a croquet mallet. I suppose he's having what they used to call a midlife crisis.

Janice smiles thoughtfully. Bates gazes down at the insect Auschwitz happening in the coffee can.

I mean look at these cases he's been in charge of, Janice says, thrusting her gloves into a swarm of thistles and greenery. Sunnydale, that prison guard thing. These last few years, everybody paints him like a senile idiot. And, you know, he really isn't underneath it all. He's just sort of clueless and technical in his approach to everything. He's not a creative jurist. She flourishes a struggling beetle under Bates's fleshy nose before plunging it into the kerosene. These little bastards will ruin your roses, she says.

Well, he says, if it really is Tietelbaum, we'd better have some solid proof before you even think about pressing charges.

Oh, Janice says, surprised, stroking a half-open bud. Who said anything about charges.

Bates meets her eye with a querulous flutter of his long black lashes, a wry twist of his big lips.

I just assumed, he says. He clears his throat. The kerosene fumes are making him dizzy.

Janice shakes her head adorably. Sunlight glistens on her golden hair.

The difficulty is, she says, Rupert was an old friend of Buffy's, my mother's that is, frankly Buffy would turn over in her grave if this mushroomed into a big deal. Actually Buffy doesn't have a grave per se, we cremated her, she's got a little urn. But metaphorically. This could just wreck Rupert's career, couldn't it. I wouldn't want to be responsible for that. Look at all his years on the bench. His distinguished service and so forth.

But it's his responsibility, not yours, Bates says, his arms outspread. He's doing it to you, threats to your kid, turds in the mail—

Can they get DNA from a turd? Janice asks, with an air of scientific curiosity.

I'm sure they can, says Bates. I'm no DNA expert, but I imagine—

Janice inspects a final row of roses and peels off her rubber gloves with satisfaction. The gloves make a snapping sound Janice associates with her gynecologist.

I'm sure you get sick of people asking this, she says, but is that your given name? Norman Bates?

Bates crinkles his lips expressively.

What can I tell you, he says. My parents never saw *Psycho*. Or maybe they did, they both had a strange sense of humor.

Isn't it kind of a handicap? Janice nods for him to follow her to a parasol-shaded table at the end of the patio, where the maid has set out a pitcher of lemonade and some little cookies.

Maybe it puts some people off, Bates muses philosophically. I thought of changing it, but then I thought, why should I go to the trouble because of a fictional character? I mean, if they'd named me Adolf Hitler or something, maybe.

Janice gives Bates a closer inspection as he sits down at the table and stretches out his long legs. His face is weird, she decides, but not alarmingly weird. He's sort of droopy and Edwardian.

You'd think Teddy would get the stalkers, she says, practically giggling.

Bates's brow creases meaningfully.

Mrs. Wade, he says, this isn't just—

Janice, Janice tells him warmly, call me Janice.

Bates allows a coy grin to play over his lips, his eyes fixed on his cuticles.

Janice, he says. This isn't just a case of stalking, which is bad enough, it's also blackmail, a B or A felony, I forget which—

Oh, Janice says, waving away the particulars, Rupert doesn't really have any photographs of Teddy doing things with this Novelli person. If he even dreamed I'd shell out fifty thousand dollars for some xeroxed centerfolds he really must be out of the loop. Rupert probably got that name Novelli from the phone book, what do you think? Besides, she says, what if he actually did have pictures? That kind of thing doesn't faze anybody anymore. If Teddy was banging a German shepherd or something, then I might worry, canine AIDS or what have you—

The point I'm making, Bates says earnestly, whether he has photos or doesn't have photos or what he has or doesn't have it's still extortion, plus menacing, and as a fine legal point, Janice, you're kind of obligated to report it.

As a fine legal point, Janice says, wrapping Bates's large hand in her cool fingers, you're probably right, but Teddy and I would like to just keep this as quiet as possible. All we want is some concrete proof that Rupert Tietelbaum and Dave Spacey are the same individual, and then we just confront him with it and say, you know, stop the insanity, or we'll expose you to the newspapers. The tabloids. That should freak him out. Enough to leave me alone, anyway.

It's your call, Bates tells her, looking confusedly at their entwined hands on the table. But if the guy is nuts and he's deciding capital cases where people could live or die, you might think about at least making him get some, uh, treatment or something.

Janice whisks her hand away and flicks at an errant strand of hair. She toasts Bates with a tilt of her lemonade glass.

I completely agree with you—can I call you Norman? she says. Theoretically, at least. We're obviously dealing with a sick person who needs help. On the other hand, I'd hate to go down as the person who caused a mistrial in the Martinez case, can you imagine the kind of publicity? When Teddy's in the TV movie? The priority here is getting Rupert off our backs. Quietly, discreetly. I do not want to open my mail and find another bowel movement, period.

When Seth comes upstairs to use the bathroom this morning, Jack's already moving around in his frayed flannel bathrobe, the bathrobe cord whipping around uselessly like a tail, sipping coffee, forking open an English muffin to stick in the toaster oven. Seth's wearing a pinstripe shirt, with the lower buttons buttoned to cover his underpants, carrying his toilet kit. The morning levee is by now an established avoidance ritual. Usually Jack is asleep and it's Seth's problem to shower and get his other business taken care of without waking him up, but Jack almost always wakes up anyway, gets out of bed, drinks some orange juice while Seth gets ready for court, they have a little morning chat and Seth leaves and Jack goes back to bed, but this morning Jack is clearly up for the day, exuding a sense of purpose, has the morning TV news on, and outside in the sunshine there's a little hum of not-too-distant helicopters spraying malathion, and a pleasant chitter and whibble of birdsong, and occasional yarfs and woofs from the dogs across the canyon.

There's a place on Crenshaw, Jack tells him, as if to set the topic of the day, that specializes in fried turkey.

Seth finds a clean mug in the sink with the name Consuela written across it in light blue script. He fills this with coffee. He opens the refrigerator and immediately closes it, dissembling morning heaves.

Fried turkey, Seth says. Oh god I can barely face this today.

Yeah, you bring 'em the turkey and they fry it for you. Supposedly it's quite delicious, though they advise you not to eat the skin because of the fat content.

Seth watches Jack pluck his muffins from the toaster oven and gingerly drop them onto a small plate. He thinks: Jack will go on living here every day that he lives, and the places that fry turkey, and the gay clubs that open, and all the freak shows that happen here will happen for him, will be part of his life, and I will be gone, gone back, living my life back there, and even when I'm here whatever happens happens differently for him than it does for me.

There used to be a place in Watts, Seth says, standing at the floating counter, You Buy, We Fry. Seth squeezes parts of his head through his hair. I dreamed about a door, he says.

Jack spreads margarine on his muffins.

It was a solid door, oak I think, and it was . . . protecting me, nobody could get in. I had a very nice Dakota-style apartment, prewar Upper West Side kind of place. But the door had these slots or little windows in it, too many openings, like mail slots, or those grille things you look through to see who's on the other side.

Seth half expects Jack to launch one of his New York stories (as Jack often does if Seth makes too specific New York references, in too familiar a way, as if they shared them) about the six months when Jack lived in New York and hated every minute of it: that was more than twenty years ago, nothing good happened to him, and Jack's opinions about New York based on that short long-ago experience always sound deadly accurate to Seth, and make him feel that the New York turn in Seth's own life was the fatal one. But Jack isn't in the mood.

Felix is testifying? Jack asks, biting into a muffin.

Felix is testifying, Seth nods, and fucking Sheraton Pyle is still getting in every day, I suppose he's decided to write the definitive article on the Martinez trial, from the minority perspective, no doubt—

Is there a minority perspective? Jack sounds truly interested.

Well, they're Hispanic I suppose, I haven't seen that angle emphasized anywhere but I'm sure if anyone can find some racial subtext—the whole turkey? Like, deep-fried?

That's why they do it for you, Jack says. So you aren't killed in an explosion of boiling grease at home.

You're looking awfully well with all this exercise, Seth tells him. Really well.

It is sort of working isn't it, Jack says with amazement. He rubs his stomach, which isn't exactly flat, but less flabby than Seth remembers it of yore.

While Seth takes his shower Jack thinks about his screenplay. His screenplay is giving him mental anguish. He has come quickly to the conclusion that anything written in the standard format recommended in Syd Field's *Screenplay* looks like an imbecile's epiphanies, and he's beginning to suspect that the real-life Sabrina Wilcox story isn't much less stupid than it looks on the page. He is attempting to develop the character of Potter Phlegg as a more legitimate type of psychiatrist who could be played by someone younger and better-looking than the real Potter Phlegg. An Adlerian, perhaps, preoccupied with issues of control, conceivably incarnated by John Malkovich. He's also thinking Sabrina could be a little less spacey, an account executive or something like that, a Sharon Stone or Michelle Pfeiffer type.

The Adlerian is a basically decent but devious man trapped in a loveless marriage. He wants out. He has all kinds of business schemes that turn out bad. Loses money in the stock market. The tensions between him and his wife are made worse by the fact that they're both shrinks and work at the same clinic. He has this one patient, a beautiful young woman with Marnie-type phobias, or possibly vertigo, something that will come up later in the movie as a plot twist. Or, what if instead of brothers who confess they've killed their parents, it's sisters, sisters that've suffered years of sexual abuse by their father, or better still, one older Michelle Pfeiffer type sister who's strong, and escaped the abuse by fighting off her dad at a critical age, and a younger more vulnerable sister who's a little bit nuts, who the older sister is trying to protect? A kind of incest-oriented recasting of *The Big Sleep*? Maybe it's not a loveless marriage but a Nick and Nora, sophisticated team of manly therapist Nick Nolte or Tom Berenger, and sassy Freudian Holly Hunter? With a doomed romance angle involving haunted unmolested older sister Uma Thurman and violated younger sister Drew Barrymore? Jack gazes out the living room windows at the wooded hills dotted with houses all around and can't imagine anyone in them with a story worth telling. When he studies this sunny, static vista the dreadful suffocating banality of everyday life works its way into his humors and fills him with a frosty sense of isolation from the world that exists in magazines and movies, and all his ideas become arbitrary and unfeasible, and maybe he'll just die.

Seth, wet, runs past him, disappears down the stairs. Jack looks at the traffic report, miles of crawling insects filmed from a helicopter.

Later, driving downtown, Seth hears words tumbling through his mind, It's enough, No, I can't, This is enough, No more, It's enough, I can't, Enough, I'll die, Enough, No more, Enough.

They are all wearing white and everything is white around the tennis court. The wrought-iron meshwork table is white, the umbrella planted in its center is white, with white fringe dangling evenly from the edges of its white triangular sections, the deck chairs they're sitting in are white, Teddy Wade's shorts and crew-neck shirt and socks and tennis shoes are white, Cassandra's pleated tennis skirt is white, her jersey blouse is white, the sweater loosely tied around her neck is white, and, on the tennis court, Matt O'Reilley, who looks like a heavier and less Hispanic Carlos Martinez, and the actor playing Felix Martinez, Tim Chumley, fresh from a minor role in Broadway's *Tommy*, who looks a little like Michael J. Fox and nothing at all like Felix Martinez, are dressed all in white, also all white is Corey Ryan, who's been a guest star on various TV sitcoms including *Roseanne* and *Home Improvement* and who's playing the tennis coach, of course the north-south tennis court itself is green, with white lines painted on it, and behind Cassandra and Teddy Wade the swimming pool is blue, and the sky is blue, with some wrinkled white clouds in it, and then there's an enormous cluttered machinery of cameras and cables and tracks and reflectors and lights and everything else that's dense and metallic and busy with silent movement, comprising a kind of shadow blackness, Teddy Wade's wearing an artfully ill-fitting black hairpiece that crinkles in the center of his extreme upper forehead, his jowls have been slightly exaggerated with latex makeup, some weight has been added to his waist with padding, Cassandra's hair has been plumped out and given a frizzy look, a decade's been smoothed off her visage with various unguents and creamy paints, the scene is an afternoon chez Martinez, and in fact these are the Martinez tennis court and the Martinez pool, the boys playing vigorous but to their father's vigilant eye less than championship tennis, establishing that (A) they can never live up to their father's unreasonable expectations; as Teddy Wade berates Corey Ryan after Carlos misses a shot, moving in on him at the end of the lesson with understated sadistic relish, it's conveyed that (B) Fidel Martinez is a brutal businessman unmoved by sentimental considerations such as the fact that Carlos and Felix Martinez really like this particular coach, the third Fidel's fired this month; as Cassandra is seen to stifle her own softer opinion of the tennis coach and her feeling that Fidel's severity has gotten way out of hand by reaching for her wineglass and draining it with the visible desire to blot out the present as well as the past and the future, the viewer understands that (C) Peggy Martinez drinks too much, that her role in the family constellation is marginal at best, that some opportunity for reason and kindness to prevail in these posh surroundings, among these attractive but fatally flawed human beings, is being missed at this exact moment irrevocably and for all time. True, A, B and C, and the ensuing D through Z, are clumsy compressions, and there is no real magic going on between any of these actors (despite the friendly blowjob Cassandra has already given Matt O'Reilley, and the impending one Tim Chumley is going to give Teddy Wade, tomorrow night, after a dinner at Drai's), and the resulting two-part prime-time movie will fail to produce any feeling that these characters have actually lived with each other, locked up together in hermetic asphyxiating cannibalistic proximity, for years and years. Cassandra is mainly hoping that she looks convincingly young, not as fresh perhaps as she did on *Vampire Cop* but ready for solid mature parts of the kind sometimes played by Farrah Fawcett, Suzanne Pleshette, or Marlo Thomas, while Teddy Wade is hoping that his willingness to add years and a few cosmetic flaws to his ageless, flawless face and body will win him more of the serious, if not quite De Niro or Pacino quality, attention he's been getting since his surprising turn as an AIDS patient in *An Ordinary Heart* and his searing portrayal of a recovering coke addict in *Monkey on My Back.*

Like the myriad impassioned viewers or listeners who are, at the very moment when Teddy Wade is leaping up from his deck chair to growl at Corey Ryan "I don't pay people to teach my sons to play tennis like pansies" (a line Teddy thinks could be a touch more concise and less overtly homophobic), phoning in to Court TV and radio shows across the country, the cast and crew of *Dark Blood* are "deeply divided" on the question of whether Carlos and Felix Martinez actually experienced sexual and other abuse from their parents. Indeed, like most unknowable things, opinions on this issue are defended with considerably more violence than opinions about matters of provable fact. Lucas Spelvin, the director of this masterpiece, is pretty firm in his manufactured-abuse-defense-though-the-father-was-a-shit position, while his cinematographer, Lazlo Daley, takes an even firmer spoiled-sociopathic-brats line. Teddy Wade, understandably, is squeamish about the fag stuff but feels the character he's playing must have been like his own nasty, authoritarian father, whom Teddy would gladly have paid to have dumped into Lake Superior from a low-flying aircraft, had Wade, Sr., not recently suffered a massive stroke that has left him gratifyingly speechless and paralyzed on the left side. Cassandra feels—well, Cassandra's feelings are complex. She has a teenage son whose behavior patterns are at least as troubling as and possibly more antisocial than her own, and suspects at times that her formidably bad example has created a juvenile monster, though she counters these suspicions by reminding herself that she is, after all, an artist, and therefore uncontrollable in her narcissism and single-minded dedication to her art: yes, such dedication comes with a high price tag, the human costs are often higher than we would wish, especially to other people, but Cassandra is what she is, and to be other than what she is would run against her very nature and destroy her art. Because of various episodes in her long and rather variegated nurturing of Frankie, Cassandra tends to credit the hanky-panky-in-the-shower school of thinking in the Martinez case, but isn't clear about why this would be, in and of itself, sufficient motive for pat- and matricide.

Matt O'Reilley is tackling the role of Carlos with a flinching-browbeaten-simmering quality, as of one who's had too much of Teddy Wade-as-Fidel Martinez's expectations thrust upon him, though in real life, as his chum Tim Chumley's confided, it's Tim who's in line for Teddy's thrusting expectations, eager for them in a way, since Tim is the only major cast member completely sold on the repeated-rape-by-the-father scenario and plans to keep this ghastly incest secret uppermost in his Actors' Studio bag of tricks during the later-to-be-filmed courtroom scenes, sketched out sketchily in the script since the real-life Felix Martinez is only now, today, testifying in the actual murder trial. Matt O'Reilley has actually had sex with one of his many stepfathers, but as a consenting-adult type of encounter years after his mother, the actress Maureen O'Reilley, divorced the stepfather in question, who was, in any case, closer in age to Matt than to Maureen. Matt thinks it is not unlikely that he will also have sex with Tim Chumley, his screen brother, before the end of shooting, having already had sex with or at least a blowjob from his screen mother. There is no business, he reflects, quite like show business.

Now, on Friday, did you hear your brother testify that you went to the Gun-O-Rama in Venice Beach and asked about buying handguns Yes And were told there was a fifteen-day waiting period Yes Is that accurate Yes Did you do that Yes Before you left to go to Gun-O-Rama had you been practicing tennis Yes And did your brother say something that got you to stop practicing and do something else Yes Now, did you hear your brother testify that he said Just because it's a new day doesn't mean everything is fine That's more or less what he said What did you say to him that made him say that to you He came over to the tennis court and asked if I was ready and I said No, I'm in a tournament in two weeks, I don't feel like it, and he said something like I realize this is hard but this is real this isn't going to go away, this is serious, and I just didn't want to deal with it Were you thinking it was a sunny morning Yes And what were you thinking about whether it was real I thought it was real but it seemed like a bad dream The night before was a bad dream The next day the birds were chipping and the sun was shining and it just seemed like this wasn't happening So after your brother told you things were serious did you have to think about it Yes Did you agree with him Yes I agreed to go Did you think his talk with your father, confrontation, your mother telling you what she told you, that that was serious I knew it was serious but I didn't want to think about it Was there a time years earlier when your father threatened to do something if you told, had you thought about that If I told He told me what he would do if I told Told you what He said he'd kill me, he said he'd tie me to a chair and beat me to death, he said all sorts of things Did you picture what might happen if this came out inside your family, if you told Carlos No After you went to Gun-O-Rama in Venice did you drive to San Diego with Carlos Soon after When you started out for San Diego had you made any decision to buy a long gun because you couldn't get a handgun No Was there a discussion when that was decided There was a discussion before yes And you decided you had to get a gun even if it was a long gun Yes And what did you and Carlos talk about in the car The things Dad had done to me Sexual things and other things Yes And this was the first time you told him Yes The details Did you tell him all the details, everything that happened over twelve years No absolutely not What did you tell him about the sex itself Objection to the form of the question It's not offered for truth, Your Honor There's no request for the substance of it just whether he recalls so the objection is overruled What's the question Do you remember what you told your brother about what the sexual activity had been between you and your father Yes What did you tell him the sexual activity had been Objection Objection sustained to the form of the question, calls for hearsay It's not being offered for truth Your Honor but goes to state of mind All right This will be received only as it might reflect upon the state of mind of the person hearing the statement as to what if any state of mind he had in reaction to it All right Do you understand the question Yes Can you answer the question I told Carlos it was oral sex And did you mention any kind of violence that accompanied the oral sex Yes What did you tell him about violence I told him there were tacks and pins Dad stuck in me Did you give him the impression tacks and pins were used during oral sex Yes And did that in fact happen between you and your father Yes What did you say about weapons your father threatened you with I told him Dad threatened me with a knife Was there an occasion when you told your father no Yes Did he use a knife on that occasion Yes Did you tell your brother about threats your father made Yes Had your father threatened to hurt anybody besides you if you told anybody Yes What was that threat He said he would kill anybody I told After the argument with your mother on Saturday you and your brother went outside and had another talk, didn't you Yes What did you do after that I went up to

my room Did you take the gun I took the gun Had you changed the two rounds
you'd previously put in the gun No When you got to the room, where did you
put the gun down Beside my bed What did you do after putting the gun down I
waited around and looked out the window toward the guest house Why Looking at Carlos gave me a lot of comfort, I wanted to see what he was doing Do
you have any idea what time that was One-thirty in the morning Were you in a
condition to go to sleep No Why couldn't you go to sleep I was real tense, real
scared My nerves were fried Did you get undressed No Did you hear someone
approaching your room Yes What did you hear Footsteps Had you locked your
door Yes Could you tell whose footsteps they were I was hoping it wasn't Dad
but I was wrong After the footsteps did you hear anything else Yeah my dad
pounding my door and telling me to open the goddam door Objection Overruled as to the question but let's not refer to them as Mom and Dad, they're his
father and mother How do you refer to your parents when you talk about them
Mom and Dad Could you tell who the person was It was Dad What did your
father say He pounded the door with I guess his fists telling me to open the
goddam door What was your reaction I ran to my gun and grabbed it What did
you do after you grabbed the gun I sat on my bed with my gun across my lap
What was going through your mind That he was going to break the door down
What were you going to do if he broke the door down I was gonna shoot Did
you think you'd be able to shoot I really didn't think so Why not I was frozen I
knew what he was going to do and I thought I've gotta shoot him and I remembered I only had two shells in the gun and I was thinking Oh my god I'm
gonna die If I miss him or I hit him and my mom's still in the house, Carlos is
all the way in the guest house Did you think two rounds of ammunition would
be enough to kill someone I didn't think it would kill my dad and even if it did
my mom had a gun in her room, and I thought I'd have to jump out the
window, all these thoughts were racing through my mind How did you know
your mother had a gun Because she bought a gun the year before Did you
think there was one gun in the house or more than one No, there were two
rifles and I believe a starter pistol or a pellet gun Was that a long BB-type gun
or a pistol gun A long gun With respect to one of these rifles you said you
knew your mother bought it a year before Yes How did you know she bought a
gun the year before Because I was with her Where did she buy it Somewhere
in Woodland Hills across from the Topanga Mall, SportLand or something How
did you happen to be with her when she bought the gun We were in her
Mercedes and she said I have to buy something and we went to SportLand and
I just wandered around the store and she came out with it to the parking lot

You met up with her outside the store I only remember walking to the car and asking her what was in this long box she had She opened it up She showed you Yes What was in the box A wooden, partly engraved brown and black rifle Did you ask her anything about it Yes, I asked why she bought it What did she say She said I'm going to kill somebody Actually she said someone, I'm going to kill someone Did you ask her who she was going to kill I had some ideas Did you ask her No, I didn't ask a single question Why didn't you ask who she was going to kill Because You're with your mother and she buys a gun and says she's going to kill someone, right Yes Your family is the kind of family where everyone asks each other a lot of questions and communicates a lot No We don't ask each other questions especially my mom the way she was she did a lot of strange things and was taking a lot of medication thirteen or fifteen pills every day she disappeared a lot she went into a lot of her rages all the time, I was afraid of her, her outbursts and so on, the fact that she wasn't completely stable, I thought I knew why she bought the gun anyway Did you think she bought it to kill herself No To kill your father, to kill you, why To kill a burglar To kill a bird She didn't say why I thought she would kill one of my father's girlfriends or maybe kill Dad, I was hoping Dad You hoped for her sake For my sake Do you remember the date of this rifle purchase by your mother The summer before Do you recognize this as a receipt for a .22-caliber gun Yes It says Best Products Northridge California That isn't where she bought it You don't remember the name of the store as Best Products No You said your thought was if you unfroze enough to fire the two rounds in the gun your mother might be there with the gun she bought Yes Did you call Carlos on the telephone to tell him what was happening No Why not I didn't want them to know I was calling my brother Was there any point between Thursday and Sunday when you were not frightened No I always thought they were going to kill me You left Sunday and came back midday Yes Did you have a conversation with your brother when you came back, when he told you what he thought was going on in the house No, he hadn't gone into the house, if I remember, I said Carlos, the whole idea is for you to find out what's going on, you've got to go into the house, if you don't we won't know what's happening Did he seem afraid He was doing his usual stalling pretending he would go and I thought he was too scared to do it Did you park where you thought your car wouldn't be seen Yes in the back alley Did you leave again after talking to your brother Yes Did you get home later than you told your brother you would Yes You knew your parents, didn't you I knew them in some ways better than Carlos did Based on what he said and what was in your own head what did you think was about to happen I thought they would kill us Did you and your brother go to the house to tell your mother you were leaving Yes Can you say what happened when you got to the house We went to the kitchen to the back area Carlos went through the kitchen into the dining room it's a little different than in this diagram This is the front door you understand that Yes When you enter the house through the front door there's a living room on the right and the so-called rumpus room on the left and a dining room beyond Yes This is a staircase Yes There aren't any stairs there, and no door here, and there should be a door there And there are stairs here Yes Now this is what's called the rumpus room Yes This is a service porch and opens to the backyard Yes There's a tennis court here Yes A maid's room here Yes An exit from the maid's room to the side yard Yes but it was hardly ever used We came from the kitchen and I didn't want to go into the rumpus room Carlos went in and told her we were going out and I went through the dining room into the foyer Through a door that isn't on this diagram Yes So, you went, how did you get into the house We went through the service area and maybe through the break-fast room I can't remember Were there doors from the breakfast room going to the backyard Yes, those aren't on here either French doors There should be French doors right here Then a door leading into the service porch Yes, right there So you went through one of those and you went into the kitchen Right Between the kitchen and the dining room there was a door, wasn't there Yes You could go through that door without being seen by people in the rumpus room Yes You could however also go straight into the rumpus room from there Yes After you went into the dining room could you hear what was being said in the rumpus room Carlos was walking out of the rumpus room followed by my mom Why did he go into the rumpus room To tell them we were going out Did you cut through the dining room into the foyer Yes, right here, there's no door, only an arch, I went through the dining room into the foyer then crossed the foyer into the archway Did you see your brother or hear your brother Yes Which first I think I saw him first When you saw him did you see your mother at the same time Yes Where were they They were right in front of the bath-room and the foyer starts right there What did you hear them talking about I heard my mother tell Carlos that I couldn't go out, and Carlos asked why, and she started to stammer and couldn't answer Was there anything noteworthy in your mind about that I started getting chills right then Why Because they were saying we couldn't go out, that meant we would be alone with them in the house What did Carlos say to her I don't know I don't remember Your mother started to answer She started to say because, because, she ended up saying

Because I say so, and that's when my dad came out Where did he come from He came from the rumpus room You saw him Yes I saw him come out and say Shut up Peggy When your father came out of that room would you tell us and show us what he did He said Shut up Peggy I saw you made a gesture with your left hand Yes he used his hands a lot Had you seen that gesture before Yes he did that when he wanted someone to shut up or stop moving or wanted you to listen to him A sharp, chopping kind of gesture Yes When he said Shut up Peggy what did your mother do She shut up What did your father do He told Carlos that he wasn't going out Did he say anything else He told me to get up to my room, he said he'd be there in a minute, to wait for him in my room How did Carlos respond when your father gestured and told you to get up to your room He said No, you're not going to touch my brother, and I think he looked at me and told me to come back down the stairs, I just remember he told my dad You're not going to touch my little brother, you're not going to touch Felix, you're never going to touch him again Did Carlos say anything to you about, we're going out anyway, or something like that No he didn't say come back we're leaving I thought to myself Carlos what are you doing you're crazy don't start a fight now and I was going up the stairs really slowly When your brother told your father you're not going to touch my brother what did your father do He just jumped at Carlos, he said I do what I want in my family, it's not your brother, it's my son, and he was yelling Did he move toward Carlos Yes he walked right up to him as if he wanted to fight, I couldn't believe what was happening Carlos backed up when your father came toward him Yes, whenever Dad came toward him he backed away When your father told him that did Carlos answer him Carlos said No you're not gonna touch him but his voice was weaker Did Carlos say anything more about leaving the house He maybe told Dad We're leaving but my dad he doesn't stop it's just a rush of wind No he's my son he's not your little brother I say what goes in this family, you're not going out, Carlos saying You're not going to touch him my father saying Don't tell me what to do, coming closer, then telling me to get up to my room because I was still on the stairs Mr. Martinez what did you think your father had in mind when he said Go up to your room I'll be there in a minute I had two things in my mind When he first said it before the confrontation with your brother I knew what he was saying What in your opinion was he saying He was saying he was coming up to my room to have sex with me It's what he always did when he said that When he said what That he'll be there That he'll be where When he said to get up to my room and said he was coming up that's what he meant Would he mean that for various kinds of sex or just one kind or what For various kinds it depended really on how angry he was sometimes he said Get up to your room I'll be there in a few minutes sometimes he said Go to your room I'll be there in a minute you could tell from his tone how angry he was what type of sex he wanted to have What type did you think he was threatening you with Sunday night Sex What kind of sex in the past three years what you called sex was that something your father did in anger or something more neutral what was it It was done in anger Did it start out that way years earlier No Okay your father approaches Carlos and tells you again go up to your room, what is your state of mind at that point about what your father has in mind It didn't just change it was one and then the other I thought they were going to kill us but I thought Dad was going to have sex there wasn't any doubt about it in my mind at that point I was more afraid of him coming up and having sex than anything else Did something change after that Yeah What changed I realized from looking at Mom it was clear what was going on Where was Mom during this exchange She came up along beside him against the wall on the other side of the bathroom How did she look what did she say or do She didn't say anything it just ended with Dad saying You're not leaving the house then he went back to the den and my mother stayed in the foyer talking to Carlos she said things like You ruined this family, Carlos said something, I don't remember, something like Are you going to let this happen or Do you want this to happen, I thought he was talking about them killing us or my father coming up to my room I couldn't hear I could see my mother from the balcony her face from the stairs on the way up just from her face if you knew her different looks her face was stone, resolved, not nervous or frightened maybe a little angry not out of control she was just in a strong sort of hard look not flipping out not any of that just a resolved expression that scared me because my mom was not often in control she wasn't often completely aware of everything in her surroundings she was often paranoid or something could set her off real easy and a conversation like this where Dad was yelling at Carlos or me she took his side right away and got angry with us and either repeated what he said or just sat there but with this angry scowl on her face that this wasn't the case here So after this exchange between your mother and your brother what happens Your father comes out of where And he grabs your mother What did he say What happens next Did you hear them close the door How could you see that from the balcony So it's like an open rectangle And what you're calling a balcony is like a gallery is it not it's a straight corridor that's above the staircase and there's an opening where you can see down And you were watching your parents during this argument How carefully were you watching Now, at that point, what did you think was happening You thought both things were going to happen At that point did your brother come up the stairs And did you say anything to your brother What do you remember telling him that you recall What did your brother say to you And what did you think already, before your brother said anything, what did you think was going to be the result of that night And what about your brother, what was going to happen to him What did you think would be the condition of your brother And die at whose hands And when your brother told you It's happening now, that's what you already thought Do you consider yourself to be emotionally different than your brother Which of you did you think scared easier And over the course of your life was that true So in looking to your brother what were you trying to see Tell me what he looked like, what did you see or hear over the course from Thursday and Sunday And on Sunday How did it affect you to see your brother, who was less emotional than you, to see him that scared On this occasion when your brother appeared frightened on the stairs, could you compare that to any other occasion in your life Was it the same as other occasions Was there anything in your past that was as frightening as what was happening on Sunday night on the stairs At that point, after your brother said it's happening now, you said your thought was I have to get to the car, what was in the car All the shells The gun was in the bedroom I knew I had to get to my bedroom but I also knew from the night before that for some stupid reason I didn't load the gun and I only had two rounds so I needed the shells in the car I went to the bedroom first and got my gun and then out to the car did it occur to me to close the door and sit there with two shells in the gun and wait for them yes it flashed in my mind to barricade the room but I knew I couldn't do it because I panicked whenever something like this was happening not exactly things like this but them coming to the room a lot, before, before, almost all the times with the sex I said to myself I'm not gonna let this happen when he comes in the room I'm gonna fight him I'm gonna jump on him I imagined myself on a ledge jumping down on him all kinds of things anything to stop the sex and when he came in the room I just crumbled I couldn't do anything I didn't think I could fight back if I waited in the room because my dad is such a big guy I don't know what it was it was just my dad there was something about it I couldn't with the sex he would just come in the room and I wanted to say No I don't want to do this and I'd want to say don't touch me and I'd see him and he was like huge and he did what he wanted to do I couldn't stop it I wanted to but I couldn't I don't know why You did run out to the car Yes You did load your gun Yes What did you do with the two rounds of birdshot you put in the gun Friday I unloaded them Why did you unload them Because of what the man at the gun store told us He said they weren't good for protection Yes Did you load the gun with the new ammunition Actually what the man said was they weren't good for protection because they're these teeny little The question is did you load the gun Yes Do you remember how many shells you put in I don't remember it was dark I just reached in and grabbed them and loaded them I think it was five I think I loaded it all the way I knew how without having to slide the pump down So you put in as many as you could without doing that Yes And are you sure you put all new stuff I tried to yes At that point you had a loaded gun, correct Yes So why didn't you wait and see what your parents were going to do Because I'm thinking they're coming out I thought I only had seconds as soon as they came out of the room I would die, I was going to die, I had to get to that room before they came out of the room, if the doors had opened and they were standing there with guns I knew I was going to freeze I was terrified of them getting out of that room that they were going to take my gun, it was this stupidly big thing and it was just like they could grab it as soon as I walked in the door Did you think they were armed at that point I thought they were but as I ran toward the foyer I just kept thinking They're going to get this They're going to get the gun Yes After you entered the rumpus room what happened I just remember firing Did you aim in any particular place Just in front of me Where were you standing In front of the coffee table How did the coffee table line up with the television It was right in front So you were between the television and the coffee table or were you between the coffee table and the couch I was between the television and the coffee table How close to the coffee table were you I don't recall I wasn't close Were you closer to the television Yes When you went into the room how soon did you start firing Immediately And when you came to this position between the television and the coffee table did you keep moving or at some point did you stand still I guess I kept moving I ran into the room I guess I kept moving When you say you were between the coffee table and the television at what point was that When I finished firing That's where you ended up Yes You said you fired directly in front of you Yes If you're moving from the doors to the area of the television and the coffee table are you firing at the bookcases directly in front of you No I just fired In what direction In front of me What was in front of you My parents So you were firing at your parents Yes Was Carlos to your right or your left To my left Could you tell when you went through the doors where your parents were They were in front of us Where were they in relation to the furniture Behind the coffee table My dad wasn't but my mom was When you say your dad wasn't behind the coffee table where was he He was in front of the couch a little to the left I just saw this figure I thought was him he was right there Did you see another figure besides the figure you thought was your dad Yes What was the position of that figure To my dad's right Did you get in front of that figure Yes Am I in front of you now Yes We're not directly in front of each other No But you're in front of me and I'm in front of you, correct Yes Do you know if you were lined directly up in front of the second figure I don't know I don't know I don't know I walked into the room and started firing I didn't think about where was this where was that I just started firing and I don't know Did you fire at the second figure did you fire at the first figure do you know I don't know Did you ever get closer to either of those figures than the area between the television and the coffee table I was as close as I was I didn't think about it we ended up about two or three feet away Two or three feet away from what The coffee table The coffee table had two ends, I was maybe two feet away from the middle of the coffee table And that's where you say you ended up Yes And were you further away before then Yes The television was more than four feet away from the coffee table wasn't it Probably four feet and I was standing in the middle maybe two feet away from each The television is about twelve feet away from the coffee table isn't it Twelve feet away It's completely across from the far wall of the room isn't it Yes but the coffee table is in the center of the room the coffee table wasn't twelve feet away from the television it was four or six feet So you were between the television and the coffee table more or less More or less However far it might have been Yes And when you ended up wherever you ended up was the firing over Yes What had stopped the firing why did it stop I just fired as much as I could And how much was as much as you could did you empty the gun Yes every shell I had in the gun And after that did something happen Yes Was the room different Yes What was different about the room I didn't see the people there was a lot of smoke it was dark there was light from the hallway from the television it was eerie Was it darker before or after the shooting Before It was darker before Yes I don't understand if there was smoke in the room The smoke made it harder to see It was harder to see after the shooting Yes When you went in the room were the lights on No Was the television on Yes After the shooting was the television on Yes Were the lights still off Yes When the shooting ended could you see your mother or father Yes Who could you see My father And where was he On the couch Could you see your mother No What happened after the shooting stopped I heard a noise from my mom What was your reaction to that noise I ran out of the room How did the noise make you feel I was scared it scared me I had to get out of there Where did you go Out to the foyer to the front door Where did you go To the car When you got to the car what did you do Carlos and I were scrambling for any shell we could find and I just handed him one You found a shell Yes Was it birdshot or buckshot I didn't look You gave it to Carlos Yes Then what happened Carlos ran back in the house and I sort of followed but I didn't want to go in Did you go in the house Yes Did you go back into the rumpus room No Did Carlos go into the rumpus room He was already there by that point Did you hear anything at that point I heard Carlos firing the gun You heard the gun go off Yes Did you see Carlos fire the gun No Where were you I was coming toward the rumpus room Where was Carlos when you saw him again Coming out of the rumpus room And at that point what did you do I just sat on the stairs And what did he do He sat on the ground across from me

Frankie Lomax chews a cruller in front of Winchell's Donut near Santa Monica and Crescent Heights. Four-thirty traffic surges east and west, north and south, cars and buildings ripple slightly in waves of torched gasoline, and Frankie is thinking about putting on his Rollerblades, which hang from his shoulder by their laces, and he wonders how many people in the passing cars notice that he's only wearing sneakers, socks, a denim vest, a money pouch, and a pair of purple boxer shorts. He's also thinking of getting his hair cut real short on the bottom and getting a price coding label tattooed on the back of his neck. In the money pouch he has eleven dollars and some change and a little crystal wrapped in foil, some phone numbers smeared on paper scraps, a condom or two, and the keys to the house in Altadena. He finishes the cruller, wipes his sugary fingers on his boxer shorts. He can't resist feeling the metal balls of his new Prince Albert through the fabric: now that his dick has healed, it feels twice as sensitive as before, though he knows he probably just thinks about it twice as often.

It's the hour when everybody's leaning on his horn, stop-and-go traffic, little dramas happening in glass bubbles. Frankie decides against the Rollerblades and starts walking east toward the bars. He nods to some kids hustling on the opposite sidewalk but they ignore him. He thinks he'll do his hair blond when he has it cut, but showing the black roots. A guy sitting in a parked maroon pickup with a pink roof catches his attention as he walks past, Frankie looks back, the guy waves, Frankie lopes over to the open window. It's a nice-looking goatee guy named Ray or Ron who bought Frankie a drink once at the piano bar in back of Sabor. Eating some take-out glop from Chef Ming's with chopsticks. Frankie leans in the window. Ray or Ron, he guesses Ray, chews up a mouthful of brown stringy stuff, swallows, and says You available right now? and Frankie shrugs and says It all de pe pe pe pe pe pends.

Ray is a friendly, self-assured type of guy, late thirties, early forties, dressed in jeans and a CalTech sweatshirt and work boots, and after Frankie gets in the truck he remembers that Ray's either an exterminator or a pool cleaner, Frankie can picture them drinking scotch and sodas while a guy of about eighty sang "The Way We Were" in Sabor. He recalls being put off by the crowd in that bar, the way they were dressed more than the fact that most of them were really old. And Ray asking him if he could get into something, Frankie forgets what. It's too far back and maybe he's thinking of someone else. Ray scarfs down the rest of the take-out container and tells Frankie what he wants to do and how much he'll pay, it's kind of elaborate for seventy dollars but Frankie figures he'll snort crystal and get through it fast. Ray adds that he's just taken X and feels really, really horny.

On the way to Ray's, Ray tells him how fucking relieved he is that he doesn't have to work the next day, he's been running his nuts off and some client in Woodland Hills keeps trying to adjust her own chlorine and screwing up her water system and then expects him to correct it free of charge. Every time Ray hits a red light he reaches over and runs a hand across Frankie's bare chest and stomach, thrilled at his musculature, and squeezes Frankie's large nipples, right in traffic where anybody can see, as he does this he groans with pleasure, added to which Ray's muffler is going so the truck makes this rumbling farty noise Frankie can't stand. He switches the radio on. It's tuned to JD Owsley's drive-time program. Frankie considers telling Ray that he personally knows JD Owsley, not as a trick but socially. JD's guests are a shrink and four teenagers who killed their abusive parent or parents at various times in the middle past. Frankie tries to follow the discussion, thinking he should be on the show himself, as Ray jabbers on about the art of pool clean-ing, pausing occasionally to stroke Frankie's thigh or pinch Frankie's nipple, which eventually gets Frankie's boner sticking straight up in his shorts, an outrageous-looking tent that causes Ray to sail through a red light and almost collide with a PG&E truck. Frankie plants his feet against the dashboard and tells him to cu-cu-cu-cu-cuntrol himself, hoping his penis shrinks before he gets out of the truck.

Ray's apartment is above a garage, behind an apartment house, on a narrow street off Fountain Avenue: the drive slopes up beside the apartment house and flows into a small parking lot, where Ray backs the truck into the garage beside a gray Camry. Someone has fingered WASH ME into the dust on the Camry's windshield. There's a small door between two big garage doors, behind it a narrow stairway covered in cheap, disintegrating brown carpet. Ray apologizes for the mess as he opens the door, and it is a mess, the kind of place Frankie himself would probably inhabit if he had a place of his own. Shag carpet the same as the stairs covering the living room floor, the carpet giving the room a furry organic look, like this is the place where food and furniture come together. A glass kidney-shaped table, a small sofa the color of boiled cabbage, a fifties standing lamp, lots of fat candles in tea saucers, magazines and newspapers strewn around along with some clothes, a Lava lamp with red and yellow blobs inside it, an old-fashioned stereo cabinet in scarred somethingwood, shiny in spots where a coating of dust has been swiped by moving objects, narrow silver blinds filtering the daylight into pencil lines that slash the furniture. As soon as they're in the door Ray's pulling off his boots and telling Frankie to make himself comfortable, sticks a Judas Priest CD into a CD player, at the same time switching on a TV, Frankie slumps onto the couch in front of the TV, Ray asks if he wants a beer, Ray needs a shower first, he brings Frankie a can of beer from the kitchen and tells him to take his sneakers off, make himself at home, asks him if he wants a hit of ecstasy which he brings out in a little stash box with some roaches in it and places on the coffee table, then disappears into a bathroom at the rear of the apartment leaving Frankie there in his socks and boxer shorts, glugging beer and staring at Oprah and nodding along to Judas Priest and playing with himself in a desultory way, his dick with the shiny Prince Albert stuck through it poking out of the slit in his boxers, pretty soon he hears the shower running over the throb of the music and the little bug voices on *Oprah* so he takes a quick look at Ray's little bedroom and the kitchen, stroking his bone the whole time in a lubricious trance that hasn't got anything to do with Ray or Ron per se but rather this feeling that comes over him sometimes that the power concentrated in his prick and balls and his whole body is the only important element in the vicinity. This feeling is seldom a good augur for Frankie's customers and today is unexceptional. Frankie can sometimes bend his idea of fun when it registers that someone else is really there, important in some way, but he resents Ray fingering him in the truck, and the lack of posh in Ray's life generally from the looks of this apartment.

There's nothing worth stealing in this place except the little drug stash.

Frankie swallows a pill with his beer, gets another can from the fridge, whips his boxers off and sticks them under the coffee table with his money belt and vest and sneakers and Rollerblades and arranges himself spread-legged on the couch, lights the longest roach he can find, sucks down a lot of smoke, cuts a loud fart while he's snorting some poppers, channel-surfs with the remote, hears the toilet flushing a few times and figures Ray, Ron, whoever, is giving himself a douche, Frankie pumps his sagging dick getting it stiff again, he pictures various people sucking him, various slick cunts and assholes and mouths engorging him, inevitably he also sees himself disabling the alarm system in the rear entrance of his father's house, it doesn't take a genius, blowing out the pilot on the gas stove, padding barefoot into the garage and pouring a trail of lawn mower fuel through the kitchen and part of the back-yard, waiting and waiting to switch on the Primus stove they used on their camping trips, he remembers running back about a mile to where he'd tied the horse to some rancher's fence and listening for the explosion as he rode the perimeter of the state park, in his mind he sees the winds spreading flames all over Malibu Canyon and sees himself rubbing his new Prince Albert over Cassandra's eyelids, sees his cum running down her face like spit, he looks down and finds Ray in a bath towel yanking at one of his socks, inhales some more amyl nitrite while Ray laps the bottom of his foot and sucks on his toes, looking up into his face questioningly, his mouth ridiculously distended with half of Frankie's foot in it, squatting on his haunches a little hairy in the legs no back hair thank God next he wants to gobble the old prong sniffing poppers Frankie gets up on his knees making Ray slide under him with his legs pointed up the back of the couch his head dangling over the edge and eye level with Frankie's cock which Frankie guides into Ray's mouth holding up the back of Ray's head the hair's still wet and pulling his face down on his dick, the angle causing Ray a lot of pain he's pretty sure, the dick keeps flapping up and Frankie keeps pushing it down and forcing it into the mouth, Lick the balls, Frankie tells him, not Lick my balls because the word "my" makes him stutter, Ray obediently licks and laps and sucks on the balls, his hands kneading Frankie's ass, Frankie's big penis rubbing his face, Frankie moves off his knees and stands up Ray's head between his legs and sits down on Ray's face, really sits on it like it's a chair or a toilet seat his asshole over Ray's mouth his balls squashed against Ray's nose, jacking himself off as Ray struggles to breathe and tongue-fuck Frankie's ass at the same time not able to really, Ray's tongue in his ass makes Frankie feel all loose and wet Oh ma ma man he says Stay like that I gotta piss don't moo moo move jumps away from

Ray's mouth runs into the bathroom tries to piss through his erection, he can't make the dick point into the toilet bowl, he runs a forest-green washcloth under the cold tap and wraps it around his meat until it gets a little soft, pisses, flushes the toilet, when he comes out Ray's changed the CD to some Ronnie James Dio thing and Frankie says Party time, le le let's gu gu gu go in the bedroom, Ray's taken off the towel they go in the room Ray lights a candle behind a Hindu statuette of some sort that throws all these weird shadows on the wall it's a small room and the bed fills most of it and after sucking Frankie's nuts and worshipping his asshole a little more Ray brings out these handcuffs and Frankie cuffs him arms forward facedown to the rungs of the bed frame and stuffs a pillow between the cuffs and the rungs Ray doesn't like this arrangement but Frankie tells him he loves it like this Ray kneeling with his ass in the air there's some lube beside the statuette Frankie squeezes some onto his fingers and works the fingers into Ray's ass Ray moaning with excite-ment he smells of some herbal shampoo and fruity soap Frankie takes his fingers out of Ray's ass and pumps his cock with the greasy fingers getting himself hard pushes two fingers of his left hand into Ray's rectum moves them around inside pushes another finger in Ray's gasping Frankie makes a kind of wedge with all five fingers pressed together and forces the bundle of fingers inside with a screwing motion gets them in up to the knuckles Ray's saying No it's too much it hurts Frankie says Relax I'm an esspert at this muh muh muh di di di dad's a proctologist giving Ray's rather modest cock a perfunctory tug, it's half-hard, Frankie keeps pressing his other hand in which moves forward a little and feels stuck everything inside there feels strange all these soft bumps and squishing velvety folds Ray's making a lot of noise Frankie pulls off the sock he's still wearing on his right foot his fist still in Ray's ass, the movement necessary to remove the sock and then stuff it into Ray's mouth causes his hand to slide deeper into Ray's curious insides, the arm goes in over the wrist, Ray's trying to scream through the sock but it sounds like Mmmm Uuuuuggg Nnnnhhhh Fuh fuh fuh fuck you Frankie screams at Ray's back, Le le le lay yu yu yu fu fu fu fuck tra tra tra tra try and enjoy yourself slapping his buttocks hard, stuff is tearing and snapping in the expanding tunnel of Ray's asshole as Frankie punches through some membrane or who knows what his arm inside now as far as the elbow what the fuck is he complaining about this is hot, Frankie pumps his arm in and out, there's a lot more give in the asshole now, Ray's making a lot of noise through the sock, Frankie's fist pops out all bloody, he wipes it across Ray's back and slides his throbbing boner in the brackish hole and fucks it for a minute or two—the Prince Albert really does enhance the sensation—then gets an idea Don't mu mu move he says runs to the kitchen and finds a long serrated steak knife, Ray's thrashing around on the bed unable to turn around completely because of the handcuffs the sock's hanging out of his mouth blood seeping out of his ass the smell of blood is overwhelming Frankie pushes the sock deep into Ray's throat and squeezes Ray's nostrils shut holding the nose tight while dancing around to avoid Ray's thrashing legs brandishing the steak knife in front of Ray's wide-open eyes Is your na na na na name Ray or Ron, Frankie asks, I got a ba ba ba ba bad me me me memory for names Ray seems to be losing consciousness, Frankie lets go of Ray's nose, puts the knife down, and starts strangling him from behind, straddling his back, Yu yu yu you are hot, Frankie says, hot fu fu fu fuck number one fuck digging his fingers into the windpipe, he takes a shit on Ray's back as he dies, then rams the steak knife up Ray's ass, giving it a hard twist when it's firmly embedded, pretending that he's cutting out a tumor or something. He thinks about sawing off the head but decides that's over the top. Frankie takes a long hot shower soaping off blood, jacks himself off under the spray finally spurting his cum in an awesome jet, dries himself carefully and fusses with his hair, wiping steam off the mirror with a towel. He returns to the bedroom and thinks about doing other stuff with Ray, give him an artificial vagina or other surgical improvement, but there is an off-putting aspect to Ray's corpse, Frankie can't tell if it's the turd squashed on Ray's back or the weird configuration of the limbs, he likes the surprised look frozen on the face and slaps it a few times with his limp cock but this isn't enough to inspire further lust. He pulls his wet sock out of Ray's mouth and wipes a little vomit off on Ray's goatee and puts the sock on his foot with distaste, goes back for the washcloth, and starts wiping his prints off stuff that he's touched. He puts on Ray's denim pants, which fit pretty good, and borrows a shirt from the closet, a nice conservative cotton number, finds his other sock in the living room, wonders for the second time this afternoon whether to put on his sneakers or the Rollerblades, opts for the sneakers again, empties Ray's stash into his money pouch, snorts some of the crystal he now wishes he'd taken an hour ago, smokes up another roach and watches Ricki Lake and *World Money Report* until it's dark outside, carefully wiping his prints off the remote when he leaves. The doorknobs, the beer cans, the poppers. Outside he risks going into the garage to rub his prints off the panel truck, even though he can hear conversations going on in the apartment house. It sounds like people are having dinner. Later, when he's tossing Ray's wallet into a storm drain on De Longpre, Frankie checks out the driving license and sees that the guy's name was actually Robert. Robert Blakely. He's terrible with names.

Are you ever going to tell me what's bothering you, Jack asks Seth, who's making a big fuss this afternoon about a lot of things, mainly the money involved in flying back to New York and getting his bills paid and Sheraton Pyle's "Black Reflections on a White Double Murder" that's apparently coming out next week in the *New Yorker* and the fact that the rap song "Kike Landlord" is no. 10 on the *Billboard* chart, Jack's bracing himself for a night in the cab with a small tumbler of jalapeño vodka and Seth's also mildly critical about that, You were doing so well, he says, look at how clear your skin is and everything, Oh says Jack it's just a gift, which is true, last night one of the women in his political group who's decided to turn herself in for a 1972 bank holdup gave everybody a bottle of the flavored vodkas she's been marketing for the past six years, Everything's bothering me, Seth tells him, trying a shot glass of the vodka, mmmm, delicious, Maybe you just need to get laid, Jack suggests, get your friend Bobby to come over and hide the salami, Well I would, Seth says, but I can't afford it, Bobby charges one fifty, I thought you said he gives it to you for free says Jack He does says Seth but I prefer to pay him, God, I really can't believe, you know, it says Kike and Hebe and Little Jew rat and it's number ten, The thing is, Jack says, you can't go overboard with this health stuff, if you push too far in one direction you're liable to swing back too far in the other, Yes but Jack at least leave the gun here, No but what is the main problem, Jack wants to know, I wish I could tell you, says Seth, the main problem is I'm crawling out of my skin I need a Valium or Remember Jack says suddenly when you were doing Paulie Crumpet? Seth looks at him blankly and then starts laughing Oh right, that's rich, Jack, I was a child, I had no idea that a junkie never gets hard no matter how many hours you blow him I'll bet that's one blowjob he never forgot oh God what was Paulie Crumpet's real name, Jerome, Jack says, Paulie Jerome, Yeah and I did him in Lizzie the Loser's walk-in closet with the Murphy bed in that dump on Divisadero Street don't tell me he's still alive? Sure, Paulie's teaching Video Art at Northwestern I get a card from him every Christmas

———

Norman how absolutely bizarre you should call, I was just about to phone your bleeper I got another—

Call from Dave Spacey, he finishes for her.

How on earth did you know. He wants the money dropped in a specific trash can on level 7 of the Beverly Center parking garage. He called me, I love this, "you white bitch." Like now he's supposed to be black or something—

Janice can you hear the street construction?

Street—that noise yes—

Were you hearing that sound when Dave Spacey called you?

Norman you're a genius absolutely that drilling I didn't even realize that I was aware of it—

Rupert Tietelbaum used this phone not five minutes ago Janice and furthermore, get this, he was wearing a wig and sunglasses—

This is so exciting Norman it's like an Alfred Hitchcock thriller isn't it why do you suppose he had a wig on what sort of wig—

Well he's obviously got a screw loose somewhere the next step is getting the phone records on this pay phone I also want to double-check that the recorder's working on your phone.

Is that hard? Getting the phone records?

I have a friend Norman says A friend at the phone company.

God who would believe it two hours ago I was watching him on television.

Life is strange, Norman says.

He's kind of a Jekyll and Hyde Norman wouldn't you say?

I'm not a psychiatrist Janice.

That's probably a good thing Norman now tell me what exactly did the wig look like?

I thought his last thing was pretty lame, the woman says. Appalling, the man agrees. Well, he's signed his Faustian pact out here that's for goddam sure. Jack has picked them up at the Bel Age, an elegant couple, him in a light-colored suit, her in a frothy Lacroix thing, in from New York by the accents. Not young and probably older than they look. You mean the one where the daughter with second sight sees a murder or something, the man says. Let's face it Ben has no flair with that type of material. You mean suspense, the woman says. He has no feeling for suspense. There was too much music, the man says. He's too old to be influenced by MTV. But that's the style now. I don't think she had second sight, the woman says. Yes she did, the man says.

No I thought it was the father had this near-death or what was it he came out of a coma and could smell things, the woman says. You're thinking of the other thing, the man says. The daughter saw the father getting shot by her mother's boyfriend even though the father himself didn't see who it was and he comes out of the coma after ten years with this heightened sense of smell. He knows his attacker's smell, and the daughter saw it, but she's repressed the memory. Who can remember these plots of his, the woman says. Don't let him get on to Machu Picchu, I heard it already. Well he is writing that Thornton Wilder thing, the man says. Ha, says the woman, Thornton Wilder, that should be a real epic. He should do it in Smell-o-Vision. Jack pulls up to the canopy of El Coyote. As the man pays him he tells the woman, Remember this place? Right, right, the woman tells him, Sharon Tate's last meal, Ben mentioned it on the phone. The food here is vile if I recall, the woman laughs. It certainly is, the man chuckles. So I guess that was a pretty awful evening all the way around, says the woman. Jack realizes they're doing this dialogue for him, so he laughs too.

Are you ready for a change? Wouldn't you like to slide into a new body? With my career I have to stay in shape, so I'm always looking for a better way to work out. Now I've found Slim Slide, I get great results, and wait until you hear the price! Sliding is the newest craze in aerobics on the West Coast. Why? Because you burn that fat. Up to three hundred calories in twenty minutes. And it focuses shaping where we need it most. Our lower bodies. Sliding is a great cardiovascular workout. The Slim Slide firms your lower body and tightens your buttocks and even slims your hips. I never thought that working out could be such a blast! The Slim Slide is made of Space Age resins, and stores so easily! And it comes complete with my workout video, featuring a fun sliding routine and my fantastic toning session. Other slides can cost up to $80. But you get the Slim Slide with two covers and my workout video for three easy payments of $11.95.

Seth is afraid of the dark in Los Angeles. He fears the encircling vegetation of Los Angeles houses. He fears the alleys behind Los Angeles apartments. He fears the unbalanced delivery boy, the stranger with the suspicious flat and the tire iron, the stalker lured by placid windows. Fear embarrasses him. But he knows all manner of things move through the dark in Los Angeles, striking at random. Tonight, alone in the house, he can't work in his basement room, with its several screened windows set high on the wall. Small animals rustle outside in the undergrowth. Because the basement and the ground floor connect by a narrow, spiral metal staircase, he fears getting trapped down below by an intruder. He keeps all the lights burning in the open kitchen/living room area, sets up his Powerbook on the coffee table facing the large television screen, within reach of the sofa, from where it's possible to keep an eye on the door that opens into this area as well as the nearby adjacent door of the porch and the living room door that opens into the porch. Thanks to the porch light, he can see all three doors from the sofa. He also has the mobile telephone within reach. It's his habit when staying in on a night when Jack is out to supply himself with food and cigarettes and anything else he may need before Jack leaves, or at least before the sun sets, because if he drives to the liquor and variety store at the bottom of the hill after dark, he could encounter some nameless menace on his way out of the house to his car, or find this nameless menace coiled in the backseat, or might surprise a burglar upon his return, or fall victim to someone lying in wait, at the same time when Seth is within the house with all the lights burning, he's afraid that someone lurking outside can see everything that he does, this imaginary person could be watching from the road, or watching from the front yard, or watching from the sloping woods at either side of the house, or behind the house, calculating the ideal moment to strike, Seth figures that ideal moment would be when he's given up waiting for Jack's return, which happens often, since Jack usually visits a few bars after knocking off work, that ideal moment, Seth thinks, would come when Seth's numb from vodka and convinced that he's paranoid and wasting electricity with all these lights, when he decides he doesn't care to betray his fear to Jack by nodding out upstairs on the sofa, for there is always a moment when exhaustion overtakes fear, when one surrenders to the possibility of being stabbed or throttled or shot through the brains as part of some disturbed person's arbitrary rampage in order to get some sleep, but quite often, in fact always, whether Seth stretches out fully clothed on the couch or goes bravely downstairs and undresses and gets into bed, and whether he sleeps fully clothed with all the lights on or naked with the lights off, Seth wakes up minutes later from nightmares of horrendous mayhem, peopled by various human monsters he reads about, not exactly the same monsters but monsters he's crafted from the horrific accounts he's addicted to, lately it's this freak in Florida who cut a woman's head off and put it in front of a mirror "so the head could see the body." At other times it's Richard Ramirez, who actually did pick houses at random, often in out-of-the-way neighborhoods like the one Jack lives in.

In his dreams at the secure Marmont, Seth is invariably the perpetrator, in his dreams at Jack's house he's always the victim. Jack's doors have flimsy locks. The house itself looks like a cheaply filled-in wooden shell whose Sheetrock walls would burst open with a strong kick. When Jack leaves his gun at home, Seth keeps it near him at all times, sometimes even carrying it to the refrigerator or into the toilet. It's a hefty, black, disturbing object, cold and faintly oily to the touch, an object with a life of its own. When Seth holds the gun he feels it could fire by itself, that he could shoot Jack, or himself, by mischance, that the gun might decide to kill somebody and even go off while lying on the table. At the same time, he's pretty certain that he wouldn't have the nerve to fire it if Richard Ramirez popped in. He always replaces the gun in the laundry hamper before Jack gets home. Tonight Jack has taken the gun with him in the cab, so Seth feels extra jumpy. He's pretending to write, having switched on his Powerbook and scrolled to a not very interesting assortment of notes for a novel he might write if he ever gets the nerve, but is really calming his nerves with little shots of Stoli, which he bought to avoid drinking Jack's special vodka, and playing the TV with the sound off while reading *Julia Child and More Company*, imagining that he will, at some bright moment before he leaves for New York, prepare for Jack and a few friends "Butterflied Pork for a Party," a dish that will include celery root rémoulade, whatever that is.

As he reads that celery root, also known as celeriac, knob celery, turnip-rooted celery, and celerirave, is "simply a variety of celery that is grown for its great bulbous bottom rather than for its stalks," a breath of arctic wind penetrates the wilting heat. A shudder seizes him, just as the soundless TV, its screen looming behind his computer monitor, displays the surreal overcrowding of a penguin rookery in Tierra del Fuego. He feels an adrenal rush he can't account for, and then something moves in his peripheral vision, a cloth, a thing. Out there. Something shifting in the malarial glare of the porch light, visible through four inset windowpanes: a person, a face he doesn't know, a figure, a man, though it could also be an animal, Seth's instantly on his feet and rushing across the room for a knife or a frying pan or some solid lethal object, he forgets the phone, forgets all the ways he prepares himself for exactly this kind of surprise, pulls out a kitchen drawer and claws through clanging spatulas and wire whisks and slotted spoons and grabs a pair of scissors and moves to look through the glass. It's a young person with black hair looking in, tapping the glass, saying something Seth can't make out, Seth's fist tightens on the clasped scissor blades as he crosses to the table and seizes the telephone, meanwhile the figure outside makes faces, maybe imploring faces, maybe the grimaces of serial killer insanity, Seth sees that he's good-looking just like the Night Stalker, he's saying something, Seth switches on the phone, moves closer to the door, I'm calling the police, he announces in a scalding voice that sounds incredibly faggy to his own ears, the phone weightless and sticky from something Jack spilled on it earlier, the guy at the door makes a different face, waves his empty hands, which flutter whitely like strange wings, in a loud voice he says something else, What do you want, Seth shouts, and the voice that answers wobbles like a sunburnt splice of magnetic tape, Fa fa fa fa friend of Jack. Seth moves closer, feeling the bones in his legs shift, part of his fear melting. Is Ja-ack home, the voice asks clearly, and something in the face, some alarm in its eyes, causes Seth to pause with his thumb on the 9 of the push button. He steps closer to the door. His body feels like rubber. Who are you, he demands again, miming distrust with his lips peeled back over his teeth. The boy swallows and smiles and makes a face that says, sort of, "I didn't mean to scare you," but the look is also scornful, as if a nifty surprise gift has been meanly rebuffed. I'm Fra fra frankie, tell Jack I cay cay came by okay? The name stirs some muzzy association just out of reach. Seth battles with contradictory impulses. As the kid turns to leave he opens the door, still clutching the scissors. You could give somebody a heart attack, he says.

As he steps outside Seth slides the scissor blades into his pocket. In the fading trail of porch light Frankie resembles the kids Seth sees sauntering up and down Santa Monica Boulevard every day eating pizza and leering into traffic. Angel-faced hardbodies with scrambled eggs between their ears, this one swinging a pair of shiny plastic Rollerblades by their thick twined laces, which makes Seth think of Mark, shirt untucked, sleeves rolled, baggy jeans, ripped sneakers, face perspiring in the evening heat, shirt clinging to sculpted back, the body turned half-expectant, half-poised to shrug its way down the oleander-shrouded flagstones to the gate. Seth says, neutrally, Where did you park? noticing that the only space that's ever free on the parkable side of the hill is empty. Frankie waggles the heels of the Rollerblades in reply, a wormy grin tossing out youthful indifference, signaling that he could now roll himself off to Long Beach if the mood took him. The kid's adorable. Seth thinks of sex with him immediately and hates himself for getting turned on by any good-looking thing that lands in his path, to the point where the only question he seriously considers is Will this guy kill me or not. A filmy image of his legs spreading wide for this stammering vision whisks through his mind: friend of Jack, and unless he's the youngest, comeliest speech-impaired Marxist-Leninist revolutionary in Southern California, this boy's connection to Jack has to have dick in it somewhere. If he's now so willing to leave, Seth figures, he's probably harmless. What are the odds, he wonders. What are the statistical probabilities. Writer found dead in Mt. Washington. Of course if he's murdered out here it will give the *New York Times* an excuse not to run his obituary.

Listen, Seth says, trying not to visibly betray his sudden interest in Frankie's corporeal package, Why don't you come in and have a glass of water? Nah, says Frankie, clocking all the stuff Seth's doing with his face, I shuda called I just took the ch ch ch chance. But he doesn't move, and a ripe look passes between them. Well Jack'll be home later but I don't know how later, Seth tells him. He teethes his upper lip. You're welcome to have a drink or something. Frankie shrugs. Looks at the street over the low chain-link fence overgrown with weeds. Looks at Seth. Okay, he says.

Seth says he quickly assumed that Frankie Lomax was a rent boy, one of the pushy kind that show up at your door unannounced when they're broke, though in his experience they actually usually do call first, Seth also says this surprised him because Jack, by his own account, was in the habit of obtaining sex of various kind through phone lines and over the Internet without ever paying for it. Curiously enough, Seth had been told a number of things about Frankie Lomax by JD, but as he had never seen Frankie Lomax in person, and had not paid very close attention to the stories JD told him, he did not put Frankie Lomax together with these stories, even when Frankie's speech impairment became obvious. Seth says it would not have mattered, in any case, since JD's Frankie Lomax stories were fairly benign and amusingly freakish. Nothing was then known about the unfortunate Robert Blakely in the garage apartment on Alta Vista Boulevard, or about several other unlucky tricks whom Frankie Lomax had decided to take out not long after taking out his father and his father's wife and their twins Amethyst and Amber in an arson fire in Malibu Canyon. Seth's notion that Frankie Lomax was sexually available brightened an otherwise edgy evening. He was not put off by Frankie's stutter. He found the boy intensely attractive and yes sensed something dangerous about him, some wild rambunctious quality is the way he puts it, and for this very reason decided to domesticate him by enlisting Frankie in the spontaneous preparation of the "Butterflied Pork for a Party" recipe he'd been studying earlier with the nebulous intention of doing something nice for Jack in the middle future.

This way he could do two noble things at once: prepare the festive and elaborate meal for Jack this very evening, and reserve for Jack first dibs on the pork of Frankie Lomax. Though his harshest feelings of guilt (the continual haunting memory, a certainty of cosmic punishment) about the accident had begun to subside, with a little queasy help from the sheepdog scenario, Seth was looking for opportunities to sacrifice himself to the well-being of others. He had done something terribly wrong, as usual something alcohol-related. It could not be put right in any usual way, but Seth believed that he could, through selected acts of spontaneous altruism, eventually rearrange his karmic bank balance. (At such periods Seth exhibits less than his usual scorn of Eastern religions.) Seth brought the pork roast idea up casually, as Frankie sat on the couch beside him, knees spread lewdly, chugging a Budweiser. Do you like to cook? Frankie's answer was somewhat convoluted and unintelligible and Seth finally interrupted him. Oh it's easy, listen, if you want to stick around here, Jack's usually in no later than three and anyway I'm sure it's cool if you want to crash out here tonight, what I'd like to do, *and you can help me,* Seth told him, becoming for a bright moment Miss Jean of Romper Room, *is cook this recipe for pork.* According to Seth, Frankie's self-absorbed expression lifted at the prospect. He got the idea that this was precisely the problem, i.e., that Frankie needed a place to crash. This explained why he hadn't called first. It's easier for people to put you off over the telephone. Seth showed Frankie the recipe, which Frankie studied without comment. We'll have to drive to Ralph's, Seth cautioned, or the Pioneer Market, somewhere there's a butcher on duty. Then we'll come back here and get everything ready. Jack will be *astonished.*

While trying to follow the precise instructions of the pork butcher at Ralph's on how to effectively separate the five-pound pork loin into two uneven sections, Seth, stoned from a hash joint Frankie produced in the car, reflected that hustlers such as Frankie often came from such miserable family backgrounds that they nuzzled up to any saner-looking domestic situation. And what could be saner than the overlit aisles of Ralph's, sparkling with beautifully packaged sustenance? (Actually, at that particular hour, the people prowling Ralph's did not, for the most part, evoke sanity or comforting domestic situations. But still.) Seth strained to understand what the butcher was telling him—really, the man rattled on like a game show host, this Lech

Walesa lookalike who kept asking Do you follow me? and looking skeptical when Seth said Yes as he rolled the lump of meat around on the counter, making imaginary slices with the side of his hand.

Seth tells this story often, with little significant variation. Sometimes he describes stopping at his favorite ATM on Glendale Boulevard and feeling a chilly presentiment. Sometimes it's the detail of a small serrated knife and the way Frankie held it as he peeled the knobby, grit-pocked bulb of the celery root, with his thumb pressed along the blunt side of the blade, Frankie's eyes considering his work in a kind of humid fixity. Sometimes he adds his own efforts at paring the oily fleece of fat from the loin muscle, the meat's slipperiness, the fact that Bowie's *Pin-Ups* and the first Ministry CD played continually as they ransacked Jack's cabinets for bowls and saucepans and various cooking arcana. There was the marinade and two vegetable side dishes to consider, an array of cooking times, myriad ingredients scattered in no particular order along the long wall counter and the floating counter. He felt unbelievably stoned, more stoned than the joint would warrant, as if they were operating in a time warp, tripping on acid, the overall meal pulling in and out of focus, as his attention zoomed in on crushing pieces of garlic or washing and draining the collard greens.

He felt telepathically attuned to Frankie Lomax. A heavy sexual vibration passed between them. Seth spices this story up for certain people by claiming he made it with Frankie Lomax before Jack got in that night, but if you follow Julia Child's recipe carefully (pp. 51–66, *Julia Child and More Company*) you will see that they didn't have time for that.

On Wednesday, Judge Tietelbaum, acting on a motion from defense counsel, admonishes the jury to consider the testimony of Dr. Judith Rampling, a psychiatric expert called by the defense, independently of certain incongruous verbal utterances and possible physical gestures of Dr. Judith Rampling, who suffers, Judge Tietelbaum explains, from coprolalia, copropraxia, and echopraxia, three distinct manifestations of Tourette's syndrome. It has been successfully argued by defense counsel, with only minor objections from the prosecution, that despite the potentially disruptive or distracting effects of Dr. Rampling's condition, she is the country's foremost crime scene analyst as well as an eminent authority on child abuse and therefore her exclusion from testifying on the basis of her handicap would be prejudicial to the defendants.

The sufferer of coprolalia, Tietelbaum informs the jury in his most enlightening avuncular manner, while engaged in ordinary conversation, or in this case examination on the witness stand, may suddenly mutter or shout an inappropriate word or phrase, including ethnic or racial epithets, or utterances referring to bodily functions, sexual acts, parts of the body, but these utterances do not reflect the actual thoughts or opinions of the person saying them. In the case of *corpro*praxia, Tietelbaum continues, a complex motor tic compels the sufferer to make obscene gestures, or to grab or point to the person's own or to someone else's genitals, breasts, and so on. People with echopraxia, Tietelbaum further explains, often involuntarily imitate other people's gestures. While these conditions are somewhat controlled by medication, says Tietelbaum, it is entirely possible that Dr. Rampling, while testifying, may be unable to suppress such utterances or gestures, so it is important that the jury as well as the questioning attorneys distinguish between obviously inappropriate words or gestures and applicable testimony, and as far as possible ignore these words and gestures, and I am further ruling, notes Tietelbaum, that such words or gestures be stricken from the record to avoid confusion.

Needless to say, this jury admonition or what have you creates a lot of sick-humored anticipation in the courtroom, which everyone tries to dissemble so as not to be thought of as amused by a person's handicap, and one feels, Seth says, particularly admonished on this score when Dr. Judith Rampling is called, since she looks like everyone's kindly and slightly out-of-it maiden aunt, a skinny woman of medium height with impossible hair tortured into a bun, wearing a really dull gray pleated skirt and an office blouse with a pattern of little blue cornflowers, glasses of course, in frames you could get at Woolworth's, and a splash of generic red lipstick, the kind of old gal, as Seth claims someone else says later in the pressroom, who just isn't getting any but wouldn't hold it against you if you were, in other words Dr. Judith Rampling wins a lot of good wishes right away, when she installs her drab pathetic self in the witness box, where she offers the court a game and ominously self-assured smile as Lauren Nathanson examines her about her credentials and background and how she was picked by a study group to examine the Martinez crime scene and facts of the case, not manifesting in any of her answers, delivered in a clear grainy voice that has a taste of Texas in it, the bizarre behavior Judge Tietelbaum has more or less promised the audience in his admonitions, and it goes from there to the developmental disorders of abused children, all hypotheticals of course, Lauren Nathanson's wearing her flame-red whatever it is with the big buttons up the front and her hair, this morning, looks teased especially wild to torment Judge Tietelbaum, and she's going for her deeply concentrated and strictly professional types of expressions, reading from a lot of notes typed on white paper rather than the notes she scrawls on yellow pads, with long strategic pauses where she pretends to have lost some vital piece of paper among the notebooks and stapled motions and everything else on the defense desk, letting various things sink in with the jury before resuming.

The anxiety this kind of parental behavior creates, does it have a long-term effect on such a child? Lauren Nathanson asks, meaning, an abused child such as Felix Martinez.

It affects various developmental aspects, says Dr. Rampling, because it's carried into each developmental stage.

What do you mean by that?

As children develop, there are tasks they have to master, for them to evolve to the next task, that's generally how you look at child development, so when you have the anxiety, that is also going to influence those phases.

Is there evidence that a child coping with trauma and stress from an early age can't get out of the past somehow?

That's exactly the problem, their minds continually return to the abusive scenario.

How does that interfere with learning?

It interferes because the mind keeps retreating back, it doesn't push on into present and future. Good mental health generally looks at people who can stay present- and future-oriented.

You said that one coping strategy is this notion of dissociation or numbing. Is that the same thing, or are they different?

They're very different.

Dissociation is like sending your mind somewhere else?

That's more a cognitive function, whereas the numbing is much more a physiological feeling affect type of phenomenon.

So in a numbing coping response the child doesn't feel things physically, or does he not feel things emotionally also?

Yeah, they really are separated from a thought, they're cut off, sometimes it's described as cut off from their feelings.

Let's assume you've got a child in this sort of environment where they're exposed to these traumas, do they just dissociate during trauma, or does this become a habit of mind?

It really can become a habit.

When you examine the background of such a child are you looking for evidence of this dissociation outside the actual abuse incident?

Yes, I am.

What do you often find?

You find a number of reports that this is going on. It won't be spelled out as dissociation. It will say the child isn't concentrating at school, or seems to daydream a lot, or seems to be looking out the window, or isn't able to follow activities in the classroom.

This is what dissociation looks like from outside?

Yes, what another person would observe.

This other concept of numbing, does the literature reflect the idea that abused children tend not to relate the incident with a great deal of emotional affect?

Yes.

Is that related to the concept of numbing?

Yes.

Can you explain that?

Well, they uh are cut off from feelings so when they describe what happened, they're able to do it in a fairly perfunctory way, and we say that the affect doesn't necessarily match the statement, and that would sometimes be in the initial phase of an evaluation.

Ultimately, perhaps, the children get back in touch and are able to be emotional?

That's the purpose of therapy.

When a child with this history is put in a new stressful situation, would you tend to find such a child using these dissociating and numbing strategies?

Yes.

Like, if they're testifying in a courtroom trial where their life is at stake, would you tend to think they'd rely on old defenses of dissociation and numbing?

Yes.

Objection, improper, Quentin Kojimoto snipes from his seat, barely raising his ass for form's sake.

Objection sustained, Judge Tietelbaum reflexively rules, the answer is stricken. Judge Tietelbaum has been following this line of questioning with a look of owlish alarm, perhaps expecting more objections from the prosecutors than are, for their own reasons, forthcoming.

Is the structure of a courtroom, Lauren Nathanson proceeds unflappably, and the method of examining a witness, something that produces anxiety usually in people on the witness stand?

Yes.

If courtroom witnesses have a history of being particularly sensitive to stress, could it cause them to fall back on coping mechanisms from the past?

Yes, certainly it could.

You've spoken about brain recoding, which is an actual change in the genetic structure of the brain?

Yes, the transmission of the message.

Can the brain be recoded back to normal, do we know?

Whether it can be recoded back, I'm not sure we have that data, but we have efforts to influence the brain chemistry through medication.

But short of intervention through medication, the brain won't just automatically recode itself if the stress-producing situation stops, for example?

No, but when there's a reduction of the stress situation that's a major step forward, that's what you always try to do in any situation.

So these people may get better?

Yes.

And could their tendency to hypervigilance dimimish over time?

Yes.

Would that occur even without therapy?

It generally requires therapy.

Now, you've said that the symptoms couldn't usually be treated with talk therapy.

Yes.

You've said there are some adaptations abused or traumatized persons make in order to survive in an ongoing way?

Yes.

If something changes, a new element or crisis comes in, do those adaptations work?

No, they do not.

And then are these people likely to experience fear reactions?

Yes they are FUCK

A ripple of astonishment prods people higher in their seats. It takes a moment for everyone, including Judge Tietelbaum, to recognize this last utterance, which comes out in a loud growl, as a manifestation of Dr. Rampling's coprolalia, and as there's of course a lot of whispering Tietelbaum sharply reminds the audience of his previous instruction and that excessively noisy or expressive persons will be removed by the bailiff. Dr. Rampling's confident smile remains fixed. Lauren Nathanson is also smiling. Fawbus Kennedy's mouth hangs open like the Lincoln Tunnel. A nervously alarmed glance between Quentin Kojimoto and Marlene Quilty, who immediately huddle together in panic, is caught by the Court TV camera and duly noted by twenty million viewers.

Going back to the notion of trauma learning, Lauren Nathanson proceeds, as if nothing happened, how long does the impact of this last on the child?

It can be SHIT long lasting.

This time the entire courtroom has to suppress an involuntary upsurge of incredulous laughter, and Tietelbaum's hand strays toward his gavel, then shrinks away from it. Tietelbaum never touches the gavel except at the end of each court session, because of his obsessive-compulsive disorder: the gavel must be lined up on his blotter flush with the top edge of the blotter, its right hammerhead pressed against the fake-leather blotter holder, or something terrible will occur during the session, and if he does use the gavel he must strike it once and instantly replace it exactly where it forms a kind of M or sideways E on the blotter surface. If he forgets to do this his mother will die.

What are some of the behavioral impacts that you see? Lauren Nathanson notes Tietelbaum's reluctance to use the gavel, something she's noted many times in the past and wondered about.

You get what we call FUCK the more internalizing types of reaction, where there's withdrawal symptoms, depression, serious suicidal ideation, then you can get the more externalizing symptoms, Dr. Rampling says, suddenly clutching her left breast and vigorously rubbing it for a moment, showing of the distress in a behavioral way, schoolroom classroom kinds of symptoms, acting up, not sitting still, things in which children's behavior is problematic.

Now certain people, in fact many people, reporters, jurors, Carlos and Felix Martinez, and various other spectators are deliberately slumping back in their seats and holding their hands over their mouths trying for sober serious kinds of looks, trying to keep straight faces, but this is not such a disturbance that Tietelbaum takes any note of it. Seth and the reporter from the *Sacramento Bee* are trying not to look at each other because if they do they're both going to explode and get thrown out of court.

What effect does it have, says Lauren Nathanson, suddenly sweeping the courtroom with a fierce approbation that chills the atmosphere, on the child's concept of self?

It's a very negative impact on the concept of self, it makes the child feel worthless, helpless, all those negative feelings come into play.

Though maintaining her tight cooperative smile, Dr. Rampling brings this answer out in a sad resigned way that forces everybody to connect the answer with her own uncontrollable predicament on the stand, sending embarrassment into the hearts of those who've reacted oafishly to her distress.

This theme of helplessness runs through traumatized people of many types?

Yes it does.

There's a term usually applied in battered women cases, learned helplessness. Does anything similar happen to abused children?

Yes. Dr. Rampling points to her crotch. You find a nonassertive, not able to defend themselves, you see a more passive presentation with children.

A child in a situation where they can't fight and can't flee, does that child approach problem solving the same way that a child who can influence what happens to them does? Lauren Nathanson cocks her head.

No, they don't. Dr. Rampling cocks her head in exact imitation of Lauren Nathanson. Their problem-solving skills, which all relate to how information comes in, they just haven't got them, they're focused on other things so they may perceive situations differently, they haven't had the same experience as nontraumatized children.

Let's go back to the battered wife, Lauren Nathanson says, tapping two fingers against her chin, a gesture Dr. Rampling instantly copies, when the question is posed, Why doesn't she just walk out of the home, the theoretical answer is learned helplessness. Are there more reasons why children don't just leave?

They may have nowhere to go. They may have no safety SHIT FUCK aspect, they certainly may be small and they can't, and they're also very connected with the parents. There are a lot of mitigating factors, the child still believes the parent is the most important person in the world and they feel very connected to the parent.

Is learning to be helpless something that continues into adolescence and even into young adulthood sometimes?

If it isn't interrupted, certainly.

So even if those children are old enough, theoretically, to walk out the door, does helplessness play a part?

Yes.

What part does it play?

It keeps them tied to the situation, they don't see any options, they can't think of what else to do, so we do see that phenomenon time and time again.

Do most abused children run away or do they stay in the situation—there are studies, are there not, especially in the incest and home abuse setting, that focus on domestic abuse rather than abuse by strangers?

Yes. Dr. Rampling touches her right breast.

And there are statistics, are there not, to assess the extent of various forms of child abuse in this country and state currently?

Yes.

Do abused and molested children tend to leave the home?

Do abused and molested children tend to leave the home? Dr. Rampling mimics Lauren Nathanson's voice, then answers her own question, No, they don't.

Do people experiencing this trauma have a feeling of isolation?

Yes.

What causes that?

What causes that? Again, Dr. Rampling reproduces Lauren Nathanson's precise way of speaking, like a nightclub impressionist, then goes on in her normal voice. Their isolation is often imposed by the abuser, to keep the child from people who they might be able to talk to. So you see family situations where the children are kept away from friends and other family members.

When you say kept away, do they have to be totally shut off, permanently, to have a sense of isolation from others?

No, it can be the way it's laid FUCK HOLE out in the rules of the family.

By this time the spectators are beginning to edit Dr. Rampling's eruptions out of hearing, or hearing them as one would hear a series of hiccups, fighting down laughter, though a few people in the Martinez family side of the courtroom are doubled over, Aunt Thelma for example is choking on her own stifled laughter, tears running into the handkerchief she's holding over her mouth.

Children who have trauma learning, who've been terrorized by an abuser, do they tend to be easier to control by rule-setting?

Yes they do.

I think you've indicated that abused children, sexually molested children, tend to be compliant.

Objection, says Lester Kojimoto, rising fully this time to remind the jury of his presence in court.

ASSHOLE, exclaims Dr. Rampling, rising from the witness chair in clear imitation of Quentin Kojimoto.

Rephrase the question, says Tietelbaum.

Quentin Kojimoto sits. Dr. Rampling sits.

You've indicated that sexually abused children, for there to be long-term abuse, tend to be passive and compliant.

That's correct.

Is that because they enjoy it?

No.

Do they enjoy it?

No, not at all.

What is serotonin?

Serotonin is an important brain hormone that modulates and regulates and keeps at an even keel the neurons transmitting back and forth, it's an important chemical part of the brain.

Is it believed that people who've undergone the genetic changes due to exposure to trauma have a lower serotonin level than nontraumatized populations?

Yes, they have a lower level.

You talked about medication as an intervention, is this one of the areas where they seek to medicate to raise serotonin levels?

Yes, you can raise serotonin by prescribing various medicines.

Which medicines are effective in doing that?

There are several, Prozac is one, Zoloft, Wellbutrin—

These medications are prescribed to traumatized people to help overcome what this genetic remapping may have done?

Well, it's done for depression and suicide-ality as well as the other traumatized populations who benefit from it.

Is there a substantial body of research regarding fear in traumatized persons?

Yes there is.

Does this research describe common patterns of how sexually molested children, war veterans, rape victims, accident victims, and other traumatized people deal with fear?

Yes, there is.

Would you describe that behavioral model?

The behavioral model describes various symptoms SHIT including the hyperarousal, being on guard, the scanning of the environment, Dr. Rampling grabs her right breast, evoking this time no visible reaction in the courtroom, and also what's called the startle reflex, these traumatized persons would have a higher level of being startled. There are other symptoms as well, what we call anxious symptoms, avoidance symptoms, and other symptoms.

What kind of behavior demonstrates avoidance?

Avoidance behaviors would be considered withdrawing from activities, being depressed, all the way to suicidal ideation, suicidal thoughts.

Is there also a behavioral model for the intrusive thought, or what we call flashbacks?

Yes.

What are those things considered?

The type of treatment generally used is talking therapy, psychotherapy, cognitive therapy, a wide range of models.

What is that symptom of recurring thoughts or full-blown flashbacks with very little cuing?

They are considered recurring thoughts, and they may also have been treated by a more behavioral model, where they'd try to extinguish the thought, it's called thought-stopping, they would encourage the person the minute the thought came into the mind to put it out of the mind.

In this behavioral thought-stopping, is the purpose of talking therapy to get inside the person to understand why they're reacting?

Yes.

In traditional therapy, if a person has an insight into their behavior they can then modify it?

Yes.

Are talking therapies effective with traumatized people to stop intrusive thoughts or get rid of these hyperarousals, scanning, startles, anxiety—

They don't work on traumatized persons.

Based on that, is that when you and others began looking for a biological explanation for why these things weren't responding to therapy?

Yes.

You told us a little about this system in regions of the brain that control a person's reactions to fear stimuli. There are two charts here on the board, one is a schematic, the other is a cross section of the brain, is that correct?

Correct.

Can you use those charts to explain to the jury how information processing in this area of fear operates in the brain?

Yes. You can see from this picture of the brain, there are all these layers here. In this section, the limbic area, is a large cortical area, this is a simplified version of the limbic system, which is very important in terms of the three areas within all of these structures. This is the hypothalamus, this is the hippocampus, and this is amygliose complex. This is very critical because this sits at the base of the brain. The three brain regions most important in the limbic system are the hippocampus, the hypothalamus, and amyglioid section, which contains a bundle of nerve cells, these neurons are very important regarding the fear component.

Do we know how fear information such as, A truck is about to hit me, where that information goes in the brain?

Here is the base of the brain. This is the amyglioid section. There are lots of nerve cells that start at this particular point, but then it activates, those neurons start shooting out messages, it starts to activate throughout the limbic system.

When this information activates, is that the physical response, the release of hormones? Is that what the body does?

Yes, as it goes out through the rest of the brain, it activates the brain's stress hormones.

Now, that happens to everybody?

Yes.

I believe there are stages of this processing of fear response.

Yes.

What is the first stage called?

The first stage is the preparatory stage.

What is the biological activity going on in the preparatory stage?

That's when the first signal that there is danger in the environment comes into the brain.

The release of stress hormones, is that part of this stage?

Yes, it alerts the organism that it must do something.

Why must the organism do something?

Because the most basic instinct in any human is survival, and that is the purpose of this alarm system, to protect the individual from harm in order to survive.

And that's why it has to do something when the truck's coming down the street.

Yes.

What's the second stage?

The second stage is what the person actually does, the flight-fight, they take action, the body's prepared to act, it must act against danger or it must retreat, flee the danger.

What thinking is going on as we understand it, what rational processing of alternatives and options, goes on when the truck comes down the street?

There is no thinking. Automatic response.

Has this component, the fact that there is no thinking, in what situations has it been found that—

Aplysia snail.

What is an aplysia snail?

A sea snail.

Why are we interested in snails?

In the base of the brain it has larger nerves and so forth to study, so from a research standpoint it provides a nice viewing of these nerves for research.

How does studying snails tell us there is no thinking but automatic instinctive survival activity going on?

We've studied the avoidance, the fleeing part of that, and found that with some stimulation of these nerve bodies the short-term memory will last up to an hour, with more chronic or prolonged stimulation of these nerves there has actually been noted the genetic recoding, it goes from RNA to DNA, one being the transmission, one being the translation.

Hypothetically, you're driving and someone cuts you off, are you cognitively thinking, I better turn the steering wheel?

You automatically respond. You do not think. Hopefully you respond in a way that avoids the danger.

This has been noted in all situations, that people and animals just act. The snail studies actually prove there are automatic changes in the genetic structure as a result of trauma?

Yes, they do.

So it supports the biological notion that these activities are automatic and not, what is the main function of the cortical area of the cerebral cortex, that area on the top of the limbic system?

That's our thinking. That's where cognition and thoughts and the whole way we organize thinking is housed.

Do these snail experiments indicate that in response to prolonged stress, signals don't even get into that cognitive part?

Well, in snails we have no evidence of cognitive activity.

But there have been other animal experiments.

The importance of the lower-level animal and snail experiments and so forth is that we do share these survival brain structures. So that's very important in this research, on the basic universal instinct of survival.

You say we have a survival brain? Humans still have a survival brain?

Yes, we actually have three levels to brain, this has been well documented in the literature. We have a triune brain in evolution.

A what brain?

Triune brain in evolution.

So even though we've evolved, we still have that original survival brain?

Yes, we do.

Like the snail?

That's correct.

Are there efforts made with people who have to work under traumatic conditions, to take advantage of this automatic response?

Yes.

What are those efforts?

Well, people who work under high stress need to be prepared to automatically respond, that includes such populations as soldiers going into combat, nurses in emergency rooms, to be able to automatically respond when a stress situation occurs.

So they don't fight or flee, but do what they need to do?

Yes.

So this is an attempt to override the automatic response?

Yes, you want them to stay calm and attend to the task at hand.

I take it that's not something people in this fear response are able to do?

That's correct.

What does the research show happens to severely traumatized people, either in one big event or repeatedly, that makes their reaction different than the ordinary model?

What begins is, they read the cues differently, this is called rewiring, they read more danger into cues than nontraumatized people.

You've mentioned hypervigilance. Let's take a hypothetical. A battered woman knows that on Friday night when her husband gets home from the bar that if they didn't have his favorite beer he's going to beat her up, and the husband comes home from the bar and says, They didn't have Budweiser, hypothetically she can start having a fear reaction because she has this special knowledge of what They didn't have Budweiser means.

Yes.

Now, if she then becomes very fearful, she's not wrong, is she?

No, she has this knowledge of the situation.

So when we talk about different people reading cues differently, they're not necessarily being irrational when they're fearful.

No.

They can also be startled easily because of their reading of cues. So research into brain structure has shown what?

That as you increase or have chronic fear, that this is the explanation for the genetic recoding or rewiring or whatever, that they're now going to react very differently and there's a neurobiological basis to what's been observed.

So they actually have different cells than they had before, or different content to their cells keeping them at this pitch of anxiety and arousal?

It's the coding that's different, it's the message that gets sent. Our neurons send us messages, and that's what goes back and forth in the brain.

So it sends a higher level of arousal messages?

Yes.

So there's also reason to believe that even the general anxiety state is because they're constantly sent a fear message of some kind?

Yes, they may keep a person at a very high anxiety level.

Is there an understanding of what happens to traumatized people who can neither fight nor flee?

Yes.

And what happens to them?

They go into this third phase, the numbing phase, and stay quite numb to ongoing activity.

Can you give us examples of people in situations where they can neither fight nor flee?

Children, certainly, are a good example, of people who don't have the ability to fight or flee, people trapped in hostage situations, concentration camp persons, even natural disasters I suppose.

Let's focus on children. The study of children in situations where they can't fight or flee, specifically what kinds of children have you studied in this connection?

Children who've been abused.

Well, she got through the fukkin snail part without any problem, remarks Dirk Chandler of the *L.A. Weekly* over a Japantown lunch.

Pam Harrison from Pacifica Radio cracks up all over again. The poor woman, she says, gasping, I mean couldn't they find somebody else?

If you think about it, Seth tells her, SHIT she's probably a big asset.

Dirk Chandler thinks about it. Pam Harrison waves and motions for the waiter to bring her another Sapporo beer.

Well, in the sense that FUCK the jury's just about forgotten about Fidel and Peggy Martinez, says Dirk Chandler. I can see that.

Yeah, well, says Pam Harrison, they don't sound like they were any day at the beach, their friends aren't exactly lining up to give testimonials.

What friends, Seth says. I mean besides the exercise partner.

Well, there's what's-her-name, Pam Harrison says. The secretary at the funeral. I take it back, two friends. Charming couple.

Are you still FUCK going back to New York? Dirk Chandler asks Seth.

Sorry? Oh, yeah. I've got um SHIT some stuff to take care of, then I'm coming back.

What should we do about your press pass, Pam Harrison wants to know, pointing at her crotch.

That's right, says Dirk Chandler, you guys are on a, what, rotating basis?

De jour, says Pam Harrison, cupping one breast through her T-shirt emphatically, but not de facto, or however that goes.

If you can cover for me, Seth says. I mean find somebody to use it so my seat's not ambushed by one of Fawbus Kennedy's readers.

Fawbus Kennedy's readers, says Dirk Chandler, shuddering. I'm not going to touch that.

I could fuck the bailiff, offers Pam Harrison.

You're in for very sloppy seconds from what I hear, says Dirk Chandler, whistling up a fresh Sapporo for himself. She won't leave Rampling to Kojimoto I bet, just you watch.

Quentin should do something with his hair, Seth says idly, holding up two fingers to double the drink order.

He should grow it out, says Pam Harrison thoughtfully, fingering her own Louise Brooks coif, and dip the ends in . . . little drops of heroin.

We never got a drug angle in this case, did we, laments Dirk Chandler.

We seem to be getting trashed, Seth remarks as two more beers land on the table.

What fukkin difference does it make, says Dirk Chandler. The tape's running in the VCR, as we speak.

The drug angle, says Pam Harrison, sniffing her own hair, is like who's taking what right now. Felix is on fifty milligrams Xanax, Lauren's dropping twenty every morning, Sarah's body manufactures its own as far as I can tell, Quilty's taking Prozac, the witness is on Haldol, who knows what Tietelbaum takes but he certainly looks glazed in the afternoons, somebody saw him lunching at Hillcrest with Mary Tyler Moore, have you heard that?

How does he get to Hillcrest, Dirk Chandler wants to know.

Freeway, suggests Pam Harrison. Booking us a table? That's thoughtful, Dirk.

I mean how does he get to Hillcrest and get back here, Dirk Chandler persists.

Pwactice, says Pam Harrison, doing a bad Jackie Mason, pwactice.

Seth walks over to the federal building after lunch and goes through the plaza of the federal building and walks around the dried-up fountain in the plaza of the federal building and out to the street through the immigration building and into the underground mall under the county courthouse across the street and while he walks he's thinking about the flies in the house in Mt. Washington, an invasion of houseflies that arrived the day after Frankie did, he thinks about the ease with which Jack laid claim to Frankie as his "friend," about the awkward, apologetic diplomacy that preceded the fact of Frankie and Jack sharing Jack's bed, about Frankie lounging around the house all day wearing only a pair of cut-off denims, maybe letting Jack do him once or twice in the course of an afternoon, Seth considers that the house has become even less his house, even more Jack's house, because of Frankie being there, and though Seth himself is gone all day it seems to him that Frankie never leaves the house, that Frankie spends the whole day listening to Metallica CDs and watching talk shows and swatting flies and helping himself to any food booze dope that happens to be in the house, pulling his dick out for Jack in idle moments, he imagines too that Frankie rifles through all of his belongings downstairs whenever Jack leaves the house in the daytime, he also supposes that Frankie's found where Jack keeps the gun at the bottom of the laundry basket, Seth wanders back to court thinking about the flies and Frankie and the gun, how annoying the flies are, how desirable and now unavailable Frankie is, how tangible and disturbing the gun is, he feels that Jack's success with Frankie is somehow a judgment on himself, that if he were truly clever or even halfway attractive he could alienate Frankie from Jack, pry Frankie loose from Jack, or at least knock off a quick one with Frankie behind Jack's back,

at the same time he misses a complicity with Jack, the confidences that usually occur between them when Jack has a lover or Seth has a lover, which
Frankie's constant presence in the house makes impossible, Seth has hardly
had a minute alone with Jack since Frankie arrived, in fact, Seth furthermore
perceives something abnormal about Frankie staying in the house all the time,
Seth has gotten quite edgy about it and resentful, too, because he'd like to
book a date with Bobby but doesn't want to have sex with Bobby or anybody
else if Frankie's in the house, and it turns out Bobby's living with some queen
on Franklin Avenue and can't do in-calls, at various times Bobby's suggested
they check into the baths at the same time or do it in the stockroom at the
7-Eleven, but Seth wants to do it in a bed, specifically Jack's bed, because
Jack's bed is wider than his bed, he wants to take a large hit of crystal
beforehand and snort amyl nitrite while Bobby's ploughing him, he wants it
long and complicated with Bobby, he wants to do it while Jack's out driving
the cab, and he wants Frankie to leave. Seth thinks if he goes to New York that
Frankie will be long gone before he comes back, he even suspects that Jack is
prolonging Frankie's visit as a way of trumping Seth's busy career with his,
Jack's, superior sexual allure. This is paranoid. Seth knows it's paranoid. He
is sick of himself for being afraid of everything and suspecting everybody of
evil. But maybe they are evil. Maybe he's evil too. It's hard to tell.

It's that Marlene Quilty moment. Today she is a flame woman, all in red, red
skirt red jacket red blouse, dressed to panic livestock, and she's done something new with her auburn hair, had some highlights rinsed in and swept it up
and back at an angle where it's pinned to one side and resembles the whorl of
a nautilus shell, and her features today look androgynous and hyperthyroidal,
Quilty is almost pretty, and in the cold courtroom light her face looks like
liquid marble, and of course Dirk Chandler called it right, no way is Quentin
Kojimoto getting to do cross on Dr. Rampling, talk around the courthouse is
that Quilty's had quite enough of Quentin's softball approach, it's time to get
mean, time to turn the screw, the district attorney is not happy, the district
attorney has no plans of returning to embalming or whatever he does in civil-
ian life, a little impromptu poll by the *Los Angeles Times* has the district
attorney running a poor third behind a West Side councilman facing fraud
charges and the head of Legal Aid in next year's elections, the Lester-inspired
strategy of not calling rebuttal psychiatric witnesses is clearly a losing propo-
sition, as far as Quilty can tell they've already blown the first-degree death

penalty convictions the D.A. desperately wants to campaign on, the best hope now is second-degree murder on Peggy and voluntary manslaughter on Fidel and that's only a hope, mistrial would be more like it, 7–5 jury split on Carlos and an even split down the gender line on Felix if Quilty's any judge.

I believe you testified about the organic or biological modifications of the brain as it relates to fear, says Quilty pertly.

Dr. Rampling smiles her maiden-aunt, even grandmotherly smile, her lipstick looking game, her eyes flashing behind the harlequin glasses.

Correct, she says.

Now when you talk about trauma, the kind of trauma that causes your genetic restructuring, what kind of trauma are you talking about, being afraid to cross-examine or getting hit over the head?

Dr. Rampling's expression undergoes a slight shift: as if she is, for the first time, sizing Quilty up, measuring her for a straitjacket, deciding to rear-end her car in the parking lot.

I'm talking about a situation, says Dr. Rampling, suddenly squeezing her right breast, that overwhelms a person's usual capacity to cope.

The breast squeeze is noted by most of the courtroom, though not by Judge Tietelbaum, whose fingers are busy lining up exactly so the staples and paper clips attached to various documents on his blotter: sometimes, when these little bits of metal run askew, the risk of an 8.3 earthquake with its epicenter somewhere near Temple Street, or the possibility of morphing, right here, into the three-hundred-pound Dave Spacey, complete with orange wig and failing kidneys, becomes dramatically present to Tietelbaum's mind, and at such times the Martinez trial strikes him as an utterly frivolous waste of his time and precious life essence.

When you talk about the biological response to that, are you talking about a response where you get a spurt of adrenaline because a truck is about to hit you?

It's an example most people can identify with because that's just what they feel, when distress hormones get released.

Is it distress hormones that cause this ultimate biological restructuring?

Only in a continued fear situation, you don't necessarily get that in the example you cited, with the truck it's a onetime situation, you'll feel the effect of the stress hormone for a limited time, unless you get into the accident.

If every time I get in my car I have an accident I'm going to have this continued buildup of stress hormones, and then eventual genetic recoding—

Some people BITCH can't even get back in their car after an accident, says Dr. Rampling, the BITCH sounding like a hiccup, yet in timbre somehow different than the expletives she emitted during direct exam.

Well, what kind of trauma is necessary to trigger the genetic recoding, says Quilty, with a certain impatience, signaling, just slightly, her lack of sympathy for Dr. Rampling's condition.

Dr. Rampling points excitedly at her crotch.

If you're talking about children, she says, you have to look at the age, continued exposure to highly fearful situations over a prolonged time period has a capacity to raise that person's ability to recode for danger.

What kinds of situations are you talking about?

There could be situations where the child is repeatedly frightened, held in certain positions, not made to feel secure, some of the early years in terms of bonding and holding and all that can frighten a child for lack of security, lack of safety.

The failure to be held could trigger this biological restructuring?

If the activities that go along with it, hitting the child, physical abuse, starting early with children—

Is the kind of fear one feels watching a scary movie enough to cause this biological restructuring? Quilty brays. She's a brayer. There's no other way of putting it. Contempt is her element. In Quilty's world *scary movie* has the same familiar meaning for everybody, whereas *biological restructuring* and *genetic recoding* carry the alien menace of complicated science.

That's at a later age PISS HOLE certainly children STUPID GUINEA who are constantly exposed, Dr. Rampling cups both breasts with her palms, rotating them defiantly counterclockwise, children who're constantly exposed to frightening movies CUNT FACE generally are able to avoid seeing them, they take themselves out of the situation.

What about the children who seek out *Friday the 13th* and the sequel after that and the sequel after that, are they exposed to fearful situations?

They may not be interpreting it as fearful.

Would it be fair to say the level of trauma necessary to cause this response varies from individual to individual?

Generally it has what's known as an idiosyncratic aspect but there are situations considered traumatic to most people, that's why definitions exist on what is child abuse, what is child maltreatment.

When you talk about trauma, are you lumping together all kinds of child abuse or only physical, sexual, what kind of child abuse are you speaking of when you use the term child abuse?

Child abuse FUCKING MORON you have to narrow it down to specific acts another type of frightening experience for children is to witness overwhelming experiences, a parent in a domestic violence situation, a parent's suicide, witnessing a killing—

Is one experience like that sufficient to cause this genetic recoding?

Enough to trigger symptoms, we see a wide range of symptoms in children who've even experienced one traumatic event.

But is it enough to cause this genetic recoding?

Generally it's repeated exposure that causes it.

Is there any way to evaluate how much repeated exposure is needed?

Is there any way to evaluate how much repeated exposure is needed? Dr. Rampling mocks.

Is there any test you can give to see if they've undergone this recoding?

Not per se CUNT we talked about that but certainly there are studies that speak to the lower biochemical reaction there's a fair amount of research TURD FACE because that's where some treatment methods have come into play.

But as far as a blood test or a brain scan or something of that sort is there any way to tell if a person has actually undergone these changes?

Not on the genetic restructuring, that's been noted in animal research.

You spoke about studies on snails, is that correct?

That's one of the studies.

Is there a difference between the brain of a snail and a human being?

This is in the brain stem, the reptilian brain, that's why researchers are able to make the suggestion, because it does share a similar function in the human brain.

But does the human brain have features that the snail brain does not?

Oh yes it has higher-level cortical functioning.

A human being can reason.

Yes it has a cortical function sure.

And a snail can't.

Well, we don't think the snail can.

What you're saying, then, is that studies with snails show that when they're exposed to trauma there are biological changes which occur in their brain stem.

When they're stimulated that's what it shows and they see what's called the avoidance pattern, if the snail moves away, goes back in its shell or whatever, that's an avoidance pattern, that seems to last for an hour, then with chronic stimulation of their fear center that's when they get into this RNA and DNA, the transmission and the translation factor, the messages that go back and forth in the neurons.

So they're scaring the snails, basically.

Dr. Rampling grabs her pussy through her skirt.

They're stimulating the fear, she says, bringing her hand to her nose.

How do they do that?

They use some kind of electrode and the snail goes back inside its little shell.

So they shock it with electrodes.

Yes.

Would it be fair to say that human beings are exactly like snails in this regard?

No, I'm not saying, research on animals is very important to understand the structures in human brains, the fear response, because it's such a basic and universal response in both the animal world and the human world, the learning part is very important.

There's no way to conduct the same studies on human beings as you do on snails because it's unethical to do so right?

Yes.

You're not supposed to poke human beings with electrodes to see what their chemical responses are, correct?

That's correct.

Likewise, you're not supposed to dissect their brains to see if there's been any sort of recoding, correct?

That's correct, but they are doing studies on people who have major problems, they use imaging techniques and so forth, there are ways to replicate brain activity.

This particular case, there's no test you can give these defendants to determine whether or not they have undergone genetic recoding in response to fear?

That's correct.

I believe you indicated the animal response to fear is fight or flight.

Yes.

What determines the choice?

It's automatic, and the most RIMIT automatic is to flee just to get away from danger.

When you talk about automatic response are you talking about snails or humans.

We're talking about a wide range, RIMIT snails, animals, a rodent, a mammal—

So the preference in this biological response is to flee the adverse stimulus.

That's correct.

Now are there any studies coding the frequency of suspected genetic recoding in child abuse victims, by child abuse I mean generic child abuse. Strike that question. Dr. Rampling, you've testified as to types of homicides.

Correct.

What is a rimit, Pam Harrison whispers.

You've testified there are approximately thirty-two types of homicides.

Correct.

Maybe she means, like, rim it, Seth whispers.

I believe the manual indicates there are four basic types of homicides and each type contains subtypes, is that correct?

That's correct.

The first would be called Criminal Enterprise Homicides, which appears from the manual to be homicides for some material gain, is that correct?

That's RIMIT correct.

The second kind would be a Personal Cause Homicide, which is a killing resulting from emotional conflict.

Maybe it's like a frog, whispers Pam Harrison, maybe she means ribbit.

Well, it's specific GRIBIT to the person.

One person versus a group of people.

That's correct.

Now it's gribit, Seth whispers. What does that mean, gribit?

The next would be the Sexual Homicide, correct?

Correct.

That's the kind traditionally associated with serial killers, correct?

Yes.

It has to be some kind of sex thing, Pam Harrison whispers. A sex killer thing must be a gribit. In her own mind, I'm saying.

And the last group is Group Cause Homicide, where groups of people for nonfinancial reasons commit homicides to further their goals.

That's correct.

So in this particular case I believe you classified the crime as a Personal Cause Homicide, because you classified it as a domestic homicide.

Correct.

Now when you talk about preliminary classification of crime scenes, there are several factors that go into the investigation besides the crime scene, correct?

As one goes into the investigation, correct.

From the crime scene other avenues are pursued, correct?

That's the whole goal, to identify suspects.

One of the ways to do that is to look at the victims, correct?

That's true.

And look at people who might have a motive to kill the victims?

That's correct.

Crime scene investigation is just a starting point.

That's correct.

Now when you participated in this study, the point of it was to aid investigators in solving crimes?

Correct.

Not to aid criminals in committing better crimes.

Correct.

The information you've given these two juries, is that information that you've ever lectured on to groups of criminals to help them improve their skills?

Not knowingly.

So you have no way of knowing if the average criminal is familiar with the years of research you did in order to arrive at these classifications?

No, I don't.

You have no way of knowing if these defendants were familiar with the classifications and other studies you've done?

Well, it FUCK was published back in '85.

When someone talks about a perfect crime, what in your mind is perfect about a perfect crime?

I have no SHIT idea.

You've testified that in your opinion the disorganization of the Martinez crime scene was—

I said it showed a lack FUCK of planning.

At least she's getting back to normal, whispers Pam Harrison. Seth nods and grabs his balls through his trousers.

Is there a difference between lack of planning and poor planning.

We talk of a lack of planning, we don't FUCK give it an adjective.

Well, lack of planning to me means, you didn't plan, whereas poor planning means you planned, you maybe planned a lot, but you didn't do it very well.

You can't say FUCK that about a crime scene.

You can't make that distinction.

No.

So for a first-time killer there could be lots of planning, but it was poorly executed because the person had never done it before?

Objection Your Honor calls for speculation.

Sustained.

I'll be back in no time, Seth tells JD on Thursday night.

No, you won't, JD says.

What makes you say that?

A certain feeling I have, says JD.

Well, stifle that feeling, says Seth. I mean I will, no question.

Why do you have to go back at all?

Seth can't think of a good answer. They're in the courtyard of the Spike surrounded by men in leather. The air reeks of poppers and beer. Looking at the silhouettes of palms rising above the roof in the night air he thinks: because of this. Because it reminds me. It reminds me of everything.

I just have some issues to resolve, Seth says, hating the sound of this. Anyway Jack has a friend staying there I've got no privacy whatever.

You can always stay with Zorah can't you?

I'm not going to stay in West Adams getting shot at.

He thinks that in all these years JD has never offered his own apartment and wonders about this, wonders what precise reservations JD has about him, it occurs to Seth quite suddenly that after all the eons of time they've filled in each other's company JD still doesn't trust him, doesn't trust something about him, and if this is the case, why would it be JD he had to confide in?

Who's Jack's friend?

Some kid, Seth says.

I said you were welcome to stay till the trial's over, Jack tells him half-belligerently Friday morning, in the downstairs bedroom. Frankie's asleep upstairs. Seth's filling a suitcase on the camp bed. And I meant that, he adds, so I hope if you are leaving that you're not leaving because—

Jack, Seth stops him, I'm only going back for a few days.

Don't tell me something isn't wrong because I can see that something is.

Nothing's wrong, Seth says. He sits down on the bed and lights a cigarette. Jack's brought him some coffee. He sips the coffee. Drags on the cigarette. It crosses his mind that Jack doesn't wish to be alone in the house with Frankie, whose presence has become, in some ineluctible way, onerous, heavy, and complicated, despite his allure, his social blandness.

I've got to think some things through, he says.

Well, I sort of thought that's why you came out here, Jack says. Tell me what you're feeling.

I feel like a blind person running his hand along an endless wall, Seth says. He smiles tightly at Jack and as he does remembers that he acquired this particular tight smile from a woman Jack was briefly married to many years earlier. He hated the smile on her and hates it even more on himself and came to imitate it as a way of disparaging whole areas of feeling that he has no use for, or no talent with.

I used to be so full of hope, he says, but I think I played my hand wrong.

Seth is crying. He hates crying, hates how it makes his face look. Jack holds him. The embrace is less awkward than physical contact between them usually is.

I played every hand wrong, Jack whispers, rocking them, the rocking like the gentle motion of two children swinging in a hammock.

No matter what you do, Seth chokes, you wind up guilty of everything.

Yeah, says Jack, no shit.

In New York his apartment has the stark dead pall of abandoned space, his objects clustered in psychotic-looking lumps, mounds, stacks, several months' worth of mail taken in by a neighbor fills a malignant cardboard box, he dumps his luggage on the kitchen floor and insensibly gravitates through his four doorless rooms to the answering machine beside the bed, as if he's returned after one hard night instead of many months, sees that the machine has stopped recording after thirty-four messages, he stretches out on his captain's bed still wearing the thin jacket he wore on the plane, and he looks at his sneakers, feels suddenly too weak to unlace them and kicks them off with difficulty, Seth tries to think about everything that's happened, tries to narrate the previous months to himself, and finds his mental movie jamming at strangely empty moments: Teddy Wade stretched out beside the Marmont pool, waning sunlight striking the dashboard of the Mazda, Felix Martinez angling his head to smile at his cousins. If he wills it, he sees himself and Bobby screwing, sees himself yanking cash from the ATM on Sunset, sees himself drunk with JD. But not exactly. He is invisible to himself in all these choppy scenes, a camera swimming through overlit, overcrowded space, and because he does not see himself, Seth's suspicion that he does not really exist turns the film livid and unbelievable, its colors impossibly rancid, and he begins to doubt if anything he's lived belongs to him truly.

There are many people Seth could see in New York. Assuredly. But for three days he sees no one, pays bills, tries to watch television without switching to the trial on Court TV. Is there nothing else? Nothing left? In the square screen at the foot of his bed, Sabrina Wilcox with her Barbra Streisand hair and shiny eyes, a big-boned girl, a boy's girl, de-brainwashed slave of love, a crystal gazer, a contemplative, possibly an idiot, an amalgam of Southern California tics and moods and intricately inflected obsessions, stares back at him in ruthless self-absorption, while Peter Fagin, the tall soft-spoken gray-haired auxiliary Carlos lawyer, asks her questions, in his velvety flat voice that sounds like his vocal cords have been poached in oatmeal.

Did Dr. Phlegg represent to you that he had several businesses?

Yes.

Let me show you exhibit number 540, do you recognize this piece of paper as containing a sampling of Dr. Phlegg's business cards?

Yes.

Did he provide these cards to you during the course of your therapy with him?

Yes he did.

And is one of these cards Robertson Psychiatric Center, Dr. Potter Phlegg?

Yes.

Is another card the Metaire Financial Systems, J. Potter Phlegg, President and Chief Executive Officer?

Yes.

Is another card Lopate and Phlegg, Furniture and Novelty World, 703 South Powell, Portland Oregon?

Yes.

Is another business card provided to you during your therapy with Dr. Potter Phlegg something called Cyberquest, J. Potter Phlegg, Chairman of the Board, President and Chief Executive Officer?

Yes.

Did he provide all those cards to you in the course of your therapy?

Yes he did.

In providing those cards, did he propose various business ventures?

Yes.

Did you during the course of your relationship with him tape-record telephone conversations in which he called you and proposed these ventures?

From my answering machine, there are tape-recorded calls.

And when did you begin recording calls from him?

I started keeping tapes in September 1989.

Why were you recording the calls?

I wasn't recording the calls.

How did they end up getting recorded on your answering machine?

I had this answering machine that had its own mind, it would just record and stop recording at its own will, and also like I also left the recorder on all the time because I didn't have phones in every room. I only had a phone in my bedroom, and if I was in the front part of the house I wouldn't hear the phone or else I would hear the phone and I'd pick up the one extension which was in the kitchen and so if we started talking before the outgoing message was finished the answering machine just assumed we were leaving a message, it didn't know we were having a conversation. So that's how I came by the tape recordings.

After you had a meeting with Detective Zabar, was there another period of time when you were recording conversations with Dr. Phlegg at the specific request of the Beverly Hills Police Department?

Yes.

In fact, did the Beverly Hills Police Department provide you with what's called a body wire, that you could wear to record conversations with Dr. Phlegg?

Correct.

That was in March of 1990?

Correct.

The dream of Los Angeles burns off his psyche like coastal fog, and though he's not yet engaged, not yet caught in the web of glue he's secreted over years in Manhattan, strands of it have begun to wobble stickily in his vicinity.

*What's being referred to there? He says you have two weeks to get it to-
gether, what's he talking about?*

*When he left the message I might not have been aware what he was talking
about. He had a new idea every day.*

It's snowing outside: plump watery flakes dropping through a metal-gray
afternoon sky, a sky the color of Peter Fagin's hair, comforting snow, theatrical
snow, that will melt on contact with the sidewalk and not accumulate.

*He says on that tape he refers to some project involving big money do you
know what he's referring to?*

He was going to start up Spanish-speaking psychiatric clinics.

What was your role in that business scheme?

I didn't have any involvement.

*Why was he phoning you and explaining he had some scheme involving big
money?*

*He likes to tell everyone how brilliant he is in business, he was just calling
to brag.*

*When he called to brag, starting in October, did he start to call up and
start expressing a certain obsessiveness?*

Objection.

Sustained.

Did Dr. Phlegg in October start making lots of phone calls to your house?

I'd say it started before October.

When did it start?

Um, probably in mid-August, early September, is when they became—

*He's testified that those phone calls reflected on his phone bills were made
because you started pressuring him to call him back all the time, is that true?*

No.

*Did you go through his phone bills and your phone bills to establish what
pattern there was if any for the phone calls made by him as opposed to the
phone calls made by you?*

Yes I did.

*He has testified there were phone calls that took for example 289 minutes,
do you recall conversations of that length?*

There were times when he kept me on the phone all night.

What was he calling about when he kept you on the phone all night?

*He would just be badgering and haranguing and manipulating and trying
to make me say something or do something that I was resisting, and he
wouldn't give up until I would say it or do it or agree. If that took three*

*hundred minutes or six hundred minutes, however long it took for him to break
me down, that's as long as the conversation would last.*

To break you down in what way?

To do what he wanted.

Seth has lost his looks and youth and his cleverness at getting other
people to do what he wants: it is, increasingly, what they want that takes
priority, whether it's money for love or writing for money, and as he watches
Sabrina Wilcox, who will not be prime meat all that much longer, he wonders
if this sadly perky woman will find true love with someone who isn't a psychopath before she is too old to find anyone. She has, he decides, a better chance
than him.

Which was what?

It could be anything, from, just to do whatever he wanted me to do.

And that occurred over a long period of time?

Correct.

Was it true he'd call and disguise his voice as someone else?

Yes.

And ask what you'd been doing, and if you'd been out with other men?

Yes.

Did you create this document?

Yes.

How was this document created?

*My attorney obtained Dr. Phlegg's phone records through discovery, and we
took his phone records and my phone records and listed them on the computer
and created this document which I think all of them except for December is in
the order in which the calls came or were placed.*

When did the calls from Dr. Phlegg begin?

*These calls only reflect calls made from his home number, not his office
number. His office number to my home or my business was a local call.*

Among other things brought on by three days of total solitude: the realization that he has, since his brief spurt of sobriety after the accident, been
drinking more compulsively and harder than he ever did before, without pleasure, to kill his memories and soften the razory edges of his days; further, that
the resulting watery consciousness oscillates almost exclusively between the
Martinez trial and Mark, his former mania, who has somehow reappeared in
his mind idealized, a sparkling possibility spattered, like a defaced Greek

statue, by reeking projectile guilt. He cannot, he tells himself, go back in time and deconstruct the accident, any more than Felix and Carlos can delete the irrevocable seven minutes for which they must, inevitably, in one fashion or another, atone for the rest of their lives.

When did the calls from his home begin?
June 18th.
How frequently were the calls made?
You mean the whole time period?
Would he call once a day, once a week?
Oh, several times a day.
All hours of the day and night?
Yes.
For hours at a time, sometimes?
Yes.
During that time he was providing therapy?
Sometimes.
Was he also talking to you about your personal relationship?
Yes.
You said that you and your attorney were involved in preparing that document, did you at some point sue Dr. Phlegg?
Yes.

But he could, perhaps there is the chance that he could, put right this one small abomination, revisit the scene of this one crime and somehow alter the forensics, change the conclusion.

Did the pattern of calls end in December?
No.
Sometime around October, were you still involved with Dr. Phlegg in a relationship?
Yes.
On October 30, did you go out of California with Dr. Phlegg?
Yes.
You went to Mexico?
Yes.
Before you went to Mexico did you have information that Dr. Phlegg was going to meet with Felix Martinez on the 31st?
I've never been clear if that phone call came just before we left or the day we returned.

Jack looks up from his legal pad, underscoring "Mexico" as he notes somewhat apprehensively that Frankie, who's wearing a pair of Jack's blue jeans, Jack's USC T-shirt, and even a pair of Jack's socks (magenta, Gap), is helping himself to a second glass of breakfast scotch (also Jack's) on the rocks, diluting it a splash with Canada Dry lemon-lime seltzer. Frankie's smiling his abstracted smile as he mucks about in the kitchen, a smile Jack associates with many young people he has known, a pleased private grin of contented, unconscious narcissism, something animalistic about that smile, Jack thinks, he thinks this because, since Frankie has been staying in the house in Mt. Washington, what began as a charmed interlude has been turning, stroke by small stroke, into something more enigmatic, a situation that no longer fills Jack with a sense of tenderness and comfort, eros gratified, or any of the other hopeful stimuli Frankie's generous physicality and easy presence occasioned in the first place.

Which calls are you referring to?

From my apartment, Phlegg had picked up his messages from his wife Maggie, and learned that Felix wanted to talk with him. So from my place he called Felix and set up an appointment.

Did he indicate to you what the nature of the meeting was going to be?

When he hung up the phone he said he hoped he wouldn't hear what he thought he'd hear, and when I asked him what he thought that would be he said he thought they'd say they killed their parents.

Your understanding was that Felix Martinez was a patient of Dr. Phlegg?

Not at that time, no.

You were a patient of his at that time?

Yes.

Was it unusual for Dr. Phlegg to be talking to you about his other patients?

No.

In fact, you had tape-recorded conversations in which Dr. Phlegg revealed the nature of his clients' problems, correct?

Correct.

Objection, irrelevant.

Objection to the form of the question sustained.

Did you tape-record a telephone call from Dr. Phlegg in which he discusses confidentiality problems of a patient?

Yes.

Objection.

Overruled.

It seems to Jack that Frankie looks content because Frankie has no idea what Jack is thinking about him. Namely that Frankie is thoughtless, insensitive to Jack's feelings, proprietary about Jack's belongings yet often indifferent or cruel to Jack personally, that Frankie's cheerfulness has begun to seem a desperate mask pulled down over all kinds of twisted things Jack can't even guess at. Lately, apparently inspired by Seth's pork roast surprise, Frankie's continually rummaging through the Julia Child cookbook and coming up with ever more elaborate, time-consuming treats, handing Jack a shopping list whenever he leaves the house. However Jack might like to view this meal-sharing as a form of intimacy, a sign of happy domesticity, he recognizes it as a sort of compulsion on Frankie's part, an obsessive messy activity, like a child playing in mud.

I'm showing you a tape you prepared in which Dr. Phlegg tells you about a woman doctor and the nature of her sexual problems.

Correct.

I'm showing you another tape you obtained that reflects a conversation in October in which he refers to someone he calls a studio guy—

Correct.

Was that uncommon for Dr. Phlegg to reveal to you the problems of his patients?

No.

Would he actually name the patients?

Sometimes.

And sometimes he would just refer to someone as a doctor, and tell you what the person's problems were?

He would give vital information that you couldn't mistake who the person was.

Seth presses Mark's number, experiencing something like a carnal thrill. He knows he'll get the machine, he does get the machine, and the odd thing is that Mark's voice has never sounded like Mark's voice on the machine, it doesn't this time either, yet knowing that it is Mark's voice, that Mark still has the same number, is presumably still living in the same apartment on Avenue B and Ninth Street, brings an ashen comfort, on the order of: *at least he hasn't moved, made a lot of money, become famous, written a successful screenplay, met up with a rich boyfriend,* another form of: *I hope to god he's still waiting tables, I hope he's unhappy, I hope he's suffering,* though of course the mere fact that Mark has his old phone number, that he leaves the same type of greeting on his answering machine, signifies none of these things, signifies nothing, in fact, besides Mark's continuing presence in the world.

Around October 30, he told you about a plan to meet with Felix Martinez?
Correct.
He indicated to you he hoped it wasn't what he thought it was?
Correct.
And that conversation was with you, it wasn't with his wife, correct?
No, that was between Phlegg and myself.
Where were you when you had that conversation?
In my bedroom.
While you were in Mexico, did you have an argument about whether your romantic relationship was going to continue?
I had broken off the relationship that Friday.
Why were you going to Mexico with him if you'd broken off the relationship?
Because on Saturday when I hung up the phone he raced over to my store and did a whole number on me and somehow I ended up going to Mexico, and in Mexico we had a big confrontation about how the relationship needed to be different.
Did you tell him the relationship was going to end?
Yes.
You did. You had already told him that when he told you about this meeting with Felix Martinez?
I had told him prior, prior to the discussion about Felix.

Seth presses the off button before the beep. He slips a fresh tape into the VCR to record Sabrina Wilcox's testimony. He opens his address book and finds the number for Nathan Greenglass's dealer.

How did he accept that the relationship was going to end?
He didn't believe it or accept it. He laughed a lot and just did his manipulations.
When you say he did his manipulations, was he trying to keep you in the relationship?
Yes.

Jack sets aside his legal pad. He slides a new tape into the VCR to record Sabrina Wilcox's testimony. Frankie chops scallions for tuna salad at the floating counter, stuttering out a suggestion that Jack's heard twice before, that they try bondage sex, and Jack again laughs and tells Frankie he's not into it, and Frankie tells him again that he wasn't into it at first either but after trying it a few times realized it was really hot. With a bla bla bla bla blindfold,

Frankie stipulates. He could be serious, he could be joking, Jack can't tell the difference with Frankie, and thinks this is a dangerous sign.

How was he doing that?

Just by the things he said, then when this phone call came up, and he asked me to go there and be there for him, that this was like the one last thing I could do for him, and if I did this, it would show that all this work he'd put in on me wasn't for nothing, that if I did this, it would show I had learned something.

Lorna, Seth says, his voice seductively low.

Hi Seth how are you. Hers clipped for business, as if syllables were money.

I'm just fine Lorna and yourself?

Oh it's the usual craziness around here.

When you say "did this," what was he asking you?

He was asking me to come and be there in case something happened to him, so I could call the police or call an ambulance.

Look, I'll get right to the point, I've got a smallish painting here that Nathan gave me years ago and he made me promise I'd sell it if I were ever strapped for cash so I decided to call you. As I'm a bit cash poor at the moment.

Things that bad? Lorna says sweetly, contemptuously.

Not *that* bad, Seth quickly counters, I just thought if you were interested it would be a nifty way to raise some Christmas money.

Are you offering this to me or do you want me to sell it for you?

Well, Lorna, if you wanted to buy it that would simplify things.

Did he give you instructions on what you were to do?

Yes, he did, he had said that he was going to leave the doors to the other offices, there are three offices, he was going to leave the doors to the other two offices unlocked so I could go in there to use the phone, and he just told me to pay attention and listen carefully and if I heard anything that sounded like he was in danger that I should call the police.

What's it look like, what period?

It's a little bird with some, you know, dots, and that drizzled atmospheric effect—

That's lucky, there's a lot of people interested in those birds.

Did he put you in fear as a result of telling you information about Felix? Definitely.

Did you in fact go to his office on October 31?

Yes.

What time did you arrive there?

A little after five.

What size is it exactly—

Oh, I would say, let me guesstimate, I'd say a foot and a half on one side—

Dr. Phlegg testified he didn't recall you being there on the 31st, he also said that after he had the session with Carlos and Felix Martinez he drove to your house and told you about the session for the first time, is that true testimony?

It's an outright lie.

Had you gone to work that day?

I went to work on October 31.

What time did you get out of work that day?

Phlegg called me I would say around four-thirty and he was with Felix at the time, he said he was checking to make sure I was going to be there, and insisted that I leave at that moment, which I did.

Janice Wade admires her garden and swimming pool while lounging in her Balinese morning room, her attention fluttering now and then to the large Sony screen and the Martinez trial, or to the thick open manila file Norman Bates has provided, full of phone records, typewritten reports, the Dave Spacey letters and cards, and numerous surveillance photographs of Judge Rupert Tietelbaum, seen getting in and out of his Lincoln Town Car in a wig and funny glasses near various public telephones, the telephoto lens even picking up the sound-altering device Tietelbaum clamped to the phone receivers. Norman has gotten several good shots of Tietelbaum rummaging vainly in a trash receptacle on level 7 of the Beverly Center parking structure, looking for the money Janice decided, at the last minute, not to place in a nylon zip bag as per the instructions of Dave Spacey. Has captured, in fact, the look of angry surprise when Tietelbaum discovered, inside the nylon zip bag, the very turd Janice received from him weeks earlier courtesy of the U.S. Postal Service, which Janice thoughtfully moistened with peanut oil to restore its original texture. Possession of this file acts like a sedative on her recently frayed nerves, for it fills her with a sensation of limitless options. It can be sent, for example, sans cover letter, to Tietelbaum himself, like a little package of Semtex. Or it can go via overnight express to one of Buffy's more durable contacts in the District Attorney's Office. It could even arrive, at some strategic moment in the downwinding trial, on the desk of defense attorney Lauren

Nathanson, who would probably have more fun with it than anyone else Janice Wade can think of.

Did you take anything with you, for your own protection?

I went to my house, and I got a gun from my next-door neighbor.

Who was your next-door neighbor, how was it that he had a gun?

I don't know why he has a gun, but he has a gun, and I borrowed it from him.

Was that a handgun?

I believe it's called a .357 Magnum?

Was it loaded? Did you take a loaded gun?

It was loaded, and he showed me how to shoot it.

Why did you take a loaded gun?

Because Phlegg had made me very fearful.

One of the tech people has set up a miniature Sharp near the craft services table in the general area of the trailers on Woodrow Wilson Drive, and Cassandra, Teddy Wade, and several others stand around the tiny screen, enjoying roast beef sandwiches and coffee, waiting for the ambulance to pull out of the driveway, as Lucas Spelvin and Lazlo Daley, standing several yards away, mull over the script of *Dark Blood* and discuss how and what to shoot around Tim Chumley, who has just experienced a mild speedball overdose in one of the many Martinez bathrooms and is presently wheeled out of the $3.5-million mansion on a gurney. Cassandra and Teddy Wade have become very close in recent days, despite their difference in age, drawn together by a shared spartan professionalism that transcends the kinds of debilitating personal problems besetting certain younger members of the cast. They have both fucked Tim Chumley and agree that he has a lot of potential, but real problems with follow-through. If he could just hold it together, Teddy Wade sighs, Tim could be the next River Phoenix. I think he's even sexier than River, Cassandra opines, as the ambulance crunches across the driveway gravel.

When you spoke to him on the phone before you left work, did he tell you anything that Felix had said to him?

At that time no.

You were fearful because of something he told you before that conversation?

Yes. The fear was generated from the conversation we had after the first phone call.

When you got to the office what time did you think it was?

I would estimate five-fifteen.

What did you do when you got there?

I went into the waiting area, and there are little buttons on the wall, I pushed the Phlegg button and I sat down and waited.

Cassandra has heard nothing from her love muffin, as she sometimes refers to Frankie, for seven or eight days. She pictures the little scamp in all sorts of arcane trouble but expects he'll come gliding into the house in Altadena on his Rollerblades any evening now, which he probably should, since she's had two or three visits from an arson investigator who needs to clear up a few routine questions before they can process a life insurance payout that happens to fall in Frankie's favor because Frankie's father never changed the beneficiary.

What happened then?

Phlegg came and stuck his head out the door and said it was as he suspected—

What did you take that to mean?

I took it to mean that they had killed their parents.

After he said It's as I suspected, what happened then?

I believe he went back to the office with Felix for a while.

And what did you do when he did that?

I just waited in the waiting room.

Could you hear any noises at all?

At that time?

Yes.

No.

How long did you wait before you did something else?

He came back out and said that he was having Felix call his brother, that he didn't want Felix to tell Carlos that he had told him outside of his presence, that he wanted Carlos to be there when he found out, and that Carlos would be coming shortly, and that I wasn't to talk to him.

Did in fact Carlos come shortly after that?

Yes.

Were you still in the waiting room when Carlos arrived?

Yes.

Did you have any conversation with him?

Yes.

What was the conversation?

He came in, and he pressed the Phlegg button, then he picked up a magazine and started leafing through it, and he asked me if I had been waiting long, and I made some stupid comment back, "You know how doctors are," and that was it.

Then did he go into the inner office?

Phlegg came out and got him and they went back into the inner office.

Did you remain in the waiting room or go somewhere else?

I went somewhere else.

Where did you go?

I went into the hallway to go into the office beside his but the door was locked so I tried another office and that door was locked.

And you were in the hallway at that point?

Yes.

And what did you do next?

I stood there confused and stunned because the doors were locked.

Could you hear anything in the office from the hallway?

Yes.

What did you hear?

Carlos was angry and he was yelling at his brother that he was angry at him, he was upset and couldn't believe he'd done this or said this.

Anything else?

Not that I recall.

How long did you stay in the hall?

Just a few minutes. Then I went back to the waiting room.

Then what happened?

Timewise I'm not sure, but the next thing was, Felix ran past me, he went down the stairway, and then Carlos came out, and then Phlegg came following Carlos, and they went to the elevator.

Is the elevator on the same floor as Dr. Phlegg's office?

Yes.

Could you see the waiting room where the elevator was?

Yes.

What did you see?

The two of them stood in front of the elevator, Carlos was closest to the door and Phlegg was behind him.

Did they have a conversation?

Yes.

What was the conversation you heard at that time?

Carlos said something about I can understand that he needed to or some-

thing like that and Phlegg said you really ought to stay and come back into the office and you have to understand about confidentiality or something and Carlos just wanted to go take care of his brother.

Objection.

The answer is stricken.

Did Carlos Martinez say anything about what his intentions were about wanting to leave?

He said he wanted to go take care of Felix.

And what did Phlegg reply?

Phlegg just wanted them to come back into the office, the elevator was coming and Carlos said Take care of yourself to Phlegg and got in the elevator and Phlegg jumped on the elevator after him.

The statement by Carlos take care of yourself was before he got in the elevator?

Yes.

And Dr. Phlegg testified that that conversation took place downstairs near the car. Was that true?

I wouldn't know, I didn't go downstairs.

Did Dr. Phlegg tell Carlos that Carlos needed him, words of that sort?

Yes.

In what context?

Exactly I'm not sure, but he was trying to convey that Carlos needed him.

Did Dr. Phlegg say something about feeling threatened, his perception was that he was threatened?

At the elevator? He said, Are you threatening me, is that a direct threat?

And that was in response to what that Carlos Martinez said?

Take care of yourself.

When you heard that, did it seem to you Carlos said Take care of yourself in a threatening way?

At the time I heard it I didn't think so, but then Dr. Phlegg came back up and told me it was a threat, that I just didn't know a threat when I heard one.

But not based on what Phlegg later told you, but based on your own observation, did it seem to you that Carlos Martinez was threatening Dr. Phlegg?

Based on my observation I would say he was trying to get away from Dr. Phlegg.

Was he menacing, in your opinion?

Not in my opinion but later Dr. Phlegg said my opinion wasn't accurate.

Lorna Michael's gallery looks like a spaceship, all gleaming surfaces, panels of opaque glass blocking visual access to the inner sanctum, burgundy velvet theater ropes with just the right degree of elegant sag stretched across doorways, and Lorna Michael's employees look like aliens aboard the spaceship, some teeny-tiny like Lorna herself, others soaringly tall, each with a face sculpted at a major teaching hospital or foreign clinic, poreless skin, every hair manicured at the cost of a small imported automobile, the clothing exactly what's being worn in this month's *Details*, *Vogue*, and *GQ*, and because Seth is vaguely known, because Seth is expected, his costume of not very carefully selected winter clothes, the torn paper bag he is carrying, and his expression of stricken urgency excite nothing more than a little guarded smile from the receptionist, a male in his early twenties who appears to be three feet tall. He presses a button on the underside of his work area which activates a red light on Lorna's telephone. Before Seth can open his mouth, Lorna strides into the outer office on Bennis Edwards pumps fashioned from some endangered species, brandishing the terrifying smile worked into her repertoire by a plastic surgeon in, if Seth remembers correctly, Mexico. Like many of her artists, Lorna has been refashioning her face and various other problem parts of her body at six-month intervals for many years, getting bits snipped and scalpeled off, other bits suctioned of fat, and the results, though spectacular, have kept Lorna and her circle arrested in time, while the world has grown old around them. On the ever-rarer occasions when Seth actually sees Lorna Michaels, he feels he's talking through a special time tube to someone inhabiting 1982.

Come in and show me what you've brought, Lorna beckons, heading straight back into her office. Seth steps around the space console of bright young things and their sleek designer office supplies to confront what is surely the world's largest empty desk, behind which Lorna has installed herself in the world's largest office chair. Looming behind that is the world's largest Sigmar Polke, primarily pink, with a swipe of fecal viscosity tinting its upper regions. Seth has the option of sitting on an extremely narrow iron sculpture which may or may not be a chair, or standing. He stands. He removes a bright yellow Tower Records plastic bag from the torn paper bag and unwraps the small Nathan Greenglass painting that has languished unobserved for many years by all but a happy few, who have, Seth reflects, often remarked, after orgasm, what a pretty little thing it is.

He gave you one of the good ones, Lorna remarks, did he sign it on the back?

Seth's never bothered to look. He looks.

No, he didn't, he says.

Lorna waves her hand.

Doesn't matter, she says. If somebody wants to buy it Nathan can scribble in the signature.

She is no longer looking at the Nathan Greenglass. She is now looking pointedly at her watch, a gold Rolex.

Tell you what, Lorna says. It's worth forty, I'll give you twenty.

Paula Cooper told me it was worth sixty.

Maybe Paula Cooper should buy it from you.

I'll take twenty.

I sort of thought you would.

They both laugh, the first funny moment of the day.

What happened then?

Then he said they had killed their parents, that they had threatened him and everyone connected to him, and that it wasn't safe, and he needed to have his wife get out of the house and get the kids out of the house and then he started making phone calls.

He said that you were in danger?

Yes.

Did he say why?

Just because I was there and I was connected to him.

Were you afraid as a result of what he told you?

Yes.

Did you think you needed Dr. Phlegg because of the danger he was making you feel?

Yes.

That he could help you out of the danger?

I felt that he was my only chance.

That was because of information he gave you?

Correct.

At a point when your relationship wasn't going so well?

Correct.

Later in March when you had a tape-recorded interview with him at the behest of the Beverly Hills police you told him, I don't think you're afraid of the Martinez brothers, didn't you?

Correct.

And he says on that tape, I don't think I'm afraid of anybody.

That's accurate.

Did he seem afraid after he'd been with the brothers?

No.

Were you afraid?

Yes.

Did he start to phone people?

Yes.

Who did he phone?

The first call was to his wife, then other people, I don't know their names, but he told me they were all connected to an ethical board of psychology or something.

And what was the tone of those conversations?

He talked and laughed with some of them, but I thought that might be a cover.

He was laughing on the telephone?

Yes.

How long did he talk?

A long time.

Oh, this is *rich*, says JD, storming through his apartment in search of a cigarette lighter, his flagging phone batteries crackling and seething in Seth's ear.

No, says Seth, *I'm* rich, for the next twenty minutes or so. He presses and holds down the rewind on his TV remote, Sabrina Wilcox reversing on the screen through a blizzard of zigzagging scan lines. I can come back and stay at the Marmont on my own nickel if I want.

You should.

I will. Except you know what, I think I'll stay at the Roosevelt.

Tell me the rest of it.

So I go to that stupid bar, and I'm already in this existential panic, JD, about drinking too much all the time now, I feel like that character in *The Long Goodbye*—

The one who always orders gimlets, JD says.

Right, and he talks about people ordering their first drink of the evening, trying not to knock anything over with their hands—

I haven't had a drink in five days, says JD, but you know something, I'm going to mix one up right now.

And he's *there*, JD, I can't believe I fucking did this, I was trashed, he was talking to some gorgeous young creature, and at first he was going to ignore me, but I got right in his face, reached across him in fact to order a nice big screwdriver, and I said, you know, Oh hello Mark I didn't recognize you, and he says kind of diplomatically or whatever I haven't seen you in a long time, so I said Well I've been in L.A., this that and the other about the Martinez trial, and he says Oh them and I say What about *them* and he says Well what's your take on all that or something like that and I said Life is a mystery like Madonna says everyone must stand alone, he kind of laughs nervously and his friend gets up to go to the bathroom—

You don't mind if I take a shit while we talk?

I *wish* I could take a shit right now, be my guest, anyway this *conversation* happens in which I think I actually managed to be just as odious to him as he always was to me, I don't recall very many details, I do remember him saying something like, I really wish we could've been friends—

"You mean, Blanche, that all this time we could have been friends?"

—exactly, I *burst* into "Writing a Letter to Daddy," *his address is heaven above,* and as you can hear my fucking vocal cords are so ravaged from four million cigarettes a day that I actually can do a decent Baby Jane Hudson, Mark didn't even get the reference, but of course all the time I'm putting on this maniacally detached front I've got this boner burning a hole in my pants, and I'm thinking He's so beautiful, he's so beautiful, I'm thinking how much I still want him, and inside, my evil twin is telling me if I can't make that face light up with ecstasy I can make it look really, really unhappy, I can ruin this kid's day, I have that much power in the situation, anyway, he tells me he's *writing,* he's had some little poems *published,* funny thing is I know he's had a few things published by this friend of Caitlin Donoghue, this tub-of-lard editor he's probably given a toss or maybe just kind of flirted with more likely, and I said, JD, you will love this, *By the time I started writing I was no longer pretty enough to publish poetry,* which is one line anybody truly witty could drive a fertilizer truck through, but instead he *blushed,* I swear to God—

I've been having the most turgid fucking bowel movements—

Don't *describe* it, JD, even the concept of shit is enough to make me puke today, my point is, I go out *searching* for this little jerk to like *apologize* for all my bad behavior, and then when I actually see him all I want is to smack him in the mouth—

Well, the best-laid plans—

Well I wasn't laid was I, that's the subtext—

No, sweetie, that's the *con*text—

But it was never just about *sex,* I *liked* Mark, I genuinely did, but you know, I can't just pretend it's not an issue when I desire him and he's got his legs in the air for half of Manhattan, especially when he handed *me* all that demure crap about breaking up with his old boyfriend and being so fucked up around that that he couldn't even think about another relationship, so I said to him, We could never have been friends, this brings a sad look to his face, he's still real pretty, JD, and I guess he's been pumping himself up a little at the gym, his friend meanwhile has come out of the toilet and is sort of hovering over at the jukebox, like maybe he knows who I am and he's heard Mark's side of all this a million times and doesn't want to involve himself, so Mark says, Just out of curiosity why not, and I said Because you're a nice middle-class white boy who's never known what it means to lose, you're gonna write your little poems and your little grant proposals and get yourself a nice safe teaching job and find that perfect little boyfriend and if I know you, Mark, and I think I do, the two of you might even *adopt a child* to make it more real for yourselves, some traumatized infant from a *Chinese orphange* or *Romania*— then he says I don't have to listen to this and I say No you don't, I'm sure it's very disagreeable to hear and I'm actually *sorry* to be saying all this, I had actually hoped to tell you something different, but now that I see you this is all I have to say.

Wow.

Lacan was right, Seth says. Language is always a substitution.

That's it?

No, that's just the beginning, the sequel is, the next night, I go to the fucking *restaurant* with a bunch of people I barely know, some kid who's, get this, writing his doctoral thesis on my magazine articles, if you can credit that, plus his, I don't know, boyfriend, and some friend of theirs who's a *fan,* you know how I love all that sort of thing, and I get up and go over and try to talk to him and he's, how can I put it, unctuously civil, distant, inaccessible, so we order a pitcher of martinis, and this kid's grilling me about my so-called career, thank you, and after about seven drinks the food arrives, all heaped up in a pile like they do in that place, and at a certain moment Mark sort of drifts by the table, and I picked up the plate and threw it at him.

Did you hit him?

I think some salad hit him.

You should've thrown the pitcher.

Oh, JD, what right do I have, when you get down to it. He's just a kid.

A kid who broke your heart, let's not—

Well, fuck it. It's just more scar tissue isn't it. Of course they weren't about to throw me out, we all just finished our meal and left. *Then,* to top it all, I go into that bar the following night, and he's there again with his little friend, only this time he turns his back very pointedly, I'm sitting next to this good-looking man, who inserts himself in a conversation between myself and the bartender—we were making up limericks, or trying to, and this stranger tried to complete one of these limericks with what he obviously considered clever wordplay, which it wasn't. Even though he wasn't clever I pretended to find him so because I needed a sort of ally, if you see what I mean, anyway, naturally, the very day after I make a scene in a restaurant, I would have to meet a so-called restaurant floor manager with a whole philosophy about the dining experience, someone absolutely obsessed about his so-called *theme restaurant*—to be fair about it, I did draw him out on the subject, I was actually quite eager to hear about his work, until I realized this was a person absolutely crazed on the subject, and of course when he said it was an *American-style restaurant* with *family fare,* I could just imagine the kinds of atrocious things they served, and from his descriptions of the staff I could tell they were all gay, or fag-hag types, for want of a better term, with a keen interest in *drag,* since according to him they have all these theme nights or costume nights, in the end he couldn't shut up about his philosophy of dining out, which had an entirely authoritarian cast to it. His main concern seemed to be that patrons of his restaurant meet particular standards of behavior for dining out, which he and his staff *strictly enforced.* He was for example not at all inclined to give special treatment to celebrities or stars, *they have to wait for a table just like anybody else,* he said, which is stupid business, really, since celebrities or stars, however they behave, spend more money than anybody else.

What's Mark doing all this time?

Mark is making a big show of his indifference, Seth says impatiently. It is a fact, he goes on, that waiters and restaurant managers and bartenders are more starstruck than anyone else, they pretend to be jaded and indifferent about their daily contact with well-known people, but in fact they brag to each other and everyone else about who comes into the restaurant or who comes into the bar, Seth says, not all waiters or restaurant managers or bartenders of course, but for a vast majority, to be spoken to by a well-known person gives them a feeling of intimate association with that person, but of course at the same time the waiter or restaurant manager or bartender knows that this well-known person would never recognize him again, would certainly never recognize him outside the restaurant or bar, in fact, most people can't tell one waiter, restaurant manager, or bartender from another, and this interchangeability is a source of unending resentment for people in the so-called *service professions.* Most waiters, restaurant managers, and bartenders in New York and Los Angeles, Seth says, are in a state of constant resentment and barely contained revolt against their condition as servants, precisely because their servitude brings them into contact not merely with ordinary people to whom they feel equal or even superior, but also with well-known people to whom they feel utterly inferior. Because they see this well-known person drinking and eating and using the lavatory *just like anybody else,* they get the idea that this well-known person isn't so extraordinary after all, and that they themselves, the waiters and so forth, could easily do whatever this well-known person does. This leads to the delusion that they could actually achieve far greater things than the well-known person—who is simply eating his dinner and completely unaware of the raging resentment his presence is causing—has achieved. They begin to believe this well-known person is a fraud, a fraud who is *taking up the space* that rightfully belongs to the waiter, restaurant manager, or bartender. Before this well-known person entered their restaurant or bar, it seemed perfectly natural for the well-known person to be well known. His accomplishments were secure. But now the waiter has a chance to observe this public person gratifying the same prosaic needs which everyone on earth has to gratify, and perhaps the servant, who already resents his servitude as a matter of course, has a chance to observe the *personal pathology* of the public person. It's a fact, Seth continues, that most well-known people are even more fucked up than the general run of humanity. They are driven to accomplish extraordinary things because they are deeply and dangerously wounded in some part of their being. They are impelled by their own pain to impress and dominate others with their accomplishments, and the people they are driven to impress and dominate are precisely these waiters, restaurant managers, and bartenders who envy and resent them.

Of course, Seth goes on, quite often the servant imagines himself a master who's *biding his time.* By the time a servant is thirty or thirty-five the will to become an extraordinary figure has been beaten out of him, and he begins to view himself as a servant for life. On the other hand, Seth says, at Mark's age, at twenty-four or whatever he is, it's far from unreasonable to imagine oneself an extraordinary person in the making, with his little poems for instance, he can tell himself he's educating himself for an entirely different sort of existence. At Mark's age the well-known persons who wander into his ken are potential role models and mentors. He believes if he studies them long enough and carefully enough, the secrets of their extraordinary gifts and talents will reveal themselves, will uncover something in himself, transform him in some essential way. He sees himself as a Felix Krull type, no doubt, using his good looks and his native cunning to coax from unwary older people the keys to a successful life. At Mark's age there is nothing very urgent about this transformation, and nothing too specifically important about which mentor or role model he gravitates toward, at Mark's age, Seth says, the psyche is soft and infinitely permeable. It's also hypersensitive and any insult to the fragile ego contained in it causes the person to flee from the source of the insult. At Mark's age, when one is good-looking as a matter of course, one has a mobility that allows one to go from one figure to another without any lasting pain. At Mark's age, a person who disappoints you, however extraordinary that person might be, can be discarded and forgotten about in no time at all. Everyone is good-looking and mobile at twenty-four, says Seth, even quite homely people, even hideously ugly people are attractive at twenty-four. Mark, for example, is extraordinarily good-looking now, and at thirty he will still look desirable. By the time he's thirty-three or thirty-four, he may not appear so extraordinary, because he has the kind of face that seems beautiful at twenty-four, becomes merely good-looking at thirty, and by age thirty-five becomes merely the object of a specific taste in faces. Even at thirty, he will find his sexual options and his sexual mobility diminished. Because he is naturally reserved and introspective, he will not be able to objectify himself and invest his energy in his physical appearance. He'll let it go, Seth says, as I did, possibly. Unfortunately, Seth says, the libido doesn't vanish at the moment when you no longer like your body. The libido never vanishes, Seth tells JD, yet we stop liking our bodies even before we're middle-aged. We get sick of our body after thirty-five years of having to feed it and water it and tend to its problem areas, its excretions and secretions, its smells, its swellings, all the little demands it makes. People who worship their own bodies, Seth says, especially after thirty-five, live in constant denial of reality. They are trapped in their bodies like weasels in a cage, Seth says, especially homosexual men, who have taken body worship to its most extreme and Nazified point of ridiculousness. Every homosexual man who doesn't look like a movie star, Seth says, believes he is worthless and unlovable, and spends half his life trying to hide the truth from himself and everyone else. Instead of accepting the inevitable decay of his body, the homosexual male, Seth says, wastes half his life attempting to arrest or reverse the aging process. We are born with a mortal illness, Seth concludes, and spend half our lives or all our lives denying that we have this illness. The aging process is the visible symptom of this illness and we devote our whole lives to *masking the symptom.*

Rewind on Sabrina Wilcox.

He told me the Martinezes were his best friends.

That they were his best friends?

And the reason he was calling the boys and going to the memorial service was that Fidel was his best friend and if this had happened to him Fidel would be there for his daughters.

Did he mention anything about money how much the estate was worth?

Yes.

When did he mention that.

Shortly after the parents had the memorial service.

What did he say about that.

He said they were worth fourteen million dollars and these boys would inherit fourteen million dollars and they would need his guidance and his assistance to invest the money properly and find the right accountants and the right lawyers.

Did he have any specific business ideas in mind that he discussed with you?

He said if we needed any money to start anything he could persuade them to put up the money.

If you and Dr. Phlegg needed any money to start any of your joint businesses that he could persuade them to put up the money?

Correct.

Did he say anything else about how he was going to help them in that respect?

To invest this money, find people to handle it for them.

Did he seem excited by this prospect?

Yes.

Did he continue to talk about this in October when Felix came in for his session?

It came up again at that time.

Before you went to Dr. Phlegg's office you say he stayed overnight got up and went to his office, did he come back to your house the next night and spend the night with you?

Yes.

Did he usually spend the night with you?

The only time he spent the night was when he felt he was losing control of me or suspected that I was seeing someone else.

Objection.

Sustained.

Did anyone force you to write this Valentine's Day card?

I was frightened into writing it yes.

How did someone frighten you into writing it?

Phlegg frightened me into writing it because he was dissatisfied by the first Valentine's card I sent him, so I said I sent you a nicer one to your office, I was afraid since you were opening Valentine gifts in front of your wife and the kids if I gave you too nice a one or something I was just trying to cover myself because when I displeased him he said there was no reason for me to be alive if I wasn't going to make him happy.

But you also didn't want him opening your mushy card in front of his wife.

Oh his wife and I talked about sex with Phlegg quite often, so there wouldn't have been a problem with a mushy Valentine card in front of her.

In your direct testimony you indicated on March 5th 1990 you went to the police department and had a conversation with Detective Zabar.

Correct.

Since that time you've given a number of statements about what you knew about the Martinez case to the police, the Court, and the press, correct?

Correct.

I believe on March 6th you participated in what you knew to be a tape-recorded conversation with the Beverly Hills Police Department and a deputy district attorney, correct?

Correct.

You also subsequently spoke to someone from 60 Minutes, *a television show aired on CBS.*

Correct.

When is the first time you spoke to anyone from 60 Minutes, *do you recall?*

When was the airing of that show May 17 I believe.

May of 1990, is that correct?

The reporter approached me she came into my store I believe the day before or two days before the airing of that show.

Then there was another show aired on August 30, in which you are shown speaking during the show, do you recall that?

Yes.

When you talked to the reporter did you tell her the truth?

Yes.

At that time you weren't under oath, right?

No.

Were you making any attempt to fool her?

No.

In addition to talking to her did you have any other conversations with her?

I'm sorry what is the time frame?

After this second show was aired were there any further shows that featured you on 60 Minutes?

I believe the interview they taped was aired on more than one show.

What was your motivation in talking to 60 Minutes?

At the time the reporter came to my store Phlegg was trying to extort money from me, and when I spoke to the district attorney who was handling it at that time all of a sudden, where before they said they were going to take care of me and protect me and do all these things, all of a sudden it was How do we know this, and I was sort of abandoned and left to fend for myself against Phlegg, so I was very afraid that Phlegg was going to kill me, and now the police and the District Attorney's Office had gotten everything they needed from me, so they certainly weren't interested in keeping me alive, and I felt the need to have some public awareness of the danger I was in to try to distance Phlegg from me, because regardless, they told me they had called Phlegg's lawyer and told him to stay away from me.

Miss Wilcox, would it be fair to say that when you went to the police in

March 1990 your primary motivation was that you wanted Dr. Phlegg prose-
cuted?

Correct. He was the one who committed crimes against me, not Carlos or
Felix Martinez.

So your motivation was that you wanted police and the District Attorney's
Office to arrest Dr. Phlegg and prosecute him, correct?

Yes, for legitimate crimes committed against me.

And you were very disappointed when the District Attorney's Office failed to
do that, correct?

I am very upset that the law seems to decide who they will prosecute and
who they won't, I thought the law was supposed to protect all innocent people.

And you are very unhappy with the Los Angeles District Attorney's Office
because of what you perceive to be the failure of the District Attorney's Office to
prosecute Dr. Phlegg, correct?

Correct.

Now when you went and talked to 60 Minutes, *what was your motivation,*
was it solely to protect yourself from Dr. Phlegg?

Correct.

And I believe you sued Dr. Phlegg, was your motivation a desire to be
protected in suing him for money?

I wasn't interested in the money, lawyers are the ones interested in the
money, I was interested in proving that I was telling the truth, that Dr. Phlegg
is a liar, and that I had been terribly victimized and had real criminal charges,
criminal acts committed against me that no one was paying attention to, they
wanted to whitewash him and make him look like a good person when he
wasn't.

Were you given any reason from the District Attorney's Office as to why they
wouldn't prosecute Dr. Phlegg.

Yes, because they needed him as a witness.

Ah, no, Miss Wilcox, weren't you told by the District Attorney's Office that it
would be difficult to prove a rape allegation, were you told it would be your
word against his?

The one thing that stands out in my mind was about giving him immunity
for any crimes, that if they had to give him immunity they would.

You understand that Dr. Phlegg wasn't given immunity in this case.

And we both know why.

Miss Wilcox, you were very upset with the District Attorney's Office because the District Attorney's Office had not filed rape charges against Dr. Phlegg, correct?

There were more than rape charges.

Weren't you very upset with the District Attorney's Office because we would not file rape charges against Dr. Phlegg?

There were more than rape charges.

Were you or were you not upset with the Los Angeles County District Attorney's Office because we would not file rape charges?

My being upset was about all the behind-the-scenes things around this, it isn't because you didn't file those particular charges, it's because of all the other things that went on behind that.

Did you give an interview to a writer named Fawbus Kennedy?

Yes.

Were there any inaccuracies in that article?

There were a few, which I believe right after the article came out I made a list and sent them to him.

Do you have a copy of that list?

I may.

In addition to talking to Mr. Kennedy and 60 Minutes you also signed this affidavit.

I don't know what you're talking about.

How many times was this document corrected before you signed it?

I signed it on the fourth version three times before I sent it back.

Did you make corrections that were then incorporated into the next typed version?

Yes, then the new version would come back with new mistakes.

It appears that on page one you crossed out four lines is that what you did?

Correct.

On page two we find the initials SW.

Correct.

On page three there appears to be a correction of spelling on line twenty.

I didn't make that correction.

You made some other corrections here, to change the word "cars" from the plural are these your initials?

Yes.

Is that the way you make your initials?

Yes.

Here there appears to be another typographical correction instead of saying on therapy it says in therapy, is that the kind of correction that you would be in the habit and custom of making in other words are you the kind of person who would correct a typographical error?

I don't know if I'm that kind of person or not.

And it indicates here, right above your signature, I certify on penalty or perjury as provided in Section 201.555 of California Civil Procedure that the foregoing facts are correct, was that statement there when you signed the document?

Yes.

And did you understand when you signed this document you were in fact signing it under penalty of perjury?

Yes.

There was also a statement you made in a courtroom, correct?

Yes.

You were told not to discuss your testimony with either the district attorney or the police, correct?

Correct, I did not discuss my testimony but I did say something when I came out of the court that I had like disappeared in the courtroom and didn't really know what was said or done but I would like to talk to them about it as soon as the judge said that I was able to, I wanted them to let me know.

But you never did that did you.

I was never notified that that was allowed so no, we never discussed this and I still have no memory of that testimony.

When you testified in Santa Monica in July 1990 did you have to raise your hand and take an oath to tell the truth?

Yes.

And did you understand that you were testifying under penalty of perjury?

Yes.

And did you tell the truth?

Yes, I told the truth as I believed it at that time.

Would you claim your memory today four years later is better than your memory was in July 1990?

In some aspects yes, because I now have my own memory not the memory Phlegg planted in me.

When you testified in Santa Monica did you tell the judge that you were testifying from a memory that had been implanted in you by someone else?

At the time of that testimony I was not in therapy yet I hadn't been diag-

nosed, I was actually in denial, I believed I was perfectly fine, that nothing was wrong with me, it was my appearance in that courtroom and my inability to know what went on, the dissociation that happened frightened me and as a result of that I then agreed to go into therapy.

When you refer to dissociation what are you talking about?

Apparently what I've learned about that incident was when I came into what I perceived as a hostile environment and something that was part of the initial trauma that I'd suffered which was coming and being in a room with the Martinez brothers, I did something which is called dissociating, where I somehow separated myself and I was there and answered questions from some element of my consciousness.

But you weren't really there?

I'm not a psychologist so I'm not really the person to ask about what happened, I'm just the victim.

You were brainwashed?

I was told over and over, Sabrina, this is what you heard, just as I was told over and over, Sabrina you tried to commit suicide, there's proof on your medical records, and when you look at the medical records it says written out by the doctor, "not suicidal."

Did you ever stage a phony suicide at your home so that Dr. Phlegg would find you?

Yes.

Would you tell the jury what you did?

First understand that for Potter Phlegg, love equals suicide.

You opened up your oven correct when you wanted it to look like you were trying to commit suicide.

Yes.

What other physical things did you do?

I opened the oven but it was never turned on.

Did you lie on the floor?

Correct.

Did you want Dr. Phlegg to find you in that situation?

Dr. Phlegg wanted to find me in that position.

Did he tell you beforehand, Hey, Sabrina, it might be fun if you pretended to commit suicide and I came in and rescued you?

Not in those words but yes he did.

Oh, so he told you to do that.

Correct.

But he was very concerned after he found you, correct?

No, he was very elated and thrilled that I had finally demonstrated what true love was.

So during the course of your relationship with Dr. Phlegg, I take it it would be your testimony that you were the one who was perfectly sane and it was Dr. Phlegg who was behaving strangely, correct?

It was very unhealthy on my part to be involved and participate and be manipulated into the things I was manipulated into.

While in the hallway I heard Carlos's screams coming from Dr. Phlegg's office, then in quotes, underlined, is the following, starting at line five, I can't believe you did this, I don't even have a brother now, I could get rid of you for this, I hope you realize what we're going to have to do, we're going to have to kill him and anyone associated with him who knows we're associated with him. Felix was sobbing, in quotes the following occurred, I can't kill any more, anyone else, I can't stop you from what you have to do but I can't kill any more. Now, you signed this affidavit under penalty of perjury, correct?

Correct.

And it's now your testimony that you didn't actually hear that?

I heard a portion of it, the last thing I heard was him saying I could kill you for this and then Felix started crying and then I couldn't tell what Carlos was saying and then Phlegg interrupted and the last thing I heard, it wasn't I can't stop you it was more like What do you want to do or What are you going to do and I got the rest of these words and sentences from Potter Phlegg.

I take it that one of your motivations for testifying is that you would like to discredit Dr. Phlegg further.

I did not have any motivation in testifying. I did not want to be here. I made a specific request not to be here.

But you are here, correct?

I was subpoenaed, and I asked my attorney, and he said I had to appear.

And you are aware that this particular trial is televised nationally?

Yes.

And you are aware that 60 Minutes was broadcast nationally?

Yes.

And when you went to 60 Minutes *you wanted them to help you discredit or protect you from Dr. Phlegg, correct?*

I wanted some public knowledge that Phlegg intended to kill me so that when I showed up dead they would know where to look.

Now, you no longer believe Dr. Phlegg intends to kill you, do you?

I do believe he intends to kill me, I was very concerned about coming to this court because he would have knowledge that I would be here, and I make sure I have people around me at all times. You don't know the lengths I've gone to hide my whereabouts from Dr. Phlegg, Phlegg most recently attacked me on October 5—

What did Dr. Phlegg tell you that night about what the brothers said about the killings of their parents?

Have you ever heard Phlegg drone on and on, this was hours and hours of dialogue, I can't under these conditions try to repeat what he said word for word.

So it's your testimony that you cannot or will not repeat the details of what Dr. Phlegg told you?

I think you're asking something that is quite impossible to do considering how verbose Dr. Phlegg is.

Dr. Phlegg is verbose, is that your testimony?

What a normal person can say in ten minutes takes him ten hours, do you want a summation of what he said, just be more specific.

The place where the guns were bought they may have videotaped the purchase and they were fearful the videotape would disclose their identity or they would not be able to get rid of the shotguns they checked to find out and they told Dr. Phlegg the place holds on to them for three or four months and then tapes over them after purchasing the two shotguns they returned home to carry out the remainder of the plan—so Miss Wilcox, did you overhear this particular description?

No, I did not.

So when you signed under penalty of perjury all of these details you were lying is that correct?

The district attorney kept telling me that that didn't really matter, that it *wasn't important, that there were parts of things I heard and parts of things I didn't hear so he said it couldn't be written that way, it was represented to me that this was just the way it had to be written, so, there are parts of things I can say yes and parts that I can say no.*

Are you saying there are things I just read to you that you heard with your own ears?

There are things that were told to me over and over to the point where I didn't know if I had heard them or if I was told them.

Is it your testimony then today that you never heard either of the defendants discussing any details with your own two ears is that correct?

I would say that considering that I've had no reason to examine all this to determine what is right at this point in time that I would be most comfortable with saying that I can't be responsible and say that I heard them because of what Potter Phlegg did to me as far as implanting memories and ideas that didn't exist.

When you talked to the police in March 1990 you said several times that you thought Dr. Phlegg might have brainwashed you, didn't you.

I didn't know the extent I knew something strange and unusual that he was doing something strange to me and I didn't know the extent I was discovering all the time things Phlegg planted in my mind.

Didn't you tell the assistant district attorney, quote, I never thought I believed in evil but when I heard those boys speak I did.

Correct.

When you told him when I heard those boys speak did you mean to convey that you actually heard them speak?

I spoke to Carlos in the waiting room, there were many times I've heard them.

Did Dr. Phlegg tell them he would help them fabricate a defense?

Something like that.

Miss Wilcox you have said many things here in front of the jury about Dr. Phlegg, isn't it true the reason you're saying these things is because you were in love with him and he was married and wouldn't divorce his wife and marry you?

It is not true at all.

But you wanted to marry Dr. Phlegg at one time.

No I did not and I have proof of that, statements I made to other people long before, it was Dr. Phlegg who wanted to marry me, not me marry him.

Do you remember telling the police that Dr. Phlegg had talked you out of having children?

Oh yes he knew I wanted to have children and he lied to me claiming that he, he tried to make himself be everything I wanted.

But you wanted to have children.

I do not want to have children that look like Dr. Phlegg, do not try to alter what is true about my situation with Dr. Phlegg, it was not a relationship that stemmed out of meeting in a social environment and having a mutual attraction to each other Dr. Phlegg had his own plans about what he wanted me to serve in his life and I can provide you with a great deal of proof to substantiate everything I say about Dr. Phlegg, he made a tremendous effort to convince me my mother was trying to kill me and poison me, I would never marry Dr. Phlegg, I told his own children when they asked me.

You've finally succeeded in getting what you wanted, which was a national forum to slander Dr. Phlegg.

Objection argumentative.

Sustained.

Miss Wilcox isn't it true your motivation in going to the police was not to solve the Martinez murder case but to get Dr. Phlegg.

No, that is not true.

And isn't it true that you are now on national television being able to slander Dr. Phlegg the way you've always wanted.

No, that is not what I wanted, I have wanted justice, I have wanted the district attorney and the police to do their job for everyone not just for selected people.

Redirect of Sabrina Wilcox.

I think you said when you went to the police your motivation was to have Dr. Phlegg arrested because of something he did to you.

Arrested for crimes he committed against me yes.

And I think you referred to those crimes yesterday and indicated he had done other things besides rape you is that right.

He abducted me from my house, he drugged me, he had forced me to stay in his home against my will, he had threatened my life.

Why did you feel as strongly as you did about going to the police in 1990?

Because on the night when he was strangling me and I was blacking out I said to God if I'm supposed to die now all right if I'm not, if you let me live, I will make sure this man cannot do these things to anybody else, I will do everything in my power within the law to see that the truth is known about him and he cannot continue to do this because I have knowledge that he had done similar crimes to other women before me.

Miss Wilcox when you went to the police you felt you'd been the victim of a sexual assault is that correct?

On two occasions he raped me yes.

And when you went to the police you were there primarily to provide the police with evidence in the Martinez case?

No not at all.

Did you care at all about the Martinez case when you went to the police?

No, other than telling them who committed those crimes, that was not my purpose in being there, my purpose in being there was to report the crimes against me.

Were you given certain assurances that the police would follow up on your information about these rapes and assaults?

I was told Potter Phlegg would be arrested.

For the crimes against you.

Yes.

And were you told the police would take a formal police report?

I believed that but I was there for seven hours and they kept getting off onto the Martinez thing and I believed I was reporting Potter Phlegg.

After you gave the initial information did you ask if a formal investigation would be undertaken concerning his crimes against you?

I later learned from someone, it came to my attention, it was represented to me that they were investigating these crimes.

In fact it was later indicated that the police or the district attorney waited until July 1990 to investigate your charges.

Objection.

Overruled.

Did you at some point complain to the District Attorney's Office that nobody had investigated?

That's true.

And did someone indicate that they'd get around to it?

They indicated to me that it was lost.

And is that the Beverly Hills police, did someone come and take a report?

I believe they had to go back through the whole thing and file this time *another complaint, I guess since they never filed the first one it wasn't really another one—*

Did you read that police report?

I read it only once it made me so upset I couldn't look at it again.

You said at some point that you were upset at the District Attorney's Office because of all the behind-the-scenes things that were happening, what did you mean by that?

I don't want to get into the details.

Why did you distrust them?

Because I know that Miss Quilty would lie knowing that I would tell the truth, that she said in fact she would deny something she said to me and that she would make me out to be a liar if I repeated it—

I called to see if you were really coming back out anytime soon, Jack tells him the week of closing arguments, specifically during day two of Quentin Kojimoto's closing argument in front of the Felix jury, a closing argument which is doing awful things to Seth's blood pressure, and something in Jack's voice raises an alarm, for Seth is always listening for the downfalling tone that would signal some worsening of Jack's health.

I'm just booking a ticket, Seth says. He's given quite a lot of thought, these past days, to not going back at all. He could refigure his self-generating agenda of projects, get involved with something here. There's the book he wants to write, should write, now that he's had the experience of killing. Instead he hears himself tell Jack: I'm trying to get a flight on Saturday. Unfortunately that means I'll have to watch all the closing arguments on TV. The thing is I'm thinking about a hotel, Jack, for what I need to do your place isn't very central though you know I'm always grateful to stay there—

Hotel's gonna cost you a lot of money.

Yeah, well, I got paid for, you know, a job.

I think this is the first time, right now, in about ten days, that I've had this place to myself.

You're not sick are you?

Luckily not. I had a throat thing for a few days but it's gone.

You sound really freaked out, is there something—

Things have been pretty weird here—

Frankie still staying with you?

Frankie, Jack says, has not only been staying with me, he's become this permanent fucking fixture, and even if that has a certain happy aspect to it namely his dick, I'm starting to believe that Frankie is a little bit, how can I say it, I get the impression Frankie's lift isn't going to the top floor.

Why, what's he doing?

Nothing specific enough to tell you, it's his whole, I don't know, I guess if I were a shrink I would call it lack of affect—

I'm not sure that counts, Jack, almost everybody I ever went out with suffered from lack of affect. Present company excluded. Or I should say had it and *didn't* suffer from it.

I wouldn't characterize what I've been doing with Frankie as going out. As a matter of fact I don't think he's been outside this house since he got here until this afternoon.

Where's he gone?

Altadena, he said. To pick up some clothes.

Where is Altadena exactly.

Oh, you know. Up there somewhere. *Out* there somewhere. Not on my route generally.

Does that mean he's moving in?

I guess what I'm trying to say is I don't know what it means because I didn't invite him to move in and I actually don't want him moving in but none of that seems to cut any ice with Frankie himself.

You haven't discussed it? He can't just move into your place without your permission, Jack.

I tried to have a conversation about it, the thing is, you talk to Frankie and he slips out of dealing with the subject at hand, somehow his focus is somewhere else and you find yourself afterwards in this dense confusion about what you just talked about, I can't describe it, it's like he's really stoned or something.

Well, tell him. I'm very sorry, but you can't live here. You can fuck me from time to time, if my schedule permits, but you can't live here.

Thing is, it would make it easier I think if I could tell him you're coming back, you know, and it's just too much with three people.

Jack, you can tell him that anyway.

I'm afraid he won't leave.

Wait, what is that I'm hearing in your voice. What are you saying exactly?

I'm afraid he won't leave.

There's some principle I'm not grasping here, Jack, it's your house.

What I'm saying is that he scares me.

What do you mean he scares you he's just a kid.

I'm saying he's a scary kid.

On Saturday he is on the plane. Like a transit passenger in a dream, he can easily forget what precise place he is leaving and imagine he is headed somewhere besides his actual destination. The convenient morning flight is full. The 747 cabin has no diverting characteristics, it's the usual off-white plastic shell with the usual blue seats and paisley antimacassars covered with thin tissue, the usual projection screen running CNN, the usual runner carpet, the perky yet drained-looking flight attendents in beige jackets and white blouses. There is the customary safety lecture which no one listens to, the crinkled flight magazines in the seat pouch in front of him, the unintelligible greetings from the captain over the P.A.

He's buckled into an aisle seat five rows from the back, a middle row away from the windows. He's given the people beside him a cursory inspection: two large men who might be soccer players, Australian by the sound of them, and on the other side of them an Indian woman wearing a varicolored sari and a bright red caste mark in the center of her forehead, with a small male child in the seat beside her. Although it is ten-thirty in the morning the Australians sound and smell as if they've been drinking. The one beside him keeps up a running commentary to his friend on all the little events happening around them: the plane is fifth, then fourth, then third for takeoff, then suddenly picks up speed on the runway, and between the moment of liftoff and the retraction of the landing gear the Australian's meaty hands grip the metal parts of his armrests in colossal terror. Seth catches the man's glance without meaning to, and the guy says:

This part always takes the piss out of me.

Seth tries out a placatory, distancing smile and turns back to his book. He's reading Michael Tolkin's *Among the Dead,* and he wonders suddenly what he will tell the Australian if he asks what the book's about. *"Frank,"* Seth reads, *"flight two-twenty-one crashed about an hour ago. It exploded in midair just south of San Diego, and crashed into a crowded neighborhood. Everyone in the plane was killed, and we don't know how many people on the ground were killed, possibly fifty or sixty more, possibly many more. The plane was at twenty-eight thousand feet when it went down. I'm sure they never knew what happened.*" But they would know, he thinks, we would know, just for a second or two, maybe, while a fireball or whatever came smashing through the cabin, we'd know we were going to die then and there.

As insurance against the Australian he fishes his Walkman out of the carry-on bag, inserts the little headphones in his ears. He's taped the closing arguments, the final bits of the Martinez trial, and starts playing with the rewind and fast-forward as the drinks wagon comes rolling down the aisle, and finds himself flipping through the book, which he's already read, for the most evocatively horrible passages. *Imagine the destruction to a body, to a face, exploded out of an airplane, and bounced against the roof of a house, or slammed into a chimney. What happens to a ten-year-old when he's blasted through a hole in the wall, and then a thin sheet of metal from the plane's tail catches him around the shoulders?* He reflects that the closest he's ever come to death, perhaps the only moment when he actually thought, unequivocally, *I'm going to die right now*, was when the car flipped over on the Harbor Freeway. No, he thinks, it happened a few seconds before that, in the underpass, when I lost control of the steering and the car began careening between the overpass pylons. Because the next part, when the car actually made it out of the underpass and went flying up the landscaped escarpment, flipped over and landed on the roof and flipped over again and yet again, was some kind of miracle: it should've crashed in the underpass, and if it had, he would certainly have died.

Why didn't he die then? He peers down the aisle where two flight attendants fill drink orders from their cart. Bloody Marys, G&Ts, single malt on the rocks. He remembers a flight between Chicago and Pittsburgh, a few years earlier, in serious weather, another trial story, about a set of arson fires in overinsured warehouses, when a flight attendant suddenly buckled up in the seat beside him. What's the worst that can happen, he asked her, in this type of weather? The worst that can happen is we can crash, she said matter-of-factly. And if that drink cart isn't secured, it weighs half a ton, it could cause some really serious injuries.

On the opposite side of the aisle, about three rows forward, a man in an expensive suit is talking very loudly, obstreperously, insistently, into one of the AT&T handsets that now come with every seat on this particular flight. Seth can hear him through the mellow tones of attorney Peter Fagin, *you look on the body in a gun-shooting case at where the injuries are,* and the man in the suit, the man on the phone, seems to be saying, *You can tell Fernando he's got a window of about six hours and ten minutes.* The drink service rolls up blocking Seth's view. He cannot see the man on the phone but the flight attendant bending over him looks nettled, flustered by some unexpected request. Her expression goes a bit further than airline protocol for conveying displeasure at a passenger. *"If we had known that Fidel Martinez was a child molester, we would've prosecuted him," that really is missing the boat by a wide mark here, because the question is* Yes, there's some sort of disturbance down there, he can see the man's sleeve, the handset in the manicured hand, the Rolex, the flight attendant saying something firm and a bit strained, then fishing out several mini bottles of brown liquor and stabbing the air with them, he takes the earphones out, but suddenly everything returns to normal.

About fuckin time for the cocktail hour, the Australian says conspiratorially. The second Australian is attempting conversation with the Indian woman, asking obtuse but friendly questions about India, to which she replies in a voice below audibility.

Well I can use one, Seth says, giving in to what he fears may become four and a half hours of exacerbated boredom.

Pete from Australia, the Australian tells him after securing two mini gins and a Heineken beer. My mate and I, Tom here, been traveling since last March. Shot a documentary over in Cameroons. Tom's the cameraman and I'm the A.C. Wrapped in March and we've been up hill down dale together ever since, you name it, Athens, Moscow, Berlin, party hardy all over the fuckin planet.

You headed home? Seth attempts a clinical appraisal of the degree and quality of relief the double vodka he's drinking spreads through his system: after one belt, two, three, and so on.

No way, says Pete. We're hanging out in L.A. for two weeks and after that it's South America. A tragically confiding look washes across Pete's face, which Seth has trouble bringing into focus despite being sober. Fact is, he says, my wife left me one year ago and ran off with my best friend. Trite fuckin story, hey? Instead of facin the fuckin situation I takes off for England where I buy a motorbike and crack it up straightaway, plate in my head now, met up with Tom the week I get out of hospital, if I face the fuckin facts I've been running away from myself for a year and I'm still running away from reality, is how I see it. It certainly looks that way, don't you think so?

I don't know, Seth says, wondering what litany of soothing words would lull Pete's demons into silence until LAX. If she left you, what's there to face, really?

Well, there's the kid, Pete says. You've got to take the kid into account.

I wouldn't be too hard on yourself, Seth ventures. I mean everybody runs away when they've got . . . too much on their plate.

Pete, absolved, beams. He catches the attention of the retouring drinks cart and its custodians, ordering two more of everything for both of them.

I like the way you put it, Seth, he says, pronouncing the name *Syeeeth*. Because that's the plain and honest fuckin reality of it, here I am tryin to provide and keep a relationship going, keep food on the table and shoes on the kid's feet, one day I walk in and my best mate's fuckin the woman I worship right in the fucking arsehole.

That's harsh, Seth says, twisting open his vodka miniatures.

Harsh ain't the bleeding word for it, Pete says before glugging his second beer. Fuckin hair-raising if you ask me.

Even for a loud, vulgar asshole like Pete from Australia there is someone. Someone who leaves, people do leaves, but there will always be others. Who wouldn't want a braying, alcoholic, self-pitying, probably violent jock keeping their toes warm at night? Yet I, I, am somehow indefensible, peculiar in some insupportable way, and it's not the drink, all the same things happen when I haven't touched a drop for months. If I hadn't thrown the plate at Mark I would've strangled him and it would've been justified homicide. As Pete pauses to jabber at Tom, Seth slips his earphones back in and holds his book under his nose. *The court's going to give you an instruction which reads, Evidence has been received in this case which may tend to show that the character of the alleged victims' violent or otherwise abusive behavior may be reason that a person of such character for violent or abusive behavior would be more likely to act violently or abusively on any given occasion.* The loud gentleman in the expensive suit waddles down the aisle in search of more booze. No knowing what will happen in those jury rooms, what fate awaits Carlos and Felix, and the whole thing hinges on what you believe can happen, what you know from your own experience does happen, Seth flashes on an evening he spent in Mt. Washington getting trashed with Frankie, watching videos, adoring Frankie's body in nunlike immobility and praying for the nerve to make a move, and instead they started talking of their families, Frankie's stutter thickening and making him crazy frustrated, there came this dumb still minute after Seth said, What's the worst thing that ever happened to you? Knowing the words that would come, clearly, enunciated with no difficulty at all: *My father fucked me.* And the words that would come from himself, that he'd never said to anybody: *So did mine.*

Somewhere over Topeka, when the drinks cart wheels through the cabin as preface to the meal service, shortly after the conclusion of *Father of the Bride Part II*, the man in the suit, the man on the phone, whose name, they soon learn, is Kittel, a Mr. Kittel from a very prestigious New York brokerage house, who looks, Seth thinks, like the guy who turned out to be the murderer in *Klute*, rushes down the aisle in his shirtsleeves, rushes up to the cart, unable to wait his turn, demanding liquor from the flight attendants, and people are straining in their seats for a better look, because however firmly the two attendants state the rules of the airline, Mr. Kittel is far too drunk and belligerent to comprehend anything they're telling him, *I got bumped from first class,* Mr. Kittel growls, *because of fucking airline policy, don't give me fucking airline policy,* commotion spreads through the cabin, other flight attendants abandon their duties to cluster around their colleagues, *Now listen Mr. Kittel you are breaking federal law,* an exuberantly blonde flight attendant struggling for control of a tray of liquor miniatures tells him, as a tall, unformidable male attendant brings up the rear, saying, *You will be arrested on landing if you continue this,* in fact nearly the entire crew is talking at once, using language culled from a flight attendant manual, *Mr. Kittel you're compromising the safety of your fellow passengers and the entire flight,* Mr. Kittel isn't listening, Mr. Kittel's shoving people's arms away, Mr. Kittel's chugalugging a little bottle of Hennessy he's managed to extract from the grip of one of the flight attendants, and of course they're all clogged in the narrow aisle, spilling into people's seats, and many passengers are leaving their seats and scrambling for safety, Seth's view becomes temporarily blocked by an enormous woman in a corn-flower-blue dress, the Australians are standing in their seats, Seth climbs up on his, just in time to witness Mr. Kittel leaping onto the cart, *I don't have to take this shit from you fucking underlings,* Mr. Kittel brays, though not everyone later agrees if the word was underlings, some heard it as underthings, now Kittel is standing atop the heavy wagon, knocking napkins and cocktail stirrers and other items into the seats around him, Seth hears *Oh no Mr. Kittel!* before he can actually see the short, middle-aged, important-looking man lower his trousers and boxer shorts atop the drinks cart, more or less simultaneously extruding a large bowel movement, which he scoops up with both hands and brandishes at the flight attendants, who back away in horror and confusion. *You're the ones who have to take shit from me!* Kittel declares triumphantly, and even from where Seth stands, the seat shifting under his feet, he can smell the rank aroma of the excrement, thick and gooey in Kittel's fingers, droplets of it flying around the cabin as he flails his arms, spattering the overhead luggage compartments, apprently striking some of the passengers as various revulsed noises rise from Kittel's general vicinity. The flight attendants have clanned in two groups at opposite ends of the aisle. At Seth's end, the big blonde, fighting hysterics, consults with the cockpit over a telephone. Kittel, meanwhile, relishing his rout of the airline personnel, blithely consumes several more liquor miniatures, smearing his face with his feces.

Panic has seized nearly everyone. People have cleared out around Kittel, some climbing over their seatbacks. At last the pilot's voice, in its most authoritative tone, comes over the P.A.: *Ladies and gentlemen we have a situation aboard the aircraft for your own safety please remain in your seats,* Kittel's face is a rictus of idiocy looming above everything, he's even clowning now, giving a sort of vaudeville salute to the passengers with his shit-covered hands, *Sometimes you gotta take action,* he gurgles, *take that bull by the damn horns, never mind that safety trigger—* In the faces around him, Seth sees a kind of awe, the situation has become static and now they are locked in mute contemplation of something no other people, in all probability, have ever beheld. A man who was in control a few hours ago, a man who was making deals at thirty thousand feet, a man one might plausibly find profiled in the plastic-bound copies of *Forbes* offered by the airline, has lost his mind on what journalists would describe, if they did not have something bigger to report that day, as a routine flight to Los Angeles. *Don't think you're better than me,* Kittel wails, wagging a brown finger at God, or whatever. *Keep your hands off me, I've got credit cards.* A navy-blue blanket is flung over Kittel's head from behind, and suddenly the man is gripped by an extra large flight attendant, who hauls him down from the cart and drags him, kicking and screaming, into the narrow galley in midplane.

The plane touches down at LAX at 2:53 P.M., and ten minutes later Jules Kittel of Fairfield, Connecticut, is escorted off in custody of two federal marshals wearing bright yellow rubber gloves and protective masks. First-class passengers unboard a few minutes later, followed by business and economy. There has been no food service on the flight because of potential human waste contamination. The passengers look, and are, irritated, bewildered, haggard, dazed by their shared ordeal. As they file into the terminal, several reporters tipped by the Federal Marshal's Office move in on them, primed for the most disgusting filler story of the week, possibly even feature story, as this is a slow news week, what with both Martinez juries in deliberation.

Seth uses his expertise in deflecting journalists: look crazy. He presses through the knot of avid witnesses and reporters wearing a mask of poisonous rage and heads for the baggage area and the bus to the rental car franchises. A weight has lifted from him, quite mysteriously, in the course of the flight. The terminal concourse and the warm air, the movement of human traffic, the pink neon of a bagel kiosk, even himself, suddenly, as a body inhabiting space, an actual person whose existence is not negligible, whose claim to a certain measure of happiness might not be at odds with the scheme of the universe, all of it has become, in these blank minutes, strangely solid and credible to him. Perhaps it is arrival, once more, always as if for the first time, the slate wiped clean, awaiting a new inscription which could, with luck, and age, and experience, and a degree of conscious effort, look different than anything written there in the past. He steps onto the escalator and begins his descent to a place that feels, finally, like home.

The event occurs at 3:27.

At 3:26, at the house on Woodrow Wilson Drive, a much chastened and sheepish-looking yet adorable Tim Chumley, standing in the driveway beside the blue 1987 Trans Am, in frame with Matt O'Reilley, loads, with blank buckshot cartridges, his Mossberg pump-action shotgun, frenetically, dropping shells, breathing fast and heavily, both actors aping panic, filling the shotguns with five cartridges each. The camera glides on an aluminum track around the driveway as the boys bolt for the French doors on the far side of the house facade, Academy Award–winning cinematographer Lazlo Daley peering through the eyepiece. Both actors, running, are thrown to the gravel as the ground shifts, and Daley himself is pitched off the camera, as the mansion windows shatter and various weight-bearing walls inside collapse. Behind the house, Cassandra Lomax has been lounging beside the pool, waiting for a shot scheduled for 5 P.M. As the foundation beneath the pool cracks apart, a multipaneled plate-glass window flies out of its frame at the rear of the house, spraying the pool area with razor-sharp shards. Exploding like shotgun pellets, several dozen lodge themselves in Cassandra's body, puncturing a lung, her spleen, her heart, and wreaking unbelievable damage to her face.

JD catches the quake during his broadcast. As shelves of tapes and recording equipment rattle and spit things into space JD dives under his console. Acoustic ceiling panels rain around him, bits of the studio snap apart, topple, smash against other bits. Everything shakes. The noise builds and builds, the familiar abatement isn't happening, the floor feels suddenly unanchored, twisting, a big chunk of ceiling pounds the console, and now he's like a nail being hammered uselessly against a bar of metal, cascades of heavy debris cracking the console apart, through the hole where the ceiling was, an office chair on castors rolls into the void smacking down on JD's skull, followed by a file cabinet and pieces of a water cooler.

Janice Wade has been showing Norman Bates the bug room. The vitrines full of beetles and butterflies, hopping and flying and humming insects, all dead, all impaled, suffused with a strange beauty. She had not been planning anything more involved than a friendly thank-you tea, but now his amazingly large cock is inside her, fucking her with great delicacy and mature skill from behind, herself bent forward with her cheek pressed against a glass bin full of ladybugs and so forth, and as Norman's penis hammers her pleasure center over and over again Janice moans and whimpers like a dog, occasionally whining, *oh, Norman, fuck me in the ass, fuck my asshole Norman,* and at the very moment when Norman reluctantly withdraws from her juicy honeypot and slides his bone-hard shaft into the tighter, more recalcitrant bud, the upper floor of the Wade home, with its myriad rooms full of period furniture and objets d'art, collapses at a 45-degree incline, sending lamps and wall panels and chinoiserie screens and several tons of woodwork and metal beams into the bug room below, like a funnel.

A gas main along Hollywood Boulevard has exploded. A trail of fire is spreading from Frederick's of Hollywood all the way down to Mann's Egyptian. Another main has exploded under Wilshire, next to the subway tunnel. Palm trees ignite like flares. The city continues shaking, collapsing houses like spoiled soufflés. Seismographs in Northridge place the epicenter around Normandie and Santa Monica.

Jack is trapped. Jack is trapped and he cannot make sense of his house. His house was around him and now it's on top of him and somewhere up there, which used to be downstairs, Frankie is moving around, and Frankie has the gun. A moment before they were arguing and Frankie got this look in his eyes and bolted into the other room and Jack knew Frankie was going for the gun. He believes something's happened to Frankie's legs because the sounds Frankie makes are crawling noises, crawl and a bump, crawl and a bump, and Jack thinks the bump must be Frankie hitting the former ceiling or whatever it is Frankie's moving on with the butt of the gun, as far as Jack can tell the house has *rolled down the hill,* fallen off its stilts and rolled, landing upside down, and Jack himself is pinned under the spiral staircase, which cracked loose and came down hard on a lot of wooden debris, some of which he was under. He thinks some of his ribs are crushed and his right arm is definitely broken, it's hard to breathe, he's not sure if the taste in his mouth is blood if he's bleeding internally or what, he is focused exclusively on the slow scuttling and scraping and bumping overhead, Frankie dragging his shattered body across the debris field of Jack's life with the sick determination of a maniac, which Jack has recognized, a little tardily, Frankie is.

The event continues and continues. It is a shallow-focus event unaccompanied by volcanic activity. The plates of the San Andreas fault, differently magnetized, are releasing pressure that has built up.

Trapped in a pitch-black cavern between the escalator stairs and a ton of rubble resting on the escalator handrails, Seth thinks, he even says aloud, *I'm still alive.*

ABOUT THE AUTHOR

Gary Indiana's previous novels include *Rent Boy, Gone Tomorrow,* and *Horse Crazy.* He has published two short story collections and, most recently, a collection of essays, *Let It Bleed.* His plays include the award-winning *Roy Cohn/Jack Smith, The Roman Polanski Story,* and *Phantoms of Louisiana.* Indiana has directed many works for the stage, including recent adaptations of H. M. Enzensberger's *The Sinking of the Titanic* and John Lennon's *In His Own Write* and *A Spaniard in the Works.* He lives in New York and Los Angeles.